When There Were 9

C.A. Larmer is a journalist, editor, teacher and author of four crime series, two stand-alone novels and a non-fiction book about pioneering surveyors in Papua New Guinea. Christina grew up in that country, was educated in Australia, and spent many years working in London, Los Angeles and New York. She now lives with her musician husband, two sons and a cheeky Blue Heeler on the east coast of Australia.

Sign up for news, views and giveaways:
calarmer.com

ALSO BY C.A. LARMER

The Murder Mystery Book Club series:
The Murder Mystery Book Club (Book 1)
Danger On the SS Orient (Book 2)
Death Under the Stars (Book 3)

The Ghostwriter Mystery series:
Killer Twist (Book 1)
A Plot to Die For (Book 2)
Last Writes (Book 3)
Dying Words (Book 4)
Words Can Kill (Book 5)
A Note Before Dying (Book 6)
Without a Word (Book 7)

The Posthumous Mystery series:
Do Not Go Gentle
Do Not Go Alone

The Sleuths of Last Resort:
Blind Men Don't Dial Zero
Smart Girls Don't Trust Strangers
Good Girls Don't Drink Vodka

PLUS
*After the Ferry: A Gripping
Psychological Novel*

An Island Lost

C.A. LARMER

When There Were 9

The Murder Mystery Book Club
(Book 4)

LARMER MEDIA

Published by Larmer Media
Northern NSW, Australia
calarmer.com
ISBN: 978-0-6452835-2-5

Cover design by Stuart Eadie & Nimo Pyle
Cover photography by Andreas-Saldavs
Edited by The Editing Pen
& Elaine Rivers

For my family, for always being there.
And Elaine Rivers, for her generosity and support.

And for all those brave 'firies',
who run towards the unforgiving flames...

PROLOGUE

As the flames licked the tops of the rainforest trees, virgins to this kind of ferocity, he knew what he had to do. It was like a gift from God—or Mother Nature at least. Whatever it was, he wasn't going to look it in the mouth. This was a once-in-a-hundred-years inferno, and he would not waste a second of it.

He took a step back and cleared his throat. "Come on then, lad, get in there. It's not gonna douse itself, y'know."

"Yeah, right," scoffed the younger man, his eyes trained on the fire, waiting for the punchline.

"I'm deadly serious," the older bloke persisted. "You like playing with fire. Here's your bloody chance."

The younger man turned and stared at him, incredulous for a moment before something crossed his face, something that started as shock, then turned to shame and, finally, utter clarity.

He knew what was going on.

He knew where he was headed.

He knew he would not be back.

And yet he did not flinch, not for one moment. It was the penance he was prepared to pay.

He pushed his hat down low, picked up his gear, and marched towards the unforgiving fire…

C.A. LARMER

CHAPTER 1

From her cosy corner of the half-empty train carriage, longtime member of the Murder Mystery Book Club, Claire Hargreaves, sipped from a reusable coffee cup as she glanced through the first few pages of Agatha Christie's *And Then There Were None*.

It was a fabulous whodunit—the last of the Christie novels they would be dissecting—but she couldn't focus on it now, her mind twittering in all directions. Claire was thrilled to be heading away, but it had very little to do with the book in her lap. That was not the real reason she was making her way up the lush mountain towards the clifftop lodge where the club had agreed to meet. She had an ulterior motive—a rather shocking one—she just wasn't sure how soon she should reveal it.

Claire smiled as she recalled the letter she had received. The lovely, crisp stationery! The carefully drafted proposition! A rather shocking proposition that she simply couldn't get out of her head, as much as she had tried.

She knew it would cause a fracture, a *death* really, but she had spent far too long playing it safe. It was time to take a leaf from Dame Agatha's book and take a chance. It was too intoxicating an invitation to give up. Or at least she hoped it would be…

As the train hurtled past walls of tangled forest, she glanced out the window and felt the first few tugs of regret. Then worry. Then fear.

What was she doing? Why had she agreed?

Did she really want to destroy the Murder Mystery Book Club?

The train suddenly swerved straight towards the forest and was swallowed up by a long, dark tunnel, and as the lights flickered out, so did Claire's smile.

~

From his seat at the other end of the carriage, Simon Crete tried very hard not to ogle the woman with the stunning feline eyes and the creeping frown. She was truly beautiful, despite the increasingly worried expression, with an extraordinary sense of style; she could almost have come from the 1940s. Her glossy black hair was set against a baggy red beret that matched the belt she was wearing around a houndstooth-patterned dress. His eyes darted downwards to her peep-toe heels, then back up to that hair, that luscious, luscious…

"Stop it, you fool," he told himself, dragging his eyes away. "You're not here for pleasure. This is serious business."

He had to keep his eye on the goal.

Sneaking another glance, he turned his thoughts back to the book he'd recently read. *And Then There Were None.* Not a bad read, as far as mysteries go, but he preferred something a little grittier, more Nordic noir. Still, it had proven to be quite lively, certainly surprising, and had given him some of his best ideas. Some very good ideas indeed.

He just had to work out how to keep it all on track until the final denouement…

~

Lynette Finlay bit into her lower lip and tried very hard not to ask her sister, "Are we there yet?" This train ride was taking an eternity! And it didn't help that it was packed with people of a certain age.

She glanced around the carriage, miserably.

The twenty-something had nothing against the elderly, but if this was a sign of the next instalment of the Murder

Mystery Book Club, it might be time to hang up her badge. There were some crinkly blokes in hats, multiple cardigan-donning grannies, and the only good sort—a swarthy fifty-something—couldn't keep his eyes off Claire. *Hmm.*

Men were normally drawn to Lynette—her thick blond hair and long, tanned legs worked like a magnet—but this guy hadn't glanced her way once. She didn't begrudge Claire, really she didn't, and not only because it had been a long dry spell for her book club friend.   But there was something a little, well, *odd* about this ruffled Greek god look-alike who was pretending to ignore Claire.

Something a little *off…*

He seemed too rigid, she decided. Too wound up. Like he was holding something in and trying hard not to explode. Probably last night's souvlaki, she decided, as she returned her gaze to her iPhone and began scrolling through Instagram.

~

Florence Underwood sat upright, half-knitted beanie in her lap, staring at the underdressed lady across from her, immersed in her screen. What was it with youngsters these days? They were like zombie moths attracted to the flame.

That was one of the main reasons she had agreed to join the Murder Mystery Book Club. More books and reading were exactly what the doctor ordered.

And more peace. That too.

She recalled the letter their club had sent her and Ronnie, courtesy of the Balmain Ladies Auxiliary in, frankly, messy handwriting, which had put her off entirely until the sentiment caught up.

Dear Ronnie and Flo,

We do hope you remember us! We met during the terrible tragedy at the Balmain Moonlight Cinema, and you helped us solve the mystery of the dead woman on the blanket (with a little help from the police, LOL)—

Flo stopped knitting. LOL? Were they illiterate, or was that how all young people spoke these days? And how young *were* they exactly? She studied the girl still hypnotised by her gizmo, then resumed knitting as the letter flooded back...

We have several openings in our book club and thought you'd make a wonderful addition as you clearly love mysteries—both fictional and real life. If this sounds like your cup of tea, please don't hesitate to get in touch. We will be advertising for other members next week but would like to give you two first dibs. We're thinking of heading away somewhere cosy and remote for a mystery weekend so we can get to know each other while dissecting the latest book on our list. Please call or email us directly... et cetera.

Flo had hesitated at first, but the more she thought about it, the more it all sounded just dandy. She wasn't getting any younger. It would be one final, memorable adventure.

As the needles kept clicking away, she looked through the window and noticed thick scrambler vines, reaching out like they were trying to drag the train in. She shivered and pulled her cardigan tighter.

The place was alive, she knew that.

Alive with possibility...

~

As she watched her friend Flo knitting up a frenzy in the seat beside her, Veronica Westera's mind was getting itself into knots, but it wasn't the weekend she was thinking about.

It was the past, the long-distant past, which was coming to her now in fragments—swishing crepe, tinkling pianos and the bubbling of expensive champagne.

And a man, a handsome hunter she should not have taken a fancy to.

Ronnie gave herself a small shake and pulled out her journal and pen but could not focus long enough to write anything. Instead, she glanced past Flo and out the window to a clump of soaring Antarctic beech, but that only made things worse.

Why did it leave her feeling so melancholy? The rattling train too?

And why did the sound of Lyle's Rainforest Lodge send her heart into a tailspin?

~

Missy Corner pulled out a plastic container of trail mix and reached across the aisle to offer it to the two older ladies, one knitting like a madwoman, the other lost in her thoughts. They both shook her off with a polite smile, and she beamed back at them.

She could not be any happier!

This was like all her dreams rolled into one—heading away for an *entire* weekend with her favourite people in the whole wide world (well, apart from her family, of course, but the book club were like family now and she couldn't imagine her life without them). And now they were broadening the fold. She looked at the ladies again and had to restrain her smile.

She just *knew* they would make a wonderful addition to the Murder Mystery Book Club. And useful too! She remembered how helpful they'd been on the club's last case—the one at the outdoor cinema—and was looking forward to their unique insight. Their rich history and experience.

Of course those were the very things that the other "young one" in the club, Lynette, seemed to hold against them. Like the older generation could not contribute. It was silly, really, and Missy knew better. Had met more than her share of switched-on oldies at the library where she worked.

Missy also knew that Lynny hadn't had a chance to meet them properly as she and Claire had. What a shemozzle their departure had been. The train had arrived early at Central Station, and some of them had almost missed it, so there was no time to be properly introduced before they all clambered aboard and scurried to their seats, but there would be time enough later.

A *whole* weekend with her fabulous book club would be delicious enough, but add those two ladies to the mix, and it was sure to be a treat. They were whip smart, she remembered that. Especially Ronnie...

Or was it Flo?

Missy shrugged and stuffed her mouth with raisins.

~

As the now-platinum blonde twitched beside him, unable to contain her excitement at the weekend ahead— he adored that about Missy, how central they all were in her life—Perry Gordon was stroking his chiselled goatee and thinking about the two elderly ladies across from them, or more specifically, the taller, skinnier of the two. The one who wasn't knitting.

She had a leather journal on her lap and the name V. A. WESTERA engraved across the front. He recognised the name; he just couldn't remember from where. And it had nothing to do with Balmain or books.

Probably the Sydney Museum where he worked, he decided. Women of a certain age were a regular fixture there. As Ms Westera reached a hand up to smooth away an ash-blond curl, Perry noticed what looked like a diamond bracelet popping out from the sleeve of her cardigan.

Now why did that look so incongruous?

She caught him staring and gave him a bemused smile. He smiled awkwardly and shifted his eyes to the view.

~

Alicia Finlay gazed out at the view and frowned. She usually adored train rides—the infamous Orient Express was at the top of her bucket list—but this trip was making her queasy, what with the steep incline and all the tight bends.

Or perhaps it was the thought of the weekend ahead.

Alicia hoped she had made the right decision, convening their first meeting at a remote and isolated location. That was the point entirely, but now she had to wonder—what did they really know of the new members? Perhaps they should have vetted them properly before locking themselves away together for an entire weekend. What if they were too chatty or, worse, too dull?

She chewed her lower lip and darted her eyes around the carriage. It had all been so rushed when they got to the station, no chance for proper introductions, so she could only guess who amongst the passengers belonged to her group. She vaguely recalled Flo and Ronnie from that night at the outdoor cinema, but they had seemed more vibrant then. Right now one looked lost in fairyland, the other was scowling at Lynette.

As for Simon Crete? She had to assume he was the tall, dark-haired man in the farthest corner, the one with the crumpled linen shirt and the fixation with Claire.

Oh dear, she thought. Book club romances were never a good idea. Hadn't she learned that the hard way?

Alicia tried not to think of Dr Anders Bright, who had gone from dishy new member to devil's advocate in the flick of a page. Every book club needs a voice of caution, she knew that, but his had become a screeching brake. And this new member, if indeed this was him, looked a little tentative too. A little wound up, perhaps. And not at all as his letter had suggested. Oh it was such a magnificent letter! So light and breezy but packed with passion. Simon had answered their classified advertisement quickly and written such an extraordinary monologue about crime writers of all persuasions, but especially Agatha Christie, with information on her background and his own love for a "good, tantalising read." But from her perspective, he looked a bit like a closed book.

As for the other gentleman, some businessman called Blake Morrow? Who knew what he was like? Alicia had spoken to him by phone, and his enthusiasm had eventually worn her down. The club had decided that eight members was enough, but he had badgered her with calls and begged her to let him join. Then he'd dropped the AC-card, insisting that Agatha Christie was his all-time favourite author, her mysteries his "*raison d'être.*" Lynette had done the rest, bemoaning the group's female population, and so she had agreed, but then he'd texted last minute, informing her he'd drive himself up. That left her worried. Would Blake be a good team member, or would they be stuck with a renegade at a remote lodge for two days?

Lyle's Lodge... That put the smile back on Alicia's face.

She plucked their brochure from her handbag and flicked through it. It looked absolutely perfect, and the manager had made such a good deal—offering them a full weekend package, all food and lodgings, for a song.

She just hoped the Murder Mystery Book Club Mark II were all singing from the same hymn sheet...

CHAPTER 2

"**W**hat a grand old dame!" Claire said, eyes wide as she surveyed the richly textured interiors of Lyle's Rainforest Lodge. "Isn't she divine?"

"Yes, she is," Ronnie agreed as a chill ran through her bones. She now had a fully blown case of déjà vu.

Claire had mentioned the venue at their last book club meeting, so no one who knew Claire was too surprised to find themselves standing in a softly lit lobby with what Christie would call "creaking wood and dark shadows and heavily panelled walls."

It was like stepping back in time. The room was plush and velvety and smelled of old winter coats, with a shiny mahogany front desk and a red baroque Tiffany-style stained glass table lamp. There were several taxidermic animals hanging from the panels—a brushtail possum, a large green catbird and what looked like an endangered spotted-tail quoll—and between them framed pictures of the Lyle family clan, with plaques underneath to reveal names and dates. Missy tried to keep her eyes from the poor dead creatures as she stepped across to the oldest photo, a black-and-white image of a man by a horse with a dog at his side. All three dead now, she assumed, but at least they didn't have the indignity of being stuffed and hung on the walls.

"Is it true we have it all to ourselves?" asked Flo, knitting bag still in hand.

"Absolutely!" gushed Claire. "Apart from a skeleton

staff who will prepare meals and clean the rooms, we are completely alone."

"There's skeletons here, that's for sure," muttered Perry, who might be a palaeontologist but preferred things alive and kicking outside of work.

"They're about to renovate the lodge," explained Alicia who'd run with Claire's suggestion and placed the booking herself. "They're going to massively increase capacity, so we got it cheap before that all starts."

"Such a pity," said Claire. "I just love it like this."

"You do?" said Simon, stepping in with the last of the luggage and glancing about.

"Well, apart from the dead critters, of course."

He nodded, locking eyes with the quoll.

The train journey had lasted two hours and taken them from central Sydney to the quaint, heritage-listed village of Lyleton halfway up the mountain, where they alighted to find the town charming and the temperature jarring. It was an unseasonably warm summer, and the heat hit them like a hot flush, so they began peeling off layers just as a woman with a floppy hat and an efficient smile dashed towards them.

"Might as well keep all that on, if you're coming up to the lodge," she called out. "It's cooler at the top and even chillier in the van." Then she glanced around the group and said, "I'm Mrs Flannery, chief cook and bottle washer. Who's for Lyle's?"

That's when the formal introductions were finally made. As each club member stepped forward to greet Mrs Flannery and place their luggage in the vehicle, they also greeted each other, and Alicia got to see that she was only half-right. Simon Crete was the handsome stranger who'd been ogling Claire, but he also proved to be less stuffy than she thought, and they'd enjoyed a lively chat as they left Lyleton behind and continued northward.

As the incline got steeper, the road got narrower and

Mrs Flannery's foot got heavier on the pedal. She took the hairpin bends like she was running late for dinner, and the van's tinted windows couldn't hide the sheer drop down on one side, the thick shrubbery even struggling to hold on. By the time they reached the lodge, one breathtaking hour later, the small talk had stopped and the startled looks were in full flight.

They were greatly relieved then, when Mrs Flannery pulled into the lodge's long driveway and crunched to a halt outside the old "dame."

"Here we are, folks! Don't forget to grab your bags," she announced, sliding the passenger door open with a whoosh of air that still felt shockingly warm despite the altitude. At least to Alicia, who thanked her as she paused to soak up the view while her hair soaked up the humidity, turning from coiffed pixie cut to ball of frizz in seconds.

Lyle's Lodge is situated 800 metres above sea level, on the only flat piece of land on the mountain—with subtropical rainforest falling away dramatically on three sides and reaching upwards to the west. It was built back in the 1930s, mostly of massive Tallow wood slabs, shiny local slate and stringy bark shingles. Having already done her due diligence, Alicia knew there were lodgings here for forty-plus guests, each a cabin-style room set off the main building, with en suite bathrooms and private decks overlooking the view to the east, back down the mountain. This weekend, however, there would just be the nine of them, as well as two staff members—Mrs Flannery and the manager who was nowhere to be seen as they surveyed the interior.

"Why do people always have to mess with history?" Claire continued as she peeled her red beret from her head. "It has such solid bones. I hope they don't pull out all these grand fittings and modernise the place."

"I hope they *do*," said Lynette, her eyes less glowing. "Grand my butt, Claire! It's dusty and moth-eaten."

Simon looked around and squinted, as if hunting for

moths, while Alicia glanced around and smiled. The place had history all right—a dark, disturbing history—but she would keep that to herself for now. No point unsettling the troops.

"Good afternoon and welcome to Lyle's!" came a booming voice above them, and for a startling moment, Alicia felt like she was back in the pages of the Christie novel they were here to dissect. If the voice had started laying out their individual indictments, she would not have been surprised.

But of course it was not the recorded ravings of a madman but the real-life voice of the lodge's manager, a relatively sane-looking elderly gentleman called Vale. Like Mrs Flannery, if he had a first name, he was not sharing it, but he did offer them a small smile as he deftly descended the staircase.

"I am the hotel manager, Vale. My sincerest apologies. I was not expecting you quite so soon."

"The train was early," Alicia told him.

"Then Mrs Flannery wanted to see if she could break the land speed record," added Perry. "That's quite a climb you got there!"

Vale swept his eyes to Perry and lingered for just a moment on his clipped goatee and black stud earring. "I can assure you it's a vast improvement from the early days, sir." He waved a hand to the framed photo Missy had been inspecting. "To collect guests back in the forties and fifties, our dear founder, Arthur Henry Lyle, had to take the horse and cart down that steep mountainside. The return journey took four days."

"Thank heavens for the automobile," Perry muttered, twiddling his earring self-consciously as Vale turned his eyes to Alicia.

"Ms Finlay? Please step this way. I will get you to sign in, and then we'll settle you into your rooms."

He crossed the foyer to the reception desk and tapped at the computer, bringing it to life. "I have your details on file, but I will need a credit card from each of you."

They all agreed except for Simon, who told Vale gruffly, "I'll pay cash. I always pay cash." Then, in case he was going to argue the point, Simon added, "You can check my bar fridge for pilfered items before I leave if that's what you're worried about!"

Vale bowed his head and said, "As you wish, sir," without displaying any hint of annoyance. Then he reached below the desk and produced a leather-bound guest book. Opening it, he slowly slid a finger down the page and then tapped on a fresh line. "We have a little tradition here. We ask all our guests to sign in before they go to their rooms and again when they depart. If you don't mind."

It wasn't exactly a request, and Vale's eyes were fixed firmly on Simon as he held the pen out. Simon hesitated for a split second, then snatched the pen just as Ronnie gave her forehead a slap.

"Now I remember!" she announced, eyes sweeping the room. "I've been here before! Oh, it was such a long time ago!"

"Really?" said several of them, including Vale, who looked almost alarmed, like he couldn't believe she had forgotten so easily. It was hardly a ringing endorsement, but then Ronnie explained.

"My memory's getting rusty in my old age, and it was just the one visit, a very long time ago. Just before the Great Fire, I believe."

"Great Fire?" echoed Missy, intrigued, while several of them glanced at Alicia, who was now writing her name in the book.

"And it had a different name back then," continued Ronnie. "I'm sure of it…"

"It was once called Lyle's Hunting Lodge," said Vale, his voice desert dry.

Ronnie clapped her hands. "Of course! The Hunting Lodge, that's what we called it!"

"That'll explain the carcasses then," said Perry,

not bothering to mask his distaste.

"Oh I didn't come for the hunting, dear, I came for the lovely dances. I think they held them every few months or so, as a way of keeping the young hunters entertained at night. They were quite *de rigueur*! Flo dear, did you ever—?"

"No, Ron," Flo said, looking embarrassed by her friend's outburst as she clutched her knitting bag tighter. "I was a poor farmer's daughter, remember? Not really my style."

"Pity that! It was such a lot of fun! One of my girlfriends talked me into it even though there were perfectly good dances back in Sydney. Still, I had a fine time. The owner's wife used to run them…" She clicked her fingers. "Now what was her name?"

"Lydia?" offered Missy, who was inspecting another framed photo of a smiling woman standing beside a bandmaster.

"That's it!" She clicked her fingers again. "Lydia Lyle! It had such a lovely ring to it, and she *was* lovely! Very beautiful too, but oh so young, I remember that! Far too young to be running a place like this."

Vale cleared his throat. "Jack Lyle was running the place at that time, madam, with help from myself and his extensive staff."

"You've been here since *then*?" Ronnie looked gobsmacked.

"Coming up to fifty-five years this August, madam. I started as the bellboy. Mrs Flannery joined us in 1982. Now, if you don't mind…" He waved a hand at the guest book, and Ronnie stepped forward to sign it.

"That brings us to eight guests," Vale said, his eyes back on Alicia. "Are we missing one?"

"Yes we are." She glanced through the large glass entrance way.

Now where was book club member number nine?

~

Blake Morrow was thoroughly enjoying the journey up the mountain, feeling like a touring car driver in his white vintage Mercedes and its screeching tyres, the smell of burnt rubber around him. The thin, winding roads, the shockingly sharp bends, the sudden appearance of GIVE WAY signs, each one designed to test you. You never knew when you'd round a corner to find another vehicle careering towards you. It was just like an obstacle course. He came within inches of a lorry full of linen at one point. The look on the driver's face was priceless.

After forty minutes, however, the thrill was starting to waver—one more nagging GIVE WAY sign and he would charge straight at it. His vehicle's air-conditioning was on the blink, and even with the windows down and the breeze slapping his face, the heat felt stifling. The higher he climbed, the thicker the rainforest, the more suffocated he felt, and it was with a rush of relief when he finally spotted signage for Lyle's Lodge, then the turnoff.

Okay, deep breaths, he told himself. *Time to get your game face on.*

Blake was not there for the drive, or books for that matter. He was more like the hunters from the lodge's distant past, but a hunter of a different kind, and he had a lot of work ahead of him. If he pulled it off though, it would all be worth it. There was a giant rainbow at the end of this road. He glanced at the folder on the passenger seat, the laptop beside it. Then he reached for a blanket he'd dumped in the back ages ago and pulled it over and across. Didn't want to give the game away.

Or send his prey scuttling.

Finally, after another ten minutes of more mindless meandering, the lodge appeared at the top of the driveway, and he steered his car up and into a parking spot behind a white van. He applied the handbrake, grabbed his overnight bag, and leapt out.

Inside the foyer, a motley mixture of people were milling about, staring his way, some of them with frowns.

He clocked the stunning blonde who was already preparing her eyelashes for batting, then turned to the two older ladies and gave them his million-dollar smile.

"Wow," he said, shaking his thick, golden hair and baring his freshly whitened teeth. "That was quite a drive, hey ladies? Gets the old heartbeat racing!"

They both smiled back, one of them almost cackling, and he thought, *Nothing like throwing a cat among the pigeons.*

"Blake?" said another woman, midthirties, bit of an early Meg Ryan look-alike. "I'm Alicia Finlay, and this—"

"Must be the Murder Mystery Book Club!" he cut in. "Forgive me, please, I'm sorry I'm so tardy. I couldn't wait to meet you all, but I wanted to take that road nice and slow."

"Good thinking," said Lynette. *Wouldn't want you to come to any harm*, was what *she* was thinking. That and the fact he was much more the younger Finlay sister's style.

Blake was older than Alicia had suggested, in his early forties judging from the very fine lines around his sparkling blue eyes, but other than that, he was perfect. And it wasn't just his handsome looks, although they were breathtaking. He had a certain energy about him, a vivaciousness that left the others looking taxidermic.

Lynette waited until everyone had been introduced, then said, "You don't look like the typical murder mystery fan, Blake."

"Hey, watch it!" He winked. "I dig all crime, especially the big AC. My gran used to read her to me before bed. Gave me nightmares, of course, freaked me right out, but I've loved her ever since."

Alicia frowned at that comment, just as a crash sounded behind them, and they all turned to find Mrs Flannery standing at the other end of the lobby, an empty tray now hanging in her hand.

"Oh my goodness me, I'm so sorry!" she squawked. "I was bringing out refreshments... I must have... I must have tripped on the carpet…"

As several of the club ducked down to help pick up the broken pieces, Vale produced a brush and tray and handed it to her with a stiff smile, then promptly shooed them all away.

"If you'll be kind enough to collect your luggage and follow me," he said, stepping around the broken cups and heading for the long, creaky corridor that led from the lobby to the back of the lodge and the guest accommodation.

They filed in behind Vale and gasped again, this time at a series of exquisite murals that were painted on the walls along the corridor. Now old and fading, even chipping in parts, they revealed a series of lush interiors—a luxurious ball room, a plush library, a glittering indoor pool—which all looked better suited to an English mansion than a rainforest lodge Down Under. Amongst it all, a series of doors opened into various rooms that Vale pointed out as they passed.

"Through the double glass doors on your right is the library," Vale told them. "There's refreshments available in there all day, as well as a wide selection of books, newspapers, board games and a billiard table. Please make yourself comfortable there at any time. And to your immediate left you will find the bar, which operates on an honesty system, and beside that, the dining room and outdoor terrace. Breakfast will be served in the dining room from eight a.m., and dinner is at seven p.m. *sharp*."

He said the final word like it was onomatopoeic and then slapped a quick glance at Blake.

The latecomer tried not to snort as he shared an eye roll with Lynette.

"Goodo," said Flo, knitting bag now hanging from her bony shoulder. "That gives me time for a walk."

Vale's eyes narrowed. "As you wish, madam. You will find the entrance to the walking tracks down the driveway, in the direction from which you came. There are three main walks, all well sign posted, and we do ask that you stay on the tracks at all times. This is a national park, so it is very important that you do not go *off-piste*, so to speak."

Lynette shared another silent snigger with Blake. *This is going to be fun*, she thought, a skip in her step as they continued down the corridor.

~

Vale's heart skipped a beat as he swept back to the reception desk after showing the guests to their rooms. His mind was in a lather, his anxiety growing by the second.

One guest had been a complete surprise. *He was not expecting that.*

Tapping furiously at the computer, he scrolled through his emails, then typed some words into Google. It didn't take long for hundreds of searches to come up. He glanced towards the guest quarters, then back at the computer and clicked a page open, reading it quickly and frowning to himself. Then he glanced down at the guest book and the scribbled handwriting and back, a deep frown now smashing through an already wrinkled forehead.

Did they think he was a fool? Was that it!

Or was there something more odious going on?

CHAPTER 3

As soon as Claire had unpacked her lovely weekend wear into the tiny closet, she checked her mobile phone. What a nuisance! There was no signal, yet she had an important message to send out. Her first impressions were imperative.

She swept open the door to the small balcony, a rush of hot air suddenly invading the cool interior, so she quickly stepped out and secured the door behind her, before holding her phone high.

"Bit more to the left and you might be in luck!" came a voice from below, and Claire looked down to find Simon standing on the walkway, straw hat on his head.

He swept the hat off and gave her a wave. "Sorry, I was just exploring the place and saw you up there on your Juliet balcony."

"Romeo, Romeo, wherefore art thou Wi-Fi?" she called back, laughing. Then she shook her glossy black locks. "You would think I could survive without it, right?"

"Can anyone these days?"

Claire placed her elbows on the balustrade and leaned down. "Oh, I think Flo and Ronnie would be perfectly fine without it."

"I'm not fine at all!" came a croaky voice to her left, and now Claire was grimacing. Ronnie was also on her balcony, waving her smart new iPhone about. "Not all oldies are Luddites, you know! My lovely nephews have got me right up to speed, although I can't seem to reach them, more's the pity…"

"Sorry, Ronnie!" Claire called back. "That was meant as a compliment!"

She swapped a mortified look with Simon, who was swallowing back a chuckle as he continued on his way.

~

From her own balcony on the other side of Ronnie, Flo was chuckling, too, but mostly to herself. She *liked* that the coverage was poor. She wanted to be far away, in the middle of nowhere. Uncontactable. She liked the heat up here too, even though it was more humid than she was used to.

Still, it reminded her of the farm. Of the good old days. When life was so much simpler…

Sighing, she reached across her bed and into her small suitcase, pulling out a floral bath bag that rattled as it went. Then she put it aside and picked up a photo of a handsome man in uniform, brushing some dust from the frame. She placed it by her bedside, then turned her eyes outwards to the extraordinary green vista beyond the balcony.

"Not long now, my love," she whispered. *Not long now.*

~

Alicia heard the rat-tat-tat on her door and pulled it open to find Lynette standing there, walking boots on her feet, a wicked glint in her eyes.

"He's bloody *gorgeous!*" the young blonde said, sweeping into the room.

"I'm guessing we're not talking about Vale," Alicia replied as Lynette glanced around.

"Yeah, right. Hey, your room's bigger than mine!" She fell onto the bed and scowled. "And your bed's queen size. I'm sure mine's just a double."

Alicia groaned like it was a bad thing. She felt guilty enough for not inviting her boyfriend Liam Jackson along. She recalled how keen he was to come; how hard she had put him off. But this was *her* book club, not his, and it was important to keep the two things separate.

If the past had taught her anything, it was that.

"Don't worry, you'll survive the weekend without each other," Lynette said, reading her mind as she often did.

The two sisters had lived together for years, and while there was a six-year age difference, they often behaved like identical twins—finishing each other's sentences, ribbing each other regularly, having each other's backs.

"I'm glad you two have lasted," Lynette added, and Alicia feigned offence.

"You didn't think we'd last?"

"Did *you?*"

Alicia laughed. Nah, of course she didn't. As she returned to hanging her clothes up, Alicia thought about Jackson and all they had been through, and she wasn't thinking now of the cruise ship murders where they first met. After a positive start, their relationship had quickly unravelled—in her mind at least. She had begun to imagine the many weird and woeful ways the Detective Inspector would let her down, including an affair with his no-nonsense, but irritatingly attractive, colleague Indira Singh.

Yet here they were, many months (and several murders) later, happier than ever.

Lynette watched her sister unpack and wondered why she bothered. They were only here for a few days, and she was happy enough living out of an exploded suitcase. Unlike most chefs she knew, Lynette wasn't the least bit fastidious.

"So what's the verdict? Are you pleased with our new acquisitions?"

Lynette was referring to the new book club members and Alicia knew it.

"Early days, but I think so. It's a better balance

I suppose. We have the two older ladies, Flo and Ronnie. They seem like good fun."

Lynette said nothing. She wasn't so sure about that. Ronnie seemed a bit scatty—how could she possibly forget this place? And Flo? Well, she looked better suited to an aged-care home.

"And then we have the two new men," Alicia was saying. "One a little older and stiffer, one slightly younger and…"

"Hotter?' said Lynette, eyebrows nudging high.

"More gregarious I was going to say. And off-limits, I'm afraid."

Lynette's eyebrows dropped. "Why?"

"Have you learned nothing from Anders and me? Mixing book club members does not work."

"Hang on a minute!" Lynette sat up straight. "Just because you two locked horns doesn't mean the rest of us have to bear the scars. Besides, a brief holiday fling can't hurt."

"It can if you have to face each other at book club every fortnight after that. Take it from me, Lynette, it won't be worth it. Club will become very awkward very fast. Then we'll have to advertise for new members again and be back where we started."

Lynette groaned. Her sister was right. She was always right, but she wasn't yet ready to give up on the gorgeous newcomer, and she had a feeling this one would last the distance.

"He looks like he'd be up for a mystery if one dropped in his lap," Lynette said. "And a massive fan of the big AC, hey?" She laughed. "Not your typical cosy mystery fan."

"Yeah, about that," Alicia said. "Didn't you think it strange that he said her books gave him nightmares? Freaked him out?"

"So?"

"So, they're not called cosy mysteries for nothing. They're hardly very scary. Even my incredibly impressionable brain doesn't blink."

"He did read them as a kid, remember? Besides, he was just making small talk. Come on, let's go for a you-know-whatie before I go out of my skull with boredom!"

Alicia laughed. "We've been here all of five minutes! And I think you can use the word 'walk' now. Max can't hear you."

Max was their beloved black Labrador, named after Christie's faithful second husband Max Mallowan, and he adored their daily walks. They could never casually mention the word without him dancing in circles, then galloping for the nearest leash, walking shoe or sock.

Lynette jumped back to her feet. "Come on then, grab your hat and sunscreen and I'll meet you at the start of the track in five. Might see if anyone else wants to join us."

"By anyone you mean our new hottie, right?"

Lynette looked indignant as she showed herself out and headed straight for Blake's door.

~

Ten minutes later, four members of the club were waiting at the start of the walking tracks, down the road from the lodge's main entrance. There was Alicia, Lynette, Blake and Flo, who had a collapsible aluminium trekking pole and was glancing worriedly at the setting sun. The heat was still aggressive, but its bite would not last long and nor would its light.

"I do hope we don't get caught out in this," she said.

"We can always turn back after twenty minutes or so," Lynette replied, but Blake assured them there was no need.

"This track splits into several different walks, so we just have to take the shorter one when we get to it. It'll get us back in under an hour."

"A good thing you're so informed," said Flo, giving him a curious look.

"Let's get cracking," said Lynette, pulling her cap

lower, but Alicia was squinting in the opposite direction, up the driveway that swept past the lodge, to the ancient Antarctic beech trees that clung to the top of the ridge.

Unless her eyes were playing tricks on her, she swore she'd seen someone walking that way, and so she glanced back at the wooden signpost.

"This is the only track, right?"

Blake nodded. "They all start here and break off after about two hundred metres."

Alicia raised her eyebrows. "Somebody's being naughty and going off-piste then. Vale won't be happy."

Then they chuckled as they walked towards the forest.

~

Simon knew he was heading in the wrong direction, but that was the point entirely. Nothing was going to avert him from his mission. He had an important deadline and, everything depended on it.

As he pushed through the thick foliage, the smell of lemon myrtle thick in the air, he found himself on the edge of a rocky escarpment with little more than a rotting handrail to stop him from tumbling downwards. Hugging the mountainside closer, he edged his way along, then peered down at the steep slope and the dusty vines and palm trees clinging to it, and what looked like the official walking track below.

This must be the spot.

Pulling out his mobile phone, he took a few photos, then glanced down and then back up again, waiting. After another minute or so, he could feel his patience waning. Maybe he had it wrong? Maybe if he moved a little further out...

Hang on a minute, what is that?

Squinting, Simon could just make out what looked like some kind of shed at the other end of the escarpment, right out on the point. No, not a shed, a hut, a wooden cabin, in fact, with a small chimney and an outhouse tacked onto the side.

Now that's interesting…

As he watched, someone appeared from inside, and Simon stepped back quickly, the stones crunching under his feet. He frowned and watched for a few more minutes as his blood began to simmer.

So that's what he's been hiding, hey? How very, very disturbing…

Although now it was starting to make sense. Now he knew exactly what he had to do.

Checking his phone one final time, Simon slipped it back into his pocket and carefully retraced his steps.

~

The first sign of danger was so subtle Flo didn't notice it. She was too busy thinking how impatient young people were.

Wouldn't kill them to wait for us, she thought as she watched Lynette and Blake stride ahead on the track, which had meandered under a dark canopy of rich, remnant rainforest and was now winding its way along a sun-drenched ridge, fern-shrouded rock face at one side, sheer drop on the other, the smell of eucalyptus around them and the sound of a barely trickling waterfall close by.

At least Alicia had waited for her, and apart from some comments on how dry it all was, they had lapsed into a lovely silence, which suited her just fine. *Who needs idle chatter? Really, silence was so underrated.*

For her part, Alicia's mind was anything but silent. Part of it was wondering whether Lynette would heed her words and keep away from handsome Blake (she too had noticed how quickly they'd scurried off), and part of it was assessing the many dangers that lay ahead.

It was a habit she had nurtured since childhood, borne

of an anxious mind and a lifetime's devotion to murder mysteries, although she wasn't sure which came first.

Snakes were Alicia's current concern, and she wondered whether the lodge had any antivenom on the premises or if they would have to rush back down the mountain should one of them get bitten. She was just imagining the hair-raising drive when something else made her hair stand on end. It started with a heavy crunch and then a soft sprinkling of dust.

What on earth is that?

Alicia glanced up to see some rocks toppling down the slope towards them, followed by what looked like a sizeable boulder. Before she knew what she was doing, she was hurling herself into Flo, who was so startled by Alicia's attack she had no time to react. Instead, the two women went flying forwards, the rocks missing them by inches. A second later the boulder came crashing down on the path they had just trodden before it continued on its journey, smashing down the steep incline, sending dust and foliage flying.

The women stared after it, gasping.

"Goodness me!" Flo said eventually, still clutching her pole as Alicia took deep steadying breaths. "Whatever was that?"

"A landslide, I think," Alicia replied, brushing herself off, then helping Flo to her feet as Lynette and Blake came running back towards them.

"Are you guys okay?" Lynette cried out.

"We're fine!" Flo called back, thanking her mother's good genes for the fact that her bones were still intact. All she had to show for the fall were a few grazes.

They took another minute to catch their breaths as Blake and Lynette stared up and then down the slope where the boulder had now settled between overhanging trees.

"Thank you, Alicia," Flo said. "If you hadn't pushed me out of the way, I would have been pummelled!"

"It may not be the last of the falling rocks. I think we better get off the track," said Blake. "Seems dangerous."

"It's deadly!" Lynette concurred. "You could have been killed!"

Yes, Alicia thought as her brain began exploding. *Was it an innocent accident or had someone set that boulder flying?*

As they turned around and made their way off the sunny track and back into the darkened canopy, venomous snakes now forgotten, Flo started to feel woozy, so they found the nearest tree trunk and stopped to let her catch her breath.

While waiting, Alicia squinted back through the trees to the ridge above, where the rocks had come from. Squinted some more. Was that…?

She felt a sudden chill run down her back. There was someone standing up there, she was sure of it! Yes, a tall figure, a man perhaps. Hat on head, arms on hips.

"Hey guys!" she hissed. "Look!"

By the time Lynette and Blake glanced up, the figure had vanished. Alicia tried to explain what she had seen, but they both looked at her like she was hallucinating.

"The shape of the trees is messing with your head," said Lynette. "Wouldn't be the first time."

Alicia ignored that and turned to Blake. "What's up there anyway?"

He had clearly researched the tracks earlier, but he looked confused now, even a little flustered. "No bloody idea," he said, his tone verging on cranky. "Come on, let's head back." Then he went to assist Flo, but she waved him off.

"I'm perfectly capable, young man!"

Her mood had also darkened, and who could blame her? If Alicia hadn't glanced up when she did, their lovely walk might have turned out very differently.

~

From the top of the ridge, someone was watching the walkers and frowning. That should not have happened, not at all. Nothing was going as planned.

There was a sigh of weariness, then a sense that life had come full circle. The future had been written, and the ending was but the flick of a page.

Or the roll of a crunching boulder.

CHAPTER 4

The lobby looked abandoned when Alicia stepped inside, and she fluffed her wet hair up as she glanced about. It was almost dinnertime, and everybody must still be getting ready, she decided, noticing the large clock above the reception desk. She had washed and dressed quickly, keen to report the rock fall, but there was no one about. Noticing a small gold bell sitting atop the desk, she stepped across and was about to tap it when she heard voices coming from what she assumed was an office behind reception.

"...any idea *why*?" came a woman's voice, followed quickly by a man's.

"Not exactly, but... my theories."

Alicia couldn't hear every word, but she could make out Vale's haughty tone. The woman's voice was not as clear, but their mutual annoyance was obvious, so Alicia reached for a pamphlet and stepped away to allow them to finish their conversation. She heard the words "imposter" and "fraudster" and then "think we're complete idiots!" before somebody humphed loudly.

After a few seconds, the woman said, "So what are you going to do?"

Another pause and then Vale said very clearly, "Confront them, of course! And I need to warn—"

There was an abrupt silence, and then Vale suddenly materialised, catching Alicia by surprise. He must have sensed her presence, but luckily she was still browsing the pamphlet, or at least pretending to, so she glanced up at him innocently, slapping a breezy smile on her face.

"Sorry to disturb," she said.

"Not at all, madam," he replied swiftly. "You're looking for the dining room, I presume?"

"Actually, no, I just want to report an incident on the track. But I can come back—"

"That won't be necessary." He glanced back briefly, giving the slightest shake of his head, before stepping out and towards her. "Is there a problem?"

"I'm not sure."

She told the manager exactly what had happened, and he listened intently, eyes darkening with every sentence.

"That is precisely why I asked you all to stick to the lower, signposted tracks."

"So that is a track up there?"

"A very old one, I can assure you. Repentance Way. But it has not been in use for years; it's far too dangerous."

"Well I'm pretty sure it was used this afternoon. I definitely saw someone up there. Could they have caused the rock fall accidentally or…?"

She didn't need to finish that sentence; he was already looking horrified. "I can assure you, madam, that if someone had strayed onto the track, it most certainly would have been an accident. I really don't see why someone would want to cause any harm to you or your friends."

Alicia smiled. He was right. Of course he was right. Her imagination was getting ahead of her again. "Still, I thought I should tell you."

"And I'm glad you did. I shall remind your party of the importance of staying on the correct tracks."

It wasn't flying boulders he was thinking of now though. It was the threat of history crashing down upon them.

~

As Mrs Flannery placed the first course before them—a hearty pumpkin soup with a scoop of sour cream in the centre and a chunk of hot crusty bread beside it—Vale was as good as his word and stepped to the front of the long dining table and tapped a wine glass gently with a knife.

"If I could have your attention please, everyone." The group settled down, and he gave them one of his awkward smiles. "I have a few housekeeping announcements, and then I shall leave you to enjoy Mrs Flannery's fine cooking."

"It smells delish!" Missy said while Lynette raised an eyebrow.

It did smell delicious, that was true, but "fine" was not the word she would use. It was more country provincial; practically peasant food.

"Firstly," Vale began, "we do want you to enjoy the surroundings, but I ask—*again*—that anyone going on a bush walk, please stay on the marked tracks. The walking paths start at the lower edge of the driveway and are clearly signposted. Please, we ask that no one take any other routes. There is an older trail that winds above the lodge at the northern end of the driveway, but it has not been maintained for many years and can cause harm to yourself or others."

He glanced at Alicia, and she nodded her appreciation. Then, eyes still on her, he said, "I believe your club will begin proceedings tomorrow morning?"

She nodded again, then addressed the group. "I was thinking we could start around ten thirty, what do you think? That'll give us all time for a sleep-in or a walk if you prefer."

"But stay on the right track!" added Flo, her tone a little huffy.

Vale continued. "I believe you will be most comfortable in the library and will prepare it accordingly. Mrs Flannery will provide both morning and afternoon tea and will leave a light lunch in the fridge at the back of the library, which you can help yourself to as required. But please, if you do need anything else, anything at all, do not hesitate to tap the bell in the foyer or use the internal phone and I will be able to assist."

"Have you got Wi-Fi?" someone called out. It was Ronnie, eyes wide.

"We do of course have internet connection on the main computer, madam, but we like to encourage our guests to unplug while they are here. We find it makes for a much more relaxing experience."

"Really?" she said, looking like she'd never heard anything so preposterous.

Blake was also frowning while Simon glanced at Claire, and they shared a smile, remembering their encounter on her balcony.

Vale went to leave, then had a sudden thought and stepped back. "One other thing, if you don't mind. It has been a very dry season. Exceptionally dry, in fact. We haven't seen it this dry since…" His voice faltered as he glanced around the group anxiously. "We are not concerned, not at all, but we do ask that you are conscious of water usage at all times. Please be sure to turn taps off securely and reuse towels where possible." He nodded and said, "Thank you for your patience and *bon appétit*."

As Vale returned to the kitchen, Lynette turned to the people around her. "What's Vale so freaked out about?"

"They are on tank water, Lynny," Missy replied, reaching for her spoon. "They have to conserve it but, really, honeykins, we should *all* be conserving water all the time no matter who we are and where we live. It's about protecting resources—"

"Actually, dear," said Ronnie, "I think he's more concerned about the immediate future and bushfires; having enough water should we find ourselves in the middle of one."

Lynette darted her eyes to Alicia, who was deep in

conversation with Claire. *Good*, she thought. They were all seated together at one table, but it was a very large table, and most of them had broken off into smaller conversations. Alicia and Claire were chatting at one end while Perry and Simon were listening to something Flo was saying at the other, and in between sat Blake, studying his meal like a food critic.

"Is that the Great Fire you mentioned earlier?" asked Lynette now. "What happened?"

"Well," said Ronnie, swallowing a mouthful of soup, then leaning in like it was a government secret, a lock of ash-blond hair dropping into one eye. "It was at least forty-five years ago if my memory serves me well, and we all know it's very creaky."

"Fifty, actually," said Blake, who was no longer staring at his bowl. He added quickly, "Or so I hear. I was hoping to learn more about it in the library, but the place is nothing but outdated encyclopedias and dust bunnies." His own eyes darted around the dining room now, his lips drawn downward. "This place could really do with a makeover, it's so old school. If I were the new owner, I'd rip it all down and start again."

"There's a new owner?" said Lynette.

"Hell yeah, why else do you think they're revamping? The Lyle family have barely touched the place since they built it almost ninety years ago. Stuck in the crusty old days, they are, with their stuffed animals and stiff family portraits. Pity the fire didn't take half the place out. At least now it'll get a new lease of life."

"*Anyhoo*," said Ronnie, flashing him a surprisingly vehement frown, "the fire was just after I visited, I believe, back in the *crusty old days*." Her frown flashed again. "It had been such a lovely dance too, and poor Lydia Lyle, she must have been devastated when it happened. The dances were all her idea, you see…"

"What happened?" Lynette asked, keeping her on track. She had a feeling there was going to be quite a bit of that with this particular club member.

"The fire, dear!" The woman looked at her like she was dim. "Vale's right of course. It was extremely dry that year, I don't believe they'd had their usual rains, and the year before hadn't been much better. Bit like now, actually." Her own lips smudged downwards. "The undergrowth was like tinder, so when a fire started down the gorge, well, it swept up like…"

"Wildfire?" Blake offered, and now she squinted at him, not sure if he was mocking her.

"What *happened*?" Lynette asked again. "To the lodge and the guests?"

"Oh they got lucky, dear. The place was spared, but I heard the fire came within inches! Although there might have been some lives lost, I'm not quite sure…"

"Just the one," said Blake, no longer sniggering. "A man in his early twenties, a staffer, employed to lead the hunt. He went to fight the fire and never came back." Then, to their raised eyebrows, he added, "I'm a bit of a news junkie. Checked it out before I came up."

Ronnie was frowning suspiciously at him now. "A hunter, you say? Hmm…"

"Yeah, well you won't find any pictures of *him* amongst the 'happy snaps'," Blake said, using his fingers for the inverted commas. "And if you check out the lodge's timeline in the library, you'll find no mention of the fire, let alone the poor bastard who died for this place. Like it never even happened."

"It's not something we like to celebrate," came a tight voice behind Blake, and he turned, startled, to find Mrs Flannery standing there, a bottle of red wine in one hand, a bottle of white in the other. "Hardly the best publicity for the place." Then she forced her lips into a smile and said, "So, Mr Morrow, what's your poison?"

~

At their end of the table, Claire was grilling Alicia about another natural disaster, a smaller and more recent one.

"I heard about the landslide. Are you okay?" she asked.

"Oh, I'm fine," Alicia said lightly. "We just got a good dusting, that's all."

Claire dropped her head to one side. "It's me, Alicia. How are you *feeling*? Has it freaked you out?"

Alicia smiled. "I can't put anything past you lot anymore." She released a heavy breath of air, causing her fringe to rise up. "Truth is, I was a little spooked. It came out of nowhere."

"Fair enough. That could have been so much worse. Tell me, any idea how it happened?"

"Vale says there's a disused walking track above the one we were on. It's eerily called Repentance Way."

"Oooh, that is eerie."

"I know! It's been shut down because they've had rock falls in the past."

"So that's why Vale got all snippy about the tracks before dinner?"

She nodded. "We must stay on the beaten path!" She squinted. "Except, somebody didn't." She glanced around, then back. "I saw someone up there."

"Who?"

"Couldn't tell from that distance, and they slunk away before I could show the others. But there was someone up there, I'm sure of it. It was probably the same person I saw heading off in that direction, up the driveway, just before we started our walk."

Claire looked doubly startled. "Really? And you didn't recognise them?"

"I only got a fleeting look. They had a hat on, but I think it was a man. I saw a flash of him before he vanished into the forest. You didn't notice anyone heading out this afternoon, did you?"

Claire frowned. Yes, she had, but she almost didn't want to mention it.

"Hmmm, I did see Simon walking about outside."

Alicia glanced across at him and back. "When exactly?"

"While we were all unpacking. I was trying to get mobile reception and was standing on my balcony. He was striding past and had a quick chat."

"Which direction was he striding? Down the driveway or up?"

She hesitated. "Upwards, last I saw him, but he wouldn't have meant any harm, Alicia, you must know that. It would have been an accident."

"Of course, Claire. He must have got the tracks mixed up. Now I think about it, it's a relief. At least I know I'm not seeing things again!" She laughed. "As long as we all stick to the lower track, the *official* track, we should be safe. And I really want to take a good long walk at some stage tomorrow."

"Me too," said Claire, eyeing off the steamy pot of coq au vin that Mrs Flannery was now placing on the table, Vale behind her with bowls of creamy mashed potatoes and green beans sprinkled with what smelled like parmesan. "I think I'm going to need the exercise!"

Alicia waited until both staff members were out of earshot, then asked, "What do we really know about this Simon fellow?"

Claire shrugged. "Not a lot, but isn't that the whole reason we're here? To get to know each other better." Then she glanced across at the man and back. "Apart from the fact that he might have inadvertently killed you this afternoon, I think he seems quite lovely, actually. Why do you ask? What are you worried about?"

Alicia followed her eyes and shrugged. "Oh, nothing. It's just something I overheard…"

~

As the two women huddled together whispering, Simon tried to keep his attention focused on something

Flo was saying. Something about the perfect way to pluck a chicken—start with the drumsticks, apparently, and work your way down. But his eyes kept straying to Claire and Alicia. He was sure he had heard his name mentioned, and they had both looked over at one point. There was no doubt about that.

He tried to mask his frown.

Surely they hadn't worked it out yet?

He couldn't bear it if they had. He still had so much left to do, so much left to learn…

~

Almost two hours later, when the casserole was consumed, followed soon after by a brandy-laced pudding, the group polished off the last of their wine and began to peel away—one to the library, one or two for an evening stroll, the others to their rooms.

It would be many more hours before everything settled down and silence finally descended, but eventually it did.

Eventually the time was right.

It was bang on two thirty a.m. when a door slowly opened. Two seconds later and a head poked out, eyes looking left then right, then left again.

Another few seconds, then a soft step into the hallway, a hand hanging low, clutching something sharp and shiny.

A few more tentative steps down the corridor towards the lobby. Then hesitation again, listening for sounds, looking for movement, before continuing on, more determined this time. Anxious now to mete out some justice that was many years in the making.

A long-awaited act of atonement.

CHAPTER 5

Alicia woke the next morning, feeling groggy and out of sorts. She had not slept well. Strange, violent noises kept interrupting her slumber—creaking and scuttling and what she could only assume were flying foxes screeching outside. Whoever said the country was quiet must have been wearing earplugs.

It didn't help that the rockfall kept playing over in her mind, the way that boulder came rushing towards them, the way that stranger stood watching silently from above. Not so much as a friendly wave or a bellowed apology.

In Alicia's dreams it wasn't Simon standing up there. It was someone else entirely. A shadowy figure with a dark face and a floppy white hat on. It was little wonder then that she was filled with relief when her alarm finally gave her permission to get up.

After a cool, sobering shower, she dressed in casual gear, grabbed her room key and headed to the dining room, where she found most of the group already gathered, now in groups of three at various tables. The only ones missing were Blake and Lynette, and as she sat down beside Perry, Alicia found her mind straying again, this time into X-rated territory.

Surely they hadn't hooked up?

The group had been exhausted by the time the three-course meal was done and had all decided on an early night.

Or had they?

She tried to think back. Alicia had nicked into the library before bed, but Lynette wasn't with her. Had she gone straight to her room? *Or had she remained in the restaurant for another glass of vino, a handsome newcomer at her table?*

"Hey, sis, you don't look like you got much sleep!" said Lynette, breaking into her thoughts as she took a seat while Perry was helping himself to the buffet.

Blake was not trailing Lynette, and Alicia took that as a good sign. She said, "What about you?"

"Slept like a baby. Although speaking of which, I miss our pooch! Max would love it up here. Such a pity we couldn't bring him."

"It *is* a national park, Lynette," Perry said, dropping a plate of scrambled eggs and bacon in front of him. "Get in there, girls, it all looks delicious!"

Lynette studied the eggs on his plate and must have liked what she'd seen, because she promptly jumped up to help herself to the cooked breakfast.

Alicia stuck to the pastries, her stomach still unsettled, then reached for her empty cup as Mrs Flannery appeared from the swinging kitchen doors with a pot of fresh coffee. By the time she reached Alicia's table, however, the pot was empty, and Mrs Flannery glared at it like it was its own damn fault and then strode back into the kitchen. When she returned, she had a platter of fruit but no coffee, and Alicia hid her disappointment as she turned to Perry.

"How did you sleep?"

"I always sleep well, honey," he said, although it was a lie this time.

It wasn't the noises that had kept him up, it was the name Westera that was playing like a loop in his head. *Now why was Ronnie's name so familiar...*

It was just as Perry was finally drifting off that he remembered. He was right! It had nothing to do with Balmain and the moonlight cinema. The way Ronnie spoke of the old Hunting Lodge, the incongruity of her dress sense, it finally dawned on him—she was one of the Museum's biggest benefactors! Or at least her family was. He was sure of it.

He'd spent the next hour tossing and turning, trying to recall the name of her husband and how they'd made all their dough. Pharmaceuticals was it? Or something to do with mining? In any case, Ronnie came from serious wealth, the kind that left you gasping. Only last year she'd donated a cheque for close to a million dollars.

He glanced across at Ronnie seated at her own table and noticed the simple cotton blouse, beige pleated trousers, the slightly scuffed sandals, and couldn't help smiling. She might dress like an ordinary granny, but she was the richest person in the room by a long shot.

Was she deliberately hiding her background, he wondered? Did it even matter?

"Morning guys!" came a booming voice from the front door, and they all swept around to find Blake standing there, walking shoes on, a camera around his neck. "I've already done the four-kilometre return trek. How about you?"

"Oh, stop showing off, laddie!" Flo called out, and Blake chuckled as he made his way across the room to inspect the buffet.

He leaned down and back. "Not bad," he said to no one in particular. Then, catching sight of Mrs Flannery, he added, "I'm going to need a cup of coffee, thanks, Mrs Flannery. Quick as you can."

As she nodded vaguely and returned to the kitchen to get the pot, Perry turned back to the sisters and said, "You'd think Blake owned the place, the way he swans about, roaring up in his fancy car and ordering the staff about."

"What staff?" said Alicia. "There's barely anyone here. I think poor Mrs Flannery is flying solo this morning."

"You're just jealous, Perry," was Lynette's take. "I like a confident, athletic man myself."

"That'll make a change from the dithery fools you usually date," Perry retorted, and they began flicking napkins at each other until Alicia's low growl stopped them, as it usually did.

"Besides, Vale's probably catching up on his beauty sleep," Lynette said. "He was up very late last night."

"How do you know?" asked Alicia.

"Oh, I'm just assuming…," said Lynette as her eyes slid sideways.

~

As Mrs Flannery returned to the kitchen, she was swearing under her breath but not at the bossy guest.

Where the blazes was Vale?

He was usually a lot more helpful than this. Cooking might be her domain, but he always stepped in when she needed it. Was never above that. She frowned as she checked the brewing coffee. The mysterious guest must have thrown him off-kilter, and she couldn't blame him for that. They'd both been out of sorts of late. Ever since the place had gone up for sale. It had put everyone in a lather.

She exhaled. No point worrying about that now. Perhaps Vale needed a decent sleep-in. She could do with a rest herself. She'd been dropping the ball a lot lately, was beginning to let things slide. Couldn't *believe* she'd forgotten to collect the mail yesterday! She blamed the early train for that. It threw her schedule out completely, and now she had no choice but to make the windy drive back to town. She was expecting an important letter, hoping for one at least. Vale might want to go down with the sinking ship, but she had plans. Grand plans, and they did not involve Lyle and his blasted lodge. Not anymore.

The sooner it was all over the better.

Straightening her apron, Mrs Flannery pulled the coffee from the percolator, wedged her lips into something resembling a smile, and then returned to the dining room.

~

Simon stood and nodded goodbye to his fellow diners, Flo and Ronnie, who, like him, were also up early and first to take in breakfast—not that Flo had consumed much, just a cup of something and a piece of buttery toast. What they didn't know was that he had been up for hours, wandering the premises, getting all his ducks lined up.

He didn't get caught this time though. He had seen to that. Stretching, he glanced across the dining room and tried not to stare.

Be cool, he told himself. *All good things come to those who wait.*

~

As Missy nattered on about her *fabulous* new apartment and the "killer deal" she got on what sounded to Blake like a cheap and nasty sofa, he glanced across to Lynette and tried to catch her eye. There was no room at her table, but he had enjoyed their digestif last night.

Soon after dinner was done, as everybody else scattered like Cinderella before midnight, he found his way to the tiny bar and was delighted when Lynette promptly joined him. It was a poky room, with a door leading into the corridor and another into the dining, and it was darker and dingier than his usual drinking holes, but the wine selection was good, and he poured them both a giant glass of cabernet sauvignon while Lynette began jotting their names into the small notepad provided.

"I guess they charge us at the end," she said, but he had tsked at that.

Blake hadn't wanted to jot anything down—"They'll never know!"—but Lynette proved to be more vanilla than he'd anticipated and insisted they account for the bottle they ended up consuming. He was suggesting they grab another when they heard a creak in the corridor outside and then spotted Vale striding in the direction of the lobby. He had a bag in his hands and a grim look on his face.

A few minutes later they heard the entrance door open and then close again.

Lynette had pondered where the manager was heading at that time of night, but Blake already had a pretty good idea. And the kernel of a plan.

Feigning a yawn, he said, "On second thoughts, I think I'm gonna head to bed," and he was sure he'd seen a glint of disappointment in the beautiful blonde's eyes.

He sniggered. Business first, then there would be time for pleasure.

"Hey Blake! Tell us more about the guy who perished in the fire!" said Missy now, her voice rising to break through Blake's reverie. "The one you were talking about last night, the hunting chap!"

Blake looked up just as a cup clattered loudly to its saucer near the buffet table. His eyes darted towards it, but it wasn't Lynette he was looking at now, it was someone else entirely. They were mopping away spilt coffee, blushing and frowning and trying to look blasé.

But that blush suggested otherwise.

Blake's eyes narrowed further as his brain ticked over and he began to do the maths…

CHAPTER 6

Eight fresh copies of Agatha Christie's *And Then There Were None* had been placed on the polished red cedar coffee table in the middle of the room, and Alicia felt a wave of warmth wash over her as she stepped into the library, a sheaf of papers under one arm, a battered copy of the book under the other. She didn't realise the lodge would provide free copies, and it was such a sweet touch! Still, they were one short, so she was glad she'd brought her own.

Then she glanced at the clock above the billiard table and got busy.

It was right on ten o'clock, but she was chairing today's discussion and wanted to get the room in order before the meeting started. Alicia felt like a curator, putting everything in its place, making everything just right.

She already knew that Lynette and Claire were heading off for a vigorous power walk, and that Flo—or was it Ronnie?—was photographing the extraordinary murals along the corridor. She wasn't sure where Simon or Blake had got to, but she could see Perry now, stepping through the open glass doors to the library.

"I won't get in your way, I promise," he said. "I just want to read up on the history of the place."

He was pointing to the Lyle family memorabilia that also adorned these walls.

"Go right ahead," Alicia said, reaching into her folder to produce a set of questions, which she now placed in a neat pile beside the books. "I brought spare pens and paper in case anyone wants to take notes. And of course I have the usual prompts, all neatly typed, in case we get stuck. I had so much fun creating the questions for this one. There are *so* many talking points! Things like vigilante justice, atonement and retribution, regret and revenge…"

Perry wasn't listening. He was staring mesmerised at the framed image of a young man, a black-and-white portrait hanging beside the fridge.

"Well hello, handsome!" he said as Alicia stepped across. "It's the founding father, Arthur Henry Lyle," he told her, reading from the inscription then, mimicking Vale's clipped tones. "Our founding father who had to ride for a hundred years in an old horse and buggy!"

Alicia slapped him lightly on the shoulder. "Be nice. It would have been very tough back then. I can't imagine how they dragged everything up here to even build the place."

"Probably sourced most of it from here," Perry told her. "Would have had first pick of the old-growth forest. Green gold they called it, and I can see why."

"Just as well it didn't all come down in the Great Fire then. Not that you'll read much about it in here."

On last night's visit to the library, Alicia had already discovered, as Blake had earlier, that amongst the many framed articles, there was nothing on the Great Fire of 1970. Yet she, too, had done her research and knew that the flames had come teeth-chatteringly close. If it hadn't been for the "tenacity of a few good men," the whole place would have gone up like a bonfire.

"Any closer and we wouldn't be standing in this lovely old library," she told Perry, who eyed her suspiciously. "Yes, okay, I already googled it before we came. You know me, I like to know what I'm up against."

He did know her, very well indeed, and he dropped his head sideways and said, "It's ancient history now, Alicia. Nothing to worry about."

"I know that," she said, chuckling as she turned away.

Yet it didn't put her mind at rest. Alicia had done one walk. Had already seen how dry the undergrowth was, and hadn't Vale confirmed as much last night?

She tried not to think about roaring fires as she returned to her curation.

~

Half an hour later, the rest of the group were scattered around the library, some of them helping themselves to the refreshments that Mrs Flannery had left on a sideboard—tea, coffee, pound cake and brown sugar and cardamom biscuits—others settling into one of the three deep leather lounges that encircled the coffee table. Missy plonked in the centre of one lounge and was quickly bookended by Perry and Lynette while Claire settled in beside Flo and Ronnie on another. She and Missy had enlisted the two friends, and she wanted to be close should they need some guidance.

Alicia pulled a lone side chair from against the wall and placed it in front of the group, then watched as Simon and Blake sat down at opposite ends of the third lounge, looking awkward beside each other.

They were like yin and yang those two, she thought. Like polar opposites. Blake was now sporting cut-off blue shorts and a tight-fitting T-shirt with the words I HATE IRONIC T-SHIRTS printed across the front; Simon was in a crisply ironed Chambray shirt and long, tanned trousers. The former looked ready for the beach, the latter for the boardroom.

"So how does this work?" Simon asked, and Alicia held up her hand.

She waited until everyone had quietened down and then said, "Hello everybody, and welcome to the Murder Mystery Book Club, Mark II!"

A boisterous cheer erupted from the group while

Flo called out:

"Whatever happened to the first book club, love?"

Perry mock shuddered, splayed fingers at his chest. "Trust me, you do *not* want to know!"

"One of our early members was a total fraud," said Missy, pushing her glossy black spectacles into place. "And then there was dishy Dr Anders. We all *loved* him, but he could be a bit, well…"

"*Anyway!*" said Alicia, cutting in with a strained smile. "That's not important now, thanks Missy. From today we're moving forward with a whole new group. We've gone from five of us to nine, and I for one am *très* excited!"

"And then there were nine!" called out Missy proudly, like she'd been rehearsing the line all morning and waiting for just such a moment.

Perry groaned, Lynette rolled her eyes and Missy erupted into giggles.

"Anyway," Alicia said again, shooting Missy a smile this time. "As you all know, we're not just here to discuss one of Christie's mysteries—the final one we'll discuss before moving to a whole new author—but also to get to know each other better, and I really hope we get a chance to do that. Now, before we start, and at risk of sounding like Vale, I have a little housekeeping of my own."

Perry groaned again, pretending to stab himself, and now Alicia was rolling her eyes.

"Settle down, it's nothing dramatic. I only want the new members to know that there are very few rules in this club. We want everyone to be relaxed and comfortable, so speak up as much or as little as you like, and feel free to help yourself to refreshments at any time."

"Alicia had a dreadful experience at a previous book club," Claire whispered to the two women beside her. "Way too stuffy and regimented."

"I don't mind things a little regimented," said Simon, and Claire smiled back at him.

She didn't mind it either, if truth be told.

"The key is to be yourself and let the conversation flow," Alicia explained. "I have jotted down some questions, but they're a guide only, so if we scoot off in a different direction, that's perfectly fine too."

What Alicia didn't realise as they reached for the questions and settled in to begin discussions was that those words would come back to bite her.

~

And Then There Were None turned out to be a contentious choice.

Its earlier racist title had evolved over time, but Perry, for one, was not in a forgiving mood.

"She might have been a wonderful writer, but the Dame was a tad bigoted, wasn't she?"

Claire gasped. While this book was darker than she normally liked, she would not stand for any Christie bashing.

"It was just the times, Perry. There was a lot of unchecked bigotry back then."

"Yes, I'm afraid there was," said Ronnie.

"Oh well, that's all right then." He sniffed, his voice dripping with sarcasm.

"No, it's not *right*," Simon said, "it's appalling, but Claire is quite correct. We have to take the context into consideration. This book was written back in the forties I think."

"Actually it was 1939," said Missy, her voice barely audible as a phone in the foyer began ringing.

Alicia jumped up to close the library doors, hoping to block out the sound, while Flo said:

"It really was a very different time, you know. Ronnie and I could tell you stories! You spring chickens have no idea how good you've got it. Back in my day…"

And off she went, telling of the hardships of growing

up in rural Australia with an alcoholic father, a downtrodden mother, five siblings and barely "two pennies to rub together."

Alicia found her story fascinating, but it wasn't the story they were here to discuss. She smiled and discreetly checked her watch, wondering whether the relaxed rule should be a little less, well, *relaxed*. The closed doors did little to muffle the ringing phone, and she could feel a headache coming on.

"That's not even the worst story I could tell you," Flo said, and Alicia held her hand up.

"If you don't mind, Flo, we really need to return to this particular story." She tapped her book cover. "Or we'll never get through it. Did you know this is Christie's best-selling book?"

"I did!" said Missy. "It's actually one of the world's best-selling mysteries. Still! Can you believe it? After *all* this time. And did you know, kittens, that Dame Agatha said it was the hardest book she ever sat down to write?"

Lynette smiled and turned to the newcomers. "We're not sure there's anything about the queen of crime Missy doesn't know." She frowned. "But I'm surprised it's her best seller. I mean, it's a gripping tale—ten people stuck on a private island with a madman bumping them off, one by one—what's not to love about that? I just missed the meddling Miss Marple and the fastidious Hercule Poirot."

"They're not in it?" said Blake, glancing at the book in his lap. "So who investigates the murder?"

The golden-haired businessman had been silent until then, and now Alicia had an inkling why.

"You mean *murders*, plural," she said, wondering if he had read the book. "And there's no *investigator* as much. At least not until the epilogue. And even then, it's a couple of unknown detectives from Scotland Yard."

"The author couldn't very well throw Mister Parrot or Jane Marple into the mix, could she?" said Flo, also looking at him aghast while he tried not to snigger at her pronunciation. "Everybody carks it by the end of the book, in case you don't remember." She gave him a pointed look. "Agatha couldn't bump off those two. Her readers would never forgive her. I know I wouldn't."

Blake's eyes widened, and he turned the book around to scan the back blurb.

Alicia shared a frown with Flo and brought up the next question—one on retribution and whether everybody deserved what was coming—but she couldn't help wondering what Blake was playing at. *He clearly hadn't read the book!* Why would he beg to be part of the group and then not do his homework?

"Don't know about racist," Lynette said, "but Christie was certainly no feminist. Did you notice how around the middle part, after the cook has been bumped off, the two female guests promptly take over kitchen duties and the men get to swan about and smoke cigars?"

"They helped clean up!" Missy said.

"Plus it was the times," Flo added. "Women *did* do the cooking duties in those days. Like it or lump, that's just the way it was. And I for one didn't mind a jot. I'm a very good cook, I'll have you know."

"So am I," snapped Lynette. "It's my profession. But that's not the point."

"I'm pretty handy in the kitchen myself," said Simon, smiling at Claire. "In my line of business you have to be a jack of all trades."

"And what business is that?" Blake asked, squinting at him now.

"Bit of this, bit of that," he said, his smile dissolving.

"Shall we get back to the book?" Alicia said again, trying to keep the impatience from her tone. It was almost lunchtime now, and they were only up to question three. Besides, the phone was still ringing off the hook and her head was beginning to throb.

"I'll get back to the book," said Claire. "Did you notice there was some violence towards women too?"

"Oh for heaven's sake," said Flo.

"That's right!" said Perry. "When young Vera gets upset about all the murders—as you would, frankly—Dr Armstrong walks up and belts her across the face!"

He stared at Flo as if waiting for her to defend that, but Missy was now doing the honours.

"It was more of a slap," she said, "and only because the poor thing was hysterical."

"Well, it's hardly best practise is it?" said Perry, and Missy shrank back in her seat.

Alicia's hand was up again, but now she was waving an invisible white flag. "Let's break for lunch, shall we?"

She hoped a full stomach would slap them all back on track.

~

As the group dispersed—some to their rooms to freshen up, others helping themselves to premade sandwiches, quiche and mineral water they'd found in the back fridge—Alicia wandered out to the foyer and straight to the front bell this time. She didn't want to be caught eavesdropping again, but she really needed something to alleviate her headache.

The phone was blessedly quiet as she tapped the gold bell. She waited a few minutes, then tapped it again. There was no response. She then leant across the desk to the room behind and called out, "Hello! Anybody there?"

There was only silence.

Surprised, Alicia turned and stepped towards the internal staircase from which Vale had appeared the day before, noticing a small sign that read PRIVATE: STAFF ONLY. She wondered if there was another office up there and if Vale was so busy he hadn't noticed the phone, which had started up again and sounded increasingly like an angry toddler.

Glaring at it, Alicia considered snatching it up, then

shook her head. It wasn't her job to answer their calls. Maybe Mrs Flannery could help.

She made her way back down the corridor, past the library and bar, to the dining room and, once inside, noticed the morning's breakfast had been cleared away but the tables were still separated and had not yet been laid for dinner.

"Hello!" she called out again, crossing to the kitchen at the back and pushing the swinging doors wide.

That's when she got the first inkling that something was not right.

The place looked like a bomb had hit it. The dirty breakfast plates were piled high in the sink, and the leftover buffet was still spread across the bench tops and beginning to attract flies. She noticed what looked like a scribbled shopping list, lying near the stove, and beside it an almost empty bottle of red wine.

"Mrs Flannery?" she called out to no avail.

After glancing around one more time, Alicia turned back, the strange fluttering in her stomach now drowning out the throbbing headache.

~

Back in the library, most of the group had returned and were now gathered around the buffet table, chatting idly.

Watching them from the library doorway, Alicia felt her heart lurch. Everybody seemed happy. Everybody seemed relaxed. Why couldn't she do as she had instructed and relax too? Why was that always so hard for her?

After failing to locate Vale, Alicia had returned to her room to scrounge for paracetamol. She eventually found an old packet at the bottom of her handbag and quickly swallowed two, then added some gloss to her lips and returned to the library. Like Missy, she had been so looking forward to this weekend yet couldn't shake the dread that was creeping through her veins.

Perhaps it was yesterday's rock fall and the ghostly image of the man on the ridge. Perhaps it was the blasted phones that had been screaming all morning like they had the answer to some question nobody had thought to ask. Perhaps it was just her imagination up to its usual tricks…

Ever since she could remember, Alicia's mind was like a disaster movie on high rotation. Where others saw a car driving innocently down a road, Alicia saw a madman about to climb the pavement and take the pedestrians out. An overhead plane was a Spitfire, and a dragging wave a devastating tsunami.

It's not that she lived her life trembling, it's more that Alicia's brain lived a life of its own, and it was probably the reason she had turned to Agatha Christie in the first place. Cosy mysteries fed Alicia's imagination without taking her anywhere too dark.

Still, that didn't always stop the dark thoughts from descending…

Alicia gave herself a quick shake, slapped a smile to her lips, and stepped into the library to resume proceedings.

~

The second half of the session was a little more productive as the club waxed lyrical about their favourite clues and red herrings. Missy was particularly in thrall to the character called Mr U. N. Owen—Mr Unknown—she thought that was a hoot! But now Alicia was the distracted one. She simply could not focus.

The phones had finally stopped ringing, and that was a blessed relief, but she hadn't heard anybody moving about in the corridor or seen any cars pull up through the library window that faced the driveway. There was not so much as a flash of Mrs Flannery or Vale, and that didn't feel right. Did they always vacate the lodge during the day? Or was there some emergency she hadn't thought of?

"Sorry everybody," she said suddenly, desperate to

calm her brain. "I just have to find Vale. Please, keep going, I'll be back in a minute."

Making her way out to the lobby again, Alicia noticed it was still empty, so she retraced her steps to the dining room and then the kitchen. Nothing had changed there either. The tables were still in breakfast mode, and the kitchen was still a shambles.

Feeling disgruntled now—*they might be getting a discount, but it didn't mean they shouldn't get some service!*—she swept back to the reception desk and smacked the front bell several times.

"Gone AWOL has he?" said Simon, and she started. "Sorry, I didn't mean to scare you."

"No, it's fine." She patted her beating heart. "I can't find Mrs Flannery either. I already checked the kitchen; she's vanished."

"Well, they can't have got far."

He opened the front door, and they both stepped outside and glanced about. There wasn't so much as a gardener in sight.

"Wasn't there a lodge van here yesterday?" Simon said, pointing to the empty car space in front of Blake's white Mercedes.

She nodded. Yes, there was.

"Everything all right?" came Claire's voice behind them, Perry beside her, eyebrows high.

Alicia explained the situation, and Perry waved a hand dismissively.

"Oh, Mrs Flannery's gone into town. I saw her van take off this morning, just before book club started."

"There you go!" said Simon. "Probably getting supplies for dinner."

"So where's Vale?"

That had them all stumped.

"Did anyone see him at breakfast?" Simon asked, drawing them back inside. When they all shrugged, he said, "Maybe he's caught up somewhere on the property, doing some maintenance. I wouldn't worry too much."

Except it was too late for that. Alicia's worry was now a whirlwind, and images of Vale in distress were whizzing through her brain. She peered up the private stairwell, her ears craning.

"Could be having a nana nap," said Lynette, who'd also appeared and was following her sister's gaze.

"Yes, but who could sleep through all those phone calls?" said Perry, eyebrows still high.

Who indeed? thought Alicia.

"Do you need him for anything in particular?" Simon wanted to know, and she shrugged.

"I'm just curious, that's all. It feels like we've been deserted or…" She glanced upwards again. "What if something's happened? What if a filing cabinet's fallen on him or something and we're blissfully unaware?"

Claire turned to Simon and said, "Alicia has a very active imagination."

"Radioactive, you mean," said Perry.

"There is one way to find out," said Simon. "Shall we go up and check? Put your mind at ease, Alicia?" She nodded, and he waved towards the stairs and said, "Ladies first."

~

That was all a bit of a debacle, thought Flo as she watched most of the group slink out of the library. Claire and Missy had promised her a slick operation, but this mob was clearly distracted and they'd barely had a good discussion about anything other than all this politically correct nonsense. "I'm heading back to my room," she told Ronnie, who also seemed very distracted.

Ronnie nodded vaguely and watched her go, then her face lit up like Christmas. Good, she had the place entirely to herself! She got to her feet and took the opportunity to do a little scouting of her own. Earlier, she had noticed a glass cabinet full of what looked like vintage guest books, various years scribbled on the front, and she wondered, gleefully, whether her own signature might be in there amongst them. She didn't exactly remember signing the book in her day, but she must have, surely? Didn't Vale say it was tradition?

Ronnie glanced through the glass doors and spotted one tagged "1969" and smiled. She was sure that was the year she had come. Or was it 1968? The problem was, the blasted cupboard was locked. She rattled the doors and then reached a hand upwards, looking for a key.

"What are you up to?" Blake asked, making her jump. He was standing behind her, a wicked glint in his eyes.

"Goodness! You could give a lady a heart attack, creeping up on her like that."

"Looks like you're the one doing the creeping," he said, glancing at the locked door pointedly.

"Am not! I just… Well, I wondered whether my name was in one of the old guest books, that's all. Thought I'd have a skip down memory lane."

He rattled the locked door. "Why don't you break in?"

Ronnie looked horrified at the suggestion, and Lynette didn't look too impressed either. She had returned to the library while the others headed upstairs. She wasn't keen to find Vale *in flagrante*, so she left them to it.

"Don't listen to him!" Lynette called out as she scooped up her iPhone. "I'm sure if you ask nicely, Vale will give you the key." Maybe he'd give her the Wi-Fi password while he was at it.

"Yes, except no one can find Vale, can they?" Blake called back.

"How do you—?" began Lynette before she was interrupted by a bloodcurdling scream that sounded like it was coming from above.

The book club members stared upwards, and Lynette's eyes then widened as she said, "I think that was Alicia!"

CHAPTER 7

If it wasn't for the pungent odour, Alicia would have sworn the hotel manager was doing just as Lynette had suggested and sneaking in an afternoon nap. She almost hadn't knocked on the door marked MANAGER, almost hadn't opened it and, worse still, had almost turned away when she realised this wasn't Vale's office they were invading, or even his living area. It was his bedroom, and he was still tucked up under the covers.

Mortified, she went to shoo Simon out when that smell smashed through her subconscious. She turned around and took a second look, noticing a puddle of something disgusting by his head. Had he come down with food poisoning?

Walking slowly across the room, Alicia called out, "Vale? Are you okay?"

She approached the bed and reached down, still thinking at this stage how embarrassed he would be when she woke him. But of course Vale was not okay, and before she knew what she was doing, Alicia was jumping back and screaming at the top of her lungs. In retrospect, it wasn't the smell that had startled her, or even his deathly features. It was Vale's body—as cold and stiff as an ice block.

Within seconds, Simon was pulling Alicia away and reaching down to take the man's pulse. Seconds later he looked back at her, head shaking.

"He's dead," he said, his voice flat, his eyes disbelieving.

"What's going on?" came Perry from the doorway, followed immediately by Claire.

Then they all looked to Simon, who was now covering Vale's face with his bedsheet. He shook his head firmly and stepped back towards the bedroom door. "I'm sorry to say, but our hotel manager has passed away."

Claire flung a hand to her lips. "Goodness me! Oh how *terrible!*"

"Alicia!" cried Lynette, racing up the staircase. "What's all the commotion? Are you all right?"

She nodded. "But Vale's not." Then, noticing them all crowd in, she said, "I think we should keep our distance, folks."

Alicia wasn't sure there was cause for suspicion, but she had seen enough corpses in the past few years to know that you needed to keep pawing hands away.

"Good idea," said Perry, who was also scarily familiar with crime scenes. "Let's preserve any evidence."

"Evidence? What are you talking about?" said Blake, who was just behind Lynette. He peered past the group and stared at the figure on the bed. "Jesus, is that Vale under there?"

Simon ignored that. "Let's not jump to any rash conclusions, Perry. The man most likely died in his sleep."

"What of?" demanded Ronnie, who was coming up the rear, Flo beside her. "He seemed perfectly fine last night."

"Old age?" suggested Blake, earning himself a scowl from the older woman.

"Could've been bitten by a snake," said Flo, and Alicia was now nodding.

That was a very good suggestion! The vomit on his pillow indicated that something was not right. For the first time since Anders had left, she wished he was amongst them. The dashing doctor could be an annoying voice of caution, but he was also very useful, especially at times like these.

As it turned out, Ronnie proved useful too.

"Step aside," she said crisply as she bustled her way through. "I used to be a nurse back in the dark ages. I'll check his body for bite marks."

"And I'll see if I can find Mrs Flannery," said Flo.

"Don't bother," said Perry. "She's gone into town."

"Well, I'm going to call the police," said Simon, and Alicia nodded vigorously.

That was the best suggestion yet! *Let's bring in the professionals and hand this one straight over.*

~

As Ronnie began to inspect Vale's body, the rest of the group returned downstairs, some to the library to get the kettle boiling. After that shock, they could all do with a cuppa, although Flo insisted they would need something stronger and headed into the bar to "have a little fossick."

In the lobby, Simon scooped up the main phone and began tapping in three zeroes. As he did so, Alicia and Perry held the front door open and scanned the steep driveway, desperately searching for signs of Mrs Flannery.

Why wasn't she back yet?

It was now midafternoon, and the cook would have to start preparations for dinner soon, surely? Not that anyone would feel hungry tonight.

"It's not working," Simon called out, holding the phone towards them.

Alicia glanced back. "Of course it's working. It's been ringing hot all morning."

"You probably just have to find an open line," said Flo, a bottle of brandy in one hand. "Ronnie might have been a nurse as a wee lass, but I was a receptionist before I got hitched. I'll get us sorted."

She dropped the spirits on the desk and snatched the receiver from Simon, then began pressing buttons and clicking it on and off. Then she, too, held the phone out, scowling. "He's right, I'm afraid. Landline's disconnected."

"How is that even possible?" said Alicia. "It was ringing so much my head was hurting!"

"Yes, but then it stopped, remember?" said Simon.

Alicia stared at him, blinking. He's right. She had been so relieved when it finally went quiet, but now... She took the phone from Flo and then glared at the dead dial tone.

"Do you think someone's cut it?" she asked, and now Flo was doing the glaring.

"Don't be so melodramatic, love. Phone lines go down all the time in the country. Back in Gulargambone we lost it every other week. The power too if we weren't lucky."

And now they were all looking at the overhead light as Lynette and Blake wandered in, cups in hand, from the library.

"What now?" Lynette asked, tracing their eyes to the ceiling.

"Phone lines are down," Alicia told her. "We can't call out."

"That's a bummer. How about the internet? Maybe we can call via Skype or something?"

Lynette stepped behind the reception desk and clicked the computer to life, hand still holding her cup as she began tapping at the keyboard. Then she too was looking at them all blankly.

"No internet connection either. I wonder if that was also cut."

"It's probably ADSL and comes in through the phone line," said Blake. "Pity they haven't got decent satellite broadband."

Simon was staring at the younger man strangely. "How do you know so much about this place?"

Blake shrugged. "I know how internet cable works. It's not rocket science, old boomer." He sniggered.

"In the meantime," said Alicia, "what do we do with poor Mr Vale?"

"Nothing," said Ronnie from the top of the stairs. "No one is to touch a thing."

"What's going on?" said Alicia.

"Did you find bite marks?" asked Flo.

Ronnie shook her head. "I found one mark, but I don't think it's a bite. Alicia, will you come and take a look for me?"

Alicia nodded and raced up the stairs while the others swapped worried glances.

~

Up in the bedroom, Alicia was trying hard not to inhale as she inspected Vale's left arm below where his short-sleeved pyjama shirt ended. Ronnie was right. There was just one clear bluish-red dot with swelling all around it, the skin puffy and inflamed.

"If he had been bitten by a snake, he would have two puncture wounds from the animal's fangs, not one. I think it's an injection mark," Ronnie told her. "And it was done fairly recently."

"Are you sure?"

"I've given plenty of injections in my time, dear. I know an injection mark when I see one."

"You think he's a drug addict or... maybe a diabetic?"

Ronnie cocked her head sideways. "I can't see any other signs of drug usage. No, I think this was a one-off."

"Suicide?" Alicia suggested hopefully, and now Ronnie was giving her a sympathetic look.

"Did he seem suicidal to you? Besides, where is the needle? I can't see any paraphernalia, which makes me think it was not self-inflicted."

Alicia surveyed the immediate vicinity. Apart from the inflamed skin and the puddle of vomit, there was nothing else suspicious. Nothing on his bedside table or under his sheets or on the floor below his bed. She noticed a small en suite bathroom and stepped across, checking around the sink and in the plastic bin below it.

"I've inspected the cabinet," Ronnie called out.

"Apart from some multivitamins and cough syrup, I can't find anything even remotely suspicious amongst his toiletries, nothing to indicate a preexisting condition. No vials of anything nasty."

"So, let me see if I can catch up," Alicia said, returning to the bedroom. "Vale has an injection mark but no obvious signs of how he could have been injected. Maybe... I don't know... Mrs Flannery gave him a shot of something down in the kitchen—maybe it's a regular thing—and then he came up here and had a bad reaction to it."

Ronnie did not look too impressed with Alicia's theory.

"How about this then: Maybe it's completely unrelated. A red herring, so to speak. For all we know, Vale could have had a heart condition or cancer or a sudden stroke and just passed away in his sleep—irrelevant to that injection."

"And yet, as I said, there's no heart medication or the like anywhere, dear. Nothing to indicate a chronic condition that might bring on immediate death. I don't think he was more than seventy, a bit young to just die in your sleep."

Alicia nodded and stared down at the man again, a hand now covering her nose and mouth.

"He released his bowels," Ronnie told her matter-of-factly, and Alicia stepped back involuntarily.

She did not know how anyone could be a nurse, let alone a forensic doctor. She took her hat off to the lot of them. "So... so what do you think it all means, Ronnie? What's your gut feeling?"

The woman stared down at Vale with a frown. "I don't know for sure, of course, and a postmortem will be required..." She looked back at Alicia. "I can see this has upset you, dear, but I don't know how else to explain it."

"*What?*"

"I have a terrible suspicion our hotel manager has been poisoned."

CHAPTER 8

"**W**here the bloody hell is Mrs Flannery?"

This was a sentiment echoed by both Perry and Simon as they walked part of the way down the driveway, looking out for her vehicle. Any vehicle would do, they just wanted to make contact with the outside world. They had skirted the exterior of the property, looking for signs of life, but apart from a few foraging brush turkeys and a couple of scuttling water dragons, they could find none.

As far as they could tell, the Murder Mystery Book Club were completely alone at the top of the mountain.

Eventually the men returned to the lobby where Lynette and Claire had just finished a search of the interior. There was not so much as a cleaner lurking, they told them. It was just the nine of them, if you didn't count the corpse.

"Anything?" Alicia asked as she and Ronnie returned downstairs to join the club who were now milling about the reception desk, looking confused, alarmed or both.

"The place is like a ghost town," said Perry, and Alicia felt herself shiver.

"So what's the prognosis?" Simon asked Ronnie, rubbing his hands together.

"Unclear at this stage," she replied smoothly, her eyes sliding across to Alicia.

They had agreed to keep Ronnie's theory to themselves for now, because that's all it really was. A theory. There was no actual evidence, and they didn't want to unduly startle the others. As they re-covered Vale's face with the sheet again and secured his bedroom door, even Ronnie had to admit, it was all quite unbelievable. Who on earth would want to poison the longtime hotel manager?

"Do we at least know how long he's been dead?" Simon pushed.

"He wasn't around at breakfast, I remember that," said Flo. "Mrs Flannery looked mighty flustered; quite run off her feet, she was."

"Do you think she *knew* about Vale then," said Missy, "and didn't want to alarm us? Maybe that's why she took off, to fetch the doctor?"

"Explains the disgraceful state of the kitchen," said Lynette, who'd seen the dirty dishes for herself. "A good chef always cleans up after cooking."

"Oh for goodness' sake, you two!" said Perry. "Mrs Flannery wouldn't take off and leave her guests with a corpse! Surely she'd tell at least one of us what was going on. Besides, I saw her leave just before ten this morning and the phones were still working then. If she had found Vale, she would have phoned for an ambulance."

Alicia nodded. That made sense. Which meant that Mrs Flannery was not a "good" chef and was probably zooming back from town now with nothing more helpful than bags of groceries.

"Any idea *when* he died?" Simon turned to Ronnie again, determined to get details.

"I am only a nurse, Simon, and even then, I haven't been a nurse for decades. I can't be expected to know something like that."

"Of course, Ronnie. My apologies."

He shared a quick smile with Claire. Around Ronnie, he felt like a naughty schoolboy, being constantly slapped across the knuckles by the headmistress.

"Blake and I saw Vale up and about at around midnight last night," said Lynette, quickly adding, "And don't get in a flap, Alicia, we were just having a quiet drink in the bar when he walked past."

She looked for Blake for verification, but he had vanished.

"Anyway," Lynette continued, "it looked to me like Vale was on a mission. I'm sure I heard him go outside."

"And he was fit as a fiddle when I saw him get back around one this morning," said Flo, her tone matter-of-fact.

"Get back?" said Alicia. "From where?"

"What were you doing up at one in the morning?" was Perry's query.

"I rarely sleep, dear. One of the pitfalls of old age, I'm afraid. You'll find out soon enough." She looked him up and down. "I was sitting on my deck, enjoying the moonlight, when I spotted him scooting back along the pathway, the one he'd distinctly told us all to avoid."

"Repentance Way?" said Alicia. "The one that leads up the driveway and into the forest?"

Flo nodded. "I thought that was a bit cheeky of him, but there you have it. He was carrying one of those bags. You know? Those ugly things we've been bullied into taking to the grocers. Quite inconvenient, really. I can't be expected to have a bag on me at all times."

"A green bag?" prodded Missy.

"That's the one! But it was clearly empty as it was all scrunched up, and he had a thermos, you know, for holding hot tea? It looked like he had gone for a long walk or a picnic or something."

"A picnic? At midnight?" said Alicia, then, "So *that's* why you thought it might be a snake bite?"

"I wondered whether he'd been accidentally bitten on his walk. My sister, Jan, got bit by a tiger snake while putting the chickens away when she was a young 'un. Her own damn fault, really. Should've put the chooks in before nightfall like Mum asked. Hard to see snakes in the dark."

"Did she *die?*" asked Missy, intrigued, while Lynette sighed.

"No dear, but she might've wished she had a few times.

It's very nasty, what happens to a body after a snake bite. First the sweating, then gasping for breath, then everything starts to shut down—"

"*In any case*," said Lynette, trying to steer them back on track, "it still makes no sense why Vale would walk that track so late at night."

"He might have been going to check on the area where the rock fall happened yesterday," Alicia ventured.

"In the dark? With picnic supplies?"

"Who knows what he was carrying but maybe he needed to tick the job off before today's activities? They are down to a skeleton staff."

"What does any of this matter?" said Ronnie, also losing her patience. "Vale clearly returned from his walk, alive—unless Flo saw herself a ghost, and I wouldn't put it past you, Flo. You believe all that silly nonsense! But no, he obviously made it to bed, where he passed."

"*And then there was one!*" Missy said, ominously. "One staff member that is!"

Then she giggled behind her hand while Perry rolled his eyes and said to the newcomers:

"Don't mind Missy. She always gets a little silly when she's freaked out."

Her "silliness" used to irk Perry but now he knew that was also her strength. Like Miss Marple, Missy was rarely taken seriously by outsiders, and she often used it to her advantage. Many a past suspect had ignored Missy and lived to regret it!

Giving Missy's back a reassuring pat, Perry turned his eyes to Ronnie. "You know, all of this *does* matter. Because now we can pin the time of death to somewhere between one in the morning when Flo saw him and…" He looked at his watch. "Three this arvo, give or take. Now we just need a doctor to tell it all to."

"I'm onto it!" announced Blake, walking in with a plaid flat cap on his head, a laptop bag hanging from his shoulder, and car keys jangling from his fingers. "I'll whizz down the hill and see if I can't rustle up some help, maybe touch base with my boss and grab a decent espresso while I'm at it."

He grinned at the older ladies, and Alicia felt like clocking him. A man had just died, the phones had also carked it, and he was worried about work and coffee!

"Thank God one of us has a car," said Simon, opening the front door for Blake. "Tell them to send help pronto, and see if you can locate Mrs Flannery while you're at it. That woman should be up here, taking care of all this. It's not the book club's responsibility."

Simon was the antithesis of Blake. He seemed almost offended by the day's proceedings. Like Vale's death had ruined his lovely weekend getaway.

Perry was also feeling grateful for Blake. He had already checked the out-buildings, and apart from a few golf buggies, a tractor-trailer, and an oversized ride-on lawn mower, Blake's Mercedes was the only vehicle capable of making the arduous drive down the mountain.

"Can I go with you?" asked Lynette, and Alicia stiffened.

She didn't know what was going on, but she didn't want her sister *whizzing* anywhere with a virtual stranger. Fortunately, Blake was shaking his head.

"Probably best you hang tight here with your book club friends," he said. "Especially if there is a madman out there—or a *madwoman*, let's not be sexist!" He gave the women a pointed look, then chuckled again. "I'm just messing with you guys! Take a chill pill, play a game of Cluedo or something. I'll race down and be back with cavalry in no time."

"Don't drive too fast," Flo called after him. "Those roads can be treacherous!"

~

"Game of Cluedo indeed!" said Perry as he stormed

into the library to help himself to the afternoon tea they had not yet got to. "Anyone else feel like smacking him across the head with his stupid David Beckham cap?"

"He is very blasé," agreed Alicia, trailing behind, but Lynette was scoffing.

"Not everybody jumps to the worst conclusions like you two. Vale's obviously died in his sleep, and the phone lines go down constantly. I'm relieved one of us has a car and can bring back some help."

"If he comes back at all," said Perry, and Lynette looked scandalised.

"Of course he's coming back! Honestly, Perry, I don't know why you're so nasty. Is it because he's younger and better-looking or because he's not remotely interested in you?"

"Didn't seem too interested in you either just now, young lady."

She shrugged a shoulder at him, pretending Blake's rejection hadn't hurt. But it had.

Why wouldn't he want company for the long drive down the mountain? She was sure there had been a spark between them last night. She thought they had really bonded...

A sudden crack came from the other end of the library, and they looked around to find Ronnie with a set of pliers and a guilty expression. She had broken through the lock on the doors of the glass cabinet and was now reaching for one of the guest books.

"How else am I going to while away the time?" she said, shrugging.

"We could keep dissecting this book?" Missy said, holding up the Christie novel, but Alicia was shaking her head.

"Nice idea, kiddo, but I think it's a waste of time. We were distracted enough before. There's no hope for us now."

~

It was like stepping into a time warp.

As Ronnie located the correct guest book—1969, she was sure it was 1969—she couldn't help toppling back to another era full of lively string bands and long, floaty dresses and handsome young hunters all vying for her attention. She remembered a flash romance with one of them—so scandalous, so naughty!—and tables laden with exotic orchids and gelatin-encased salads and icy buckets of Dom Perignon.

She pulled the book from the shelf and wondered where to read it. The library was large enough, but it could do with a decent makeover. She would break up the main setting, for a start, and position several plush armchairs around the place. Libraries were for quiet reading, not sitting in a group gasbagging! Besides, she wanted to check this one out on her own, without any prying eyes. Apart from the main coffee table, the only other option was the billiard table, so she strode across and placed the book carefully upon it, then smiled as she peeled the hard cover open.

Now where was her lovely handwriting?

As she scanned the pages, Ronnie smiled at the flowery messages and the funny doodles and the pretty names that now seemed positively antiquated. That's when she noticed a familiar name, but it wasn't hers. She stopped and glanced back at the book club, who were chatting amongst themselves, then smudged her lips sideways.

It's a common enough name. Has to be a coincidence, she thought idly as she kept scrolling...

~

Standing at the northern end of the driveway, Claire held her phone out and groaned while Simon watched from a distance.

"Still no signal?" he said, stepping closer.

"Nothing," she replied. "How on earth do they survive

all the way out here without any communication?"

She had made a similar comment yesterday, and a dark shadow now flitted across his face.

"You have to remember there's usually a working phone line and internet reception, and you can get good mobile reception if you head up Repentance Way." He coughed. "Or so I hear... but I'm not sure that's correct..."

Claire looked delighted. "Shall we give it a whirl?"

"No!" he burst out, then blushed. He really had to get his emotions in check. This woman was stirring him up! "Sorry Claire, it's just that Vale did say that track was dangerous. I would hate for you to get hurt. There's been more than enough excitement for one day."

"As long as nobody's walking on the lower trail, it should be fine, don't you think?"

Still his head continued to shake. Should he say something? He wasn't yet sure...

"What's going on?" Claire asked, eyes narrowing.

"There's... well, there's something I haven't told you." He plunged his hands into his pockets. "I didn't mention it yesterday because I know what happened to the others, but, well, I was the one who walked the forbidden track."

He paused to gauge her reaction, but Claire did not seem outraged or angry or even surprised, so he forged on. "I honestly don't think I caused the landslide. I mean, I didn't feel the ground give way or hear anything, and if I did, it wasn't my intention. I'm mortified if I hurt poor Florence..."

Claire reached out and touched Simon's arm, and he felt a jolt of electricity. She must have felt it too because she snapped her hand back, and now she, too, was blushing.

"In any case," he continued, coughing and clearing his throat, "I didn't get very far because I spotted a man."

"A man?"

"Some old guy, living out there in the middle of the

bush." He saw Claire's eyes widen. "I didn't approach of course, but he seemed a bit, well, *rough*. He's got a little settlement out there. Maybe that's his home or maybe he's squatting? In any case, I think we should keep our distance. Just in case he's… well, you know… *dangerous*."

Claire agreed. "Do you think that's why Vale warned us off the track?"

"Maybe," he said, hoping she'd forget all about the rockslide.

"Okay, but did you get any phone reception while you were out there? Perhaps if we go together—"

"No! That's the thing, see. I took my phone while I was walking, and there was no signal. None at all. It's a furphy. Complete waste of time."

"Oh, that's a pity."

And he blushed again, this time at the lie he had just fed her.

As they turned back towards the lodge, Claire gave the stunning view a final look, then stopped and looked properly this time.

"Simon!" she called out, a hand above her eyes, the other raised and pointing. "Down there. Am I imagining things or…?"

Simon followed her finger and frowned. "Oh dear," he said. "This day goes from bad to worse."

~

Alicia checked over her shoulder, then whispered to Perry and Lynette, "Ronnie thinks Vale's death is suspicious."

"Really?" said Perry.

"Seriously?" said Lynette, sounding sceptical.

"Ronnie was a nurse once, Lynny. She thinks he's been injected with something, perhaps some kind of poison. There's a suspicious mark on his left arm."

Pity Dr Anders had left the group, she thought for the

second time that day. He wasn't only a doctor, he was a poisons expert and would know exactly what they were dealing with.

"Poison is all a bit retro isn't it?" said Lynette while Alicia threw a finger to her lips to quieten her. "Who would do such a thing? *Why?*"

Alicia leaned in closer. "Listen, I didn't think anything of it at the time, but last night I overheard Vale talking to somebody. Probably Mrs Flannery. They were standing behind reception." She leaned in closer again. "Vale sounded cranky."

"I hardly knew the man, but I have a hunch 'cranky' was his default mode," said Perry, twiddling his ear-ring again.

"Yes, but crankier than normal. He was saying something about an imposter, a fraudster I think he said. I got the impression he was talking about one of us."

"Us? Like someone in book club?" said Lynette.

She nodded. "Vale said something about how he wasn't stupid, like he'd worked out who it was, and then he said he was going to confront this person and warn somebody or other, but I didn't hear any more than that before he caught me eavesdropping."

Both Perry and Lynette stared at Alicia, digesting that for a moment.

Then Perry said, "An imposter, hey? He must have been talking to Mrs Flannery. Who else? They're the only staffers, right? The only other people here?"

Lynette nodded while she swished her hair into a top knot, an eyebrow high. "This is all very clandestine."

Alicia agreed. "I'm telling you what I heard, and I have no idea if it has anything to do with his death."

"Except you *obviously* do," countered Perry. "And it does add an element of suspicion to the whole matter. Vale says he's going to confront someone and then Vale shows up dead."

"Poisoned, if you believe Ronnie," said Lynette who

was still not sure she did. "So who do we think this imposter is? I mean, it has to be either Simon, Blake, Flo or Ronnie, right?"

Perry scoffed now. "I sincerely doubt Flo and Ronnie have anything to do with this."

"Now who's being sexist and ageist?" Lynette snapped back. "I think Flo's got a few secrets under that blue rinse of hers."

"Really?" said Alicia. "Like what?"

Lynette shrugged. "It's a sense I'm getting... Still, I can't really picture her doing it. How about Simon? He was the only one who wouldn't give a credit card when we checked in, remember? That was odd."

"That's right!" said Alicia. She'd forgotten about that.

"That doesn't mean anything, Lynette," said Perry. "Just because you Millennials will hand over your private details at the drop of a hat, doesn't mean the rest of us want to. Cash is still an acceptable form of payment last time I looked. Nope, sorry, I think Blake is the dodgy one."

Lynette frowned but Alicia had to agree.

"He did clear off at the first opportunity."

"He's the only one with a car! He's gone to get help!" Lynette spat back as her sister continued.

"Think about it, Lynny. Of all of us, he's the square peg in the round hole. He doesn't seem to belong. I mean, why is he even in this club? Why did he call and beg me to sign up? Does he even *like* murder mysteries? He clearly didn't read the latest book."

"Oh, shock, horror, somebody didn't do their homework," said Lynette. "He told me he came here to prove himself, show he's more than just a pretty face, that he has a brain too. He's not a *murderer.*"

"Shh," Alicia said. "Keep your voice down. We don't know for sure that Vale has been murdered, and I really don't want to upset the newbies."

"Except it could be one of the newbies who killed

him!" said Perry. "Like, er, *Blake!*"

"You've had a grudge against him from the moment he walked in," said Lynette.

"And you're letting his pretty looks cloud your judgement," Perry hissed back.

Lynette rolled her eyes. "Fine. Okay, I'll hear you out. What's your problem with him, Perry?"

"Apart from the fact that he's the only one who's buggered off at the first opportunity? And didn't let any of us go with him? That's extremely suspicious, but there is something else." Perry sat forward, lowering his voice considerably. "Do you remember when we first arrived and were checking in at the front desk, and Mrs Flannery appeared with the drinks?"

Alicia gave it some thought. "Yes, she dropped her tray when she saw us."

"*Au contraire.* She dropped her tray when she saw *Blake!* He had just made his grand entrance, remember? Had swept up in his flash Mercedes—which is actually not that flash, people. They don't call them 'thirty Mercs' for nothing. They practically give them away when they get to a certain age."

"Get on with it," said Lynette, grumpily.

"Well, he waltzed in like he owned the place, and then Mrs Flannery came in, copped one look at the guy and dropped her tray like she'd seen a ghost!"

"She tripped on the carpet," said Lynette. "That was also around the time that Ronnie remembered that she'd been here before. For all we know, Mrs Flannery could have been reacting to that news. Now that I think of it…"

Lynette glanced over her shoulder again to see Ronnie still studying the guest book at the other side of the library. "*Ronnie's* the one who's got history here, acting like she didn't remember coming. She's the one who's snooping about, breaking into cupboards. Look at her over there. What's she really hunting for in those old guest books? It's more likely that Mrs Flannery suddenly recognised her.

Maybe Ronnie's the fraudster?"

"Well, I don't know about fraudster, but she is definitely hiding something," said Perry, his voice barely a whisper. "Our dear Ronnie comes from serious money. I mean, *serious* serious money. She makes the Queen look like a pauper. She's one of my museum's biggest benefactors. Married into wealth, I believe. Her husband was in shipping maybe? Or was it shopping centres?"

"You wouldn't know it," said Alicia.

"Doesn't surprise me," said Lynette, who'd also noticed the woman's bling. "So what are you saying, Perry? Because she's not flaunting her wealth, she must be an imposter? You think *she's* the killer now?"

He looked scandalised by the thought. "Don't be ridiculous. I just thought, since we're sharing information, I should mention it. Besides, *she's* not the one who's slithered off into the forest like a snake."

"Okay, settle down, you two," said Alicia. "Mrs Flannery will be back any minute, and we can ask her directly who Vale was talking about. She might also have a good idea why he's lying up there dead. Hopefully she'll tell us he had a dicky heart and that'll be the end of it."

"Until then?" said Lynette.

"There's always Cluedo," Perry said, slapping her with a smirk.

~

Alicia returned to the reception desk and scooped up the landline, hoping for a miracle and finding only the sound of silence. *Why wasn't it working?*

"Could be the fire, dear," said Flo, wandering in from the corridor, gardening gloves in hand.

"Sorry? What are you talking about?"

"Outside, you didn't notice?"

Alicia's jaw dropped and Flo said, "Oh, I didn't mean to alarm you! Don't get yourself into a bother; it's halfway down the mountain. Still, it might be what took the phone lines out."

As Alicia rushed outside to check, she ran into Claire and Simon, who were returning indoors to inform them.

"Now don't panic," Claire began, but Alicia was already racing past her and out to the edge of the steep driveway to see for herself.

"Bloody hell!" she said, peering towards the distant plume of smoke. "How long do we think that's been burning? And how close do we think it is?"

Nobody had a clue, but there were no clear flames at this point, which gave them some degree of comfort.

"I'm sure it's miles away," said Simon, not sounding at all sure.

"Looks closer to town than to us," offered Claire, also sounding uncertain.

"Damn it, this is just what we need," said Alicia. "Do we at least know which direction it's headed?"

Simon noticed Claire's lovely black hair fluttering away from her face as they stood staring towards the smoke, and unless the wind changed, that did not bode well for them. If the wind was heading their way, the fire would be heading in their direction too.

He decided to keep that shocking thought to himself.

CHAPTER 9

The Murder Mystery Book Club were standing in one line at the very top of the driveway, staring out at what would otherwise be a magnificent view if it wasn't for the ominous plume of smoke blighting the forest below. They were already getting wafts of it in the gentle breeze, and the hotelier was, for now, forgotten, as their thoughts turned to Mrs Flannery.

"At least we know why she's not back yet," said Simon. "She's obviously caught on the other side of that smoke."

Lynette thought of Blake suddenly and gasped. Missy was gasping too, but it wasn't Blake she was thinking of.

"Do you suppose that's why the phones were ringing all morning?" Missy said. "Maybe Mrs Flannery was cut off and was calling to warn us of the fire, but none of us picked up."

"It wasn't our job to answer the phones," said Simon. "We weren't to know."

"If *only* we'd picked up!" she said. "Now we're stuck in the middle of nowhere, all alone with a fire raging towards us!"

"We're not *all alone*, Missy," said Claire. "There's nine of us, and it's not raging. Is it?"

"Eight!" said Lynette, but Claire was looking to Simon for an answer.

He gave her a reassuring smile. "The fire is far away, I'm sure of it."

"And the firies will be onto it," said Flo.

"The whaties?" asked Alicia.

"The Rural Fire Service, dear. Volunteer firefighters. We call 'em firies where I come from. Every country town has 'em—a scrappy crew of guys and gals who sign up to fight fires in their local area. They'll be onto it toot sweet. Will stop it in its tracks, don't you worry about that."

"And if they don't?" asked Missy.

"Then we enact our fire safety plan of course."

"What's that when it's at home?" asked Perry.

"It's what you do when a fire breaks out," she told them. "Growing up in the country, we all had to make one. You had to decide whether you were going to stay and fight the fire—"

"Yeah, *right!*" said Perry, trying not to punctuate that suggestion with a derisive snort.

"Or," she continued, flicking him a frown, "pack up and leave, and if so, what were you going to pack, and how soon were you going to choof off? There comes a point, you see, when it's too late to go. And you certainly don't want to get caught on the road in your vehicle. That's possibly the worst place to be."

Lynette gasped again. *Did nobody remember Blake?*

Perry said, "What vehicle? I don't think the golf buggies will get us far."

"I can drive a tractor," said Flo. "Used to drive my dad's old one."

The woman was the size of a sparrow, but for some reason that didn't surprise anybody.

Simon was holding up a hand. "Hate to break it to you, folks," he said, "but I have a terrible feeling leaving is not an option for us. If Mrs Flannery is cut off, that means the fire is across the main road. It's hard to tell from here but…"

"Oh yes, I think you might be right," said Ronnie, peeling her eyes downwards. "As far as I recall, there is only one road in and one road out. The one we took yesterday, and that's exactly where the fire's coming from. Unless anyone knows of another route out?"

There were shrugs all round.

"If we stay here and bunker down, we should all be fine," said Simon, but Lynette had had enough.

She stepped to the front of the group and turned to face them, hands on her hips, eyes narrowing with anger and disappointment. "I *cannot* believe the lot of you!" she said. "Has everybody forgotten about poor Blake? I know most of you had it in for him"—her glare was now directed at Perry and Alicia—"but he's already left the lodge, trying to seek help. For all we know, he could be caught in the middle of all that!"

Alicia flinched. Lynette was right. She hadn't even considered that possibility. She glanced at her watch. It was now almost five p.m. As far as she recalled, Blake left sometime after three, and it takes a good hour to get down the mountain. Had he made it down safely, before the fire started? The thickness of the smoke gave her cause to wonder.

What if he had got ambushed by the flames?

"Look, we've only just spotted the fire, and Blake left ages ago," said Simon, soothingly. "I'm sure he made it through and he'll be alerting them to our plight."

"And if he didn't make it through?" asked Lynette.

"Then I'm sure we'll see his car return any moment now."

As though in a pantomime, they all stopped and listened for the sound of a vehicle roaring up towards them, but all they could hear was the rustle of the wind and the call of lyre birds in the distance.

Then a lone kookaburra began to sing, mocking them with its jollity.

~

Darkness was rapidly descending, and the book club decided that worrying about Blake was going to get them exactly nowhere and it was time to get organised. It didn't take a detective to know it would be a long, arduous night.

While Lynette and Perry went to "sort out some dinner," Flo and Ronnie returned to the library to get a fire plan together while Simon said something unsettling about checking the fire alarms in case it caught them by surprise in the middle of the night.

That left Missy, Claire and Alicia, still gaping towards the smoke. They seemed rooted to the spot, unable to budge, as though by keeping a stern eye on the fire, it wouldn't dare creep up on them.

"Is it getting any closer, do you think?" Missy asked eventually. "And is that a second fire down there, on that lower ridge? Or is it all one giant inferno?"

"Thanks for that, Missy," said Alicia, shuddering. "We should have taken a photo of it earlier to compare." She reached into her pocket but found it empty. "Anyone bring their smartphone?"

The other women shook their heads. "No point," said Missy. "They're useless here. We *are* all alone!" She directed that comment at Claire. "What are we going to do? How are we even going to think about sleeping with a fire burning down the ridge?"

The others shrugged. None of them had any experience of fires.

"Flo knows fires and she's not at all worried," said Claire, "and neither is Simon."

"Yes, but with all due respect, what do they know, really?" said Alicia. "Flo's a country girl, comes from dusty flat paddocks out west. Simon's from Sydney, isn't he? The middle of the city if I remember his address correctly. Neither of them knows this particular mountain, this particular forest. It could be roaring towards us for all we know, and we're sitting here like kindling!"

Alicia had already imagined them scrambling through the scorching forest, flames snapping at their feet. Had already worked out what possessions she would grab—just her sister, her book club friends and her ragged copy of *And Then There Were None*. It had been her mother's, and they would have to pry it from her scorched dead hands.

"Actually, I know someone who might have more of an idea," Claire said, adding, "We're not quite as alone as we think we are. Simon said something to me earlier about spotting an old guy squatting in the middle of the forest. Says he looked a bit rough, but, well, if he's a true local, he might know how long we've got or if there's another road out."

Missy clapped her hands. "Oh, that's such a relief! Good thinking, Claire. We need to find him and fast! Where is he? Did Simon say?"

Claire gulped and looked at Alicia. "Yes but you're not going to like it."

~

Lynette stared into the cold room and beamed. She loved it!

The lodge was incredibly well stocked considering their low guest numbers; almost as well stocked as the inner-city restaurant where she cooked. There were crates of fresh fruit and vegetables, boxes of the basics—tinned goods, cereals, flour, rice, pasta—as well as multiple smaller sealed plastic containers all perfectly labelled with enticing words like Persian Fetta and Lyle's Own Pesto. All with dates scribbled across them.

"Looks like you've got plenty to work with," said Perry.

"I guess these remote places have to keep supplies up," she said as she stepped in to inspect some cherry tomatoes.

"So why would Mrs Flannery need to drive into town?"

She shrugged. She didn't care. She was going to have fun whipping up dinner tonight.

Swooning at an enormous container of fresh goat's cheese, Perry asked, "So what's on the menu, chef?"

Lynette ummed and aahed for a few minutes, glancing around, and then she noticed a handwritten recipe sitting on the bench top amidst all the breakfast debris. She picked the recipe up and smiled.

"Looks to me like Mrs Flannery was going to whip up a Bucatini all'Amatriciana tonight."

"What's that in anyone else's language?"

Lynette smiled. "A delicious spicy tomato and pancetta pasta." She dropped her head to the side. "Yeah, why not? Let's keep it simple." Then she scooped up the almost-empty bottle of red wine on the bench and handed it to Perry. "Okay, sous chef, see if you can find some more plonk. Proper plonk, though, not this cheap cooking stuff. We opened a good cab sav at the bar last night. See if there's another. And I'll get this kitchen back in shape so we can get dinner rolling."

"I can fetch some fresh parsley if you like," said Flo, watching now from the doorway. "I noticed a lovely herb patch, just behind this kitchen."

"Really?" said Lynette, stepping to the back door and opening it wide to reveal more than a lovely herb patch. There was an enormous vegetable garden out there too, bursting with all kinds of produce, as well as a garden shed and a large chicken coop. "Grab some of those lovely ripe tomatoes while you're at it," she told Flo.

As Flo headed out, Lynette glanced towards some fresh baguettes and then reached for a bulb of garlic. If this was going to be their last meal, she was going to make it a magnificent one!

~

The light was fast waning as they made their way carefully along the forbidden Repentance Way, and Alicia decided Claire was right. She didn't like it one bit.

In parts the track hugged the very edge of the escarpment, and it wasn't simply walkers on the track below who could get hurt if the rocks beneath them gave way. One misstep, and all three of them would be hurtling downwards. The rotting railing was as good as useless.

She wished they'd thought of that before they began, wished they'd been a little smarter about it—brought a torch, alerted the others to where they were going, that kind of thing. But time was of the essence, and so they had thrown caution to the wind and set off. But the longer they walked, the more worried she became.

They didn't know who this squatter was and whether he was even friendly. Why was he living out here in the bush? Was he a loner? A survivalist? *A psychopath?*

"Do we know anything about this guy?" said Missy, voicing Alicia's concerns.

Claire went to say something, then stopped and pointed. "Look, through there, near the edge of the ridge, that must be his house."

They all took in the view. From what they could see, the house was more of a cabin—a slab hut with a rusty tin roof and a small cement water tank on one side—and on the other, the most extraordinary view, better even than the one from the lodge. Set close to the edge of the escarpment, it looked out across the blue misty highlands and the rainforest-carpeted ridges down to the sweeping valley and teeny tiny Lyleton below.

"Not a bad place to be homeless," Missy said.

"He's not homeless," Alicia retorted.

"You know what I mean!"

As they approached, the women sang out, hoping to give the stranger plenty of warning, but he did not appear, so Alicia bravely stepped forward and knocked on the rattly wooden door. An enormous Huntsman spider scuttled across the wooden frame, causing Missy to squeal and Alicia to recoil.

Other than that, there was no response.

"Maybe he's gone for a walk or something?" said Missy, swallowing deep settling breaths.

"Seems a bit late for a walk," said Claire.

Alicia felt her heart drop. Perhaps he'd seen the fire and had already cleared out.

"Oi! What do you lot want?" came a gruff voice behind them, and all three women jumped as if the spider had leapt out and bitten them.

~

After locating handfuls of fresh herbs and cherry tomatoes in the well-tended garden, Flo glanced around. They were on the western side of the mountain, at the very back of the lodge, and the view from here was not as good as the other side, the trees crowding in too closely— although you couldn't see the smoke, and that made Flo feel comforted. A pebbled pathway led from the garden to the chicken shed and then on towards an enormous fig tree where a decorative cast-iron bench seat had been placed. From there the pebbles continued, almost to the forest, before stopping abruptly—as though someone intended to head that way but thought better of it.

Flo noticed a mossy statue of a small angel perched on the edge of the herb patch, one wing smashed off, eyes rolling at the world as it glanced skyward, a smattering of wildflowers behind it. She stepped across and picked a few, then returned to the kitchen and dropped them into an old milk jug.

"I'm going to set a lovely table," she said, hoping that would cheer them all up. "Perry, will you help me move the tables back together?"

After their troubling day, they needed to be united tonight. He happily obliged and then, as he returned to sous chef duties, Flo hunted around for a pretty tablecloth and laid it out, placing the flowerpot in the centre.

It really was perfect! Just like dinners at the old farmhouse.

"Need a hand setting the table?" Ronnie asked,

stepping into the dining room.

"If you like, dear. See if you can find the silverware, and I'll fetch some plates."

~

As they quietly set the table, Flo humming a tune to herself, Ronnie's mind wandered back to the old guest books.

She kept wondering whether she ought to say something to her old friend about what she'd discovered. Did she trust Flo enough to tell her? Should she go straight to the older Finlay girl, the one who seemed to be in charge?

"What are you thinking about, dear?" said Flo, interrupting her thoughts. "You look quite befuddled. Are you regretting signing up for this lovely little club?"

Ronnie tried for a smile. "Maybe. Are you?"

Flo shook her head firmly. "Best fun I've had in ages! Better than crocheting baby booties all day, I can tell you that. Feel more alive than I have for decades. Feel like I'm finally achieving something."

Ronnie nodded thoughtfully. "Why did you sign up?" she asked as she secured a serviette beneath a fork. "What were you hoping for?"

Flo shrugged. "Bit of old-fashioned sleuthing, I guess. Why else would you sign up for a Murder Mystery Book Club?"

Why indeed, thought Ronnie, her thoughts darting off into dark corners again.

~

"Wondered how long it'd take you lot to find me," the elderly man said, his voice slow and gravelly as he yanked off his beaten-up Akubra hat and strode past them and into the hut.

He was very tall and very thin with a few white whiskers on his weathered face and virtually nothing left on his head. The skin on his neck and forehead looked like a busy road map, deep lines criss-crossing each other at multiple points. The man must have been pushing eighty, but he had a gallop in his step, and as he passed them, he left a faint trail of stale tobacco, barbecue smoke, and fresh, wet sweat.

The women glanced at each other warily, unsure whether to follow when he called out:

"I'm puttin' the billy on if you want a cup."

Alicia smiled and led the way in. He can't be too dangerous if he's offering tea, she thought, and he certainly can't be too worried about the fire.

The place was modestly decorated but surprisingly cosy with a small wood-fired stove in one corner and a plush bed in the other, a handcrafted rocking chair beside it with a checked blue-and-beige blanket flung across the top. It looked just like the one in Alicia's room. On closer inspection, she decided it was just like the one in her room, and she wondered about that. Was he pilfering items from the lodge?

On an antique bedside cabinet she noticed a dusty silver frame with a sepia-toned photo inside. It showed a beautiful young woman who looked a little like Lynette, with long, fair hair and a wide, vibrant smile. Her eyes were also wide and full of mischief.

"Coffee? Tea? Even got Earl Grey, if that's your fancy," he said, directing that at Claire.

Alicia noticed that the teabags had the Lyle insignia on them, as did the cups, and raised an eyebrow at him suspiciously.

"No, thank you," Claire said crisply.

"I'll take a tea, please, if you're offering. No milk or sugar thanks," said Missy, and he turned to make it, pouring the water from an old electric kettle.

There was obviously power to the hut, and Alicia

spotted a phone attached to the wall. He noticed her gaze and said:

"Hasn't been connected in twenty years."

She smiled weakly. *Oh well, it was worth a shot.*

"So," he said, handing Missy her cup and leaning against the kitchen sink, his own brew in hand. "Vale know you're here?"

They all stared at him, startled. In the excitement of the fire, they had forgotten all about the poor hotelier, and now Alicia felt a stab of guilt. Of course this old-timer knew Vale! They might have very different lodgings, but they were the only two men for miles. She glanced at Claire, who raised her eyebrows warily.

"Don't worry, ladies." He chuckled, misreading them entirely, his grey-blue eyes twinkling wickedly. "I won't dob you in to the boss. I know how he can be a big girl's blouse about that track."

Missy giggled nervously, then hid her face in her cup while Claire gave Alicia a more pointed look this time. Somebody had to break the sad news.

Alicia took a deep breath and stepped forward. "I'm so sorry to tell you this, but Vale passed away last night."

The man stared at her like she was joking. He waited a beat, then said, "What are you talkin' about?"

"We… we found him in his bed this afternoon. He—"

"He can't be dead!"

She offered him a sympathetic look. "I'm so, so sorry."

"Nope, nope, nope, nope, nope…" The man was refusing to believe. He turned and dumped his untouched drink in the sink, then stormed outside, the front door banging loudly behind him.

The women swapped worried frowns, then followed him out and couldn't find him for a few moments before they spotted him right on the edge of the ridge, staring out at the extraordinary view as though it would somehow make it all better. The persistent smoke suggested otherwise, but he clearly wasn't thinking about that.

He turned back to them, his eyes now red and rheumy, the twinkle extinguished, a deep channel etched between them. Like the news had just driven a fresh lorry across his face. Sniffing, he cleared his throat, then cleared his throat again.

"He was a good man, Vale," he said at last, his voice croaky. "A good friend to the end." He rubbed a hand roughly at his stubble. "What happened?"

Alicia shook her head. Unsure how much to reveal. Ronnie was not a doctor, after all. Perhaps she had it wrong.

He was nodding now, as though he knew exactly what had happened, and said, "And Joan? How's she taking it?"

"Joan?"

"Joan Flannery, the cook. She okay?"

Alicia nodded. "Yes, I mean, we think so. She left for town this morning—"

"She's not back yet?" He looked outwards. "Must be cut off by the fire then."

"That's what we suspect."

"Rightio, now it's makin' a bit more sense. You lot are scared, all alone back there in the lodge."

"We're not all alone," said Claire, indignant. *Why did everyone keep saying that?* "There are several gentlemen in our group."

"I'm talking about the fire, sweetheart. You're wondering how long you've got."

It was the elephant in the room. The real reason they had come, and Alicia felt guilty about that, of forgetting the hotel manager and thinking only of themselves.

"How long *have* we got?" she said, no longer pretending.

He turned to inspect the horizon. "It's still below Cooper's Crossing, so you've got that in your favour. Besides, it's not the seventies. They'll stop it long before it gets up here. They won't let that happen again."

"Who?"

"Firies, of course. They've got choppers now, much better equipped. You'll be right."

"What about you?" Missy asked. "Aren't you worried?"

He shook his head and smiled, revealing a few missing molars. "Nah, love. Nothing will get me off this mountain now. This is where I belong." Then he turned back to the view and said, "In the midst of life we are in death. Now where did I read that…?"

Missy recognised the line. It was straight from the Agatha Christie book they'd been dissecting; she distinctly remembered highlighting it. Gulping, she glanced at the others, wondering if they'd noticed. Had he been spying on them, she wondered?

Was he playing with them now, or was it a coincidence?

"Do you think that's what's killed our phone lines?" asked Claire, and he looked back sharply.

"Lines are down?"

She nodded.

"Very likely then." But he didn't look like he believed it. His frown was firming, his eyes darting about.

"How long do we have?" Alicia asked. "If they can't control it?"

His eyes stopped on her. "Rainforest doesn't burn fast, doesn't normally burn at all, so that's also in your favour. Plus it's almost nightfall, should slow right down now the temperature's dropping. There's no rain comin', not for a few days yet, but I suspect the winds'll change by morning. Firies should have it under control by then anyway."

"And if they don't?" asked Alicia.

He shrugged. He didn't have an answer for that.

"Okay," she said, feeling anything but. She gave Claire and Missy the nod and said, "Thank you for your time, and we're so sorry about Vale."

"Like I said, death is just part of life, love."

She nodded, then realised they hadn't even been introduced. "I'm Alicia, by the way, and this is Claire and Missy. We're up here for the weekend. Obviously."

He nodded and returned to the view, so she said, "I didn't catch your name."

"Don't worry about that now, love," he said. "Focus on getting through the night."

~

"He was rude," said Claire as they made their way back.

"And a little creepy," added Missy, wondering whether she ought to say something about the line he'd quoted. It all seemed a bit silly now. Why would an old guy be spying on them? Had to be a coincidence, or maybe it was a common line. *Ah yes, that's right. It was a prayer, wasn't it?*

"I quite liked him," said Alicia. "Salt of the earth. And he certainly knows his forest."

"Must love it too," said Claire. "He sounds like he wants to die in it."

"I can vaguely understand that," said Alicia. "He's obviously a local, was probably born and bred up here. And he's not getting any younger. Where else is he going to go?"

Claire shuddered. "Let's just hope those so-called *firies* do make it."

"Or Blake," said Missy. "Don't forget Blake. He's probably down there now, organising our rescue."

Alicia and Claire shared a frown.

~

The second dinner at Lyle's Lodge was very different to the first. As they devoured Lynette's dish—well, all of them except Flo, who seemed to have lost her appetite entirely—the group seemed reluctant to discuss dead bodies or missing people or the distant fire. It was as though they had mutually agreed to give themselves a reprieve, and instead, an eerie kind of silence fell upon the group. When they did speak, it was to compliment Lynette on the meal, which was indeed magnificent, or to ask someone to pass the wine.

What they weren't to know was that it was all that alcohol that would end up changing the tone entirely.

"Shall I hunt for more?" asked Perry, tipping the last of the cabernet sauvignon into Claire's glass.

"God yes!" said Lynette as similar sentiments echoed around the table. "Although I have a terrible feeling we've depleted the bar's supplies."

Lynette remembered her drinking session with Blake last night. It felt like a lifetime ago now.

"Check the cellar then," said Ronnie.

"There's a cellar?" said Lynette.

Claire frowned. "I don't recall seeing one when we did our search earlier."

Ronnie shrugged a shoulder. "It's an old lodge, miles from anywhere. There's got to be a cellar."

Simon nodded. "You'd hope so. I'm not nearly drunk enough yet."

He laughed apologetically, but most of them agreed. They were going to need to dull the senses to get through this night.

"Mission accepted," Perry said, getting to his feet. "Any idea where I might find this mysterious cellar?"

They all stared blankly, and Flo said, "If you do find it, dear, d'ya mind digging about for some sherry. I prefer a drop of sherry after I've had me tea."

~

As Perry strode out of the dining room, determination in his step, Simon suggested they all adjourn to the bar while he cleared the plates away. Claire smiled appreciatively. This wasn't Agatha Christie's day. She liked a man who was not afraid to step up and do his bit.

"We'll help you, dear," said Ronnie, giving Flo a nudge. They weren't used to men of a certain age stepping up at all, certainly not when it came to kitchen duties.

"And I'm going to check that fire again," said Lynette, catching her sister's eye.

Alicia scooped up her empty wine glass and said, "I'll do the breakfast shift. See you all at the bar in five. BYO glasses so we can reduce the washing up!"

After dropping their own glasses on the countertop, the sisters made their way outside and stopped for a moment to soak up the view. The moon had turned an extraordinary shade of orange. It was almost blood red.

"It's breathtaking," said Lynette. "Seems so inappropriate considering what's going on."

"It's probably *because* of what's going on," said Alicia. "The fire must be causing that, but can you smell the smoke? It's getting thicker. And is that...?" Alicia held a palm out and watched with horror as a small fleck of black landed in it. "Is that ash? Oh my God, the fire must be getting closer."

"Don't start panicking," said Lynette. "We are going to be okay."

Alicia dusted her palm off, trying hard to believe that.

~

The three new book club members cleared the table and washed the dishes in silence for a while, and then Simon cleared his throat and said, "It's been quite an initiation to the club, hasn't it, ladies?"

Flo cackled and Ronnie frowned. Initiation was one word for it. She was not sure she would last long with this mob.

"I'm having the time of my life," said Flo, echoing her earlier sentiment.

"How about this old lodge, hey?" he said. "Would you come back? After all this?"

"Oh I won't be back," said Flo, her smile now dissolving.

"I thought you were having a fine time," said Ronnie.

"I am, dear. But I think one visit is enough for one lifetime. Besides, the spirit of that hotel manager will be haunting the corridors now." She grimaced. "Not sure I want to meet up with that fellow again!"

Simon looked up from the sink, horrified.

~

Perry was feeling victorious as he made his way down the rickety wooden staircase. He was so proud of himself for finding the cellar!

It was located through a door just down from the dining room, and they had all walked past it many times on their way to their rooms, yet no one, it seemed, had noticed. Still, it had been cleverly disguised. Hidden in plain sight.

The door was low and small and obscured by the mural of a faux bookshelf that had been painted across the door and wall in the long corridor. It was only when Perry was about to hold up the white flag that he spotted the handle, masquerading as a book.

"Got ya!" he said, pulling it open with a loud, angry creak.

A draft of icy air swept up towards him, and something else, something slightly off. He grappled about on the wall beside the door until he found a light switch, then flicked it on and waited for his eyes to adjust as the dust danced about before him. That's when he saw the steep staircase reaching downwards and twisting around to the right. He smiled jubilantly and made his way in.

Despite the goose bumps now popping up across his arms, Perry really wasn't prepared for what he'd find down there.

It was only as he hit the bottom step and glanced about that he saw the body, slumped on the stone floor, one hand clutching a bottle of Jacob's Creek, a second bottle, a

Penfolds Grange, smashed to pieces on the hard ground nearby.

What a waste of a top drop, he thought before the horror of what he was staring at hit him like that broken bottle, and he staggered back, landing hard on his buttocks on the lower step.

He pulled himself up, twisted himself around, and rushed back up the staircase.

CHAPTER 10

Mrs Flannery looked like a fallen drunk, her body leaning up against the dusty wine rack, her legs spreadeagled on the crumbling stone floor in front of her, the cheap wine still holding fast in one hand.

It's little wonder then that Perry's initial reaction was so benign. If it wasn't for the deep red gash on the side of her head and the sickly smell of dried blood and something else, something he didn't understand, anyone might assume the woman had got stuck into the hotel's wine supplies and passed out. It was that thought that propelled Perry up the cellar stairs and back into the dining room.

Maybe she just needed a strong cup of coffee and a bandage!

By then the group were gathered around the bar, talking, but the conversation promptly stopped when they caught sight of Perry.

"Are you okay?" asked Lynette.

"What's going on?" said Simon.

Perry waved a hand in front of them, speechless at that point, and simply turned and ran back down the corridor.

Within minutes the group were all standing at the bottom of the cellar stairs, watching, eyes wide, as Ronnie leaned over the body, tut-tutting to herself. Eventually she stood straight, rubbed her back and offered them a resigned sigh.

There was no sugar-coating this one.

"Definitely been struck a mortal blow, most likely from the Grange," she said, causing the eyes to turn to saucers.

97

"Looks like she never knew what hit her. There's blood but not a lot of it, so it wouldn't have taken long."

"You're saying somebody deliberately killed the poor woman?" said Flo, still trying to catch her breath.

"Oh dear God," said Claire, turning to Simon, who was just behind her. He reached out and drew her to his chest.

"This is frankly unbelievable!" he said crossly, as though another body had ruined everything.

And in many ways it had. They might like to pretend that Vale's death was somehow an accident, the fire a mere coincidence. But this… this was clearly murder.

Something was very wrong.

"I don't understand," said Perry, hand grasping his chest like he was about to have a heart attack. "I saw her drive off this morning. I'd swear to it!"

"She must have come back," said Missy, her cheeks flushed as she stared at the body, but Alicia was shaking her head.

"If she did come back, then where's the van? We were just outside, and the van is still missing." She asked Ronnie, "Any idea how long she's been lying down here?"

"As I keep telling you all, I'm not a trained physician."

"But if you had to guess?"

The ex-nurse picked up the dead woman's arm and let it drop again. "There's a little rigor mortis, and that usually takes a few hours to set in. Of course it's cool down here, so that would have delayed the process. Maybe half a day, I really don't know."

"That's okay; we can work this out," said Alicia, trying to compute the facts. She was a trained journalist and liked to work with evidence. As horrific as the sight before them was, that was her way of regaining control, halting the crazy images in her head.

"So, we all saw Mrs Flannery at breakfast. Then Perry saw her van leave just before book club started." She glanced at Perry. "Around tenish?" He nodded bleakly. "So she either came back while we were discussing the book and we didn't notice her…"

"Or?" said Lynette, not believing that for one moment.

"Or you didn't see her leave at all, Perry, and that was somebody else entirely."

He gulped, gobsmacked by the suggestion. "Somebody else? Driving Mrs Flannery's van?"

"It was the murderer! Has to be," squealed Missy. "He killed Mrs Flannery and escaped in her van."

"Could a woman have done this?" asked Simon, and Claire looked startled by the suggestion and stepped away, towards Alicia.

Simon held a palm out. "I don't mean any offence," he began, but Ronnie was nodding her head.

"Wine bottles make a pretty good weapon, I reckon. Nice and solid; not too heavy. If a woman hated Mrs Flannery enough, she could probably pull it off. Did you have someone in mind?"

There was a glint of humour in her eyes, but Simon wasn't laughing and neither was anyone else. They now had two dead bodies, a murderer on the loose, and a fire on the horizon.

Their orbit had shifted dramatically again.

~

From his perch on the edge of the escarpment, the old man dragged on a rollie cigarette and wondered about Vale and the fire and the folks at the lodge and how terrified they must feel now. He had felt that terror once himself, a long time ago. Now, not so much. Now he welcomed it. Was disappointed the wind had changed. He remembered the last great fire on this mountain. Back then there was fear and disappointment, but of a different kind.

His mind drifted back further, to the way things used to be. The endless music, the excitable guests, the lovely, lovely Lydia. Oh how he had adored that woman, would do anything for her, scale any mountain, fight any dragon.

And hadn't he?

Hadn't he done all that and more?

Stumping out his smoke, he slowly made his way back to the hut. There was no use thinking about that now. It was done and dusted. The fire had seen to that.

Still, it didn't stop him from dancing with her every night in his dreams...

~

The fresh bottles of red wine and one of sherry—pilfered from near Mrs Flannery's corpse—did little to mellow the book club's frazzled nerves as they returned to the bar and replenished their glasses, trying to come to terms with how the cook had been dead all day without them realising. Not unlike Vale.

"I can't believe we ran an entire book club while the poor possum was lying down there, waiting to be discovered," said Missy.

"It wasn't an entire book club," Claire retorted. "And how were we to know? We thought she'd left."

"She *did* leave! I'm sure of it!" said Perry. "I wasn't lying about that!"

Alicia took one of Perry's hands and gave him a reassuring smile. "No one is saying you're lying, Perry. But maybe you're confused about what you saw."

"I saw the van drive off. I promise you I did!"

"Yes, but did you actually see Mrs Flannery driving? Think back. Did you see her get in? Did she give you a wave or something? Those windows are tinted, if I recall. It might have been somebody else behind the wheel."

He flung a hand to his mouth as the reality hit him. "I must have seen the killer! I must have!" His hand began to flap. "They must know that! They could come back and finish me off!"

"If the killer was driving that van, Perry, they'd be mad to return to the scene of the crime," said Simon.

"Besides, they couldn't get back through the fire even if they wanted to."

That seemed to settle his nerves a little, although it did little for Alicia's, and she grasped her wine and took a comforting gulp.

"Do you remember anything about the driver? Anything at all?" asked Ronnie.

Perry was shaking his head. "No. Alicia's right. The van windows are tinted. I think I assumed that was Mrs Flannery in there. I..." He hid his face in his hands, and Alicia gave his back a gentle rub.

Flo cleared her throat. The young ones were getting in a tizz, and even she was starting to feel fuzzy. And it wasn't just the sherry. "So, let me try to get this straight," she said, placing her tiny glass back on the bar top with a slight wobble. "Do we think that whoever killed Mrs Flannery and Vale—" She turned steely eyes to Ronnie. "Because I don't believe for one moment that man simply passed in his sleep, Ron. I mean, I might be doddery, but I wasn't born yesterday. Are we saying that there was some kind of madman up here at the lodge? Someone no one noticed. And that he killed two people and just drove off, happy as Larry?"

They all stared into their respective drinks. It did sound incredible.

"But we checked the place thoroughly," said Lynette.

"Not *that* thoroughly," said Perry. "You didn't find the cellar, did you? There could be other hidey holes."

"Ew creepy!" said Missy.

"That's irrelevant," said Simon. "We searched the place *this afternoon*, long after the van had vanished, so there could have been someone else here this morning, someone none of us knew about. They could have been staying in the staff quarters or one of the many empty rooms about the place. Whoever it was obviously had some beef with the hotel staff—"

"You seriously think two people were murdered over

shoddy service?" said Lynette. "That's what Tripadvisor's for."

Simon frowned. *Now that she put it like that…*

"He's just trying to be positive, Lynette," said Claire, rushing to his defence.

And she was right. Because if it wasn't some hidden stranger who'd since taken off in the van, then it had to be one of them, and that didn't bear thinking about.

Lynette slapped them all with a smug smile. "At least there's one silver lining in all this. At least Blake has been vindicated. Because he left *after* Mrs Flannery's van went missing. So unless he can drive two cars at once, he's in the clear."

"Not necessarily," said Perry, causing her smile to slip. "He could have killed her after breakfast, driven off in her van, dumped it out of sight down the road, then doubled back—he's fit enough for that—and then turned up to book club all bright-eyed and bushy tailed. I mean, there was thirty minutes between the van vanishing and club starting. More than enough time."

Lynette's jaw dropped. "You really have it in for that guy! Why would he even bother? Why come back and then take off again? He could have killed them both last night."

"Provide an alibi?" Perry suggested.

"Okay but answer this, smarty-pants. Why kill them in the first place? What possible motive could Blake have to want to kill two staff members? He wasn't here long enough to have a bad experience." Lynette glared at Simon. "What *beef* could he possibly have against them?"

No one had an answer for that although Perry had an idea how they might find out. He went to say something, then thought better of it and clamped his lips shut. He'd keep that to himself for now.

"There's no point getting our knickers in a knot," said Flo, stifling a yawn. "I think Simon's on the money. Whoever this madman is, he's cleared off and we're now safe as houses. I'm going to take one final peek at that fire, then I'm heading to bed. And it wouldn't hurt you lot to do the same. We could all do with a good night's sleep to settle the nerves. Who knows what's ahead of us tomorrow?"

"I'll come with you," said Ronnie. "I'm beat. Good night, folks."

They all called out good night as the two women made their way out.

"Who cares about tomorrow?" said Alicia, turning back to the others. "It's tonight I'm worried about. There were eleven of us up here yesterday, happy as Larry, as Flo would say." *Twelve if you counted the old-timer in the forest.* Alicia hadn't mentioned him yet. There hadn't been any time, and now it felt like a distraction. "Today we've got a fire roaring up the mountain, two dead bodies and one man missing."

"That leaves just eight of us," said Simon.

"And then there were eight...," said Missy, swallowing her giggle this time.

CHAPTER 11

As she reached for a tea towel to help clean up after breakfast, Alicia caught her sister's eye. She looked tired, her eyes drooping, her hair in a messy ponytail. They had bunked in together last night—there was no way Alicia was getting any sleep without her sister close by—but it was clear neither woman had had a good night.

"Are you okay?" she asked.

"Just wondering what it is with us and this book club?" said Lynette, immersing her hands in the watery sink. "Everywhere we go, there's corpses."

"A self-fulfilling prophecy, perhaps," Alicia replied.

"You think we *asked* for this?"

"In a way, maybe. I mean, all we do is talk about murder. We have a passion for it; it's like we're drawing crimes to us."

Lynette scoffed. "That's silly! I think we have a terrible run of bad luck."

"Or good," said Perry, strolling in with a basket of leftover bread rolls. "We do have a good track record of solving these crimes. And it's not like a detective can get up here anytime soon. I just checked the fire. It's still going, looks bigger to me. I have a hunch two fires have joined. But I'm not sure it's closer, thankfully." He located another tea towel and picked up a dripping bowl. "We may be amateur sleuths, but I think Mrs Flannery and Vale were lucky we're here. Anybody else would be freaking out about now."

"The others aren't freaking out," said Lynette. "Simon,

Flo and Ronnie. They're strangely calm."

"They might have experience with death too, for all we know," said Perry. "Haven't Ronnie and Flo both buried husbands?"

"Still, I wish Jackson was with us," said Alicia, now kicking herself for not inviting him.

"We don't need him," said Lynette, dropping the last wet bowl on the drying rack. "*You* don't need him, Alicia. You're perfectly capable without him."

Alicia nodded as she hung her towel on a hook, wishing she could be so certain. She glanced at the rolls and turned back to Lynette.

"Any of those lovely cold meats left over? Maybe some cheese or jam?"

"Plenty. Why? You still hungry?"

"No, but I know someone who might be."

~

Sipping a calming cup of Lyle's Earl Grey—yes, the old guy pegged her from the start—Claire was feeling anything but calm. And it had nothing to do with death and fire. She had watched her friends wander off into the forest and was now leaning against the balcony railing, drinking one last brew before facing what would certainly be a very difficult day ahead, but it was the distant future she was thinking of.

She thought she had it all sewn up. Thought she knew exactly where she was heading. Then she met Simon.

There was something comforting about the man, something so *solid*. He had been so cool yesterday in the face of all the adversity. So together, so controlled. He made her feel like everything would be okay, that he would get them through it. Oh, she trusted her book club implicitly, knew they were a capable bunch, but it was Simon she had turned to.

Simon who felt like her saviour.

Claire smiled. It was all so very silly. She barely knew the man! Yet there had been an instant connection between them; she was sure he felt it too—all their shared smiles and in-jokes. He was just so... lovely! They got along so well. And that's what had her rattled.

It was almost as though she was falling in love. Claire shook the thought away.

Don't be ridiculous, woman! You hardly know the man.

And yet, just thinking about him brought the smile back to her lips and butterflies to her stomach. And before she knew it, she was imagining the distant peal of wedding bells—something she hadn't let herself do since her first disastrous engagement; the one Perry had rescued her from that first year of book club.

Yet Claire couldn't help where her mind was now galloping—towards a romantic proposal, a glorious engagement, a stunning, vintage-themed wedding ceremony.

She giggled, Missy-like, and hid her face in her cup.

Imagine if they ended up together! Oh the stories they could tell their children about how they met and what they had endured!

Of course, it would put a serious dent in her immediate ambitions. She hadn't expected that. It wasn't at all what she was planning when she caught that train up to Lyleton. Still, she couldn't help thinking what it would be like to be Mrs Simon Crete. If she took his name—and she wasn't sure she would—she'd be Claire Crete.

Claire Crete, how funny that sounds. She smiled and took another sip of her drink.

Mrs Claire Crete. C. Crete...

That's when she nearly choked on her Earl Grey.

~

While Ronnie checked the chicken coop for fresh eggs, Flo rolled up her sleeves and dug her hands into the herb garden, pulling out some weeds.

Oh how she missed the giant veggie patch they had back in Gulargambone, her Sydney garden just a few planter boxes wrestling for space on her tiny apartment balcony.

This, this was magnificent! And it felt only right to be digging into the soil now while everybody else scurried about. They all seemed so lost and confused, and she could not believe the two sisters were heading off on the forbidden track, green bag in tow. She frowned as she plucked some fresh parsley and chewed it.

What could possibly be dragging them through that dark, tangled forest?

They looked exactly as Vale had looked late that night she had spotted him—furtive and suspicious, clutching his silly bag.

What were they all doing? What were they trying to achieve?

Didn't they know there was a fire out there, roaring up towards them? She thought about the forest, and her mind was spiralling back to another time, another tragedy.

Flo knew something terrible had happened the moment she got in from the milking. Her mother was as white as the contents of her pitcher, her father already half-tanked, a large bottle of homebrew close by. It was early even for him. It was a fallen tree, her mother told her, really just a large branch that had snapped off and snapped her brother's back in half, killing him instantly.

A widow-maker the farmers called it, but it made widows of them all. And homeless widows at that because he was the only son. It was a different time. A different era. Girls couldn't run a large cattle farm with nothing but an old drunk beside them.

That wasn't sexism. It was just the way it was.

Flo thought of the young things wandering off now into the forest, so naive, so gung-ho, like nothing would ever stop them. Like no branch could simply drop from the sky and obliterate their future.

Well, life had stopped her, or death to be more precise, and so they were forced to sell the property, and all scattered with the breeze. She blew in to Sydney soon after, scored herself the secretarial job, then found herself a husband. Had her own brood. Pretended she was happy. Then she'd lost her hubby; the cancer took Ian fast. That's when she met Ronnie and joined her fancy ladies club, and for the first time in a long time she was happy, really happy. Ronnie had also experienced loss, so they helped each other through it. But Flo had never forgotten her brother and the cattle farm and everything they had surrendered.

He seemed more alive to her now than ever. Almost whispered to her through the trees and she looked up and sighed. Oh how he would love this place! He always lamented the dusty paddocks, the scorching sun, the scarcity of trees. Of course, the irony of his death was not lost on any of them.

Flo turned back and reached for a pot she had found by the back shed, ready for planting, and gently pulled a young sapling out, the roots crumbling in her glove.

It was up to her now, she thought. She would plant a little something to honour his memory here, remind herself and the world at large, that life was bigger than all of them.

~

Lynette could not believe that Alicia was hauling a bag of fresh food along a crumbling track to feed some old geezer, especially at a time like this, but she could not dissuade her sister from her mission and so had insisted on accompanying her to the elusive cabin.

"He was so shaken by Vale's death," Alicia explained as they sidestepped a tripping root. "And he knew Mrs Flannery too, so he has a right to know about her murder. Besides, it's clear Vale's been sneaking him food;

he's probably starving. He didn't get any dinner last night."

"That's his own fault, really. He chooses to live out here in the sticks; he shouldn't be stealing food from the lodge."

"He wasn't! Vale obviously took the food willingly—he had the grocery bag and thermos that night, remember? Come on. It's also a good excuse to pick the guy's brain on this blasted fire, which from what I can see, doesn't look like it's shifted."

"You say that like it's a bad thing," said Lynette.

They had just stepped through the clearing and caught their first sight of the cabin when a strange yet familiar ringing sound startled them.

"My phone!" Lynette squealed, reaching into the pocket of her cut-off denim shorts. "It works out here!"

She retrieved her smartphone to find a dozen missed calls and text messages and grabbed Alicia's arm, holding her in place. "Do not move an inch! This might be the only place we get a signal."

Alicia dropped the cold bag to the ground and waited while Lynette scrolled through her phone to retrieve her messages.

As she did so, Lynette asked, "Why didn't any of you call for help when you were here yesterday evening?"

"None of us had our phones on us. We assumed they were useless." Now Alicia was the one who felt useless. They could have reached help so much sooner.

Lynette stopped scrolling and glanced at her sister. "Your man has left me a stack of messages."

"Jackson?"

"Unless you've got another man I don't know about." She held up a finger and listened to one message, then another. "He's obviously heard about the fire and sounds manic. You'd better call him back, babe, but first I'm going to call the police."

Alicia snatched the phone from her. "He *is* the police, Lynny!"

As she began tapping her boyfriend's number into the mobile, Lynette grabbed her arm. "Is that him?"

They both looked towards the clearing where a man in a beat-up hat was just stepping out of his cabin, now turning and peering back towards them.

Alicia nodded. "Can you take the food over while I talk to Jackson?"

"I'm not going over there alone! Are you mad? He could be the killer!"

"He's harmless," she said then, "Shh!" as Jackson picked up.

"*Lynette?*" Jackson said, and Alicia quickly corrected him.

"I'm using Lynette's phone. We've finally found some mobile coverage."

"That's a relief!" Jackson's voice sounded clear and misleadingly close. "I've been trying to get through to you all morning. I've rung the lodge; it just rings out. I've called your phone a million times, Lyn's, Claire's, Perry's, I didn't know how to reach you."

"Yeah well—"

"Listen, it's all over the news. There's a fire, just outside of Lyleton."

"Well, duh!" she said, sounding harsher than she meant to. "We have worked that out, honey. But the main lines are down so we couldn't call out. But to be honest, that's the least of our worries—"

"Look, don't panic," he said. "I'm on my way up there now, and I'll get you guys out. I've already spoken with the local RFS—that's the Rural Fire Service—and they assure me they have it all under control."

Alicia stared at the black smoke billowing from the not-so-distant fire. Twice the size it was yesterday. "Doesn't look under control to me," she said, her eyes now shifting to Lynette, who hadn't budged. Alicia nodded her head towards the old-timer who was still watching them closely. *Go!* she mouthed to her sister.

Lynette groaned, picked up the bag and made her way over.

"Apparently the winds have changed," Jackson was saying, "and it's heading back downwards, so you should be okay for a bit, but obviously we want to get you out as soon as possible. Tom Benson—that's the group officer leading the operation—tells me there is only one road in and it's blocked off at this stage. There are some old fire trails, but they're extremely overgrown and there's giant trees down, so they're having no luck getting through that way either."

"That fills me with hope," she said, watching now as Lynette reached the man and held the food bag out like a peace offering.

"Please don't worry," Jackson told her. "You will be okay. I should be in Lyleton in a few hours and I can reassess the situation then. In the meantime, Benson says to keep an eye on the fire and activate a bushfire survival plan. That's where you—"

"I know what it is," she said, interrupting him this time. She could see Lynette talking now, one hand gesticulating as the old man just stood and listened. Alicia continued, "Flo has already got us thinking about that. If the fire comes all the way up, we're grabbing our bags and heading down the other side of the mountain."

Lynette suddenly reached across and dragged the old man into a hug. She must have told him about Mrs Flannery and he must have been devastated. Alicia felt guilty that she hadn't thought to give him a hug yesterday.

"I knew Flo was a capable woman," Jackson said, remembering her from the last case. "But there's a lot more to it than that, honey. The biggest concern at this stage is spot fires ahead of the main fire front."

"Spot fires?" Her eyes snapped away from Lynette and back to the smoke.

"Embers can travel several kilometres and start random fires at different places. There's two fire fronts already and they're worried about more. I'm told it's pretty dry up there."

She glanced down at the crisp dead leaves under her feet. *That was an understatement.*

"You need to get away from those dangerous trees and back to the lodge," Jackson was saying. "It's your safest bet. You'll also need to prepare yourselves properly. Benson emailed me a list of instructions. Have you got a notepad and pen?"

"I'm in the middle of those *dangerous trees* now, Jackson."

"Okay, well try to remember some of this." He rattled off a checklist while Alicia's headache returned.

"Should I call the RFS directly?"

"Good luck with that. They're in the thick of it now. Just do as I say, and you'll be all right. Benson reckons there should be good maps of the fire trails up there at the lodge. Find them and keep them handy; hopefully you won't need to use them. Listen, I need to get on the road. The sooner I get going, the sooner I can help out."

"You're going to come fight the fire for me, honey?" she said, her tone coquettish.

"Who said I wasn't romantic?" He chuckled but there wasn't much in it. "Listen, I'll call you in a few hours when I get to Lyleton."

"No point. There's no signal at the lodge. I'll have to come back and call you from here." She took a deep breath. "But listen, I haven't told you the worst of it."

"The worst of it?" He almost chuckled again. "There's something worse than a bloody great bushfire?"

She took another breath. "You're not going to believe this, Jackson. I almost don't believe it myself. Then again, knowing our history, maybe you will…"

"What are you talking about?" He inhaled suddenly. "Oh no. Do not tell me you stumbled upon a dead body."

She squinted. "Not just one dead body. There's two people dead here, and both deaths are suspicious."

~

On the return walk back to the lodge, as Alicia tried to come to terms with everything Jackson had told her, Lynette gushed about the old-timer and what a charmer he was.

That surprised Alicia. She had quite liked the guy herself, but charm wasn't the word that sprang to mind. "You didn't catch his name, did you?"

"Of course. It's Snowy, which seems hilarious considering how hot it is around here. He was pretty upset about Mrs Flannery." She pushed some hair from her face. "Although, it's odd, he didn't seem *that* surprised. Maybe it'll hit him later. He was grateful for the food though. I get the impression all Vale ever brought him was cold soup and stale bread."

"Considering it's pilfered bread, he's lucky to get anything," said Alicia, her mood now soured.

"Still, we can't keep this up. I told him he should come to the kitchen and help himself next time he's peckish. It's not like there's anyone there to stop him. I even suggested he have dinner with us tonight—that is, if we're still stuck in this hell hole."

"Really? You think that's wise?" Alicia was happy enough to entertain Mountain Man, but she wasn't sure how Richie-rich Ronnie or even stuffy Simon would feel about a smelly old squatter joining them at the table.

"Don't worry, sis. Snowy had the same reaction. Said he'd rather slit his wrists than come to the lodge. His choice of words, not mine. He's no fan of the place, that's for sure. Did you know he was born on this mountain? Said it was peaceful before Lyle's Lodge destroyed everything for him."

"Lyle's Lodge has been feeding that man; he should be more grateful."

"No, *Vale* had been feeding him. I doubt the Lyle family ever knew about it. And I'm almost certain the new owners will put a stop to it."

"New owners?" said Alicia.

"Didn't I tell you? According to Blake, the Lyles have just sold the place. I guess that's why it's undergoing serious renovations. I do hope whoever's bought it is kind to the old squatter though. Doesn't try to move him on. He said he has no intention of leaving the mountain. Said they'd have to remove him in a coffin."

"That's depressing."

"Actually he was very sweet. I really liked him, and not only because he assures me the fire has headed back down the hill, away from us."

"That's what the RFS told Jackson. But the wind can change at any time, Lynny, so you better not get too complacent."

"With you beside me, honey, no chance."

They walked in silence for a while, both of them lost in their thoughts, then Lynette said, "So, how'd you go with Jackson? Racing up on his white charger is he?"

"Something like that. He won't get to Lyleton for a few hours though, but it's a relief to touch base with the outside world. He gave me a checklist in case spot fires break out. Then I gave him the grim news about Vale and Flannery, and that took a bit of digesting."

"I bet it did. He must be regretting ever meeting the Murder Mystery Book Club."

Alicia agreed. She couldn't believe she hadn't scared him off yet. "Jackson said to secure both Vale's bedroom and the cellar and he'll alert the local authorities."

"We're not complete idiots; we've already done that. Although we haven't really taken this fire very seriously, have we? I never thought of spot fires. Good thing he mentioned that."

Alicia nodded and focused on the path ahead. It wasn't all Jackson had mentioned. There was something else. Something to do with another white charger, but she didn't have the heart to break the news to Lynette.

~

Ronnie glanced from Flo, who was now rinsing her hands in the kitchen sink, to her sparkling Cartier watch and frowned, relieved she hadn't mentioned the guest book. The latest death had changed absolutely everything.

She placed the basket of eggs in the cold room and rubbed her aching back, giving it all some thought. Feeling almost relieved. Oddly.

They had all believed the story of the madman, and she had to admit it was a good one. It made so much sense! Of course a crazy person had killed Vale and Flannery! What other reason could there possibly be? Mrs Flannery wasn't even here until the eighties, so how could anyone connect the dots?

Still, it didn't stop her from twiddling her wristwatch and wondering how to play it…

~

It was just on ten thirty a.m., and the Murder Mystery Book Club were all twiddling cups of tea, sitting on the leather lounges in the library, staring up at Alicia again, and she felt a jolt of déjà vu. It was eerily quiet, and apart from the very faint smell of smoke and the missing book club member, you might almost think they'd gone back in time, back to that first session before everything turned to chaos.

She glanced at the empty seat beside Simon and frowned.

Things had changed, and dramatically. There was something else Jackson had told her, just before she'd hung up. She would leave that to the end. For now, she gave them a reassuring smile and said, "There's good news and bad."

"Can we have the good news first?" said Flo, whose tea was a fresh ginger-and-honey concoction, prepared by

Lynette earlier. A special request to settle her stomach. "I think we all need it."

She nodded. "Right, well, the good news is there is a tiny bit of mobile coverage out on Repentance Way, so I was able to make contact with the outside world."

"Woo-hoo!" said Perry.

"Really?" said Ronnie.

"Thank goodness," said Simon.

Claire tried to rein in her frown. She distinctly remembered Simon telling her there was no mobile coverage out there. Perhaps he hadn't walked far enough. *Or was he lying about that too?*

Simon caught her eye then, and she quickly glanced away, shifting in her seat and trying to keep her heart from hammering through her blouse. But it wasn't love that was causing it to accelerate now. It was feelings of betrayal and dismay and, if she were being honest, a tinge of anxiety.

She had a creeping feeling Simon wasn't the man she thought he was.

"So," continued Alicia, oblivious to Claire's inner turmoil, "the Rural Fire Service know we're up here; they know our situation and are battling the flames as we speak. They should also know about Vale and Mrs Flannery by now." She told the new members, "My partner, Liam Jackson, is a police officer, and he's alerting the relevant authorities."

"Good to hear it," said Simon. "That's quite a relief."

Alicia agreed. It felt like a weight had been lifted. "In the meantime, we need to do what we're already doing and stay well away from both crime scenes. Big thank you, though, to Nurse Ronnie for all her expertise and wisdom."

As they gave the older woman a round of applause, Missy suddenly had a horrifying vision of Vale's bed empty. His body missing.

Had anyone thought to check him lately? Missy wondered. See if he was still dead? Or, more precisely, ever dead in the first place? It was a strange thought, an eerie one, but hadn't something similar happened in the Agatha Christie mystery they'd been reading?

Missy shuddered and pushed the image away while Ronnie asked:

"So what's the bad news then, dear?"

Alicia took a deep breath. "Jackson confirmed that the road up is cut off, and they may not get through to us anytime soon. The winds are currently in our favour, but they may change later this arvo, so we need to enact our fire plan pronto."

All eyes swept across to Flo, who nodded. "Yes, that's a good idea. Jolly good…" She reached into the pocket of her skirt. "I did jot some things down…" She came up empty-handed so tried the other pocket while Alicia jumped in.

"It's okay, Flo. Jackson gave me a list we can work from. The most important thing is to be alert for spot fires. I've just learned that embers can fly great distances and start new fires ahead of the main front, so we have to be vigilant and watch for that."

"What do we do if there is a spot fire?" asked Perry, flabbergasted by the thought.

"We put it out of course," said Flo, like he was a complete imbecile.

"There are some water tanks about the place," said Simon. "I'll secure some hoses, maybe find a few fire extinguishers while we're at it."

Alicia produced a second finger. "We also need to get a very basic kit together in case a secondary fire becomes too big for us to handle and we have to make a run for it."

"Good golly," said Missy.

"What kind of kit?" asked Claire.

"Things like drinking water, a first aid kit and any specific medicines people need, a bit of food, some blankets, I guess in case we get caught out overnight. It took a good hour to drive up that mountain, and Mrs Flannery wasn't exactly dawdling, so it will take some time to make it down on foot. But hopefully it won't come to that."

"Actually, love, the blankets are in case we get caught in a firestorm," said Flo. "A woollen blanket can be your best mate if you have nowhere to run."

She imitated throwing a blanket over yourself and crouching under it.

"Good bloody golly," echoed Perry while Missy looked ready to faint.

"Anyway," said Alicia, clearly wishing that terrifying thought away, "the main road is not the only road in. Apparently there should be some old fire trails we can use if we need to escape."

"Fire trails?" asked Claire.

"Unmarked access routes," Flo explained. "The fire service use 'em to get in and clear the forest, do a bit of controlled burning through the year and I guess to fight the fire when one breaks out."

"So how do we find these elusive trails?" said Perry. "Do we look for bread droppings?"

Perry was joking of course, but Flo was squinting at him through her glasses now like she thought he was a galah.

Alicia jumped in. "Jackson says there should be some maps somewhere, indicating our nearest fire trails. Apparently there's at least one heading down the other side of the mountain, and he reckons it's our safest bet."

"I'll search for them," said Perry. He needed to do something to settle his nerves and stop Flo from scowling at his lame jokes. He just hoped this search didn't produce another corpse.

"Excuse me for sounding ageist now," Simon said, "but isn't the trek down going to be a little difficult for, er, some of the older members of our group?"

Ronnie looked scandalised. "I might be *old*, young man, but I'm still a very competent walker!"

"As am I," said Flo, sounding equally offended.

"Apologies, ladies," he replied, offering Claire a mock grimace, but she was no longer looking his way. He shifted in his seat awkwardly. "Hopefully it won't come to that. I'll set the hoses up around the property, maybe even get up on the main roof, see if I can clear some of the leaves from the gutters so they don't catch fire. Would hate to see this lovely old lodge go up."

"Who cares about the bloody lodge when our lives are in danger?" said Perry.

"I care," he retorted. "If we're inside the lodge when it catches fire, you'll care too I suggest."

Alicia noticed how edgy they were all getting. "Okay, let's all stay calm," she said. "I think that's a good idea, Simon, but be very careful up there." *You're not getting any younger yourself,* she might have added if she were Perry. "Lynette, can you get some food supplies together? Nothing gourmet, just some basic provisions."

Her sister nodded, and Missy offered to organise the water bottles.

"I'll round the fire extinguishers up," said Ronnie, "and keep them at the ready."

"And I noticed some good thick blankets somewhere," said Flo. "I'll add them to the mix."

"I'll look for torches, matches, that kind of thing," Alicia said. "Between us, we should be right. Thanks, everyone, we are all going to get out of this alive."

Then she smacked her lips shut, thinking of at least two people who wouldn't. And if you added Blake to the mix, there could be a third. She cleared her throat. It was time to tell them her final piece of news, this one the grimmest yet.

Avoiding Lynette's gaze, she said, "Before you all run

off, there is something else Jackson told me." They looked at her warily. "We didn't have long to talk, but the fire chief told him something that may or may not affect us. An aerial water chopper spotted something on the road down from Cooper's Crossing, which I gather is about halfway between us and Lyleton village. It's a car."

She couldn't help but sneak a glance at her sister then. "It's completely burnt out."

"A car?" said Lynette. "What type of car?"

"I don't know what type," she said, grimly. "All I know is it's a white one."

CHAPTER 12

While they headed off to attend to their respective chores, Claire approached Alicia and said, "Can we have a quiet word?"

Before Alicia could reply, Lynette was looming, arms akimbo.

"Why didn't you tell me about Blake?" she demanded. "While we were walking back, why didn't you say anything?"

"I don't even know if that *is* Blake," Alicia replied. "All Jackson knows is it's a white vehicle. Nobody said anything about a Mercedes. Apparently the chopper can't get close enough to see if there's a body in the car or if he's managed to escape." *Or double back*, she thought, a little alarmingly. "It could be anybody's car. A day-tripper? Someone else who lives on the mountain?"

In fact, she was hoping it was the lodge's stolen white van and karma had caught up with Mrs Flannery's killer. But the more she thought about it, the less it made sense. The van had left long before the Mercedes. If the van had been caught in the fire, it didn't bode well for Blake.

"You've all been thinking he was the killer and here he was, burned alive while trying to save us!"

Claire held a finger in the air. "Just because he might have got caught in the fire doesn't mean he wasn't the killer," she said, landing herself a withering look from the younger Finlay. "Sorry, Lynette, but if you think about it logically, both Vale and Flannery were killed long before Blake drove off, so he could've done it. Then got caught up in the fire. Or maybe he ditched his car and took off on foot?"

"Humph!" she replied, striding off towards the kitchen.

Claire turned to Alicia, both hands up now. "I didn't mean to upset her."

"It's probably not his car down there anyway, but really, she barely knows the guy. I don't know why she's so hung up on him. So, what did you want to talk about?"

Claire frowned. She barely knew Simon too, and now she felt foolish. As she debated whether to say anything at all, they heard a not too subtle "Pst!" coming from the corner of the library and swept around to find Perry standing by the bookshelf, motioning them over.

He had been searching for trail maps but was clearly eavesdropping. The two women shared a curious look and made their way across.

"I know how we can find out if Blake is on the level," he whispered. "But we need to act now before the others come back. And by others I really just mean Lynette."

~

Simon had no luck finding a leaf blower, but he did find several rakes, and so he hauled one to the rooftop closest to the fire front and began sweeping the dry leaves out of the gutters. As he did so, they crackled and crunched, and it sent shivers down his back.

The lodge roof and surrounds were littered with kindling. It was like a loaded fire pit waiting for a match. If a stray ember did make it this far, the whole place would be up in minutes.

He thought then of Claire, his shiver intensifying. If only he'd told her what was going on, what he was really up to.

Now... now it felt too late.

~

Sneaking softly up the staircase, Missy couldn't stop the jitters that were playing ping-pong in her stomach. But she had to be strong. She had to take one for the team. She had to see if Vale was still lying stiff underneath his covers.

It all felt very silly, really. Typical silly Missy! But Alicia wasn't the only one with an active imagination. The others liked to laugh her off, but Missy had a terrible tendency to mix real life with fiction, and right now she was mixing Vale's murder with the murder of the old judge in *And Then There Were None*.

He had been faking his death in the book. Was Vale faking too? And was Ronnie in on it with him?

The idea was so preposterous there was *no way* she was going to mention it to the others. She had to check it out for herself, and so she continued upwards.

A sudden creak stopped Missy in her tracks, and she glanced up the final few steps but could see nothing and no one. She took some calming breaths, trying to settle the ping-pong game that was now at Olympic standard, and then tiptoed up and towards Vale's door, the last one along the corridor and the only one still closed.

She passed what must be Mrs Flannery's room first, the bed neatly made, her handbag resting upon it, like she was about to head out for a shop. Then a series of empty rooms, the beds stripped of sheets, as well as several storage cupboards showing guest linen and towels, blankets and miniature bottles of all types of bathroom supplies.

Which brought her to Vale's door.

Another deep breath and then Missy slowly turned the handle, hoping for the best, which if you thought about it, meant the very worst for Vale. She pushed the heavy hardwood door open and peeked inside, across to the bed where—lo and behold—a sheet was covering what could only be a corpse. Missy knew there was a dead body under there—the violent smell, the rush of goose bumps, the clammy cold stillness of the air—yet her imagination was stronger than all of that and propelled her forwards, to the bed, to the sheet, to check he really was under there.

And then she was running back out, slamming that door, tearing down the steps, feeling as she always did, like silly, foolish Missy. When she got to the lobby, she flung herself out the front door and vomited into the garden, drenching some violet-coloured flowers in the process.

The reality was nothing like the book. And Vale really had been murdered.

~

Ronnie noticed Missy through the library window and wondered if she was doing some gardening, hovering as she was over the native wisteria. It's certainly all Flo seemed interested in right now, and she took that as a good sign.

More gardening was a brilliant idea. That would keep them all distracted!

"Milk dear?" said Ronnie. "I can't remember if you have it."

"Just a drop, thanks Ron, and a spoonful of sugar if you can find it," Flo replied, reaching for a canvas bag she had left on the couch earlier.

The two old friends had worked diligently, fetching fire blankets and extinguishers and dumping them near the front door. Then Ronnie had suggested a refreshing cuppa and now handed it to her, along with a plate of ginger biscuits.

"Found these in the cupboard," she said. "Might as well dig in."

Flo thanked her, then ignored the biscuits as she pulled out her knitting.

As the needles clicked away, Ronnie could hear Simon busy scratching about on the roof above their heads. He was nervous, she knew that. They all were, and if you

124

thought about it too closely, it *was* all rather terrifying.

Eventually she turned to Flo and said, "How long have we known each other, dear?"

Clearly lost in her own thoughts, Flo looked up with a start. "Oh goodness, who knows. An eternity?"

Ronnie shook her head. "Not that long actually. We met at grief counselling, do you remember?"

"Ah, that's right. You convinced me to join your Auxiliary. I've been madly knitting ever since." She cackled at the striped brown-and-cream beanie in her lap.

"Do you remember why we first became friends?" Ronnie persisted. "Why we became so close?"

"We were both lonely old bags?" suggested Flo, tongue firmly in her cheek, but Ronnie was not smiling.

"It was more than that, Florence. Don't you remember? We had both suffered great loss."

Flo frowned. Yes, that's right. "Are we talking about your Bert now, dear? Do you miss him terribly? Is that what this is about?"

"Of course I miss Bert!" Ronnie said, snapping at her friend as she chomped into a biscuit. But this wasn't about Bert, not at all. It was about another man, a handsome young hunter with sparkling blue eyes and hair streaked from the sun.

Flo, worried, watched her for a moment more, then continued knitting while Ronnie's eyes shifted back to her friend, wondering how she could be so blasé.

"How did you get over him in the end?" Ronnie said eventually.

"Sorry?" Flo said, looking up.

"You were heartbroken, Flo. You really were. I thought you'd never recover. But now… now you seem… so calm or something."

Flo shrugged and stared back at her wool, pulling a new ball from her bag. "I don't think you ever do get over great loss, Ron. You learn to live with the pain. What do the quacks say? You *compartmentalise* it."

"And if you can't? Live with it, I mean."

Flo shot her a wary glance. She was lost for words. Now Ronnie really had her worried. "What's really going on, dear? What are you trying to say?"

Ronnie blushed and looked away as Flo's eyes narrowed beneath her delicate spectacles. "I do hope you're okay, Ronnie," she said. "I do hope you're letting go of *unimportant* things. You must only focus on positive things now, dear. We are all going to get out of here, and we are all going to be fine. Do you hear me? Every last one of us. Don't dwell on the past or worry about the future. Do you think you can do that?"

Ronnie nodded, but she was lying. She had not forgotten. It was all coming back to her like a whirling dervish. Suddenly everything was swirling into focus—the hunter, the fire, Lydia, the misery, the murmurs and the rumours that were forgotten just as quickly. But not by everyone and not by her, not now.

It did not feel unimportant suddenly. It felt like a matter of life and death.

But how many deaths, she wondered? And would they all get out alive?

~

"Blake is halfway to Byron Bay by now, I'm sure of it," said Perry, the moment his bedroom door clicked shut behind them.

He had wanted to enact his devious plan immediately, but Alicia had got all snippy about getting fire ready first, and so they had agreed to meet in his room in thirty minutes and not to mention anything to Lynette. He had run into Missy though—she was searching for water bottles but looked like she could do with a stiff drink. When he asked her what was wrong, she shook him off and said something about "silly Missy!" then trailed him down the corridor.

Once they were all safely inside, he produced his theory, one he'd been working on all morning. "I didn't want to say anything in front of Lynette—she's blinkered, that woman—but I don't think Blake is caught in the fire, I think he *started* it!"

They stared at him, bewildered, so he forged on. "The timing is too perfect. Lynette's already told us he was up and about last night at midnight. She says he went to bed after their drink, but how does she know that? What if he stayed up waiting for Vale to return? He kills Vale but can't get access to Mrs Flannery so waits until morning and bumps her off after breakfast. He then drives her van away, hides it somewhere in the bush—hence the burnt-out vehicle—and treks back to book club to provide himself an alibi. He probably cut the phone lines—we should really check that—but he obviously didn't expect us to find Vale so fast. In any case, once we did, he took off faster than lightning, you can't deny that."

Because the look on their faces suggested they might.

"Then," he continued, unperturbed, "to cover his tracks, he stops midway down the mountain and starts the fire behind him. If the RFS look closely, I bet they'll find the burnt-out car is an empty white lodge van, and, as I say, Blake is hiding away in some luxury beach resort, high-fiving himself!"

He finished with a suggestively raised eyebrow. The women were staring at him, each with a different expression.

"That's quite a theory you've got there," said Alicia with a note of scepticism.

"I'm confused," said Claire, head to one side.

"You really think Blake is trying to *burn us alive*?" was Missy's horrified interpretation.

"It's not *personal*, Missy," said Perry. "But he would want to destroy the evidence."

"But why kill Vale in the first place? Or Mrs Flannery for that matter?" asked Claire. "What's his motive?"

"Like Simon says, he must have some beef with them or some history with this place—which, of all of us, he was the most familiar with."

"That's true," said Alicia, remembering how well Blake knew the walking tracks that first afternoon. He was also the one who'd told Lynette about the lodge's sale, how there was a new owner. How did he know that? Why was he so well informed?

Perry continued. "Who knows what his problem is, but maybe Blake infiltrated our little book club so he could come up here and wreak havoc—for whatever reason. He was using us as subterfuge." He turned to Alicia. "After Flo and Ronnie agreed to join the club, we all decided we needed at least one more member. You placed the advertisement in the *Herald*. What did it say? Did you mention Lyle's Lodge specifically?"

She thought back and gulped. Yes, she did. "I said we were getting the club together at the remote Lyle's Lodge…" She groaned. "You think I drew him in?"

It made her feel sick to her stomach, but it also made an awful kind of sense. They had lured in a criminal once before, and this time Blake had been so determined to join them. Had practically *begged* her to let him make up their ninth member.

When was she going to learn? The more desperate they were to sign up, the more she should avoid them!

"I bet it wasn't the *book club* he was keen on," said Perry, "it was Lyle's Lodge. We just provided the perfect cover."

"But you still haven't explained *why*," said Claire, rubbing her temple. "Why would Blake even need a cover? He could come up any old time and kill them both in the dead of night and slink away again, no questions asked."

Perry frowned. "Okay. I haven't got all the details sorted, which is why I've dragged you in here." He nudged his eyebrows to the right. "Blake's room is on the other side of mine. I'm going to climb across the balcony and see if I can't have a dig about."

"Ooh, naughty!" said Missy, perking up a little.

"Why don't we just get a spare key from reception?" said Alicia. "What are we hiding from?"

"Er, a killer!" he said, like she was stupid. "If I'm wrong about Blake—and let's face it, the more I talk, the shakier it's all sounding—then that means somebody else did all this, and I don't care what Simon says, that somebody else could still be here amongst us. And unless you've all been fooling me for many years now, it *has* to be one of the new book club members. I don't want to alert them to what we're doing."

They all stared at him dubiously, and he said, "Okay, that made a lot more sense in my head. Look, I'll do all the hard work. Alicia, you just need to stand outside the hallway and keep watch. Especially for Lynette. If she comes down, steer her elsewhere. She's incapable of thinking badly about brawny Blake. Missy, maybe you could guard reception, in case anyone takes a stroll outdoors—crash tackle them before they do—and Claire you scoot down to the walkway below the balconies in case someone comes around the back."

~

Claire wasn't convinced they'd find anything in Blake's bedroom. If he had taken off, surely he would have taken everything with him? But she did as Perry asked and made her way outside, standing below Blake's balcony, not far from where Simon had looked up at her only yesterday. She sighed at the memory.

It felt like a lifetime ago...

"Oi! All clear?" Perry hissed and she swept her eyes up to find him leaning across his balustrade.

Claire surveyed the pathway, then gave him a subtle thumbs-up and watched as he clambered rather awkwardly across from his balcony to Blake's.

Perry was a gym-fit forty-something, better suited to exercise bikes and rowing machines than scaling real-world balconies. Still, he managed to fling himself across smoothly, and once there, he straightened himself out, checked the internal door, then turned and gave his own thumbs-up before disappearing inside.

~

Back in the hallway between the two bedrooms, Alicia chewed her nails and tried to get it all straight in her head. If Blake was the imposter Vale had been talking about, then who was he really? And how delighted must he have been to come across her rather naive advertisement? It made her feel sick thinking of it. If only she had not mentioned the words "remote" and "Lyle's Lodge," they might still be happily discussing the book in the library now, and two people might not be murdered.

Was this all Alicia's fault? Had she inadvertently signed up a killer?

There was a sudden click, and then Perry appeared from inside Blake's room. He ushered Alicia in and secured the door behind her. Then he waved a hand around the room and said, "I think you all owe me an apology."

CHAPTER 13

Blake's room looked like it was occupied by a teenage boy. Smelled like it too. Clothes were exploding like intestines from a bag on the luggage rack, there was a wet towel lying on the bed and sweaty walking gear strewn across the floor. The small desk was cluttered with paraphernalia—pens, notepads, a knock-off Gucci watch, a thick manila folder bursting with articles and a shiny black camera with a zoom lens loose beside it.

"Looks to me like he left in a hurry," said Perry.

"Also looks like he was expecting to return," said Alicia. "That camera gear doesn't come cheap, and these—" She pointed to a dusty walking shoe poking out from under the bed. "They cost a bit. Why wouldn't he take them with him?"

"Because, like I said, he was in a hurry. Who cares about Nikon and Nike when you're locked away in prison? In any case, honey, I think you're missing the gold in the room. As you journos say, I think you've buried the lead."

Perry waved a hand at the folder on the desk, and she stepped across to open it.

It was like opening the aforementioned teenager's history project. There were old newspaper articles stuffed inside, mostly about Lyle's Lodge and the Great Fire of 1970, as well as black-and-white prints of the resort from different angles, and a variety of fading happy snaps, clearly dating from that era. Some were group shots of revellers all dressed to the nines, others were of smaller groups outdoors, dogs, horses and/or rifles by their side.

Alicia scooped up an envelope with the words Family Tree scribbled on the front. She half pulled the first page out and was surprised to find it was not for the Lyles as she was expecting but for a family called Murphy, with the names Eamon Joseph Murphy and Mary Louise O'Connor typed at the top.

A sudden tap-tap made her drop the envelope and lock eyes with Perry, who placed a finger to his lips to quieten her. He stepped across to the door and opened it a crack to find Claire and Missy staring in at him, expectantly. He waved them in, and together they continued to sift through the rest of the folder's contents.

After ten minutes or so, Claire said, "Why would Blake have all this information?"

"Could be a journalist, doing a story?" said Alicia. It looked like one of her old research folders, before Google put an end to hard copies.

"Or a private eye, snooping on behalf of someone?" said Missy.

"Or," said Perry, not liking either of those theories, "he could be related to a man called Donal Murphy and it's a lot more personal than that. Listen to this. It's dated January 28, 1970."

He began reading aloud an article in his hands.

"Bushfire Tragedy—Man Still Missing."

Perry gave them a knowing look and kept reading.

"LYLETON—Firefighters are still searching for the body of a young man who went missing during the bushfire that came close to razing Lyle's Hunting Lodge over the Australia Day long weekend. Identified as Donal Eamon Murphy, aged twenty-one, the Commonwealth Games sport-shooting champion was last seen heading towards Joiner's Ridge on the turnoff to Cooper's Crossing. Lodge manager and Lyleton's newly elected mayor, Jack Lyle, said Murphy had insisted on fighting the fire, despite his protestations, and the search party would continue until his body was recovered. 'Mr Murphy is a true hero and his sacrifice will not be forgotten,' said Mr Lyle…"

Perry didn't bother to read on, just slapped a hand at the page and said, "And yet do you see anything about this poor fellow anywhere in the lodge? Not one mention in the library, no photos, no memorial, nothing. And here's the spooky bit…" He paused again, this time for effect. "Blake, *himself*, was bitching about it all at dinner the first night, like he was offended they hadn't made more of a fuss of the poor sod who died in the fire."

"That's right! He did," said Missy. "And Mrs Flannery overheard and—"

"She dismissed it!" Perry interrupted. "Said it was hardly something to celebrate. Called it bad publicity! Well, if you are related to the guy who's given his life to save your lodge, that's gotta cut deep! Maybe he only meant to come here to fill in the family tree but her remark left him fuming, so he followed her down to the cellar and smashed her over the head—in a crime of passion. Maybe Vale said something similar?"

"Except Ronnie thinks Vale was poisoned," said Alicia. "And that takes planning. Nothing spontaneous about that. He would have had to bring the syringe and the poison with him, or find it somewhere…?"

"Okay, but Vale worked at the lodge in 1970, remember? Sure, he was young, but he was *here when it happened*. So maybe Blake holds him responsible? Maybe there's something in all his research that points the finger directly at a young bellboy." He glanced down at the articles in their hands and shrugged. "Maybe Vale was a smoker and accidentally started the fire? I don't know. But it could be the reason Blake came up here—to enact revenge on Vale—but then, after Mrs Flannery's frankly *insensitive* comment, he bopped her over the head as well. I mean, you can't deny her death seems spontaneous."

They all mulled over that for a moment, then Claire asked, "What age is Blake? He seems way too young to care so much about all of this. Was he even alive in 1970 when the fire happened? If so, he couldn't have been more than a baby."

"Exactly! Maybe this Donal fellow was Blake's *father*. You'd care then!"

"Ohhh," said Missy, loving Perry's theory. "Maybe Morrow is Blake's mother's maiden name, or maybe he changed it! Morrow is not *that* different to Murphy."

"Or he could be using a fake name entirely," said Claire, her mind skipping in another direction.

Alicia was nodding quietly. This was starting to make a weird kind of sense. "Pity Blake has taken off and the only people who can tell us the truth are both dead."

"There is Ronnie," said Claire. "We could ask her about it. She was around at that time."

"Oh she was here for five seconds and she barely remembers it," scoffed Perry.

"I know someone who might remember," said Alicia, glancing at her watch.

~

Standing in the kitchen, Lynette sorted out supplies for a potential evacuation and then began putting together a platter for lunch. But her mind was elsewhere. She didn't know why she felt so defensive about Blake, but he hadn't struck her as a killer. Sure, he was cocky and immature— she'd seen how he flirted with the older ladies, trying to make her jealous—but they'd really bonded after dinner and she had come to realise they had a lot in common.

And it wasn't all skin deep.

"You and I, we don't get our due respect, do we

Lynette?" he'd said as he swirled his glass of red wine. "We're too beautiful to be taken seriously."

She'd snorted at that but noticed he was serious.

"I'm sick of being underestimated all the time," he told her, "of being shoved to the side and treated like I can't possibly have a brain because I look like this."

He waved a hand at his chiselled jaw and she laughed then.

"Oh diddums!" she'd said, but she understood the sentiment.

Pretty people didn't get a lot of sympathy, but it wasn't all wolf whistles and roses. Lynette wasn't a vain woman, not really. She was a pragmatist. She knew she had all the bells and whistles—the pretty face, the naturally blond hair, the ridiculously long legs—all the things that others deemed beautiful. But what they didn't know, what she and Blake had bonded over, was the fact that sometimes beauty could get in the way—of promotion and true love and being taken seriously. People liked having you around but only as a decorative ornament.

It had taken Lynette years to move from the floor of Mario's café into his bustling kitchen, mostly because Mario liked having her out front, working as a waitress, all sparkly and bright and inviting. She had only just convinced him to let her cook, but even then she was relegated to pantry chef duties—preparing cold dishes and salads, never anything fancy. Even the head chef seemed blinded by her bling.

Perhaps that's why Ronnie hid her wealth and jewels, Lynette thought now. She just wanted to be treated equally. Well, Lynette's looks were like jewels, and she wished she could discard them.

It didn't help that she was living under her older sibling's shadow. Because for all their love, for all their laughter, Lynette always felt like the lesser of the two Finlay sisters. Lyn might be prettier than Alicia, but it was a fringe benefit that did not pay dividends. Sure, guys ogled Lynette, but it was *Alicia* they wanted to marry. And she didn't begrudge her sister that, honestly she didn't. It was herself she begrudged, the person she had become.

She had taken the lazy route, traded on her looks, and now it was time for a reckoning.

Blake had said something similar last night: "They all think people like us have got it easy, but actually it's so much harder. They don't have to prove themselves, but we do, don't we, babe? Over and over. Well, you know what, I'm tired of being stuck behind the eight ball. It's *my* time to shoot some holes. And I'm about to shoot a big one!"

Lynette hadn't been sure what Blake was referring to, and when she asked where he worked, he turned evasive.

"That's not the point," he told her. "I'm trying to make a grander statement. You need more than looks to make it in this world. You need a bit of dynamite and a bag full of detonators."

She thought about that statement now and decided to keep it to herself. Alicia and Perry would take it literally— proof the man was dangerous. But she knew it was just a metaphor, albeit a mixed one, because she understood it completely. Like Blake, she had ambitions that had nothing to do with beauty. It was time to step out of her sister's shadow and prove she was equally as smart.

And so she stepped out of the kitchen and made a beeline for the lobby.

~

It was just on lunchtime as they walked Repentance Way, and Alicia glanced at her watch, feeling grumpy.

"If we'd waited a bit longer, I could have called Jackson. He won't be in town yet."

"You can always come back," said Perry. "I think this is more important, frankly. Lynette's right about one thing— there's nothing Jackson can do for us right now. Right now we have to do for ourselves, and Blake could still be out there, plotting to take us down."

"But we didn't *do* anything to him!" said Missy, sounding petulant.

"We are living, breathing witnesses, don't forget. Besides, he's obviously unhinged. You don't smack a woman over the head with a bottle of Grange for no reason!"

"Exactly," said Alicia. "If he'd opted for cheaper plonk, then we'd know he was sane."

Perry flashed her a smirk. "Very funny, Ms Finlay. Let's get to this old guy and find out if he has some answers. I want to know what happened back then, who exactly we're dealing with. And it won't hurt to check my mobile messages while we're at it." Then his smirk turned to a frown. "Why didn't you tell me about this bloke, girls? Why keep him a secret?"

"Sorry," Alicia said.

The truth was, like Perry, she didn't believe Simon's theory that the killer had taken off. And not because she had any real suspicions about the others—she didn't. But her mind wasn't about to hand her a free pass. And she wasn't about to hand over the whereabouts of another potential victim either. If she had inadvertently brought a madman to the mountain, Alicia didn't want Snowy to get caught in the cross fire. The less everyone knew about him the better.

It was that final thought that had Alicia holding her hand up when they closed in on his cabin. "I think I should talk to him alone. Give him his space."

"Fine by me," said Perry, staring across at the man on the escarpment and then down at his smartphone. "I've got two bars. I'm going to—"

He didn't finish that sentence as it began singing out to him, notifying him of his messages, and he started tapping away frantically just as Missy's phone began vibrating. She squealed with delight, pulling it out and cooing at all her missed calls—like a drug addict who'd finally found a hit.

"Oh my poor mother," Perry said. "She is beside herself. I'll have to give her a quick buzz."

"Mine too!" said Missy. "And my sister Henny, and my boss! They must have heard about the fire."

Trudging on to the cabin, Alicia wondered whether the others had really come to interrogate Snowy or if their primary motivation had more to do with the mobile coverage.

Claire watched Alicia go then sighed at her phone, not surprised by its silence. Wasn't this the very reason she was changing her life so dramatically? And lying to the book club while she was at it? She tapped speed dial and waited for her assistant to pick up. Might as well see how her little vintage clothing store was faring.

~

Lynette scoured the guest book and frowned. Perhaps she wasn't as smart as she thought she was. If there had been another guest lurking, she assumed they would have signed in. Hadn't Vale suggested it was compulsory? Yet after locating the book beneath the reception desk, she had quickly scanned the names above theirs and came up wanting. Judging from the dates and addresses, there had been no guests at all last week, and the week before that accommodated a Japanese tour group from Kyoto.

Hmmm... She tapped the book glumly.

Lynette then turned her attention to the computer. Maybe there was a clue to be found amongst the files or emails or something? But the moment she began investigating, she realised it would not be much use either. The internal hard drive was password protected, and after a few lame guesses, she gave up.

Tapping her nails on the table now, she squinted at the

screen. From what she could tell, the only thing accessible was Google Chrome, but without internet connection, it was completely useless.

Or was it?

Lynette grabbed the mouse and moved it to the top of the screen and clicked on Show Full History, then smiled to herself as a page of past Google searches sprang up before her eyes. She glanced around the lobby quickly, then scanned the search history. None of the websites could be opened, but they still gave her a pretty good idea what Vale had been looking at before he died.

Except how could she be sure these were even Vale's searches? Judging from the time code, they had all been accessed the first night the book club had arrived. Any one of them could have hopped on the computer when Vale was elsewhere.

Had someone from book club searched with Google? Did he even know about it?

Checking she was still alone, Lynette scrolled down the list, mentally noting what she saw. Somebody was obviously missing the outside world as several news sights had been opened, including the *Daily Telegraph*, News.com.au, and the *Lyleton Tribune*. There were other random searches for sites like Ancestory.com, Shady Nook Palliative & Aged Care Home, and something called Living Large Enterprises.

Hang on a minute.

Lynette stared at the listing for Shady Nook again, then across to the time it was searched—very early that morning, at 1:07 a.m.

As far as Lynette knew, there were only two people still awake and lurking about at that particular hour. She clicked the page shut and tapped the table again.

~

Snowy was perched on a bespoke wooden bench seat,

staring out at the view, mesmerised, like he was watching an episode of *Survivor*. When Alicia walked up, he glanced at her quickly and back, like he didn't want to miss a minute, then patted the space beside him, inviting her to join him.

She did so, then turned her own eyes outwards, to watch the show.

And it really was entertaining. Birds swooped in all directions—rainbow lorikeets, king parrots, bowerbirds— while towering teak and cedar branches wrestled furiously with each other in some spots and sat deadly still in others, like they were in completely different settings. Ancient tree ferns dipped down into the rocky gorges as though searching for a drink, and even more ancient waterfalls stood dry, the first time anyone could remember. And all around that ominous smoke still billowed, with just a flicker of red if you dared to look closely. And if that didn't freak you out, the steady sprinkling of ash just might.

Yet for some reason Alicia felt safe sitting there beside old Snowy.

"This is the best view on the mountain," she said softly. "I wonder why the Lyles didn't build their lodge here."

"Why let bloody tourists hog the prime real estate?"

She smiled. *Good answer.* Alicia cleared her throat. "Do you mind if I ask you something else, Snowy? Something about the other fire, the one in 1970?"

He looked across at her sharply then. "What of it?"

"Were you around when it happened?"

"Course I was."

"And it came very close to here, yes?"

He nodded mutely.

"I heard that a man was killed in the fire. A guy called—"

"Donal Murphy," he said, cutting in. "Young lad, green as the valley. Giant bloody fool, that one. Not even a local.

Didn't stop him from charging towards the fire, with barely a second glance. What kind of idiot does that?"

Snowy wasn't looking at Alicia now, wasn't expecting an answer, and it was clear to her that he'd asked that question many times over the past fifty years and always came up wanting. Perhaps they all did. Perhaps they all carried some guilt for the ring-in who had died trying to save the rest of them. Perhaps they didn't advertise the man's heroics because it left the rest of them feeling too humbled.

Yet Snowy's tone had a tinge of anger in it too, and she wasn't sure if he was angry at Donal for his naivety or the fire for its ferocity or for the way life had turned out.

"Did Donal have any family, do you know? A wife and baby he left behind?"

Snowy snorted at that. "Nah, love. Too much of a lad about town for that."

"Bit of a charmer was he? Troublemaker, too?"

He shrugged. "He was an arrogant little blighter. Came up here, tried his luck and got burnt in the process."

Now Alicia wasn't sure if he was talking about the fire or something else entirely, but the description could easily be applied to Blake Morrow, and it made her shiver.

A whooshing sound caught Alicia by surprise, and she peeled her eyes downwards and could just make out something yellow and bulky hovering amidst the smoke.

"Water bomber," Snowy said. "It's back for another crack." Then he stood up, his bones creaking. "I've just been down to Cooper's Crossing. Fire's progressing but slowly. Found the maps for the fire trails yet?"

She shook her head.

"That's a pity." He turned, then turned back. "There's an old paper road on the western ridge, behind the kitchen. Most people don't know about it. It's longer and steeper, and you'll need a machete to cut your way clear. But it just might work. Now if you'll excuse me, I'm buggered."

He turned towards the hut, and Alicia was left with more questions than answers. Yet he did look exhausted, weary to his core, so she just called after him:

"How do we find this paper road you speak of?"

Snowy stopped at the hut door. "Look for the Lyle family story, love; there's a map in there. Fancy white book. Probably find it under fiction." Then he had a little chuckle at that.

"What about you? Will you come with us?"

Snowy's smile faded. "Nah, love. History is rushing towards me, and it's time for some atonement."

CHAPTER 14

Snowy's words kept echoing through Alicia's mind as she stood at the kitchen bench, preparing a sandwich from the platter Lynette had left for them.

Atonement? What kind of atonement? What did he mean by that? And what of Donal Murphy, the man who'd been killed in the fire? If he didn't leave behind a wife and kids, as Snowy had suggested, then who exactly was Blake in relation to him? And why was he so fixated with the guy? Snowy had called Donal a "lad about town," so she had to wonder—was Blake Morrow Donal's illegitimate love child?

"You still thinking of old Snowy?" said Claire, creating her own tasty concoction from the cold meats and salad, Perry and Missy beside her.

Alicia nodded, glancing around. The others had already eaten and left them to it. But they all demanded to know where the four of them had vanished to, and she had managed to put them off with a line about scouting for signs of a way out down the mountain. What else could she say? I've been hassling an old geezer about the past, and the others were checking voice mail.

Besides, as Lynette reminded them before she followed the others out, "The plan is very simple, people! We're *supposed* to be getting fire ready, not spending our precious time trying to stitch Blake up!"

Then she'd told them to "clean up after yourselves" and stormed out of the kitchen.

"She's cranky with us," said Missy, stating the

bleeding obvious.

"She's feeling on the outer," explained Alicia. "She believes in Blake's innocence, and she knows we're suspicious of him. I really don't know why she's so taken with the guy."

"About that…," began Claire just as Simon stepped back into the kitchen.

"Hey there. I thought I'd help with the washing up," he said, then noticing the awkward silence, asked, "Everything okay?"

His eyes were firmly on Claire, who reached for a sliver of cheese before turning her gaze upon him.

"We're tickety-boo, thanks *Simon,*" she said, before thrusting the cheese into her mouth and staring at him, like she was throwing him some kind of challenge.

Now Simon was the one looking awkward, blinking back at her, his hands shoved into his trouser pockets.

Alicia watched this exchange curiously, then picked up her sandwich and said, "Shall we eat out on the deck? Might be nice out there now."

"You mean hot and smoky," said Missy, clearly not reading the vibe.

But Alicia preferred hot and smoky to the frosty atmosphere that had just descended inside.

~

After brushing the dead leaves from a table and chairs on the paved terrace outside the dining room, they all took their seats and Claire looked a little more relaxed, but it wouldn't last. Perry had also noticed the tense exchange, and he rounded on her now.

"You and Mr Crete have a little tiff we don't know about?" he said.

"Mr Crete, hey? Are we still calling him that?" she replied, smirking as she chomped into her sandwich.

The others watched her furtively for a few moments,

then Alicia said, "Okay, I'll bite. What's going on, Claire?"

Claire finished chewing, then sighed. "This is what I've been trying to tell you all morning. Simon Crete is the imposter!"

They looked at her expectantly, so she ploughed on. "I had been thinking about Mr U. N. Owen from *And Then There Were None*. You know, *Mr Unknown*, the imposter with the fake name?"

"Yes? So?" said Perry, pulling a piece of onion from his roll with a grimace.

"So, I started playing with everyone's names, just testing them out." She was lying here, of course. It was only Simon's name she had been playing with, but they didn't need to know that. Claire felt mortified enough as it was. "Anyway, I kept thinking Crete was a weird name, and then I checked the guest book in the lobby, and well, it all got even weirder. Simon's middle name is Edward!"

They were munching away, staring at her, waiting for the punchline, so Claire burst out, "Simon Edward Crete. S. E. Crete. *Secret!* Get it?"

Now her friends were looking at her like she'd lost the plot entirely, and for a moment Claire felt such relief. Yes! She *was* mad. Of course Simon wasn't the imposter! He was far too lovely and far too normal.

Then Missy bobbed her head about and said, "S. E. Crete. Secret! Oh my, that does sound kind of fishy. Just like U. N. Owen. I can't believe I didn't think of that! Good work, Claire. Wow, it's all very sneaky."

And now Alicia was clicking her fingers and nodding. "And don't forget Simon's the one who refused to give his credit card when we booked in. Would only pay cash. That's a bit of a giveaway that he's faking his name. But why would he do that? What's he got to do with all this?"

"Maybe *Simon's* related to this Donal Murphy fellow?" said Missy. "His age works in better. Maybe it's Simon's dad not Blake's? And Simon's real surname is Murphy!"

"Or it could all be a coincidence," suggested Perry, who was still fixated with Blake. "People do have funny monikers, you know. I went to school with a Wayne Kerr. He had a tough time of it."

Missy and Claire blinked blankly while Alicia burst out laughing. "Wanker? Really?"

He nodded. "Poor bugger." He looked at Claire. "We could just ask Simon. See what he's playing at."

"I'm not going to ask him!" Claire gasped. "He could be the imposter that Vale was talking about. Which means…"

Her voice trailed off as her eyelashes flickered furiously. It didn't bear thinking about. Could the calm, controlled man she'd just fallen for really be a cold, ruthless killer? If that was the case, she really was the most dreadful judge of character!

"He must have some ID on him," said Perry. "You could take a peek in his wallet and check out his driver's licence, Claire."

"How am I going to do that without giving the game away? And why me?"

He nudged his eyebrows high. "I think you'd have a better chance of getting an invite to his room to look at his etchings, I mean *wallet*, than I would. He's obviously got a crush on you."

"Really? Do you think so?" She sounded almost wistful, then gave herself a shake. "I am *not* going into that man's bedroom, Perry! Especially if he is…"

Again, she couldn't say the words.

Alicia finished her sandwich and checked her watch. "Look, maybe we should leave it for now. I don't know what Simon's playing at, if he's playing at all, but I do know Lynette is right. We need to focus our energy on getting off this mountain. We keep getting distracted, but there's no point solving two murders if we end up burnt to a crisp." She shuddered at the very thought. "Once we are out of here, we can worry about who's who and what's what."

Begrudgingly they all agreed, but Claire wasn't feeling quite so agreeable towards Mr S. E. Crete anymore.

Alicia dusted herself off and pushed her plate away. "Do one of you mind taking that back to the kitchen for me so Lynny doesn't bite my head off? I'm heading back to the escarpment to call Jackson. He'd definitely be there by now, and maybe he has some good news for us."

She pulled out her smartphone and frowned. The charge was running low. She would have to be quick.

"Want us to come with you?" Perry asked.

"No, you need to hunt down that Lyle book Snowy told me about and find that elusive paper road. It could be our only escape."

Whether they were escaping an oddly named killer or a burning inferno seemed almost irrelevant at that point.

~

As Alicia stepped back onto Repentance Way, groaning at the thought of another bloody walk, someone was watching, their own irritation growing.

How many times did that woman have to trek off into the forest? What was she playing at? And how could this finally be over if she didn't butt the hell out?

A sigh, a groan, then the angry voyeur turned away.

~

Perry searched the library for the Lyle family story, but his mind kept wandering to another book—*And Then There Were None*. Was Simon Crete just trying to be clever, emulating a plot device from an Agatha Christie novel? Trying to show off to his fancy new book club?

Or was it more sinister than that?

He had his suspicions about all of them, but he couldn't see Simon as a killer. Not really. He'd put money on Ronnie before he put any on Simon. Still, he'd been wrong before and the Finlay girls were right. None of this mattered a jot if they ended up perishing in a fire.

He needed to focus and find this book Snowy had spoken of.

After wading through the biography section, he checked out nonfiction and still came up empty-handed. That's when he spotted the shelves crammed with romances and crime novels. Hadn't Snowy made some jibe about it being amongst the fiction? Alicia thought he was joking, but what if he wasn't?

Two minutes later, Perry was pulling out a thin volume with an off-white hardcover and a black-and-white family sketch of the Lyle Lodge on the front. Above it was the title *The Lyle Family Dynasty* and below it the subtitle *From Logging to the Lodge, by Juliette Lyle-Hampton.*"

"Bingo!" he said, placing it to his chest with delight.

~

By the time Alicia had made it back to the escarpment, she was sweating beneath her T-shirt, feeling prickly and irritable. She knew that the rainforest was normally cool, even midsummer, so the heat was more than annoying; it was extremely worrying.

To mollify the fire, they needed cold air and lots of rain, and they needed it fast.

It had just gone two in the afternoon, and Snowy was nowhere in sight. She pulled out her phone and noticed some new messages from her family and some friends at work, but the battery was fast draining, so she quickly texted a group message assuring them all, somewhat dishonestly, that she and Lynette were fine, then called Jackson.

The line was very crackly this time, but his relief at hearing from her came through loud and clear. "Thank goodness you're okay! I'm at RFS headquarters in

Lyleton now and ready to do what I can. How's everyone up there? How are you holding up?"

"We're fine, Jackson. Getting the place fire ready. I think all the tasks are keeping us from going insane."

"Good to hear it. I know what you're like." He braced himself and then said, "Any more bodies?"

She would have laughed, but he was being serious and with good reason. "Thankfully, no. How about you? Did the fire chief manage to get closer to that burnt-out car?" She wanted to know if it was the lodge van down there, burnt to a crisp, or if it was Blake's old Mercedes. And if that was the case, had they also recovered a body?

"Visibility is extremely low, and it's still too dangerous to check it out," he told her, "but there's no clear signs of life, so they're focusing on other priorities—which includes getting you lot out of there alive."

"Thank you," she said, wondering if he realised how triggering that sentence was.

"I asked Benson about this Blake Morrow fellow you mentioned last time we spoke, but he hasn't had any contact with anyone fitting that description or seen anyone driving around in an old Merc."

The fact that Blake hadn't identified himself when he got into Lyleton was a bad sign and they both knew it. If Blake hadn't got caught in the fire on the way down the mountain, why hadn't he checked in, called the cavalry as he promised he would?

As far as Alicia was concerned, there could only be three answers to that: Blake hadn't survived the drive, he'd survived and kept going, or he'd turned back. And if that was the case, where was he and why was he still in hiding?

"The whole town is abuzz with the fire," Jackson was saying. "The smoke here is so intense, and anyone who's not RFS has packed up and cleared out."

"Lucky them," Alicia said. "Smoke's not so bad up here; maybe we're gonna be okay."

"Or maybe it's more about how the smoke moves in

the hot air," Jackson said, making her heart skip a beat. "Listen I've got some bad news for you."

"Oh good," she said. "I was afraid things weren't grim enough."

He chuckled briefly. "Sorry, but I thought you should know—Benson says the fire is suspicious, at least in part. They're not yet sure how it started, but there are clear signs of accelerant in at least one location—Cooper's Crossing. We're lucky it's going down the mountain, not up at this stage. I'm not sure how they work all this out, and what, if anything, it means for you. I wasn't even sure I should tell you but—"

"No, I'm glad you did," she said. "Don't keep anything from me, Jackson. We need all the information we can get."

"That's what I figured. I'm sure it has nothing to do with the lodge. Teenagers and pyromaniacs start fires all the time. Occasionally they even work for the RFS— gives them a sense of purpose, excitement."

"It's certainly exciting." Her tone was droll.

"Honey, we're doing everything we can to get through to you. I'm hoping to have you in my arms by close of day."

She sighed. She was hoping for that too.

"If there weren't so many trees around the lodge," Jackson continued, "they would have winched you out via chopper ages ago."

"If there weren't so many trees, it wouldn't have happened in the first place," Alicia quipped, but she didn't blame Mother Nature for this. Not one bit. If what Jackson said was true, it was a human being who drove halfway up the mountain and set the place alight.

Or did they drive down?

Jackson took Alicia's silence for what it was and said, "Don't overthink things. Stick to the plan we talked about earlier. Get your supplies together and be ready for an evacuation. Any luck finding the maps of the fire trails?

Benson gave me one I can email across to you now, if you like?"

Alicia glanced at the phone battery and said, "You can try, but I'm low on charge. It'll probably drop out any second. Perry's onto it though." There was no time to mention the paper road—or Snowy for that matter—so she added, "We'll find a way out."

"I really don't know why the owner isn't stepping up a bit," Jackson said, his tone now testy. "They should know the tracks off hand, should really be the one phoning in too, not you. You're a paying guest!"

"Owner?" she said, not understanding. "You mean the manager? Vale? He's dead, remember?"

"No, Benson said the owner is also up there with you. At least I think that's what he said."

"We're all alone up here, Jackson. There's no owner. It's just me and the book club, unless they're keeping their identity a secret..."

She gasped, suddenly thinking of S. E. Crete.

"You okay, babe?"

"Did Benson say it was the *new* owner up here? The one who recently bought the place?"

"Um, I'm not sure, to be honest. Look, I might have got my wires crossed about that one. You're going to be okay, so please don't panic. Just hold tight, stay vigilant and—"

And then the line went dead.

~

Groaning at the disconnected call, Jackson thrust his phone into his pocket and returned inside the concrete, besser-block building that housed Lyleton's RFS headquarters. He smiled at the young girl sitting at the front desk. She was sixteen if she was a day but had a phone at each ear and was reading something out from the computer in front of her. Something to do with the humidity levels and how unseasonably low they were.

She grinned back at him, looking completely unfazed, and he wanted to pull her into a hug and thank her for everything she was doing, and all for complete strangers. He wanted to thank every single one of them, the entire motley crew—and motley was the perfect word for this lot. Apart from Benson—the town's head librarian would you believe?—there were two teenage boys, barely out of school, a young mum and her own mother, pushing fifty, a couple of local tradesmen covered in tatts, and at least two councillors, one in his midseventies. They were all members of the community, with their own homes and loved ones to worry about, yet their only concern at this point was for the guests at Lyle's Lodge. Until they got them all out safely, Benson told Jackson, they would not rest.

It filled him with so much confidence, and humility too.

This lot were volunteers and would not be paid one red cent for their efforts. At least coppers got a pay cheque and plenty of accolades. These were Australia's true heroes, he decided, swallowing back the lump that had developed in his throat.

He made his way to a small desk at the back of the office where he'd set himself up and tried to focus back on Alicia. She said she was okay, but he knew better. He hadn't asked too much about the murders, desperately wanted her to focus on getting the hell off that mountain, but he knew what Alicia was like, and he knew the book club too. There was no chance they weren't poking about the corpses, doing a little sleuthing. And who could blame them? If the killer was still up there with them, it might very well be their only chance.

His mood grew dark, thinking about that.

Like Alicia, Jackson was wondering about the missing book club member. Like her, he wondered whether Blake was somehow responsible for the murders and had conveniently cleared off or if it was worse than that and he was still up there, lurking in the woods, looking for more prey.

Most murders were logical. Jackson knew that from experience. But every now and then you came across a lunatic whose actions defied logic.

Were the Murder Mystery Book Club up against a psychopath this time? And if so, he didn't like their chances. This lot thought they were clever, and most of the time they were. But, like Agatha Christie herself, they relied on facts and clues and reasoning—all things a psychopath sneered at.

You didn't need any of that to commit murder; you just needed a thirst for blood…

Jackson wiped a hand across his face, trying to refocus. All this worrying was not going to help Alicia, but maybe Google would. He stabbed at the keyboard in front of him, tapping in the name she had given him earlier—Blake Morrow.

Who the hell was this Morrow bloke?

Expecting very little, Jackson was surprised to find thousands of search possibilities appear before him. He zeroed in on the most salacious option, a news site with words like "police statement," "blackmail," and "shattered lives" and frowned as he tapped the page open. Then he sat forward and began scanning it, shaking his head incredulously.

He wanted to call Alicia straight back, but of course he couldn't. Her phone had died and she wouldn't be contactable for hours. Groaning now, he caught the eye of the young girl and offered her a reassuring wave, then glared back at his computer.

Oh, Blake Morrow was after blood all right, just not the kind Jackson had been expecting.

CHAPTER 15

While Lynette sautéed the organic beef and onion, pre-preparing beef bourguignon for dinner, Alicia, Perry and Claire chopped vegetables while Missy stood guard at the kitchen door, chewing on a raw carrot.

Alicia wanted to get them up to speed with what Jackson had told her, but this conversation had to be done in private. She knew that Lynette wanted to focus on their evacuation, but what she'd just learned changed everything. If the RFS captain was correct and the owner was here amongst them, then it had to be one of the newcomers. There was no other explanation. So who was it and why the subterfuge?

Those were the pressing questions, and the most obvious candidate was Simon.

It wasn't simply his name Alicia was thinking of. He did have a certain air of authority about him. Blake might have acted like he owned the place, but Simon was the one who seemed most unimpressed with the missing staff member and the way the weekend was sliding, just as an owner might. Alicia wished she had encouraged Claire to sneak a peek at Simon's wallet, but Perry was now running in a different direction entirely.

"It could be Ronnie," he told them. "If anyone's rich enough to buy this lodge, it's Mrs Westera. Did Jackson say if the new owner was a man or a woman?"

"I'm not sure he said one way or the other. I didn't get a chance to ask much more because my phone died on me. So stupid of me to go all the way there without a fully charged battery!"

Alicia reached across the kitchen bench where her mobile was now plugged into a socket and checked that it was still recharging.

"Don't beat yourself up, honey," Claire said as she sliced into a zucchini. "So if the owner really is up here…" She scowled suddenly, but it was fleeting. "Why aren't they stepping up now that there are two dead staffers and a fire threatening their investment? What possible reason could they have to remain in hiding?"

"The same reason they were hiding in the first place," said Perry, giving her a *duh!* look. "They're up to something, and I have a hunch I might know what it's all about. I saw something amongst Blake's stuff earlier…"

He pushed some peeled potatoes towards Lynette and sprinted out of the kitchen. She frowned. "That man is like a yo-yo. I thought he was gunning for Ronnie, but now he's pinning it back on *Blake?*"

They had already filled Lynette in on what they had discovered in Blake's room earlier that day, and she had told them about her Google history search on the reception desk computer. But it only left them feeling more befuddled.

Alicia appreciated her sister's renewed enthusiasm but couldn't get excited about some aged-care home. She had a hunch this whole mess started with a man called Donal Murphy and ended with the Great Fire of 1970. But what Donal had to do with a mysterious new owner who was now lurking amongst them was way beyond her "leetle grey cells."

"Perhaps the new owner is related to Donal Murphy?" said Claire just as Missy suddenly coughed loudly.

Then she coughed again, giving them a pointed look, as Ronnie and Flo walked in, breezy smiles on both their faces.

"Can we give you lovely young things a hand?" Ronnie asked.

"Not at all," said Lynette. "I have so many hands I barely know what to do with them."

"I told you," Flo said to Ronnie.

"How about we set the table?" Ronnie persisted, but Alicia was already pushing Missy forward.

"No! Missy said she wanted to make it look pretty tonight, didn't you, honey?"

Missy nodded fervently although she wasn't the prettiest of table setters. She never knew quite where to put the serviette—was it under the fork or the knife? As for the wine glass, did it go at the front? To the side? And if so, which side? She didn't have the foggiest.

"See, Ronnie, they've got it all under control," Flo said, then turned to Lynette. "Can I get some more of that lovely ginger tea you made for me this morning, dear? If you're not too busy."

"No worries, Flo," Lynette replied, her eyes narrowing. "I'll get it steeping and bring it out to you."

She smiled. "Lovely. Come on then, Ron. Let's leave the young things to it."

Ronnie flashed them a look as she left, and it smacked of deep disappointment. Missy wondered how much they'd overheard or whether their ears were burning.

Alicia was thinking the same thing. "You had one job, woman!" she whispered after a few minutes.

"Sorry," Missy whispered back. "They crept up on me! Oh, and now here's Perry."

Perry was calling something out to the ladies as he strolled in, a bag hanging from his shoulder. He waited until they were safely out of sight, then pulled out some folded paper and waved it in front of them.

"This, my fellow sleuths, is a copy of the DA for Lyle's Lodge. That's a Development Application for the uneducated amongst you. It was in Blake's file, and I didn't think too much of it at first."

"Blake must be the new owner!" said Missy while Lynette glared into her pot.

"Unfortunately, it's not quite that simple." Perry pointed to the top of the page. "It's not his name on the application, or Simon's or Ronnie's for that matter. It's Living Large Enterprises. LLE for short. Whoever the hell that is."

"That was a Google search!" said Lynette. "I'm sure of it. I saw it in the computer history from the first night."

"Did you see any info on it?" asked Alicia, and she shook her head. "It's obviously a company name, which means any of them could be linked to it. It might even be the name of the architect or builder. It doesn't get us very far. What else have you got in there?" Alicia had spotted something thin and white in his bag. "Is that the book Snowy mentioned?"

Perry smiled and pulled it out. "Oh, yeah. He wasn't joking about that. I found it tucked away in fiction, exactly where he said it would be."

"That's odd," she replied, opening it. She had thought Snowy was being facetious. "How would he know where it was? Do you think he comes up here and uses the library when no one's about?"

Perry shrugged like he didn't care, but Missy's eyes had widened.

"I think Snowy does come up here," she said. "I think he's a sneaky old bugger. There's more to that man than meets the eye."

Claire ignored that and said, "I hate to keep sounding like our dearly departed handbrake Dr Anders, but who *cares* about the DA, Perry? So the owner wants to renovate; we already know that. It's not a big secret."

"Not just *renovate*, honey. They're practically bulldozing the place and starting over. Look at this." He pushed some tinned tomatoes out of the way and spread the plans out on the bench top. "It's massive. From the looks of this DA, they were going to drastically rebuild. Rip out all the old rooms, including the library, and put in a gym, a spa and a pizzeria-style café." He wrinkled his nose. "How *inappropriate*. They also want to triple the guest capacity and add a bunch of luxury villas right there on the escarpment."

"Show me that," said Alicia, taking it from him. She studied it for a minute and recognised the area where the villas were marked. "That's right where Snowy lives."

"Not if the new owner has anything to say about it," Perry said.

"They're going to boot out poor Snowy?" said Lynette, her mind wandering to another of the Google searches.

"You're missing the point entirely, people!" Perry said. "Maybe the DA got knocked back. Maybe LLE wanted to go bigger but the Heritage Council and tree huggers wouldn't let them. So they needed to 'accidentally' burn the place down. That way they could start again from scratch."

"With us in it?" said Missy, horrified.

"And *them* if Perry's story is to be believed," said Lynette, "because this mysterious owner is still amongst us, right?"

"It's not a story, Lynny. It's a theory, and maybe he or she figured we'd all be rescued just in the nick of time."

"That's a bloody big risk to take," said Alicia, "and it didn't work out so good back in 1970, remember?"

"Which brings us full circle back to Blake," he said. "Ronnie might have bags of money, but she slummed it on the train like the rest of us. Blake is the only one who turned up with his own wheels and then conveniently cleared off—*before the fire started!* So my money's firmly on him again. I reckon he's the new developer, or he's working for them most likely. That's why he has all this info—he's been doing his due diligence. Vale and Flannery obviously recognised him. How could they not? They must have met the new team at some point, right? So Blake had to take them out, and the phone lines as well, before they reported him. Then he took off and started the fire. We're just collateral damage." He brushed his goatee. "Did anyone get around to checking the phones? See if they were cut?"

"I tried," said Missy. "I didn't know where to look. But a development company, Perry? Would they really do something so evil?"

"*Of course!*" he replied, looking at her like she was demented. "Some of the biggest developers in this country are run by the Mafia. They stop at *nothing* to push their plans through."

As Missy grimaced, Alicia's brain was stewing as hard as the beef, but she bit her tongue. She'd heard some loopy plots in her time, but Perry's latest was the loopiest.

"If only the blasted internet was working," she said. "We could look up Blake Morrow and see if he's connected to LLE. Although…"

She checked her phone again. The battery was now two-thirds full. That should do it. She yanked it from the plug and then looked at her sister. "I know you want us all to focus on the fire and stop investigating these murders—"

"I don't really want that, Alicia. Especially if they're all connected. I just want to be included this time. No more lies, please. I'm more than a pretty face, you know!"

"Of course you are," said Alicia, swapping a chastised look with Perry.

"I'm being serious, guys! I have a brain and I can contribute more than good cooking!"

"I agree, honestly I do," said Alicia. "Which is why I want you to come with me back to the escarpment. We can google LLE and have the answer in minutes. Well, twenty minutes if you count the bloody trek."

Which was starting to wear thin, just like her walking boots.

"While you *brainiacs* are doing that," said Perry, offering Lynette a wink, "I'm going to do a little analogue sleuthing of my own, see if I can't trick a few answers out of Ronnie, find out what her family company is called and tick her firmly off the suspect list. Honestly, this place would be loose change to a Westera. And you, Claire, you're going to have to take Simon on."

"*Nooooo,*" she wailed.

"You've put it off long enough, honey. He clearly likes you. You're the only one who could ask him questions without sounding suspicious."

"What about me?" said Missy from the doorway. "I want to do something! What can I do?"

"You can go with Alicia," said Lynette, reaching for some fresh ginger. "I have something else I need to do."

Missy's face lit up with a smile as Alicia's deflated. She was looking forward to some one-on-one time with her sister, hoping it would bridge the gap that had suddenly— inexplicably—opened up between them.

Lynette sensed her disappointment. "Sorry, sis, but there is another member of this club that everyone has completely forgotten—Florence Underwood. I want to have a quiet word with her, if I can."

The others looked surprised by that, but she was right. Flo's name had barely been mentioned. Claire was already dismissing the notion.

"Do we really think Flo works for a development company or is going around killing people? I can't see it."

"No, no, Lynette might be right," said Missy, clapping her hands. "In Agatha Christie mysteries, it *always* turns out to be the least likely character! It could be Flo!"

"Do you see the Dame lurking about anywhere, Missy?" said Perry, dismissively. "How many times do we have to tell you? You do not live in an Agatha Christie book."

Missy shrugged, used to that remark. They all agreed it should be the epitaph on her tombstone. "Still," she said, sulkily, "it doesn't mean Flo's not hiding something under all that knitting."

"Oh she's hiding something all right," said Lynette, now reaching for the kettle. "I'm going to make her a lovely pot of tea and drag the truth out of her even if it kills me."

~

Snowy dragged the screaming kettle from its base and slapped it on the bench top. But he didn't make himself a cup. Didn't have the stomach for it. He just stood and scowled at the kitchen he'd built and the home he'd created and the mess he'd left behind.

His eyes turned to the bedside cabinet and the items he'd placed there, beside Lydia's photo. Lovely, lively Lydia. Always too lively for him. If only he'd realised that sooner, perhaps none of it would have happened. Perhaps it all could have been avoided.

He sat down on the bed and felt his body quiver. Did he have the courage to do it?

Perhaps that wasn't the right question. Perhaps what he needed to ask himself was why he hadn't done it sooner. He reached for the frame and offered Lydia a weary smile.

"Sorry, my darling," he whispered. "Just one more death, and then it will all be over."

~

Simon had one more task to tick off his to-do list. It was long overdue. He had seen the gang in the kitchen; he knew what they were up to, what they were all thinking. And he didn't blame them one bit.

They were old mates. Flo and Ronnie too. He was the ring-in. The last surviving ring-in at least. They might have wanted to blame Blake at first, but their eyes were already straying to him, that much was obvious.

And now he knew what he had to do. He checked the reception desk and rummaged through the drawers, then made his way outside, determination spurring him forward.

~

"You're dying, aren't you?" Lynette said, hugging a cup of ginger tea to her chest as she stepped through the kitchen door and out towards the garden.

Flo went as rigid as the broken angel at the edge of the herb patch, and for a worrying moment Lynette feared she had overstepped.

Was Flo feeling outraged? Angry? *Invaded?*

"I'm sorry," Lynette added quickly. "I don't mean to intrude."

The older woman had her back to Lynette, had been watering a small sapling, while Ronnie sat under a large fig some distance away. Far enough away not to be overheard, Lynette thought as she said those words out loud. They weren't just any words, and she feared they might have this effect. But when Flo turned around, she did not look angry, just sad and weary.

She sighed heavily, and Lynette saw confirmation in her watery eyes and grey features and the way her body trembled ever so slightly even though it was warm out. It didn't take a doctor to know the woman was unwell. Even before Lynette had spotted the website for the aged-care home with palliative care, she had become suspicious of Flo. The fact that the old lady kept reminiscing about the past, unable to sleep at night, yearning for nausea-busting ginger tea, had all pointed to something, but when she'd barely touched Lynette's cooking? Well, that was the final piece of evidence the proud chef needed.

Flo held out her hand so Lynette could help her, and together they made their way to a nearby bench and sat down.

"You are a little too clever for your own good, young lassie," she said eventually. "I guess that's what you get when you join a club full of mystery buffs."

"How long have you got?" Lynette asked.

"Doc reckons I'll be lucky to see the year out."

"I am so sorry," Lynette began, but Flo cut her off.

"What for, dear? Unlike many people, I've had a good, long life. I can't complain." Her face clouded over then, like she did in fact have a few complaints.

"Why didn't you tell us?" Lynette asked her. "Why all the secrecy?"

Flo looked at her sharply. "Would you have let me join the club if I had? An old battle-axe who'd only make a few meets before she carked it? You already bemoaned the other member who let you all down."

"That person was a fraud! Used us abominably!"

"Ahh yes, but then I've been a little fraudulent too, haven't I? I just wanted one final adventure, that's all." She stared off into the distance, not really seeing. "I already said goodbye to my family a few weeks ago. Gathered the whole clan together at my younger sister's place in Dubbo. She married a wheat farmer. Decent chap. Was nice to be back on the land. We had such a lovely time, sharing favourite dishes, funny stories…"

She choked then and cleared her throat.

"How long before you move into the home?" Lynette asked, but Flo was looking at her now vaguely. "Shady Nook?"

Flo waved her off and said, "Must you tell the others about this? Can it be our little secret?"

Lynette placed a hand on the woman's glove. "They won't kick you out of the group, Flo, if that's what you're worried about. And it might help explain a few things."

And she wasn't talking about Flo's loss of appetite.

"Ahh," Flo nodded. "I've seen you all scurrying about like meddling Miss Marples. What are your concerns, love? What are you worried about?"

"Apart from two dead bodies and the mighty great fire?" Lynette shot back and Flo smiled.

"Sorry, yeah, I s'pose you have a point. I guess you get to my stage of life and none of it really matters."

"It matters to us," said Lynette, peering towards the distant forest.

The fire was on the other side of the mountain, obscured here by the lodge, and apart from a lingering wisp of smoke that looked more like innocent fog, you would never know the place was in peril. Perhaps that's why she and Ronnie spent so much time out here, she thought, glancing across at Ronnie.

Ronnie caught her eye then and stood and waved, then made her way inside. Waving back, Lynette wondered if Ronnie knew that her best friend was dying.

"I'm sorry you're so sick, Flo, but I still have so much living to be done. I want to cook for a fabulous Michelin-star restaurant, not the dingy café where I've worked for years. And I want to get married one day and have kids eventually and—"

"Then you should choose your beaus better," Flo told her, voice scolding, and Lynette looked at her, eyes wide.

"Not you too, Flo!" *Did nobody like Blake?*

"He's trouble, that one."

"You think he did all this?"

"Goodness no. Not switched on enough for that! I'm just saying, he has a dark heart, that man, a devious nature. Slippery, I'd say. A bit of a snake." She squeezed Lynette's hand. The strength of her grasp was surprising. "You could do better, my dear. You *deserve* better! Don't settle for someone like him. Stop falling for fancy cars and floppy fringes!"

Lynette laughed. "*Fancy Cars and Floppy Fringes.* Now that would make a great title for a reality TV show."

Flo looked at her like she was talking gibberish. "And don't waste any more time at that dingy café you speak of either. Grab your dreams now, Lynette, with both hands while you can. Because if you're not careful, dear, your dreams will get ripped out from under you!"

"Okay, I will, I promise!" Lynette said. "If we get through this—*when* we get through this—I'm turning over a whole new leaf. I've already been thinking about it anyway. I'm handing in my resignation at Mario's. You're right, I'm not getting any younger and it's time to grow up."

"Good for you, dear," said Flo, and they both sighed together as they stared out at the misty view. One lost in thoughts of the future, one with only thoughts of the past.

~

Claire could not bring herself to face Simon again. Her heart was too tender, and she knew her strained smile would give the game away. He'd seen how distant she'd become. The man wasn't stupid. If she suddenly switched back to carefree Claire, he would smell her disingenuity a mile off.

So she waited until she saw him clambering up a ladder at the back of the lodge, rake in hand and a can of something—was that spray paint?—then she dashed to the reception desk and grabbed what she could only assume was the skeleton key for the rooms. She had spotted it hanging under the reception desk earlier that day when she was checking Simon's name in the guest book. It had a picture of a skeleton on the front, so it didn't take much of a sleuth to work that out.

Listening for the sound of the rake on the tin roof above, she checked the corridor, then raced along until she got to Simon's room. Using the key, she glanced around again, then let herself in.

Leaning up against the door, Claire took some big steadying breaths, guilt and fear rushing through her in equal measure. Then she blinked at the sight before her and could not help smiling. Unlike Blake's room, this one was so tidy it barely looked slept in. Almost a mirror image of her own. Claire spotted Simon's empty suitcase on the relevant rack and noticed his clothes all neatly placed inside the cupboard. The bathroom was also squeaky clean, just a toothbrush in the glass indicating he had even used it. Through the glass balcony door she could see his walking boots and socks airing outside—which was where they ought to be—and a towel hanging neatly on the back of a chair to dry, the one he must have used that morning.

She stepped in and searched the small desk, but there was nothing on top or in the drawers except an old Bible, a guidebook on the lodge, and some brochures for Lyleton tourist sites. Sweeping her eyes towards the bed, she noticed a few things on the farthest bedside table and snuck across, running her hand over his shiny gold Rolex and what looked like a brand-new copy of a Jo Nesbo thriller, with a small bookmark inside it. She was reaching for the book when she saw it, tucked up behind the lamp—a black leather wallet with the brand Louis Vuitton embroidered across the front.

Claire leapt on the wallet like it was a gold nugget and went to open it, then stopped, held it to her chest and closed her eyes for a moment, not sure she was ready for this. Not sure she really wanted proof of Simon's betrayal. She had been so fond of him. So sure he was one of the good guys…

The bedroom door suddenly clicked open and Claire's eyes flew open with it.

Simon was whistling a jaunty tune as he strolled in. He spotted Claire and began to smile when the reality must have hit him—she was standing in his room, clutching his wallet, invading his turf. He stopped, turned and, without saying a word, pushed the door firmly shut behind him.

Then he checked it was locked, rattling the handle a few times, and turned back to Claire, his lips no longer smiling.

~

"What have you got there, dear?" said Ronnie, reading over Perry's shoulder.

He smiled to himself as he drew her in. Hook, line and sinker.

"Oh, just a little something I stumbled upon while looking for trail maps," he told her. "It's on the Lyle family, the story of how they pioneered the mountain."

"Oh really?" She slipped onto the couch beside him. "Any pictures of the lovely dances?"

He turned the pages. "There are a few pictures, yes." But it wasn't the dances he wanted to discuss. "Lots of history of the place, how long it had taken to build, the blood, sweat and tears that went into it." He paused for effect. "You know, Ronnie, there's a lot of heritage value in this old hovel."

"Oh, I don't doubt it," she said, looking over his shoulder.

"Be a pity for it all to get ripped out," he continued, eyes locked to the book.

"Yes, I guess it would," she said, still not biting.

If she was the new owner, this was her chance to confess.

"If I ever got my mitts on this lodge," she continued, "I'd give it a good lick of paint of course, but I wouldn't want to remove the character. It's the character that makes the place."

He looked at her then. "Are you being serious? You really love this old joint?"

"Well, *love's* a strong word. But I'd hate to see it modernised. Don't you agree?"

He smiled, nodding. "Yes, Ronnie, I think I do." He flashed his eyes around the library. "It's funny. At first I thought it was all very outdated, a bit like Agatha Christie's book. But the longer I spend here, the closer that fire comes, the more I realise it would be a *tragedy* if it was all destroyed. Sometimes the past is worth saving even if it is dark and dusty."

His comment surprised her. Surprised him too. Preservation had always been his goal when working as a palaeontologist, but he'd never extended the same courtesy to the less distant past. Like the only things worth saving were a million years old.

But this lodge *was* worth saving, he knew that now, even with its shabby interiors and stiff family portraits and even stiffer creatures clinging to the walls, reminding them all what humans were once capable of and how quickly they had changed. Some of it for the better. But not all of it, he knew that too.

"I would hate for this place to be torn down or turned into chrome and glass and plastic," he said. "And heaven forbid they put a pizza oven in!"

Ronnie cackled. "My, haven't you come full circle."

He smiled again. It was time to stop beating around the bush. "Can I ask you something, Ronnie? Do you know anything about a company called Living Large Enterprises? They have nothing to do with your family business, right?"

"Goodness, no. Never heard of them. Why?"

"They're the company who recently purchased this place, want to renovate it within an inch of its life."

"Oh I do hope they reconsider. As I say, it'd be a pity to go in too hard." She glanced around. "Since my husband passed, I'm less interested in acquiring assets and more interested in helping others."

"That's why you donate to my museum."

She smiled. "I wondered if you'd clicked. I didn't want to say anything."

"Why do you keep it a secret? Why hide your background and wealth?"

Ronnie looked offended at that and sat up straight. "I'm not hiding anything, young man. But I can't see how it's relevant. In fact, I think it's rather poor taste to discuss money. Bad manners, frankly."

And there it was. She wasn't keeping her background a secret; it just wasn't polite conversation.

"Why do you ask, dear?" she said, relaxing a little.

"Oh, no reason." He kept flicking through the pages. "I haven't seen your photo in here, more's the pity."

"Thank goodness for that!" she shot back. "If my memory serves me correctly, I made a bit of a fool of myself that weekend. Drank a little too much of the bubbly, I'm afraid, and might have had a tryst with a very unavailable young gentleman. But we'll keep that little titbit to ourselves!"

She chuckled, but it sounded almost forced to Perry as he turned the pages, and he was going to enquire further when he noticed a photo that looked vaguely familiar. It was of a man with a mop of white hair, wearing a black tuxedo, a stunning blonde in a slinky dress beside him.

"That's the founder's son, right? Jack Lyle?" said Perry.

"That's him," said Ronnie, sighing. "Heir to the lodge and Lydia's long-suffering husband. He had such lovely white hair, didn't he? That's why they all called him Snowy."

~

The forest was eerily quiet when Alicia and Missy stepped into the clearing. It was close to sundown, and there was no sign of Snowy at his hut. Alicia wondered if he was still resting, but she didn't give it further thought. They were here to do some Google research, and she wanted to get on with it.

As she pulled her phone out, it began to ring, and she saw that it was Jackson.

Before answering it, she told Missy, "Can you start researching Blake and LLE? See what you can find?"

Missy nodded, perching on a dusty rock, while Alicia took the call from Jackson.

"Everyone still alive and accounted for?" he asked, his voice sounding strained.

"We're fine," she said. "Just want to get out of here."

"Okay, but before we get to that, I did a background search on that Blake fellow you mentioned, and—"

"He's a writer!" screamed Missy, breaking through Alicia's conversation.

She held a finger up and said, "Sorry, Jackson, what were you saying?"

"The guy's a journalist, Alicia. A bloody tabloid journo."

Her lips dropped wide. Hadn't that been her first thought when she'd noticed the research file on his desk? If only she'd listened to her instincts.

"Okay, that makes more sense. He was here researching a story, yes?"

"Yes. I called his boss, Gryson Dale, down at the *Tele*. He reckons Blake was investigating some dark mystery from the past, something explosive he said. But the bloke is tabloid, so take that with a grain of salt. Said Blake was about to expose someone, big time, and it had something to do with some past fire?"

"The Great Fire of 1970," she told him, already a few steps ahead.

"Yeah, well, apparently they're doing a story on it for its fiftieth anniversary, and there's some scandal around it. Some fresh angle that Blake was looking into before he vanished. Because here's the thing, Alicia. He hasn't returned to work. Hasn't phoned in. Nothing."

"Oh no," she said, gulping. "Does that mean he's caught up in the fire?"

"Yes and no. Benson's crew finally got to the burnt-out vehicle and have confirmed that it is Blake's Mercedes, but there's no sign of life. He must have got out. Doesn't mean he survived the fire though. He might have made a run for it and got caught elsewhere."

Or ditched his car and crept back, Alicia thought, then just as quickly dismissed it. Tabloid journalists gave the rest of them a bad name, but they wouldn't kill for a good story, would they? Even one that was *explosive*?

No, her guess was he got caught in a firestorm, and she shuddered thinking of it and of the lies Blake had spun, wondering if they were worth dying for. Whatever happened to him, Perry was right about one thing. Blake Morrow had been using the book club as his way in, using them to go undercover. It wasn't exactly an ethical way to gather information, but it was an easier, lazier option.

She wondered what Blake had found—what was this dark mystery surrounding the Great Fire? And what, if anything, did it have to do with the current fire and the two murders at the lodge? They had to be related, surely.

Or was it all a massive red herring?

As she considered these things, Alicia's eyes strayed downwards, and she remembered the rock fall that first afternoon. She had completely forgotten about that!

Was Blake the intended victim, not her or Flo? Perhaps Perry was right and Vale and Mrs Flannery had recognised Blake's face or byline when he'd first shown up. Perhaps he'd hassled them for quotes in the past?

Lynette said someone had searched the *Telegraph* online that evening—was it Vale, confirming his suspicions? Had he dislodged those rocks to scare the journalist away, Flo and Alicia getting caught in the commotion? No one had ever explained that one properly.

"Babe? You still there?"

"Sorry, yes, I was just thinking."

"Well, stay focused because you need to hear this next bit."

She groaned, catching Missy's eye.

Jackson said, "They're doing absolutely everything they can, but it's incredibly difficult terrain. Forest is so thick and the fire trails are as good as useless. Some heads will roll back here for not keeping them clear, but that's not important now. The point is, I can't see them breaking through before nightfall, which is any minute now."

"Right," she said, heart plummeting.

Alicia hadn't dared to dream, but the truth was she had

been secretly hoping Jackson had good news. That he would tell her they were a kilometre away, to listen for the sound of fire engines, that he was about to come charging in for the dramatic rescue.

But now…

Now they had to spend another night, wondering if a killer was still amongst them, waiting for a chance to strike.

Reading her thoughts again, Jackson said, "Stay close to your book club friends tonight, okay? And I'm not talking about the new ones. I mean Lynn and Perry and Missy and Claire. Do not leave each other's sight, and unless a fire breaks out there, do not leave the lodge."

"I don't intend to," she said, then realised that she had done exactly that. Here she was all alone in the forest. Well, apart from Missy and old Snowy of course.

Her eyes darted to his hut, but there was still no sign of the man.

"Everyone's doing their best to get through," Jackson repeated, "but the blasted fire is intense and they don't want to take any risks or lose any lives."

Not like last time, she thought. Not like 1970.

Then Jackson added, "This isn't a simple house fire, Alicia. It's a bushfire, and I'm told the most dangerous place you can be in a bushfire is out in the open. The intense heat alone can kill you, long before the flames do." Then hearing her intake of breath, he added, "Sorry, but you told me not to hold anything back. That information could save your life."

"Yes, yes, thank you." *I think.*

Alicia hung up, feeling completely rattled, and not just about the fire. Another day had passed, and they were no closer to uncovering the killer. In theory, Blake was the perfect suspect. He was slippery and conniving and, best of all, nowhere to be seen. But she had a feeling he was also little more than a zealous journalist.

She had a feeling the killer was still in their group.

And as they returned to the lodge, leaving Snowy to his slumber, Missy reluctantly agreed. "Morrow calls himself a True Crime Reporter," she said, "but most of his stuff was about B-list celebrities and vacuous scandals. Nothing major as far as I can see. His last piece was on some reality TV star's sex tape scandal. Sounds mean to say it, but he seems like a bit of a creep to me, destroying people's reputations, like it's a game and he's a player."

Or a hunter, Alicia thought, the cowardly kind. He slaughtered people from a distance with ink, under the guise of journalism.

"But that's not all I learned," Missy said, smile returning as she produced her smartphone. "Check this out, kitten. It's a picture of LLE's top dog."

Alicia glanced down at Missy's screen, then grabbed it from her hands and gave it closer inspection.

"Oh no," she said, and Missy giggled.

"I know! Claire is going to be so disappointed!"

CHAPTER 16

"Claire's missing!" Lynette burst out the second she caught sight of Alicia and Missy turning off Repentance Way and back towards the lodge.

They were hot and flushed, and Alicia felt like she'd run a marathon that day, but that very sentence gave her a shot of adrenaline, and she picked up the pace, racing to Lynette's side.

"What do you mean?" she said, glancing towards Perry, who was coming out of the lodge behind her.

"I just checked her room again," he said, also sounding breathless. "She's not there. Can't find her anywhere. But that's not the worst of it." He gave Lynette a little shove. "You tell them the worst of it."

"I'm not telling them! It was your idea to send her snooping around Simon."

"Simon?" said Alicia. "What's going on, guys?"

Perry gulped. "We can't find him either. Simon's also missing."

"And then there were six," said Missy, but she wasn't even smiling when she said it.

~

Flo was seated at the small desk in her room, trying hard to block out all the kerfuffle. It had been difficult enough giving Ronnie the slip. Fortunately, her friend had gone for a walk, and that would keep her occupied for a bit. The woman seemed intent on sticking to Flo's side, like she was worried she'd suddenly drop, or worse.

Well, Flo wasn't quite finished yet.

Still, it was hard to concentrate with all the excitement. Perry had burst in first—had she seen Claire? Then Lynette came with the same question, followed by Perry again this time wondering about Simon. Finally Flo had the wherewithal to lock her door behind them.

The young things really were like headless chooks. A suspicious bunch, their minds tangling in all directions, acting like amateur Poirots. If only they knew that life would work out for them in the end. It always did for the young and pretty. Well, almost always…

Life was rushing up to Flo now, death banging loudly on her door. She smiled, thinking of Lynette who was, indeed, young and pretty. Foolish, too, like she'd said. Hopefully the young lass would sort herself out before she went the way of others; before she brought her own proverbial widow maker down upon her head.

How clever Lynette was, though, working out her secret! Outwitting even Ronnie. Flo thought she'd been clever herself, hiding her deterioration, her nausea and loss of appetite. She still had a surprising amount of energy, but that would not last long. Her doctor had already informed her of that. Her motor skills would go first, then her mind. That was the bit she was most terrified of, which was why she had to get her skates on, as her grandchildren would say.

"Get your skates on, Nan! Haven't got all day!"

They were always in a hurry, young people, weren't they? Always in such a dreaded rush. Still, that might be where she went wrong. Perhaps she should have done all this sooner.

She reached for the official Lyle stationery and began to write them all a lovely goodbye letter…

~

The original book club members were huddled in another locked room, this time belonging to Claire, and as expected, everything was in its place. Except, of course, for Claire.

"Where could she *be*?" said Missy, perched on the edge of Claire's meticulously made bed, trying not to ruffle it.

"Let's think about this logically," said Alicia, who'd dropped into the desk chair, exhausted. "Who saw her last?"

"We all did," said Perry. "Remember, we went off in different directions? You guys headed off on the trail, Lynny went to speak to Flo, and I went back to the library and asked Ronnie a few questions."

"What did Ronnie say?" Missy asked, and Alicia held a hand up.

"Can we get to our findings in a minute. I want to know where the bloody hell Claire is. And why Simon is missing too!" She took a steadying breath. "So, we all separated, and Claire went to investigate Simon's real identity." Her eyes widened. "You did check Simon's room?"

Lynette and Perry nodded. "No answer."

"Damn it."

"I think we should tell them what we learned," said Missy. "It could be the key."

"Are you talking about Blake now?" said Lynette. "Don't tell me he works for Living Large Enterprises. Please don't tell me that."

"No, possum, he works for the Murdoch press," said Missy. "He's not the new owner, Lynny, he's a journalist."

Lynette's lips formed a perfect circle.

Perry said, "I never would've guessed."

"I would," said Alicia. "In fact I did, remember? Then you started raving about Blake being related to Donal Murphy, and one thing led to another and we got sidetracked. Turns out Blake was here to research a story for the fiftieth anniversary of the Great Fire. Sometimes,

people, if it looks like a duck and quacks like a duck..."
She cocked her head to one side. "In any case, none of this
is helping us find Claire!"

Lynette had a hand up now. "Just a second, please.
I think I need to enjoy this a moment longer." She slapped
Perry with one of her smug smiles. "Are you saying I was
right all along? That Blake is not some mad killer; he was
here for a perfectly reasonable purpose?"

"I'm not sure about *reasonable*," Alicia shot back. "He
obviously used us to come up and poke about and write
some salacious article. Jackson spoke to Blake's boss at the
Telegraph. They said he was about to expose someone or
something, didn't know much more than that, said he was
out on a limb on this one and about to reveal something
big."

"Something explosive!" added Missy.

"That's not the worst bit," said Alicia. "They still
haven't heard from Blake."

"Still?" Lynette didn't look so smug now.

Alicia nodded. "It is his car burnt-out down there, but
there's no sign of him anywhere. He's vanished from the
face of the earth. Like Claire. Which is why I really want to
try to focus on finding her."

"But hang on," said Lynette. "If Blake isn't the new
owner, who is? *Ronnie?*" She was looking at Perry
sceptically, and he shook his head.

"We had a good chat earlier, and I don't think she has
anything to do with any of this. Certainly has no
connection to LLE. She hasn't mentioned her wealth
because it's not polite, apparently. I think it's a
generational thing."

"I hate talking about money," said Missy.

"That's because you don't have any, honey," said Perry,
giving her a sad smile. "So that leaves Simon and Flo."

"It's not Flo," said Lynette. "Turns out death is not
polite conversation either."

She then broke the news about Flo's prognosis, and

that left them even gloomier.

"Oh dear," said Alicia, resting her chin in one hand. "I never would have picked that. Well done, Lynny. The poor, poor thing."

"Why didn't she *say* something?" said Missy, her eyes popping with tears. "I wished she'd told me!" She reached for a tissue as the tears became streams. "I really... like... Flo!"

Alicia pulled her into a hug while Perry gave Missy's arm a rub.

"Flo thought the truth would be a turn-off," Lynette told them. "She was worried we'd reject her from the group, and she just wanted one final adventure."

"Well, she's certainly getting that," said Alicia, and they settled into a glum silence before Alicia sat back. "Listen, it's awful about Flo, but we can't get side-tracked. We need to find Claire. If Flo's not involved with LLE, that just leaves Simon."

She turned to Missy. "Are you okay? Can you show them what you found?"

Missy nodded and wiped her eyes before producing her smartphone and swiping her way to the relevant image. It was a screenshot from LLE's company website with a list of the Executive Team. She zoomed in on the words Managing Director/Owner. Then she swiped for the next photo. It was a picture of Mr Simon Barrier BCA. He had an expensive suit on and a clipped beard, but there was no mistaking that dark handsome face.

It was the face of Simon Crete.

~

As they stormed up the hallway in the direction of Simon's room, Perry was kicking himself internally the whole way.

"I thought you'd already checked his room," said Alicia, trailing with the others behind him.

"We just knocked. And way too politely. This time I'm not going to take silence for an answer! Simon has to be in there. Where else is he going to be? And I bet you any money he's got Claire cowering in there with him."

Alicia recoiled as an image of Claire appeared before her eyes. She was chained to Simon's bed, a dirty scarf around her mouth, the fraudster looming with a shiny syringe... Her step quickened.

Perry came to a grinding halt when he reached Simon's door, and the others almost toppled over behind him. He took a deep breath, then raised his hand and began banging loudly. This time he called out as he did so.

"Open up! We know you're in there, *Mr Barrier!*" He glanced back at the others with a self-satisfied smile. "If you don't open this door *immediately*, we are breaking it down!" Then, considering the hard timber frame, he added, "Or coming in via the balcony at the very least!"

They all waited another minute, then he raised his hand to bang again when there was a soft click and the door opened to reveal Claire peering through from the other side, a meek smile on her face.

~

The luminescent blue gin looked way too festive for the occasion, and even worse when you mixed it with tonic because it turned a blushing shade of pink. Which was the same shade now covering the cheeks of both Claire and Simon, who were swallowing it down like it was water.

It was almost dinnertime, but none of them had an appetite, and that suited Claire, who steered them to the bar for a settling gin and tonic and a chance to explain.

She had been completely mortified when Simon busted her in his room earlier that afternoon, but her blush was nothing compared to his. No sooner had he spotted his wallet in her shaky hands, he had secured the door, dropped onto his bed and hung his head low, apologising profusely. He knew immediately what she was up to and didn't blame her.

"I should have told you! Of course I should," he'd said. "It's just that things started to go a little berserk with the bodies piling up and the fire down the hill. But I had nothing to do with any of that. You have to believe me!"

And for the life of her, Claire did, especially after hearing the full story. Now she was determined her friends hear it too, preferably over a drink. Perry was determined that drink be "top shelf," and with Grange Hermitage now tainted in his mind forever, he reached for Husk Distiller's Ink Gin.

"The bastards even *try* to charge us for this, I'll sue," he said, then, realising the bastard was actually amongst them, he added, "Got a problem with that? Whatever your name is?"

"It's Simon Barrier and no, I do not," Simon replied, pushing the bottle towards Perry. "Finish it off for all I care. In fact, I've already arranged for the entire weekend to be reimbursed to you all. I am so, so sorry about everything."

"Humph!" Perry said, adding another splash of gin to his tonic.

"And I'm sorry we didn't let you into Simon's room earlier," Claire said. "He was still trying to explain it all to me, and I needed to get it straight."

"*If* he's giving you a straight story!" Perry snapped back.

"Perry…," Claire began, but Simon placed a hand on her forearm.

"It's okay, he has every right to be angry with me. You all do. And it's not your job, Claire, to apologise on my behalf. *I'm* the one who let you all down, badly." He glanced out towards the corridor. "Should we wait for Flo and Ronnie before we get into it?"

"No way, *Mr Secret*," said Lynette. "I've spent the past two days defending Blake when you're the one who's been lying. I want to hear what you have to say."

"Actually, Lynny," said Missy, nose wrinkled. "If you think about it, Blake was lying too. He didn't tell any of us he was a journo. He told you he was a 'businessman,' didn't he Alicia?" She glanced at Alicia but was caught in Lynette's glowering cross fire, so she cleared her throat and said, "But that's not important now, is it, kitten? You were saying, Simon?"

He nodded. "I didn't mean to lie, not really. It all made so much sense at the beginning."

"Then why don't you start there," said Alicia, who was still struggling to make the pieces fit.

He took a gulp of his own drink, then exhaled loudly and said, "It all started with you, Alicia."

"Really?" She looked mortified.

"Yes, when you booked the club in." He stopped, swirling the glass in his hand. "Actually, scrap that. It started even before then. My company, LLE, had recently purchased this lodge and were trying to decide what to do with it. Whether to go large and seriously renovate or tread gently and return it to its former glory."

"We already saw the DA," Perry said. "We know which way you were heading, so you can drop the spin."

A wrinkle crossed Simon's forehead. "That's my business partner's dream. Not mine. He wanted to see how much he could push through council. I was leaning more towards the low-footprint option. Nothing has yet been decided. I get final veto."

Perry rolled his eyes like he did not believe him, but Simon forged on.

"That's when I hatched the plan. I'd been in our New York office when we purchased the property as part of a growing portfolio, so I'd only seen it online. I wanted to experience it for myself. And not as a VIP. You never get treated normally when they know who you are. Never get the genuine experience. I wanted to come incognito as a regular paying guest. Get a feel for the place and see what real guests are thinking—before it all gets changed irrevocably."

Perry scoffed again, and Simon shot him a frown and tried to explain.

"We'd had a bad experience with a previous investment, you see. I'd let Tommo, my business partner, run with it, and he'd gone the full monty—ripped all the character out of the place, changed the guest type entirely, and I wasn't convinced it was for the better. It's a resort in the Blue Mountains, you might have heard of it." He shook his head. "Anyway, that's not important. What's important here is that we got Alicia's booking enquiry. She wanted to bring her book club up and asked if we could accommodate them."

"You sent the booking to LLE and didn't remember it?" said Perry, surprised, but Alicia quickly shook her head.

"No. I filled in the lodge's online booking form and added a note about the book club, asking if they had a private room for us to run the meetings. That's all I did."

"Vale must have received it," said Simon, taking up the story again. "He passed it on to my personal assistant, Queenie, wondering whether we were still taking in paying guests or if he should now officially close the books. Queenie brought it to me, and that's when I saw the opportunity."

"To lie to us?" said Perry, still unforgiving.

"As I explained, I only wanted to trial the place as a guest." He blushed again and snuck a glance at Claire. "Truth is, I also loved the sound of your book club. I really did. It seemed ideal for a place like this. That's when Queenie and I hatched the plan for me to use a pseudonym and come along so I could check it all out and immerse myself in what sounded like such a wonderful weekend, have a little fun while I was at it. It's been a very trying year…"

"Oh diddums," said Lynette, not buying into the

flattery. "You've certainly had fun at our expense." She was in Perry's camp and unsure what to think of all this. It felt like a very roundabout way of researching a development project. Why not just survey the paying guests? "So you came up with the name Simon Edward Crete—Secret—and infiltrated us. You must have thought you were very clever."

"Actually the name was all Queenie's idea. She's an avid Agatha Christie fan. She'd make a great addition to your club, actually. What she doesn't know about the author would fit on a postage stamp." His eyes slipped to Alicia. "Queenie's the one who wrote that lovely letter. On my behalf. That's why it was so successful."

Alicia nodded. Now it made more sense.

"Queenie's a damn sight smarter than I am," Simon continued. "I didn't even realise what she'd done until you lot started talking about Mr U. N. Owen during book club, and that's when it hit me. She'd given me a crazy *nom de guerre*, and I hadn't even noticed! I was so embarrassed and so worried you'd all work it out and think I was playing games."

"Well, you got that part right," said Perry.

"I wasn't trying to be conniving, honestly. I just didn't want the name Simon Barrier or LLE anywhere near the booking. I'd never met Vale in person, so I didn't think he'd recognise my face, but I had a hunch he'd know the name and, as I say, treat me differently. That's when Queenie suggested the new surname. I guess she didn't figure on you lot working it out."

"We are the Murder Mystery Book Club, you know!" said Missy, but Alicia was now shaking her head.

"I think Vale did suspect something," she said, wondering if it was Simon he was referring to when he used the word "imposter," not Blake.

As Simon swigged his drink, Alicia stared hard at the developer. He had a distinguished, slightly crumpled look about him, but perhaps he was really a smooth operator.

Was he telling them the whole truth, she wondered? Or what they wanted to hear? Was the DA really his partner's doing, or was he spinning them a tale to get them off his back? And, more importantly, was he capable of killing two people to hide his true identity and force his DA through?

It seemed like such a stretch, but she didn't know who or what to believe anymore.

She said, "Okay then, Mr Barrier, tell me this. Once Vale was murdered, why didn't you speak up?"

"Or when the phones went out and the fire started?" said Perry.

"Or after we found poor Mrs Flannery for that matter?" added Lynette.

He glanced at each set of accusing eyes. "I know, I should have. I almost did so many times. I already explained all of this to Claire. I deeply regret my silence now, but I thought Vale's death was innocent, and then the fire started and Mrs Flannery was found... it all happened so fast. Suddenly you were looking at us newcomers like we were all guilty, and I didn't think confessing to using a fake name was going to exactly help my position."

"Who cares about your position?" said Lynette. "It might help us get out of here alive!"

He held up a placatory palm. "I can assure you all, Queenie is very aware of the situation and has the LLE chopper ready to winch us out if it comes to that. That's why I've been preparing the rooftop as a helipad, clearing away the debris, marking the safest landing zone up there for the chopper pilot to see should it become necessary."

"*That's* what you've been doing up there all this time?" said Claire.

He nodded. "It's the only potential landing zone for miles, but it's not ideal. There are numerous overhanging branches and a power pole that's a little too close for comfort. Plus the chopper can only take two passengers at a time, so I've been hoping the fire brigade will get on top of it and we can all leave safely together. That was my final task—making sure we had an adequate exit route—then I was going to come clean. I assure you."

"Cutting it a bit fine, aren't you?" said Perry. "That fire's still going, you know. We still have to spend another night here at its mercy."

"It has calmed considerably, and there's rain predicted. Good falls, I believe. My expectation is that we'll be out of here by midmorning tomorrow," Simon said.

"You've been sneaking off to the escarpment and speaking to Benson at the RFS," said Alicia.

"I have been calling out but not to the RFS. As I say, Queenie is my eyes and ears. I've been in touch with her, and she's monitoring it all from Sydney. The weather forecast is for early-morning rain. That will douse it, you will see."

"Okay, then Queenie must have mentioned you to Benson," said Alicia, "because he told Jackson that the owner is up here amongst us."

Simon was firmly shaking his head. "He wasn't talking about me, I can assure you. The only person who knows I'm here is my PA, and she would never betray my confidence, not without my permission. She hasn't even told Tommo what I'm up to, or our chopper pilot for that matter. He thinks he's getting ready to winch out some paying guests. Again, it's imperative that I see how the entire operation works when they think it's just ordinary folk, not the managing director."

"I'm not sure I like being called ordinary folk," said Perry.

"I'm not sure I like being a puppet in your little experiment either," said Lynette.

"Oh deary me, this is all a bit intense," came a croaky voice from the doorway, and they swung around to find Flo walking in, a light shawl around her shoulders, some pink lipstick smudged across her lips, clearly applied with a shaky hand. "Is everything okay?"

"Yes, it's fine!" said Lynette, flashing Simon a scowl as she slipped off her bar stool. "How are you, Flo? How are you feeling?"

"I'm fine, dear, now you mustn't fuss."

"Let's get you to a chair," said Simon.

"Let's move into the dining room," said Lynette. "I'll get the stew. I think we could all do with something in our stomachs other than lies and deceit."

Simon received another scowl as she padded off to the kitchen.

~

The book club took their seats around the dining table, and Alicia took one of Flo's hands and squeezed it gently. "Lynette told us your news, and I am so, so sorry."

"Oh pft!" she said, shaking her off. "Lynette never should have mentioned it. She's very naughty! Please, can we enjoy our tea without any more discussion of death and dying?"

"Of course," said Alicia, glancing towards the corridor. "Is Ronnie on her way?"

Ronnie had been glued to Flo's side lately, and now it made more sense to Alicia. She was obviously looking out for her ailing buddy.

"Oh, she said to start without her; she'll be here soon," Flo chirped, then clapped her hands as Lynette placed a large casserole dish in the middle of the table. "That smells delicious, dear!"

"That's because it *is* delicious, Flo," replied Lynette, ladle pointing at the older woman, "and you are going to eat some of it tonight, okay?"

Flo cackled and held out her plate.

For the next thirty minutes, everyone did as Flo had requested and enjoyed the heavy beef dish and kept the conversation light. But it didn't stop their brains from stewing with questions and concerns.

Missy was wondering how on earth she hadn't noticed that poor Flo was dying. And why the *darling* woman hadn't felt brave enough to tell them!

Alicia was still wondering whether Simon was lying. Like Blake, he had signed up for the club under false pretences, and like Blake, his career had a dark side. Could this developer really be trusted?

Claire was thinking about the rest of her conversation with Simon in his room before the group caught up with them. A conversation they had not yet repeated. They had both agreed to keep it to themselves for now, even though she knew how much her friends despised lying. Yet how could she 'fess up now? And was it really even important?

And Perry was thinking of Snowy and suddenly kicking himself! He went to speak, then stopped, remembering what Flo had said. No more talk of death and dying. Except this wasn't about death and dying. This was just idle gossip, right?

"You all right, dear?" said Flo. "You look ready to pop."

He pushed a hand to his lips and finished his mouthful while the others watched him curiously, then he said, "Sorry, I can't believe I forgot to tell you! In all the excitement over Claire, it slipped my mind entirely. You'll never guess who Snowy is? Not in a million years."

They all continued to stare, none of them offering an answer, so he burst out with it.

"He's Jack Lyle! The founder Arthur Lyle's son."

"Who?" said Flo.

"What?" said Lynette.

"Our hut dweller, Snowy, is really a Lyle!" he repeated, then waved a hand around them. "This place is his!"

"No way!" said Missy.

He chuckled, thrilled by their reaction. "I *know*! Quite a revelation! Ronnie recognised him from an early photo in the Lyle family tome."

"Are you sure she's got that right?" said Alicia, wondering why Snowy never mentioned anything.

And that was only her first question. She wanted to know why he was living like a squatter out in the forest when, for another month at least, he owned his own hotel with plenty of spare bedrooms and properly functioning bathrooms. Not to mention a fully stocked kitchen.

"Ronnie recognised him from his mop of snowy-white hair," Perry was saying. "That's where his nickname came from. But he was in a photo with his wife Lydia. It's many years old and he doesn't have the hair anymore, but he's just as tall and skinny. I only saw him from a distance but seems about right to me. How many other Lyleton Snowys would there be?"

Missy's head had started nodding madly. "I thought he was an odd-bod! I knew he'd been to the lodge. I reckon he helped himself to one of our Agatha Christie books."

Simon looked at her bemused, then turned to Alicia. "Perhaps *that's* who the fire chief was referring to when he said the owner was up here. Perhaps he meant the *original* owner, not me."

"Perhaps," said Alicia, chewing on her lip as it all began to sink in. It was Snowy who told her about the Lyle book and the paper road, so he obviously knew more than she realised. "Simon, did you know the original owner was living up here? Out near the escarpment?"

He shook his head firmly. "If I had known, I would have introduced myself."

"But you did see him," prompted Claire, and he nodded now.

"Yes, on my walk, soon after we arrived. I thought he was a squatter, if I'm being completely honest."

"It's too bizarre," said Claire. "Why would Jack Lyle be living like a hobo out in the bush?"

"Maybe he had a breakdown?" said Lynette. "Or maybe he sold his share to the rest of the family years ago? He did say he'd rather slit his wrists than come to the lodge. Probably just wants to live the quiet life."

"In a crusty hut?" said Perry. "It's like he was hiding."

"It wasn't crusty, Perry," said Alicia. "It was actually quite nice inside. Furnished with stuff from the lodge, so that explains that. It also explains why Vale was carting food to him. For all we know, Snowy was still his boss."

There was a discreet cough, and they stopped prattling long enough to find Flo looking at them, her face wretched with worry. "I'm not sure what you're all yakking about. You've lost me completely, but I am a little concerned for Ronnie." She tapped her watch. "She should be back by now, and if there is some hobo out there in the forest, well..."

Alicia sat forward. "Ronnie's out in the forest?"

"Yes, dear, didn't I say that?"

No. No, she did not.

"She went to talk to somebody, she said. Had her little portable phone with her," said Flo.

"Ah, probably phoning her nephews," said Simon. "She's quite fixated with them. Has been trying to contact them since she got here."

"That'll be it!" said Claire. "She'll be back soon enough, and even if she does encounter Snowy, well, he's perfectly harmless, right?"

They all nodded, but one of them less assuredly.

~

Ronnie sat in the dark hut, wincing as Snowy ranted and groaned and threw himself about the place, smashing items in his wake. When Lydia's photo hit the ground, she really began to panic.

Should she make a run for it? Try to get some help?

Or should she do as he'd asked and sit there quietly, listening, waiting, knowing the end was coming and it was going to be horrific?

~

It wasn't until the meal was finished and they were in the kitchen, putting it back into shape, that Alicia got a chance to mention her concerns to the others. She was becoming increasingly worried about Ronnie—if she was just making a phone call, why wasn't she back yet? But first she had some more questions for Simon.

As he led the charge with the washing up, she said, "So your company never knew that the old owner was still here, living close by in the forest? The Lyle family didn't think to mention it during the sale?"

"I can assure you, Alicia, it was never mentioned to me, but…" His face clouded over. "I can't be absolutely sure my partner Tommo didn't know something. He's so intent on developing that escarpment, calls it the *pièce de résistance* of the entire property. Perhaps he's been keeping it under wraps. I wouldn't put it past him. The old hut could be heritage-listed for all we know. Might put a dent in his plans."

"Why are you even in business with that man?" said Perry. "He sounds beastly."

Simon shrugged. "It's complicated. What I do know is that this lodge is held in a family trust and we've been dealing with a younger man, an Alexander Lyle, who is based in Sydney. He's a great-nephew of the original owner, I believe. Perhaps Jack is no longer part of the trust anymore? Alex certainly never mentioned any uncle Jack to me. I assume Jack—Snowy—is his uncle. It's all a bit cloudy now."

It's positively murky, Alicia wanted to tell him. "Okay, so you didn't know Snowy was a Lyle, and he certainly never said anything to us. But I can't help wondering how Snowy would feel about the sale of this place and the fact that you guys were considering building luxury villas on the very place he calls home."

"I would never have allowed it if I'd known he had

lodgings there," said Simon.

"Yes, but it was part of the original DA, right?"

"What's your point, Alicia?"

"My point is what if Snowy saw that DA? What if it infuriated him? He doesn't know you have a right to veto. For all he knows he's about to be booted from the only home he's ever known. I can't help wondering…"

She stopped and bit her tongue, feeling queasy again. Alicia had grown to like Snowy. He seemed genuine to her, salt of the earth. She leaned up against the oven and gave it more thought, but her mind kept circling back to one thing.

"I can't help wondering," she repeated, "if Snowy is somehow involved in all this."

"How so?" asked Claire, looking up from the kitchen bench she was wiping.

"What if… I don't know… he heard about the development plans and was enraged. What if he decided he'd rather burn the place down then let some big city developer come in and mess with the family estate?"

"Goodness me," said Perry. "We're going through suspects faster than a Christie novel!"

"Actually, Alicia's half-right," said Lynette, emerging from the cold room. "I don't think Snowy cares what happens to the lodge per se—he loathes the place, that's what he told me—but I do know he adores that escarpment. Said they'd have to remove him from the mountain in a coffin."

Alicia frowned. "Exactly what I'm worried about. Maybe he started the fire. Maybe that was his intention all along."

"Except…," began Missy, who'd been busily drying dishes. "If Snowy loves it so much, why burn it down?"

Alicia recalled something else Snowy had said. *Why let bloody tourists hog the prime real estate?* Would he rather destroy it than hand it to strangers?

"But hang on," said Claire, also trying to keep up.

"By that logic, you must also be saying that Snowy killed Vale and Mrs Flannery. Which seems preposterous! They were his friends; they were caring for him."

Alicia swished her lips to the side. Yes, that was harder to reconcile.

Claire turned to Simon. "What was going to happen to the staff after the sale went through?"

"We've already found most of them work in our other resorts, and we did the same for Vale and Joan Flannery. I always try to re-employ staff when we redevelop an existing property."

"Aren't you a saint," said Perry.

Simon looked at him. Hard. "You are going to have to try to forgive me at some stage, Mr Gordon."

Perry glanced away. The truth was he did forgive Simon. He was just enjoying holding on to his grudge. It was a nice distraction from what was going on around them.

Simon continued, "We offered both Vale and Mrs Flannery temporary positions at our revamped Blue Mountains resort, the one I was telling you about earlier. Then, once the renovations here were complete, they were invited to come back. Vale has run a very tight ship for thirty years, been here for almost fifty-five. I wasn't going to lose that kind of history and experience."

"So what happened?" asked Claire.

"They both rejected the offer to come back. Mrs Flannery had requested a permanent move to the Blue Mountains and was waiting on some paperwork, and Vale said he would retire, and I can't say I blamed him. He has done a great job up here, but it can be exhausting, thankless work, and he's way past retirement age. I can't think why he stayed on all these years, frankly."

"He stayed on for Snowy," said Alicia quietly.

"So why would Snowy then kill him?" said Claire. "Seems illogical."

"Maybe Snowy thought they were deserting him,

shifting to the dark side." Alicia offered Simon an apologetic smile. "That's you, you're the dark side. No offence."

He smiled back. "None taken."

"Maybe after all these years Snowy felt betrayed and lashed out at them and then the whole place by starting the fire."

"He's pushing eighty, Alicia!" said Perry.

"So? You don't think he can strike a match or inject a needle or swing a bottle of red at someone's head? He already told me he trekked all the way to Cooper's Crossing this morning. Who's to say he didn't do it the day before to start the fire? Snowy might be old, but he's very switched on and seems fit as a fiddle."

"And so sweet!" said Lynette. "He was so lovely to me."

"Yes, and I'm not saying he wishes *us* any harm," said Alicia. "He told us about the paper road, so I'm sure he doesn't. But I wonder if that's because we had no idea who he was. Maybe that very factor gave us some protection." She drew in a quick breath. "Hang on, Perry. Didn't you say Ronnie pointed Snowy out to you?"

"Yes, why?"

"What did you say after that? Did you tell her that Snowy is still alive and living in the forest?"

"Of course, but—" He gulped. "Oh dear. You don't think she went to talk to him, do you?"

"Flo said that Ronnie went to talk to somebody. Maybe it wasn't her nephews at all. Maybe Ronnie wanted to reconnect with Snowy. They have history, right?"

Perry had paled. "Oh dear Lord. She said something to me about a fling she had with some 'unavailable young gentleman' back in 1969. What a mistake that had been. I wonder if she meant Snowy?" He gulped, looking at Alicia. "You don't think he wants to hurt her, do you?"

Alicia frowned. "If she tells him she knows who he is, then… maybe?" She glanced out towards the dining room door. "If Ronnie was going for a walk, why isn't she back now that it's dark?"

They all stared through the kitchen window, looking for answers and finding only swirling shadows.

~

The lodge torches were bright, but it didn't make the trek along Repentance Way any easier for Simon and Perry as they strode back to Snowy's cabin. It didn't help that the moon was lost behind the smoky clouds and that there wasn't a single trace of cabin light filtering through the foliage.

That had them both worried.

They had volunteered for Ronnie's search and rescue, and Alicia was relieved. Lynette's stew had fortified them all, but her legs weren't going anywhere else tonight but bed.

"There it is," said Perry, surprised that there wasn't so much as a candle flickering.

It sent prickles down his spine. He knew the hut was connected to the power lines—had seen the line for himself earlier today—so he wondered why Snowy didn't have his lights on, especially if he had Ronnie visiting. They hadn't passed her on the track so could only assume she was still in there. Could only hope she was still okay.

"I wish we'd thought to bring a weapon," said Perry. "There's already two bodies. I'm not keen to be the third."

"Ronnie could be the third, let's pick up our pace," said Simon.

As they stepped into the clearing, they stopped to listen but could hear nothing other than an eerie rustling in the bushes around them and the distant coo of a Sooty Owl. No sound of chatter or laughter or old lovers catching up.

They swapped a wary look and crept even closer until they were standing outside the front door. Again, they were met with terrifying silence.

"Keep your torch ready," whispered Perry as they creaked the door open. If required, it could work as a makeshift weapon.

The darkness inside took some adjusting to, but when their eyes finally focused, they both inhaled at the same time. There were two other people in the cabin. One was coiled up on the bed, the other perched in a rocking chair beside it.

They were both so still, both sets of eyes closed, that Perry could not be sure who was who and what if anything was going on.

Then he heard a slow creak and the person in the chair sat forward and looked at him with a grim smile.

CHAPTER 17

Alicia couldn't help smiling as she flipped through the Lyle family story. She was worried about Ronnie and needed a distraction, so she had quickly showered, then grabbed the book from Perry's bag and was now curled up on a library lounge, Claire on one side, Missy on the other. The old pictures were almost dreamy and told a very different story of a very different lodge in a very different era.

"It was lovely in its heyday, wasn't it?" said Claire. "I do hope Simon retains a lot of this."

"He'll have to expunge the ghosts of Vale and Mrs Flannery first," said Missy, sounding a lot like Flo. "Where's the pic of Snowy? I want to see him as a young bloke. Can't picture it myself."

Alicia kept sweeping through the pages until she found one. It was captioned "Jack, Lydia and the children" and showed the couple standing by an old car, new then no doubt, the lodge out of focus behind them. There was a curly-haired girl at Lydia's knees and a smaller boy just inside the open vehicle, and standing stiffly beside him was a tall, skinny man with a mop of white hair.

Snowy.

He had a knitted vest on and a matching knitted flat cap, similar to the one Blake was wearing before he vanished. As his family beamed towards the camera, Lydia calling out something that could no longer be heard, Snowy was staring towards her, a bemused expression on his face.

"Lydia looks a lot younger than Snowy," said Claire.

"And a lot like Lynette," added Alicia. "No wonder he charmed her socks off."

"Whatever happened to Lydia and the kids?" asked Missy. "Do we know?"

"Hang on a minute," said Alicia, skimming through the text. "Says here that the Lyle children were all shipped off to Sydney soon after the fire. Something about boarding school..." She kept skimming. "Says nothing about the couple exactly, but check out this picture." She tapped a small photo of a woman waving a hand, the Sydney Opera House behind her. "That's Lydia." She turned the page and continued reading, then said, "Okay, so Lydia moved to Sydney's north shore... Oh no. Oh, that's interesting."

"What?" said Claire.

"Says nothing about Snowy, but it does say Lydia remarried in 1975 and had two more children." She stared at the others. "Maybe the stress of the fire killed the marriage?"

"Maybe that's when Snowy moved out and into the cabin," said Claire, tapping on a fresh image of Snowy, this time with a receding hairline and, beside him, a younger man who looked almost identical. "That's his brother Harry. Maybe Harry took over the lodge and Snowy tucked himself away, licking his wounds, after the fire and the loss of life and then the loss of his family."

"Pity he didn't *stay* tucked away," said Missy, glaring at the photo. "How did we even end up here, in a remote location with a crazy lunatic?"

They both turned their eyes to Claire.

"Hey, don't blame me! Alicia's the one who wanted to go somewhere isolated so we can all get to know each other better."

"Okay, I feel bad about that," said Alicia. "With our track record, I should have known better. Still, I wasn't the one who brought us to Snowy's doorstep. I'm sorry, Claire, but that one's on you. You were the one who chose

Lyle's Lodge, and you picked a doozy this time."

Claire was shaking her head. "Actually I didn't pick this place." She gasped and sat forward and repeated the phrase. "*I didn't pick this place!*"

"Who did?" asked Missy.

Claire paled and said, "Ronnie. The Lodge was all Ronnie's idea!"

~

"He's finally passed," said Ronnie, leaning back in the rocking chair, which creaked again beneath her like an ominous soundtrack. "It took a while, but we got there in the end."

Perry and Simon glanced at each other warily and then down to the body of old Snowy, coiled in the foetal position on the top of his covers, a plastic bucket beside him. Ronnie stood and made her way to a lamp and switched it on, the room now cast in a soft orange glow.

"He asked me not to touch anything," she said. "He's gone now, so I guess we can use the lights."

Simon shared another startled look with Perry. They could now clearly see a syringe on the bedside cabinet and a small glass vial that looked empty. And, behind all that, a silver-framed photo of a very pretty blonde whose giddy smile was still evident despite the smashed glass.

"What happened here, Ronnie?" Simon demanded.

"I found him like this," she replied.

"Dead on the bed?"

"No, but in the final throes." Her tone was so matter-of-fact, so casual, but she must have finally registered their shock because she tsked and said, more forcibly, "He was dying when I got here, of course." Again they shared a look, and now she was scowling. "For heaven's sake! I didn't do this if that's what you're thinking."

"What *exactly* happened?" Simon asked again, trying to

keep his tone level and nonaccusatory. If Ronnie was responsible for Snowy's death—and it certainly looked like it from his angle—he didn't want to set her off.

"The man injected himself with snake venom," she said, waving a hand towards the table.

"*Snake venom?*" said Perry, staggered.

"Yes, snake venom. Or at least that's what he said." She sighed heavily. Looked every one of her seventy-two years. "It's been a very long evening, and I am beat. Please, can we go back and I'll explain everything properly then?"

The two men shared yet another look as they followed her out of the cabin, careful to keep their distance and their torches ready as they trudged towards the lodge, their hearts heavy, their minds buzzing with questions.

~

"That doesn't make any sense, Claire," said Missy breezily, back in the library. "How could *Ronnie* have suggested Lyle's Lodge? She didn't even recognise the place until she was standing in the lobby."

"No, I'm being serious!" Claire was now on her feet and pacing. "It was an attachment on Ronnie's email. I'm sure of it. Oh my God!" She stopped and looked around. "This place was *all her idea*! I just clicked on the link, and that's the first I knew of it."

Alicia frowned and sat forward. "Start from the beginning, Claire. Tell us exactly what happened."

And so she did. Claire told of how she had written to Flo and Ronnie, courtesy of the Ladies Auxiliary in Balmain, on behalf of the book club. How she had asked the two ladies if they would like to sign up, and then attached her contact details at the bottom.

"I never mentioned Lyle's Lodge. I hadn't even heard of it at that point," she told them now. "All I said was that we were hoping to hold the first meeting somewhere cosy. Somewhere remote."

She stopped pacing and threw a hand to her lips. Her look of guilt mirrored Alicia's from earlier that day. "I didn't hear from them for a week and assumed they weren't interested, then I got an email from Ronnie accepting on both her and Flo's account."

"And you're sure it was Ronnie?"

"Yes, one hundred percent! She said Flo wasn't online and didn't do all that 'newfangled nonsense.' Anyway, attached to the email was the link to Lyle's Lodge, so I'd assumed she was recommending it; that's how I heard about it and looked it up. That's when I suggested it to you, Alicia, and you then booked us in."

"That doesn't make any sense," Missy said, repeating her earlier sentiment. "Ronnie definitely acted like she didn't remember the place before we arrived. Why would she recommend a place and then act like it's a lovely accident that she was here at all?"

Alicia was madly chewing her lower lip.

Why indeed?

Was Ronnie also hiding something? Had the book club been looking in the wrong place all along? Did all of this have less to do with luxury renovations and more to do with an old love affair between young Ronnie and a married man? A man with twinkling blue eyes and snowy-white hair?

~

"Snowy is dead," Ronnie said, loudly and slowly, as though giving them all a chance to digest the gruesome news.

They were all in the library now, all nursing a cup of creamy hot chocolate whipped up by Flo, with a dash of her "secret ingredient to settle your nerves"—nobody had the energy to ask—and it was delicious. But it wasn't settling anything.

They stared at Ronnie with a mixture of sadness,

concern and utter disbelief. There was also a lot of shock and distress in the mix.

"Poor Snowy," Lynette said at last. "The poor, poor man."

Somebody tsked at that, but Alicia wanted to know what had happened. "How on earth did he end up dead, Ronnie? How did you find him?"

Ronnie held a finger up and took a fortifying sip of her hot chocolate. She had already refused the stew, telling Lynette she did not have the stomach for it, but Lynette didn't take that personally. The woman looked ready to drop.

After another sip, Ronnie placed her cup down shakily and then cleared her throat. "I just went for a walk," she told them. "I just wanted to phone my nephews. My housekeeper's away and they're minding my cats. I... I just wanted to check in on them..." She shook her head, lost in her own thoughts suddenly.

"So you weren't visiting Snowy originally?" said Perry, moving her along.

"Of course not. I told you that. I barely knew the man. I met him for five minutes at a dance nearly fifty years ago. Which is why there's no way I killed him." Her eyes narrowed. "Because I know what you're all thinking, and you can jolly well think again!"

"Oh no, Ronnie, no we don't," said Flo, who was sitting beside her old friend, but Ronnie shook her off.

"Of course *you* don't think it, Florence. But the rest of them do!"

"I'm sorry," said Alicia, feeling guilty as charged. "It's been a stressful weekend, and we're all strung out. Please, tell us what happened next."

Ronnie nodded. "Fine." Nodded again. "I didn't even know Snowy was still around until Perry mentioned it, but even then I had no intention of looking in on him. I noticed his little cottage while I was chatting to Sebastian, my nephew, but it was only when Snowy started groaning…" She shuddered at the memory. "Such low, agonising groans. I thought it was a distressed animal at first…"

Ronnie stopped short and grappled for a handkerchief but couldn't seem to find one, so Missy jumped up to retrieve a box of tissues from a side table. Ronnie took one gladly and swiftly blew her nose, then continued on.

"Anyway, I told Sebastian I'd call him back and went to check it out. That's when I found the poor man, lying on his bed, thrashing about. Oh he looked quite shocking." She shifted in her seat. "He was in so much pain, so… much…" She sniffed again. "He begged me to stay with him. Begged me to hold his hand."

Missy helped herself to a tissue while Alicia asked, "Did he recognise you?"

"Why would he? Like I keep saying, we barely knew each other. No… he… he simply wanted someone to stay with him until the end, that's all. And so I did."

Ronnie shifted uncomfortably in her seat again, looking less like a competent nurse now and more like a battle-weary soldier. She had dark, heavy bags underneath her eyes, and her worry lines were like tram tracks across her face. Flo patted her hand gently, but she yanked it away and folded her arms, suddenly very defensive. She was clearly upset and not just from the experience. She was offended by their judgemental questions and horrified expressions, and Alicia didn't blame her, but what else could they think?

"And he'd injected himself with snake venom you say?" said Perry, also struggling to swallow it. "You're sure it was snake venom?"

"I told you, Perry, that's what he said!" Ronnie took a few deep breaths. "He was in a lot of pain and wasn't making a lot of sense, but it was pretty obvious what had gone down. I saw the needle by his bed. The vial that must have contained the poison. It's all still there if you want to check for yourself. But I have no reason to disbelieve him.

The way he died, the nausea, the pain..."

"How long would it have taken?" asked Simon more gently.

She shrugged. "Depends what kind of venom it was, I suppose. Some work faster than others. And if he'd been bitten before, which is highly possible living out there for so long, well he might have built up some immunity. But he had the exact same swelling on his arm as Vale."

She stopped and gave them a pointed look, and Lynette's eye widened.

"You think Snowy injected Vale with snake venom, don't you, Ronnie?"

She shrugged, her eyes sliding sideways.

"Did he *say* that?" Lynette persisted. "Did he say anything about hurting Vale and Mrs Flannery?"

Ronnie went to say something, then stopped, her eyelashes flickering furiously as though trying to decide how much to reveal. Then she folded her hands into her lap and took a deep breath and said, "Yes, actually. He did."

She swallowed hard as the others continued staring at her, lips wide. "Snowy confessed to everything. The murders, the fire. The whole kit and caboodle. He's the culprit."

"*Really?*" said Alicia, a little too loudly.

The others sat watching her, speechless.

"What exactly did he say, Ronnie?"

She shrugged like it didn't matter. "It was very difficult for him to talk, Alicia. He... he was in extreme pain. He just said something like, 'I killed the others and I started the fire, and now I want to die.'"

"Wow," said Missy, exhaling loudly. "I knew he was dodgy... but, well, wow. That means this thing is solved! We've done it!" She offered a jubilant smile, but no one was returning the smile.

Lynette, for one, could not get her head around it. "But... but did he say *why*? Did he give any *reason* for killing his two old friends?"

Ronnie shrugged. "Like I said, he was in so much pain. I didn't press him on it. I let him go. I really didn't want to know, and I'm not sure you do either."

Lynette frowned. Clearly, she did want to know, and so did Simon, his mind obviously galloping to his company and its culpability.

He sat forward, hands prayerlike in front of his lips, and said, "Was there any mention of the renovations at all? Of LLE? Of the plans for the escarpment?"

Ronnie looked at him blankly. "What? No... He never... No, nothing like that."

Simon exhaled and sat back, colour returning to his cheeks. They all suspected he was worried his company's DA had pushed the old man over the edge.

"What about the 1970 fire or the guy who died in it?" Lynette persisted, still staring hard at Ronnie. "I thought it might have had something to do with Donal—"

"No!" Ronnie's cheeks flared with colour. "Nothing to do with that either." She sighed wearily. "Look, there was obviously something else going on here that we know nothing about. It's over, folks. Can we let it go?"

"It's just—" began Lynette, but Ronnie had two palms out now, her eyes fiery.

"Stop!" she burst out, making several of them jump. She took a few steadying breaths. "Sorry. I'm sorry, but I'm exhausted and I can only tell you what the man said. He's gone now. It's done. It's over. We have our answers. Please, can we just have one peaceful night?"

"Of course, Ronnie," said Simon, giving Lynette a firm look as the older woman struggled to her feet.

"Are you okay, Ron?" asked Flo, a wrinkled hand reaching out, but Ronnie simply slapped it away and hobbled out of the room, leaving them now with a mixture of sadness, weariness and regret.

But this time there was also considerable doubt swirling in the mix.

CHAPTER 18

A very soft pitter-patter caught the group by surprise, and several of them jumped up and ran to the windows to find it was gently raining.

"At last!" said Missy.

"Such a relief," said Claire.

"We're going to need more than drizzle if we want to douse that fire," was Perry's offering.

"Don't look a gift horse in the mouth, young man," snapped Flo, struggling to her feet. "I'm off to bed too. I'm sorry it's been such a dreadful weekend. Good night, folks."

Lynette jumped up and helped her out while the others remained in the library, some heading for the sink to get the kettle boiling, some foraging through the fridge.

And Alicia remained on the couch, as confused as she'd ever been. Like Lynette, she was trying hard to digest what Ronnie had said. She knew she should be relieved. It had all been tied up very nicely. Well, not *nicely* exactly, but they had their confession.

So why wasn't she feeling any comfort? Any closure?

The fact remained, despite what Ronnie had said and what she, herself, had accused Snowy of just hours earlier, Alicia was still struggling to think of him as a killer. And she certainly hadn't picked him as suicidal.

The few times she had spoken to Snowy, he seemed resigned to his fate—like he was sitting on his perch, waiting for Mother Nature to give him her best shot. But he didn't sound like he was going to help her along.

And not in such a brutal, drawn-out way. Snake venom seemed a bizarre choice too, considering his beloved escarpment was just metres from his door. Why not simply step off the cliff and be done with it?

And why do it *now*? With all of them so close and constantly loitering on the escarpment, checking their phones?

"Aren't you relieved?" said Claire, catching Alicia's burgeoning frown as she handed her a fresh cup of peppermint. "The killer is gone and the rain is coming. All our prayers have been answered."

Alicia took the tea and smudged her lips into a smile. Yet she didn't feel relieved. She felt like they had been lured into somebody else's nightmare and been spat out the other side. It made absolutely no sense to her. She couldn't help wondering why it happened now, this weekend. It all felt so random. Whatever Snowy's issues with Vale and Mr Flannery, why sneak in and do it with guests at the lodge? Was he using them as a diversion, trying to pin it on a group of strangers? If so, why would he then confess to everything on his deathbed?

Alicia sat forward. *Hang on a minute.* They weren't strangers, at least not all of them were. And the choice of the weekend wasn't random either.

She dropped her cup to the table and got to her feet. "Our prayers might be answered," she told Claire, "but not all the questions have been. Not yet."

Then she turned and dashed out of the library.

~

Ronnie was swinging her door shut when Alicia caught up to her, and she shook her head and said, "Please, Alicia, I'm dead on my feet."

"I know, Ronnie, I'm sorry. I just have one question that needs answering."

The older woman groaned dramatically but waved her

in, then closed the door behind them, and for a moment Alicia wondered if she had just locked herself in with a killer. But she couldn't think about that now. She needed the truth, and the only truth she knew was that Ronnie was lying and had been lying long before they got on the train to Lyleton.

As the older woman dropped onto her bed and began pulling off her shoes, Alicia took the chair by the desk and gave her a moment to catch her breath.

Then she echoed Missy's earlier question. "How did we end up here, Ronnie? How did we end up coming to this particular lodge at this particular time?"

Ronnie misunderstood and said, "Yes, it was bad luck wasn't it."

"Or was it?" said Alicia, causing the older woman to look up. "Claire said you were the one who suggested Lyle's. It was all your idea."

Ronnie looked suddenly flummoxed. "Oh, I don't think so, dear. I hadn't even heard of the place until I got the official invitation, and even then I didn't recognise the name. Like I said, I knew it as the Hunting Lodge. I only recognised the place when we got here."

Or so you say, Alicia thought. "Claire got an email from you, Ronnie. You included an online link to Lyle's Rainforest Lodge."

"Did I?" She bat her eyelids, looking for the first time since they'd met, like a dotty old lady, and Alicia wasn't buying it.

"What's going on, Ronnie? Anything you want to tell me? Does this have something to do with you and Snowy? Was he the one you had an affair with? Is that why it's all come to a head now?"

Ronnie stared at her then with genuine surprise. Then she shook her head and started peeling off her socks. Alicia wondered if she was taking a moment to concoct a fresh lie.

Eventually Ronnie said, "I honestly don't recall adding

any link to my email, but if you say I did, then I must have. I forgot about it, that's all. I told you my memory was shot."

She rolled the socks up while Alicia tried hard not to roll her eyes. It was so clearly another lie.

"I know there's something you're not telling us," Alicia persisted. "I don't believe Snowy just randomly killed his two devoted employees, then shot himself up with poison."

Ronnie had reached for a large tub of moisturiser and was now lathering it up and down her arms, so Alicia forged on.

"Did you bring us here so you could reunite with old Snowy? And did it all go terribly wrong?"

Ronnie stopped lathering and almost smiled. "How many times do I have to tell you all? I met the man briefly, a long time ago."

"You told Perry you had an affair with an unavailable man—"

"Yes! A tryst with a married man called Dieter something-or-other. A dashing Dutch man if you must know. I was newly engaged to Bert then, and I really should not have done it. Wasn't my finest hour. But it meant so little I can barely remember his name! Really Alicia, you're holding on to that connection far too tightly. I was here for one weekend! What possible reason would I have to drag us all up here and start killing people?"

"I'm not saying—"

"Of course you are!" Ronnie's voice was now full of thunder. "I can see you don't believe me, and quite frankly, I'm just too tired to care. Believe what you want. I had nothing to do with Snowy's death, other than holding his hand and helping him through it. I would not wish that on any living creature, and I'm frankly offended that you'd suggest it."

"Ronnie—"

She smacked the tub back on the bedside table,

stopping Alicia in her tracks. "Everything I have done here, all weekend, has been about protecting the book club. I'm desperately sorry that Snowy felt he had no choice, and I'm furious that it even came to that. But there's nothing any of us can do about it now. Nothing! Do you hear me? We have to try to put it behind us and move on."

It felt like a warning to Alicia, some kind of veiled threat, but Ronnie wasn't finished. "Please Alicia," she said more gently now. "Just focus on the fact that it's over. The RFS will break through tomorrow, and we will all get out alive. Now, if you'll excuse me." She exhaled loudly. "It's been an extremely distressing evening, and I would like to be left alone. I am completely and utterly drained."

Alicia nodded, feeling chastened, and stood up.

She didn't know what to say. She wanted to tell Ronnie she was sorry, wanted to assure her that she didn't suspect her, but all the signs pointed her way. Ronnie had a nursing background, was the only one who would know how to administer poison or even how to find some. She was also the only one with a connection to this place, the very person who had lured them here, the one who was still clearly lying about that.

Alicia opened the door and stepped out, was about to close it when Ronnie said something so softly she barely heard it: "One day you'll forgive me..."

When Alicia turned back, the woman was snoring.

~

Simon found Claire standing on the edge of the driveway, arms wrapped tightly around herself, looking out at the smoky view. Or what you could see of it because it was such a dark night.

"Are you okay?" he asked, and she nodded, looking upwards now.

"The rain has stopped."

"Don't worry. It will start up again. More is expected very early in the morning." He stepped closer. "I'm so sorry I lied to you."

Claire shook her head. "I'm not exactly an innocent in all this."

"About that... When are you going to tell the others?"

She stiffened. "I don't know."

"They'll forgive you. They forgave me and I'm practically a stranger."

"It's precisely *because* you're a stranger that they forgave you, Simon. I'm not sure how they'll feel when I tell them I've been lying to them all and doing it from the start. That I manipulated everything."

"It wasn't manipulation, Claire—"

"It was selfish and it was greedy." She sighed and stared at the view again.

"Do you hate this place now?" he said, not wanting to hear the answer.

"Oh no," she replied, reaching out to him. "I love it now more than ever."

~

Alicia was walking past Blake's room, deep in thought, when she heard a very soft, scuttling sound coming from inside. Her heart lurched as her stomach dropped to the ground.

Was the tabloid journalist still alive? Had he been hiding out in his room all this time?

Realising the door was slightly ajar, she gently pushed it forward, reluctantly peeking in. The first thing she noticed was how tidy it was. No more dirty clothes strewn about the place. Then she glanced across to the desk and saw someone sitting there, shuffling through some papers.

"Jesus, Lynny!" Alicia said, stepping inside and pulling the door closed behind them. "You gave me a heart attack! I thought the prodigal journalist had returned."

Lynette looked up. "Sorry. No, it's just li'l ole me. I wanted to get a head start on the packing tomorrow. I'm going with the positive angle that we're all about to be rescued. Thought I'd put Blake's stuff into his bag for him. I don't know if he's alive or..." She let that dangle. "Somebody's got to clean up this mess."

Alicia nodded and sat on the edge of his bed. "Are you okay?"

Lynette shrugged. "Yeah, I'm fine. It's just..." She glanced around the room and then back at her sister. "Did Ronnie's story sound a little *odd* to you? Snowy's confession a little too good to be true? I mean, I only met the guy briefly, but he didn't strike me as suicidal."

"We can't always tell..."

"Yeah but here's the thing—this place was empty last week. I checked the guest book earlier. Not one single booking from what I could see. Why not kill Vale and Flannery then, when you had free run of the place? Why do it with all of us here? And if he was trying to incriminate us, why confess to Ronnie?"

Alicia smiled widely. "That's *exactly* what I was thinking, Lynny. Something definitely doesn't add up."

This is what Alicia loved most about her sister. They were always on the same page. Or at least they used to be. She noticed the pad in Lynette's hands and asked, "So what have you got there?"

Lynette looked down and back. "Not sure to be honest. I can't help wondering if there's more to it all than Ronnie's saying." She frowned. "I'm not saying Ronnie's lying, exactly, but maybe Snowy was. Maybe..."

She stopped and looked at Alicia again, her eyes impeaching. "I know Blake was a rotten egg. I know he used us, appallingly. I know all of that. But I also know he was onto something here, sis. That night we shared a drink at the bar, he said he was on the cusp of something big. Something that was going to turn his career around. I didn't know what he meant at the time, but I think it all

211

comes back to Donal Murphy."

Lynette's eyes narrowed. "Notice how defensive Ronnie got when I even mentioned the name Donal? She started blushing, I'm sure of it. You can't fake that."

Alicia nodded. Yes, she had noticed.

Lynette said, "I think Blake found out something important about Donal, and I think it's in here amongst his stuff." She tapped the notepad on the desk. Scowled again. "Problem is his notes are all in some kind of hieroglyphics. I can barely understand a word of it."

"Show me," said Alicia, reaching for the pad. She glanced across the page, and then the next. "Oh, it's shorthand. I studied a bit at journalism school but never needed to use it. I wonder if I can still remember..."

Lynette stood up and stretched her arms high. "While you do that, I'll finish the packing." She made her way across to the bathroom and after a few minutes, called out, "He had good taste in aftershave, I'll give him that."

But Alicia wasn't listening. Her head was spinning with what she was translating.

"What is it?" Lynette asked, returning to the main room, a bottle of Hugo Boss Eau de Toilette in one hand.

Alicia looked up. "It's what you thought; it's his notes on Donal Murphy."

"What does it say?"

Alicia glanced down again and tapped a finger on the pad. "According to this, or what I can make of this—my shorthand is very rusty—Donal had an affair with somebody while he was here, and I'm pretty sure the name Blake has written down is Lydia."

Lynette's eyes widened, and she sat down beside her sister. "Lydia Lyle? The owner's wife?"

"*Snowy's* wife," Alicia pointed out. "There's some other stuff here, says something about hunting trips and there's a series of dates..." She continued scanning. "Three dates in 1968 and two in 1970, the year of the fire."

She turned the page and peered at Blake's handwriting.

"He's written down the name Tom something. O'Brien maybe?" She looked at Lynette, who shrugged, looked back again. "Okay, well, there's a sentence in quotation marks, so I'm assuming it's a quote from this Tom guy. It says, 'Lydia and Donal were at it like... ravetts."

"Ravetts?"

Alicia peered more closely. "Rabbits!" She smiled. "They were at it like rabbits. Oooh, that's not good. Then it says..." She stopped and squinted. "It says, 'Snowy worshipped his wife. The truth... would have... destroyed him. If he found out, he would have been...' Um, what is that word? Devastated? I think it says devastated." Alicia looked up. "Blake has underlined the word *if*."

"So it doesn't say if Snowy did find out?"

Alicia shrugged as she turned the pages. "Okay, so Snowy's wife was unfaithful. That's not exactly surprising. Judging from the photos, there was a good twenty years between them. I mean, Snowy was a handsome chap, but Lydia was in another league entirely."

"So was Donal Murphy," said Lynette, dumping the aftershave and pulling a headshot from the file.

It showed a man with a mop of light curls, his face clearly sunburned, his eyes bright and lively. They could only see the top of his shoulders, but it was clear they were broad and tanned. If he were alive today, he could've modelled for Hugo Boss.

"Oh yeah, he's gorgeous," said Alicia. "And young. Looks barely out of his teens."

Lynette nodded. "He was also the hunky hunter, remember? That would have been hard to resist, especially if the boring old hubby was busy running the lodge, and didn't Perry say something about Snowy also being the town mayor? While the cat's away..." She raised her eyebrows. "Perhaps those dates Blake noted are when Lydia and Donal hooked up—the hunting weekends,

213

except they did more than hunt."

Her eyebrows dropped back. "Do you think Snowy knew? Caught them at it or something?"

Alicia shrugged. "Maybe? He certainly didn't like the fellow, or that's what it seemed like to me. I think the bigger question is, what would he have done if he did find out? And why has it all come to a head now, after all these years? Did Blake stir things up, asking lots of questions? Maybe he found where Snowy was living, like we did, and interrogated him, bringing up bad memories?"

Lynette considered that. "Still doesn't explain why he'd kill Vale and Mrs Flannery. And why set the mountain alight?"

"Maybe he was angry at how life had turned out? Looks like Snowy's marriage fell apart after the fire. Lydia left the mountain, so did the kids, and we can only assume that's when Snowy dropped out of society, moved into the cabin…"

Alicia's head began spinning, and it had nothing to do with her tiredness. She felt like the answer was within reach; she just couldn't quite grasp it.

Donal Murphy was clearly the "arrogant blighter" Snowy took him to be. He came up to run the hunting weekends and helped himself to his boss's wife while he was at it. Or at least that's what Blake's witness claimed. So how did Donal end up fighting the Great Fire? How did he end up dead when everybody else survived? And why was it all coming to a head now?

Snowy's final words to her suddenly danced before her eyes.

"History is rushing towards me, and it's time for some atonement."

Alicia gasped. "What if Snowy killed Donal?"

"What?"

"What if the fire was a ruse to cover up what had really happened. Maybe Snowy caught Donal in bed with Lydia and killed him, then buried him near the escarpment?

That's why it's come to a head now and why he can't stick around for the renovation, because they'll unearth Donal's corpse!"

Lynette was shaking her head and reaching for one of the files. "I love that theory, sis, really I do. But I'm pretty sure there's an article in here somewhere about Donal's body being recovered and returned to his hometown." She began flicking through it. "There was a funeral, a bit of a ceremony…"

As she continued trawling the file, Alicia wasn't about to be deterred. "Okay, doesn't mean Snowy didn't kill Donal though, then plant his body in the fire. Maybe Blake discovered the truth and was threatening to write an article, bring it all back up, all in time for the fiftieth anniversary. *That's* why Snowy killed himself now, with all of us here. He had to do it before the story broke. For all Snowy knew, Blake was back in Sydney, writing the whole thing. Maybe Vale and Flannery knew the truth so he had to kill them too?"

Alicia sat back and groaned. Nah, that didn't make any sense. That's the part she kept stumbling over—why Snowy would want to kill two people he had lived with for decades and trusted his secrets to.

"Maybe Blake offered Vale and Flannery a wad of cash for the tell-all?" Alicia continued thinking aloud, then groaned again. "Seems like a lot of killing to keep a fifty-year-old secret, especially one that probably can't be proven after all this time. Especially if Donal's body is now a box of bones back at home. Where is his home, does it say?"

Lynette was not listening, she was staring at an article with a small picture attached. "Check this out, Alicia. According to this news report, Donal had a bunch of sisters." She looked up at Alicia. "Do you think *Ronnie* might be Donal's sister? Do you think that's why she dragged us up here, to wreak revenge on the man who killed her brother?"

Alicia paled. This was starting to make more sense…

As Lynette kept reading the article, Alicia looked around and then back. "Is there an A4 envelope in there? It's got the words Family History across the front."

"Um… don't think so," Lynette replied vaguely. "I shoved some of it in the side pocket of his bag." She waved a hand as she continued reading.

Alicia dashed across and began rifling through Blake's bag until she found the envelope she had been looking at the first time she was in there—the Murphy family tree. She had forgotten all about that. Thrusting her hand inside, she reached for the piece of paper she'd spotted earlier with the names Eamon Joseph Murphy and Mary Louise O'Connor typed at the top. Underneath that was a branch that revealed the names of Eamon and Mary's six children—five daughters and one son.

One name had been circled in scratchy red ink, and it wasn't Donal's.

As Alicia stared at the name, her breath catching, her mind doing somersaults, Lynette was staring at a grainy black-and-white image of a group of black-clad women huddled around an open plot. Lynette counted the women and felt a trickle of ice run through her veins, then gasped as she read the name of Donal's hometown.

Both sisters turned to each other at the same time, eyes wide, lips speechless.

Then Lynette smacked the article to the table and said, "The dirty rotten liar."

CHAPTER 19

Lynette hesitated at the door to the library, Alicia just behind her. They had already agreed that Lynette would do the talking. She needed that, she'd told Alicia. She needed to prove she had the mettle—as much to herself as to her sister. But most of all she needed to do it because she was the one who had been led up the garden path and fed the most lies.

"Just stay detached and don't get too emotional," Alicia told her. That was another trick she had learned at journalism school, but it was also a lesson they might have taken from Miss Marple and Inspector Poirot.

They gave each other a comforting nod, then strode into the room to the leather couch where someone was bent over, poring through a thin white book with the words *Lyle Family Dynasty* across the front, a knitting bag beside her.

"Hello, Flo," said Lynette. "Mind if we join you?"

The elderly lady looked up at them, surprised. "Oh! Hello girls!"

Then, reading their expressions, which were now hard and a little nervous, she smiled and said, "Ah, so you've come for the grand denouement!"

"Something like that," said Lynette. But she wasn't smiling. She pointed at the book in Flo's hands. "Perry found that in the fiction section. Seems appropriate considering all the lies that have been swirling around this place."

The older woman's smile deflated. "Yes, well,

they started it. It's disgraceful, really, how little they mention Donal. Quite shocking. My brother gave his life for this place, and he barely rates a sentence. Tea, ladies?"

Now they both looked surprised, and she chuckled. "The kettle's just boiled, and I have a feeling it's going to be a long night. You might as well get comfortable. Get yourselves a pot. There's a lovely chamomile over there, Alicia. Might help with your insomnia."

"I'm fine," Alicia replied, swapping a frown with Lynette.

"Rightio then." Flo reached for her cup. "Now, you've come to ask why I did it. What could the old biddy possibly be thinking?" She swept her eyes to them and they both stared back, trying not to flinch. She shrugged. "I was thinking of my brother, of course. It's always been about Donnie."

Then she took a sip from her teacup and exhaled like the conversation was over.

The sisters glanced at each other again, then sat down, side by side, on the lounge across from Flo. Lynette took a deep breath and said, "You never got over your brother's death, did you Flo?"

"His *murder!*" Flo corrected, a spindly finger high. "And no, I did not get over it, as you so eloquently put it—like it's some speed bump I can just drive across. But I did move on, dear. I did try to do that. It was a struggle, of course. He was my baby brother. The heart of our family. The only son—"

Her voice choked on the final word, and she frowned as she cleared her throat, annoyed by her own emotion. "I didn't think I would survive at first. But you know what kept me going? The *only* thing that kept me going?" She dropped her eyes to the book. "The thought that Donnie had died trying to save others. That he'd gone out in a blaze of glory. That he would forever be remembered as a hero. Yet here they are, dousing his memory, like he never even existed." Her eyes narrowed as she looked up.

"Why would they do that, do you think?"

"Because he was having an affair with Snowy's wife?" Lynette offered as the woman's eyes hardened.

"But that's all it was, just an *affair*! A bit of silly nonsense! You think he deserved to die for that?"

"Not at all," Lynette said, placing a conciliatory palm up. "But I don't think Vale and Mrs Flannery deserved to die either."

"Ah, well, that's where we disagree." Flo drew her lips downward and crossed her arms. "I never intended any of it, you know. Not at first anyway."

The two sisters shared a sceptical look, and she caught it, shaking her head.

"It's true. I simply planted the idea of coming here, and you're the ones who ran with it."

Like it was all their fault.

Lynette bristled at the comment and was about to argue the point, but Alicia took her hand and gave it a squeeze. She had witnessed several confessions now and knew there was only one way to get to the truth. They had to stay calm and let the suspect keep talking. She also had a question of her own, one that Ronnie hadn't properly answered.

Alicia said, "You slipped the link to Lyle's Lodge at the bottom of Ronnie's email to us, didn't you Flo? Ronnie said she hadn't done it, then pretended she must have forgotten. But she was covering for you, wasn't she? How long has she been protecting you?"

Flo blew some air through her lips like it didn't matter. "Ronnie thinks she's the only switched-on oldie, like the rest of us are a bit dim. So I played along. I liked the distance it gave me. I let her agree to the weekend, then said I wanted to check her email before she sent it—it was on my behalf, so she agreed. Then, when she wasn't looking, I added the link and pressed Send before she noticed. You lot did the rest. It was really quite a dream! The way you booked it all in. Really, quite amazing."

"What if we hadn't? What if we had suggested somewhere else?"

"Then none of this would have happened, dear."

Again, Flo appeared to be blaming them, and now Alicia felt herself bristle, and the older woman smiled.

"Oh don't get your knickers in a knot, girls. That's how life turns, you see—on a dime. One stroke of good luck is another person's misfortune. Nothing anyone can do about that."

"Your brother learnt that the hard way," Lynette said, calmer now, and Flo nodded. "So you used us to come up here and wreak revenge?"

"Oh I never meant to kill anybody. That wasn't my plan at all! I just wanted one last adventure, and Claire's letter suggested you were thinking of going somewhere isolated. I immediately thought of the Hunting Lodge."

Her eyes danced around the room then. "Donal used to love this place. We all thought he came up to show off his shooting skills—he was quite the drawcard. Got a bronze medal in the Commonwealth Games, did you know that? No, of course you didn't know that."

She flashed a scowl at the book again. "His whole story has been expunged. Like he never existed. But yes, they invited him here regularly to lead the hunts, show the city folk a thing or two. Turns out he also came for some *tart*."

She spat that last word out like it was poison, then drew her lips back into a smile. "I've always wanted to visit here, see what all the fuss was about, but I never had the courage, probably never would have if it was just me. But to come with a book club, well, that seemed like a beaut idea. I wanted one last chance to say goodbye, that's all it was."

Lynette was growing increasingly impatient with the woman's nonchalant attitude. "I'm sorry, Flo," she said, "but I don't believe you. You brought poison and a syringe with you. You knew exactly what you were doing. You were out for blood from the start."

"Oh, that wasn't for *them*! That was for me."

"You?"

"I wasn't lying to you about that, Lynette. I am on my way out, and I really didn't want to spend it knocked out on morphine in some drab hospital. No, thank you."

"You're not moving into aged care, are you?"

"Aged care? Over my dead body! In fact, that was my plan. I had no intention of leaving Lyle's. I wanted to join my brother, that's all it was at first." She reached for her cup of tea and held it to her lips as she stared out the dark window, seeing only her pitiful reflection. "I always felt so bad that Donnie's spirit was stuck up here, all alone, out there."

She sipped and placed the cup back. Folded her arms again.

"They found his body down from the track we walked the first day, did you know that? Did you find that amongst Blake's notes? It took them a week to find him. A whole week! And he was so close all along. We tell people Donal died when a tree branch broke his back, a widow maker, and that's true. He was killed by a falling branch. But it didn't happen in Gulargambone. It happened up here. A burning branch fell on him while he was fighting the fire. *Their* fire, the one he should not have been fighting!"

She sat forward and plucked a tissue from the box Missy had placed there earlier. Gave her nose an irritated blow. "They shipped Donal's body back to us, the Lyles, with barely a note of apology, and we buried him on the property, but that's not him down there, not really. I've seen enough carcasses in my time to know that. It's just empty bones."

She waved the tissue towards the dark forest outside. "*This* is where Donnie took his final breath, *this* is where his spirit lives, and I wanted to take my final breath here too. Reunite our spirits. Keep him company after all this time. That's why I went for that walk with you the first day, girls. I was scouting for a lovely spot to die."

The words were quite shocking, and Alicia shivered deeply, remembering how worried she had been about snakes and the rock fall and of Flo getting hurt. Perhaps if she had not rescued the woman, none of this would have happened.

Lynette said, "So what made you change your mind?"

"Insomnia my dear, and good old-fashioned luck." She smiled, but it was ugly now. "It was just as I told you all. I was wide awake that first night. While you were in the bar, flirting with that silly Blake fellow, I was on my balcony, thinking of Donnie, like I often do. That's when I noticed Vale trotting off with his silly bag, up the forbidden track. That made me curious. I had no idea Snowy was up there! Like everyone, I assumed he'd cleared off years ago. It wasn't until Vale returned that I found out the truth. Or, rather, Blake did."

Her eyebrows lifted, gleefully. "You went to bed, Lynette, but Blake was still loitering in the lobby, snooping about on the computer. I didn't know what he was up to, so I loitered too. But I'm better at it, dear. He never even knew I was there. Like a shadow in the wind…"

She grinned. So proud of herself. "I heard Vale come back, and the two men began talking. Arguing, really. Blake was hammering Vale with questions about the fire, and I realised he must be a journalist, but Vale already knew because that's when he let the cat out of the bag, the foolish chap." She cackled softly. "Vale said he'd just warned Snowy that the press was loitering and to keep his mouth shut. I'd seen him go up Repentance Way and so had Blake, so we both put two and two together. Snowy must be up there!"

She cackled again, like it was all a lark. "Oh you should have seen the look on Vale's face! He'd effectively handed Snowy over to that snake. Because he was a snake, Lynette. A slippery, slimy snake."

Lynette took a deep breath this time. She wasn't going

to take the bait. They still had so many questions to get through. "What happened next?"

"Vale told Blake to clear out, but Blake wasn't having it. He said he had a witness who was willing to testify to the fact that, back in 1970, the eminent Mr Jack Lyle had marched my brother off to his death."

She stared at Lynette, almost daring her to dispute it, but Lynette just waved her on.

"While everyone else was urged to stay safely in the lodge, Jack led my baby brother out to the burning forest and told him to get on with it. It was as good as a death sentence. Indeed that's exactly what it turned out to be."

Her eyes were wet with tears now, and she swiped them angrily, like she'd had enough crying for one lifetime. "Truth is, girls, it wasn't that much of a surprise. The rumours at the time were rife. But I never let my mind go there, not really. I hung on to the fact that the Lyles were better than that, and my brother had died a *hero*."

Her eyes turned to the thin volume again. "It also helped knowing that the Lyles had struggled afterwards too. I heard that Lydia had left Jack and he'd handed the lodge to his brother or something like that... But to discover that he was still *here*, enjoying this mountain, occupying *my* brother's sacred space? Well, that was very disappointing!"

She slapped a shrewd look at Lynette then. "He might have been a snake, your lad, but he was also smart, I'll give him that. If it wasn't for him, I never would have twigged. I would have died quietly here and joined my brother while Snowy continued to live on, enjoying this lovely place, free of any penance."

"He had to pay," said Lynette, and she nodded. "And the others?"

"They were just as guilty my dear. Feeding him and covering for him. Enabling a murderer. They deserved a death sentence too."

Two people were killed because they fed a man some food?

223

Lynette didn't have a response for that. The woman was a monster. A cold, heartless monster. Sensing her growing distress, Alicia gave her sister's hand another squeeze, and Lynette looked back at her and nodded, so she took up the interrogation.

"You poisoned Vale first," Alicia said. "How did you do it, Flo?"

"Oh, it's your turn now is it, dear?" Flo said to Alicia, her eyes twinkling with mischief.

She was enjoying the interrogation, that much was obvious. But the constant, irritating appearance of tears told them it wasn't all fun and games. No matter how much Flo cackled and teased, how much she had enjoyed enacting her revenge, the subject matter was still red raw and her beloved brother was still six feet under.

"How did you do it?" Alicia asked again.

"Quite simple, really. I waited until Vale was asleep. He's a man, he's old, he'd just done that walk. I knew he'd sleep like a log. No guilty conscience on that one. I'd already seen him return upstairs. I just hoped he didn't lock his door, and I got lucky there. Another dime falling in my favour. I waited another hour, and then I slipped in."

She smiled serenely. "Vale's arm was so perfect, like he was inviting me to do it." She indicated with her own arm, holding it out with the veins in her elbow showing. "I had pre-prepared the syringe, so I gave him the shot and returned to bed."

"It was snake venom?"

"Ronnie's right about that. It's the venom from an inland taipan. One of the most venomous snakes in the world. Very potent. You have to remember, it was originally meant for me. I didn't want to drag my own death out. His wasn't dragged out either, more's the pity. It would have been over in less than an hour."

"He was violently sick, Flo. It would have been a horrendous hour," Alicia said, trying to keep her own emotions in check and wondering now why Mrs Flannery didn't hear his moans. The hard timber walls—all that lovely green gold—must have muffled the sound.

Later they would learn she had taken two sleeping pills that night, and he never stood a chance.

"His pain was trifling compared to the horrendous death of my brother," Flo was saying, "all alone out there in the burning forest, don't you think?" Her eyes were rheumy and bloodshot. "They told us he died instantly, but how do we know that?"

She stopped, gasped, her voice catching. "How do we know he didn't endure horrific… excruciating… agony before he… before he…"

Flo reached a hand to her eyes to swipe at them again, and the two sisters felt their first stab of sympathy, but Alicia, for one, refused to give in to it. She needed to keep on track.

"What about Mrs Flannery?" she demanded.

Flo coughed, clearing the lump in her throat. "Oh her room was locked, that was a damn nuisance! As I say, the dime doesn't always fall where it should. But I heard what she said to Blake over dinner, how *disgusting* she had been about my brother; like *he* was little more than a bad news story. A smirch on the great Lyle dynasty. I couldn't let that drop."

"Oh, Flo," Lynette said, heart plummeting again, no longer able to hold it back. "It was just a throwaway line!"

"It was my *brother* they threw away!" she spat back, the tears now streaming freely down her crepey cheeks. "Sending him to his death and then acting like he was nothing!"

"But she wasn't even here back then, she—"

"She cooked that bastard hearty meals every day for decades. That's more than my Donnie ever got! She probably did his washing, darned his socks! She cared for him, and she deserved everything she got!"

"Okay, okay," said Alicia, trying to get the emotion

back in check. "So Mrs Flannery went down to the cellar after breakfast, yes? Went to see if there was any cooking wine, is that right?"

Alicia remembered the shopping list on the kitchen bench, the empty wine bottle beside it. Mrs Flannery was probably checking supplies before heading back to Lyleton.

Flo shrugged like it didn't matter. "I have no idea why she was down there, but I wasn't going to miss my chance. I'm not even sure she saw it coming. I got to the bottom of the stairs, picked up the nearest bottle, and I bopped her over the head with it." She smiled weakly. "Ronnie's right about that too. It's not so hard if you get the swing right."

Alicia and Lynette felt sick to their stomachs, especially for the dear old cook. Snowy might have been culpable, maybe even Vale, but they were certain Mrs Flannery deserved none of it, but now was not the time to press the point.

Lynette cleared her throat and took over again. "So you drove Mrs Flannery's van away to make it look like she'd left the premises. That was quite a risk, Flo. Perry could have spotted you if he'd looked a little closer."

"Ah, but I knew he wouldn't, see? I had that in my favour." She cackled, making Lynette frown. "Oh, you're still young and pretty, dear, but you'll learn soon enough." She glanced at Alicia. "Perhaps you're already learning, love. Women of a certain age are entirely invisible to most people, certainly to men. Even men with silly earrings like *Perry*."

She spat out his name like she thought he was vermin. "I found the car keys in the woman's handbag, up on her bed. I grabbed her hat, just in case I needed it. If anyone did see me, all they would have registered was an old biddy behind the wheel with a floppy hat on."

She took another sip of her tea, and now Alicia wished she had stopped to get one. She felt drained by all of this.

She couldn't imagine how exhausting it was for the sickly woman sitting in front of her. Perhaps Flo was still buzzing from the adrenaline that came with revenge?

Flo said, "So, yes, I snuck off before book club. Drove the van down to the main road and looked for a place to dump it. That's when I spotted the old fire trail, leading in two directions, downwards and back up towards the western side of the lodge. I had to ram through an old gate to access it of course. Left a mighty great dent in the bumper bar I'm afraid, but they can always charge my room for it."

She winked and Lynette frowned back. The woman was making jokes? *Really?*

"That must be the paper road Snowy told me about," Alicia said.

Flo shrugged. "It was very overgrown, but I managed to get through and back up, parked under some bushes and found myself just behind the kitchen. That really was a spot of good luck!"

Lynette sat forward. "So that's how you discovered the herb garden."

"Yes! And a lovely garden it is. I had a little dig about, then I joined you all as book club started. It all worked out very neatly. Agatha Christie would be most impressed."

She cackled again, but Alicia was still confused.

"Why start the fire? What was that about?"

"I didn't, dear. At least not the first fire, the one that took the phone lines out. That was jolly good luck too! I noticed it when I took off in the van the first time. It was all the way down the ridge, just outside Lyleton, but it was small and I didn't think too much of it to be honest. I figured someone was back-burning."

"Again, Flo, I'm struggling to believe all these 'happy' coincidences," said Alicia.

"Believe what you like. It's all true. No reason to lie now. I did not start the original fire, but it did give me a top idea. You see, after you all found Vale's body,

227

and Blake announced he was driving into town, well, I knew I had to act. I hadn't got to Snowy yet! If Vale and Mrs Flannery had to pay, so did that man. No two ways about it!"

"Oh, so you set the second fire, down at Cooper's Creek?" said Lynette. "To buy yourself more time. You retrieved the lodge van and followed Blake down after he left."

"Got it in one, dear. See, I said you were smart! You have to trust yourself more, Lynny. And Blake should have kept his mouth shut. I wouldn't have followed him if he hadn't been so smug. He said he would be back with the cavalry, and I knew exactly what he meant by that. He looked straight at me when he said it. I think he'd already worked out who I was and he was bringing the police back."

Lynette nodded. "He had your family history amongst his stuff, and I think he used the reception computer to look you up on Ancestry.com that night."

"Did he now? Well, isn't he a clever clogs! In any case, I wasn't ready to hand myself over just yet. I needed more time, you see, a chance to walk up Repentance Way, confront that murdering bastard. But you!" She glowered at Alicia. "You couldn't keep off that dreaded path. I wondered why you didn't set up camp there, you were there so much!"

Alicia balked at that, almost apologising, but she couldn't get past the fact that the van was at the lodge all along. "Where is it now? The van?" she asked.

"Back in the bushes, behind the kitchen, where I left it. I can't believe none of you have found it yet. Really you're not as capable as you think you are."

Lynette gave her an eye roll for that comment, but Alicia couldn't help but feel impressed. The woman really was extraordinary. She was right; they had all underestimated her at their own peril. They had all looked straight through her, as if she were invisible—incapable of doing anything more than knitting beanies and reminiscing about the past.

Even when Lynette and Missy suggested Flo could be a possible suspect, none of them had taken it at all seriously, none of them thought she was up to it. In their own way, they had all been a little ageist.

"So," continued Flo, "after you found Vale, while the rest of you were scurrying about out the front, I snuck out through the kitchen, returned to the van and followed Blake down the mountain. He was well ahead of me of course, well past Cooper's Crossing when I got to it, so I stopped there and started another fire." She winked. "I trained as a firie back in Gulargambone, I did tell you all that, yes? I can get a rip-roaring fire going with nothing but a bit of bark and some dry twigs."

Lynette was gasping now. "Blake is missing, Flo! He's probably been burned alive down there in your *rip-roaring* fire!"

Flo offered her first look of contrition, a shaky hand reaching for her throat. "The winds must have picked up, dear, and the two fires must have converged. I never intended to hurt Blake, you must believe me. He was a cocky little thing, but he had the story, see? The *true* story of what happened to my brother, of what the Lyles had covered up. He said as much when he left, remember? That he was going to get in touch with his boss. I knew what he was saying, and I *wanted* the story to get out! I was just trying to cut us off from the world for a bit longer. I did not know the fire would get so out of control. And I certainly never expected the fire to catch up with Blake."

Lynette bristled again but sat back and gave her sister a look. One more cocky word and she was going to reach across the couch and throttle the woman herself.

Alicia nodded, knowingly, and sat forward again. "Tell us about Snowy then. How did you manage to inject him when, as you say, I was practically camped out on that track today?"

"I didn't dear. You heard Ronnie; that was suicide."

Lynette scoffed loudly and Alicia shook her head, but Flo looked deadly serious.

"Truly. I trekked out to him last night after you had all gone to bed. I handed him the gear and he did the rest. And don't you dare feel sorry for him, because I can see it in your eyes! I gave him a choice in the end, a privilege he never offered my brother."

In fact, Snowy had given Donal a choice. Donal, like Snowy, had taken his penance. But she wasn't to know that. The surviving witness would attest to that later.

"So you just waltzed on in and told Snowy to kill himself. Simple as that."

"Wasn't that simple, Alicia. That walk nearly did me in! It was very treacherous at night. I almost slipped at one point." She cackled. "That would not do! I still had one more job to tick off. And it's not like he wasn't expecting me. In fact, Snowy wondered what took me so long."

The sisters were both scoffing now, so she said, voice croaky, "Really, ladies, it's true. Vale had already told him that there was a journalist here, poking about, so he knew the wound was reopening. I guess you told him about Vale's death and Mrs Flannery, and he put it all together. He knew that only one person could wish them both dead. Or five people really—the surviving Murphy sisters."

Flo's face clouded over again. "My sisters never really cared, to be honest. Not like me. I mean, they *loved* Donnie. I'm not saying they didn't. But they saw his death as… almost a relief. They *wanted* to leave the farm, at least the younger ones did. But not me! I knew the true value of that property. It had been in our family for generations. That was our *birthright*!"

She sniffed and swiped another tissue. Then cleared her throat again. "But Donal's death killed it for all of us. I could not work it without my brother, not in those days anyway. Today, well, you wouldn't bat an eyelid at a group of sisters running a farm. I told all of this to Snowy, and he got it. He understood. He killed more that day than just my brother. He killed *my* dreams and hopes and future."

She paused to blow her nose, then said, "Would someone fetch me a glass of water, please? This is all very draining."

Alicia glanced at Lynette, who looked almost as drained as Flo did, and said, "I'll get it." Then to Lynette she added, "Come on, you look like you could do with a cuppa."

Dragging the truth from Flo hadn't just been draining, it had been depressing. And for one of them, at least, incredibly demoralising.

~

From their corner of the library kitchenette, Lynette watched Flo sip her glass of water while Alicia watched Lynette.

"Are you okay?" she asked, and Lynette glanced back and frowned.

"I'm good. How about you?" She sounded defensive, and Alicia pulled her towards her, attempting a hug, but Lynette pulled back.

"I'm sorry," Lynette said, wrapping her arms across her chest. "I'm just... I don't know. I just want this done with. I want to go home, and I want to get on with my life. Sick of all the *deceit*."

"I know. It's been horrible, and this isn't exactly easy, but you're doing good. We're nearly there."

Lynette shrugged like she didn't care. "The sooner she's locked up the better, if you ask me. Good riddance."

Alicia watched her for a moment. "I know you liked her, Lynette. It's okay that she became your friend."

"She didn't! I didn't!" Lynette spat back, reaching for the boiling kettle.

They slipped into a glum silence as Lynette prepared them both a cup of peppermint tea, but as she did so, the younger sister's mind drifted back to when she'd first met Flo.

Alicia was right. She *had* liked the woman. They had become fast friends. Lynette might have grizzled at the "cardigan-donning grannies" joining the club, judging them for their appearance just as she hated being judged herself, but she had warmed to them both so quickly, especially to Flo. The older woman had helped her in the kitchen, and later they had bonded over her diagnosis, but the truth was she didn't know Flo at all.

None of them did.

A weekend together didn't tell you anything. It didn't matter a jot. They were as good as strangers. And now she wasn't feeling quite so clever.

"Come on," Lynette said. "Let's get this over with."

~

Back on the couch, Flo was still looking weary, but she was determined to forge on.

"Now, where was I?" she said, her voice still croaky. "Ah, yes, Jack Lyle. Old Snowy. I went to see him last night. We had a good chinwag, and I could see that he was contrite. But it was too little, too late. It certainly wouldn't bring my Donnie back."

She glared at the sisters, defying them to suggest otherwise, but both of them looked exhausted, sipping their tea quietly.

Flo said, "So I gave the man a choice. I could administer the needle, or he could do the honours. He decided on the latter and I'm glad of it."

"How did you know he'd even take it?" asked Lynette. "He could have overpowered you. He could have made a run for it."

"Guilt, my dear. I think, in the end, he wanted it to be over. Like I said, my brother's spirit is up here. I think it's been haunting him all this time." She cackled suddenly, like she loved the sound of that.

Alicia frowned. "I'm still not sure how you got the poison."

"The snake venom? Oh, didn't I tell you? Got it from my sister's grandson. Ronnie's not the only one with useful rellies you know!" Cackled again. "Betty lives on a property in Dubbo. Her grandson keeps serpents. That's where I got the idea. Angus extracts the venom for some biomedical mob; milks them himself, he does, then freezes it and sends it off. Gets paid a pretty penny for his efforts. I guess they use it to manufacture antivenom. In any case, I pinched s. It was as easy as that."

"Ah," said Lynette, another piece falling into place. "You pinched it when you went to say goodbye to your family last month."

Flo nodded. "I chose the deadliest venom, from the inland taipan. Painful but quick. You have to remember, I was getting it for myself at first, and I'm not scared of pain, but I'm also not a masochist."

No, you're a sadist, Lynette wanted to tell her but Alicia was already shaking her head.

"I don't believe you ever intended to use the poison on yourself, Flo," she said. "It's far too brutal and you know it. You saw what your sister went through when she was a child. I think you had revenge in mind from the beginning."

Flo pursed her lips and looked away. She also looked increasingly weary and now was not the time to explore her subconscious, Alicia decided. They needed to get the full story out tonight because who knew how much Flo would clamp up when the police arrived and then lawyers started hovering?

"So you just handed Snowy the needle?" Lynette said. "And he agreed to kill himself?"

"It did take him a good long while, didn't it? I gave it to him last night! But I guess he finally found the courage. Must have done it right before Ronnie showed up."

Flo's face looked suddenly drawn, suddenly wretched. "I didn't mean for Ronnie to find him! I… I never meant to put her through that. I was hoping he was gone by the time she got there. I never… Well, I never would have wished that on my dear old friend. She'll probably never forgive me, and I can't say I blame her."

Alicia's eyes were squinting again. "I'm sorry, but I still can't get my head around the snake venom. That Snowy would willingly shoot himself up with something so agonising. I mean I know he was looking for atonement, but—"

"Atonement!" Flo bellowed, before coughing and spluttering and reaching for her glass. She took a good gulp and cleared her throat. "Do you really think anything will atone for what that bastard did to my Donnie? This is *all* his fault. None of this would have happened if he hadn't forced my baby brother to head out into a burning forest, all to pay for one little misdemeanour. So Donal played around with his wife. So what? His form of justice was not fair, not at all. It wasn't an eye for an eye, it was an eye for the entire body! More than that! It was an eye for a farm and all our livelihoods. And it wasn't *fair!*"

She coughed again and waved a hand in front of her face. Then took another swig of water and a deep breath. "That's why Snowy's marriage fell apart, I reckon. I bet Lydia guessed what he had done and never forgave him. His own kids too. It was a Lyle family secret, an ugly little secret that destroyed them all. A secret that Vale kept and Mrs Flannery too. Snowy told me that was why he hid out there in the bush, in his hokey little hut. Said he wasn't worthy of polite society after what he'd done to my brother, and he got that right! He said he was 'paying his own penance,' but I don't believe him. I think he's a coward and a bully and he should have come clean when it happened. He should have put my brother's soul to rest a long time ago."

Lynette suddenly snorted, almost laughing, and this

caught Alicia by surprise. Flo too.

"What are you smirking at?" the older woman demanded. "What's so damn funny?"

"I'm sorry, Flo," Lynette said, placing a hand to her mouth. "But if what you believe about spirits is true… If they really do wander the earth where they took their final breath. Then I hate to break this to you, but Snowy is still *here*. So is Mrs Flannery and Vale for that matter."

Lynette pointed to the shifting darkness beyond the window, a crack of lightning suddenly opening up the view, making the old woman jump. "Thanks to you, Flo, they've joined your brother out there in the forest for eternity."

Alicia gasped at the very thought, and so did Flo. She looked distraught for a few minutes, then something crossed her face and the distress vanished just as quickly as it had appeared.

She shrugged slowly and offered Lynette a small, wobbly smile. "Ah yes," she said softly, coughing a little. "But Donnie was young and strong when he died… and his soul is too. He'll make sure they get their comeuppance—all three of them. And if they don't, I'll see to it."

"You?" said Lynette. "What will happen to you?"

"It's already happening, dear…," she said, her voice dropping away.

The sisters looked at each other confused for a moment, then down at the table, to the teapot and the teacup and the empty glass of water. There was something on the saucer they hadn't noticed. It was a tiny glass vial. And it was empty too.

Lynette jumped up. "Oh my God! What have you done? Flo! What have you taken?"

"We need to get help!" said Alicia, looking around frantically. "Maybe there's some antivenom somewhere."

But Flo was holding a wobbly hand out towards them. "No point, girls. It's not snake venom. I… I… found it in

… the first aid cupboard. Not long… Please don't leave. Stay."

The sisters stared at each other aghast, unsure what to do.

"Please," she said again. "Will you do as Ronnie did and keep me company?"

"Ronnie!" cried Alicia. "We have to get Ronnie. She'll know what to do."

"No… please. She's suffered enough. Just… come. Sit with me. Humour a bitter old lady to the end."

The two sisters looked at each other alarmed, then something crossed Lynette's face and she looked calmer suddenly, more resigned. She pulled her shoulders back and sat down beside Flo, taking one of her hands into her own.

Alicia watched her for a moment, tears springing from her eyes, then she sat down on the other side of the dying woman and took hold of her other hand. They sat there for a few minutes in silence, then Flo coughed again.

"I need to tell you something else," she said, her voice barely audible.

"Flo," began Lynette, but she shook her head.

"Please… you need to hear this. I need… I need you to tell Ronnie." She swallowed hard and took a deep breath. "I never wanted to hurt any of you. Never my intention. I… I only came for Donnie… did it all… for Donnie. You will be… okay."

"We've been terrified of the fire, Flo," said Alicia, not feeling as forgiving as her sister now. "We thought we'd be murdered in our beds."

"I'm sorry. So… so… sorry." She spluttered a little. "It's why I… I laid the pretty table… and tried to make everything nice. I didn't mean…" Coughed again. "I didn't mean for it to be scary… tried to make it pleasant."

She stopped and smiled suddenly, her whole face lighting up. "Ahh… listen to the rain now. The fire will soon be over… will all be over… They will come…"

The sisters did indeed hear rain, and it was louder this time, coming down in buckets, lashing against the windowpane and making a din on the tin roof above their heads. Alicia, for one, never thought she'd be so happy to have such miserable weather. She glanced back at Flo whose eyes were now rolling back in her head, and for a moment she thought she had passed, but then they fluttered open and she said:

"Lynette? You there, Lynette?"

Lynette squeezed her hand. "Yes, Flo. I'm here."

She coughed. "Good." Coughed again. "Promise me something... please... one thing."

Lynette almost laughed at the audacity of the woman. She had set fire to the mountain and murdered two people, driven another to his grave, and who knows what had happened to Blake. And now *she* was asking for a favour? *Really?*

The older woman squeezed her hand then, and the smile she offered Lynette was beatific. "You are so beautiful, dear," she said softly, her head resting against the back of the couch. "My Donnie boy... he would have fallen for you... just his type."

Lynette smiled back, not sure how to respond to that.

"Please," Flo managed, swallowing hard again. "Tell the truth... Tell my brother's story. Make... make sure the world knows..."

Then her chin dropped onto her chest.

~

For ten long minutes, the two sisters sat there quietly, still holding the woman's hands as she passed away, tears trickling down their faces, mirroring the rain on the window nearby. Alicia couldn't seem to swallow the lump that had formed in her throat, and Lynette was breathing heavily, like it was her lungs that were refusing to work.

But eventually they released their grip and stood up.

Turned to each other and hugged each other tight.

"I'm sorry, I've been so weird lately," Lynette began.

"No, I'm sorry if you thought I'd left you out. Or patronised you or treated you like you were stupid. I don't think you're stupid. I never have!"

"I know! It's just my own shit." She sniffed and hugged her tighter. "I love you, sis. I always will."

Alicia smiled. "Good. But don't ever do that." She glanced down at the dead woman, who now looked surprisingly serene. "No matter what happens to me, don't ever hurt other people in my name. And don't give up your life for me. Really, I'm not worth it."

They both laughed at that, feeling good to have a release, then they turned and walked out of the room, into the corridor.

"I'm going to wake Ronnie," Alicia said. "I think she would want me to."

Lynette nodded and they hugged again before Alicia headed towards the rooms while Lynette headed for the lobby. The rain was now hammering the rooftop, and she smiled and stepped outside under the awning to watch as it pelted down. She hugged her arms across her chest, feeling cold for the first time all weekend, and kept watching as the rain kept coming in heart-warming, fire-dousing bursts, then she squinted, peering through it, to the dark, tangled forest beyond. She felt a slight shiver, then made a little wish.

Despite everything Flo had done and said, all the evil and the horror, Lynette could not help wishing that the woman's theory was true.

That despite everything, Flo was finally being reunited with her beloved brother.

EPILOGUE

As it turned out, Lynette would not need to tell the story of Donal Murphy and how he was marched towards certain death by an aggrieved husband in the Great Fire of 1970. Blake Morrow was found in a nearby hospital, alive but suffering burns to 55 percent of his body. He had been picked up by a neighbouring fire crew and was placed straight into an induced coma. The blanket he kept in his Mercedes was the one thing that had kept him alive. He had huddled under it and had survived.

It would be many months before Blake left hospital though, and he would never have his handsome looks again nor his arrogant, cocky nature. But that didn't bother Lynette, who had just visited him in Concord Hospital where his skin grafts were coming along nicely.

"Blake still wants to tell the story of Donal Murphy," she told the others as they gathered for another book club meeting, this one safely in Lynette and Alicia's inner-city living room. "His boss has given him extra time, of course, but he's given him more than that. He's got something to cling to now, something to live for. Blake never would have picked the ending though and says he'd like to interview all of us when he finally gets better. It's more than an article now; he's turning it into a book."

"Sounds like he might be a mega success after all," said Perry.

"Yes, but at what cost?" replied Lynette.

Since the weekend at Lyle's, she had abandoned her dreams of cooking for a Michelin-star restaurant and had applied to a local college to study business and hospitality. She still wanted the Michelin star, but she wanted it for her own restaurant. It was time to stop waiting for others to tell her she was good enough and believe in herself. And she needed to smarten up to do it.

"It's going to be one hell of a story when it all comes out," said Ronnie, the only new member of the Murder Mystery Book Club Mark II to remain with the group.

Simon had only signed up to sample Lyle's Lodge as a guest and was now too busy with the renovations to continue. He had overridden his business partner though, and they were treading gently, he'd told Claire, who relayed this to them as they sipped glasses of minty pineapple punch from a jug Lynette had prepared.

"Simon says they're going to restore Lyle's Lodge to its former glory, right down to the parquetry flooring and formal dining. They're even going to resume the dances every three months just as Lydia Lyle did."

"I hope that doesn't mean the hunting is resuming too?" said Perry, and she shook her head no.

"They're going for ecolodge not hunting lodge, thankfully."

"If only I were fifty years younger," said Ronnie, wistfully. "I'd go back and have another fabulous affair with a dishy Dutch man!" She smiled wickedly. "And you, dear? What are you going to do? Are you going to accept the job at Lyle's?"

Because that was Claire's big secret, the thing she was terrified to tell the others. It had burst out of her eventually but not until the RFS had burst in—Benson at the front, Jackson coming up the rear. Alicia decided then and there that she would never let her boyfriend out of her sight again! It was while driving back down the mountain, gasping at the charred, ruined remains of the once-beautiful rainforest, that Claire found the courage to admit what she had done.

Lyle's Lodge might have been Flo's sneaky suggestion,

via an email from an unsuspecting Ronnie, but it had become Claire's passion. No sooner had she clicked on the link, she was smitten. It was while poring over the site that she found her way to a page advertising positions vacant. Lyle's was looking for a new manager, and so she had sent in her application, not realising it would go directly to Simon's PA, Queenie, at Living Large Enterprises.

Simon hadn't realised when he joined the club that the Claire who had sent such a charming résumé was also Claire from the book club, the woman he was fast falling in love with. They only put it all together the afternoon they spent holed up in his room, and she explained all this to Alicia as the two women made the grim journey back to Lyleton. She didn't expect Alicia to forgive her, she said, but she hoped she would understand why she was accepting the position Simon had offered.

"I love my little vintage clothing store," she told the group now. "But I'm as stale as the old frocks in my shop. I desperately need a challenge."

"I completely understand," said Lynette.

"Me too," said Missy. "As sad as I am to see you go, possum, a change is as good as a holiday, my Aunty Dora always says. But..." She swallowed hard. "You're not worried about, you know, all the spirits up there now?"

Claire smiled. "I don't believe all that stuff, Missy."

"What about fires then?" said Perry, helping himself to an egg-and-cress sandwich from a spread laid out beside the jug.

Several of them shuddered at the thought of another bushfire, and even Claire's smile wavered.

"It is a worry, I do understand that. But it's oddly heartening to hear that both fires that weekend were deliberately lit—totally avoidable. The first was back-burning gone wrong. They nearly had that under control when Flo's fire roared down and set it off again. So, no, I'm not really worried, but Simon assures me they are doing a lot of clearing—especially the fire trails—and are also clearing and flattening some land near the lodge for a helipad, just in case. So we'll have an easier evacuation option if, God forbid, it does happen again."

"That's a relief," said Alicia. "So when do you go up?"

"The renos should be underway within the month, and I'll be going up to help with those. Simon wants my advice on vintage furnishings and fixtures." She smiled. "He loves my shop and wants the same inspiration for Lyle's interiors."

"Will you sell the store?" asked Perry, and she shook her head firmly.

"I'm not giving that up, not yet." Claire had been let down by love before and wasn't quite as trusting of it as she once was. "But I need a change. I really do! Simon's building a special residence for me, well, for the manager. So I can have more privacy than Vale was ever allowed."

"Good plan," said Ronnie, remembering Vale tucked up in bed. "What about Snowy's cabin? What happens to that?"

"They're demolishing it, sadly. It's riddled with white ants."

"And bad spirits," said Missy, who was holding fast to Flo's theory.

Claire ignored that. "They're repairing Repentance Way and building a small viewing platform on the escarpment; have abandoned the idea of luxury villas. Simon wants everyone to enjoy it. It really does have the premiere view."

"Speaking of Repentance Way," said Perry. "Did we ever work out who started the rock fall that nearly took you and Flo out, Alicia? Was that deliberate do we think?"

They all looked to Alicia, and she shrugged. "I've been wondering about that and whether it's related to the remark Vale made about an imposter. Was he referring to Blake? Did he recognise his byline and then sneak up the forbidden path and dislodge some rocks, just to frighten him off, but got us instead? Or did Vale maybe recognise

Flo? Did he see something of Donal in her features? I really don't know, and I guess we never will, but the truth is, I can't see Vale doing any of that. I have no idea if he had any involvement with Donal's death—I guess Blake will eventually find out—but I think harming guests would go against the hotelier's principles, his very fabric. Besides, every time I recall the shadowy figure on the ridge, I think of Snowy."

"You think *Snowy* dislodged the rocks?" asked Missy, but Alicia shook her head no.

"If anyone dislodged the rocks, it was probably Simon, accidentally, on his first walk. But I wonder whether Snowy witnessed the near miss and realised the track was getting more dangerous by the day. There was no avoiding the fact that he would need to move out and let the new owners repair it. No matter what their plans were, that was inevitable."

She glanced at Lynette who said, "Jackson spoke to the manager of Shady Nook—that's the aged-care home I thought Flo had been researching on the lodge computer. Turns out Shady Nook is based in Lyleton and it was *Vale* who emailed them that night, enquiring about a room for Snowy. Snowy wasn't suicidal. At least not until Flo got to him."

Lynette smiled sadly. "I can't help wondering about their final night together—Vale and Snowy. Vale obviously took Snowy some food and, we think, a copy of the book we were reading." She winked at Missy. "Jackson said there was a brand-new edition of *And Then There Were None* amongst Snowy's things."

"The missing ninth book!" said Missy.

She nodded. "It was probably a gift from Vale, something to get old Snowy's mind off what he was about to tell him—that a tabloid journalist was lurking, that the past was catching up with him. I can only assume that's when they discussed moving him out."

"But I thought Snowy told you he'd never leave the

mountain," said Missy. "That they'd have to remove him in a coffin."

"Yes, the *mountain*," said Lynette, "and Lyleton is still on that mountain, albeit halfway down. I reckon Snowy was just moving down to Shady Nook. That's all it was."

"And *you*," said Perry, now turning back to Claire. "What's going to happen when you move up the mountain? Isn't Simon's office in Sydney? I thought you two were now an item."

"We are," she said, blushing like a schoolgirl. "But it's early days and we're taking it slow. We'll see each other daily during the renovations and see what unfolds."

"Smart thinking, Claire," said Ronnie. "Never give your life over entirely to a man. That's where Flo went wrong. He might have been her brother, but she gave up her life for Donal. Never got over it. She might have been dying at the end, but she never really lived, not since that weekend in 1970."

"They're placing a plaque on the lookout," Claire told her. "Memorialising Donal."

"Well, good on them, but it's too little, too late," Ronnie snapped back. "If only the Lyles had done that decades ago, none of this might have happened."

They slipped into a sullen silence then, thinking of what might have been, before Lynette asked Ronnie, "How have you been faring?"

Flo's suicide had been traumatic enough for her and Alicia. She couldn't imagine what Ronnie had been through with Snowy. The older woman waved her off.

"I'm fine, dear. Don't forget I was a very capable nurse before Bert took me away from all that. I'm not going to forget Snowy in a hurry, of course, but I'm glad I was there to see him through. I know he wasn't innocent, but I'm not sure he deserved *that*."

"Why didn't he just step off the escarpment?" asked Alicia. "Why subject himself to the poison?"

Ronnie shrugged and said simply, "Penance."

Then she dropped her eyes as the word settled in around them.

"I'm sorry I lied to you all," she said eventually.

It was the elephant in the room.

"It's okay," Claire began, but Ronnie shook her head firmly.

"No, I need to say this. I need to clear the air." She smoothed her skirt down as she prepared her next words. "We met at grief counselling, Flo and I. Did I tell you that? It was only ten years ago, although it feels a lot longer. I'd just lost Bert, and she said she'd lost her husband Ian and her brother Donnie. Told me Donnie had perished fighting a fire at a fancy hotel somewhere in the mountains. She was still so consumed by grief I assumed it had happened recently. Not all the way back in 1970!"

She shook her head, remembering it. "Anyway, we became friends, Flo and I, and I invited her to join the Ladies Auxiliary. I never thought any more of it. Honestly I didn't. She didn't want to talk about it. We left it at that."

Her eyes danced around the group. "Then we met this lovely book club and you so kindly invited us to join you for the weekend. I honestly didn't remember Lyle's until I stepped into that lobby. And I honestly didn't remember Donal Murphy until Blake said something at dinner that first night that sounded strangely familiar—about a young hunter who was killed in a fire. I remember looking across at Flo and she had gone completely white. I thought she would faint. Then, at breakfast the next morning, the subject came up again, and again Flo looked startled. She dropped her cup like she'd been slapped. But he never used Donal's name, so I didn't think too much of it. Even after Vale was found, I... Well, I never really connected the dots."

She gave them an apologetic smile. "For a bright woman I can be a bit dim. It wasn't until I started reading through the old guest books and saw the name

Donal Murphy in there a few times that I grew suspicious. I recalled that Flo's maiden name was Murphy, and she had a brother called Donnie, who had died in a hotel fire. But... I guess I didn't want to believe it. Then... then we found Mrs Flannery."

She turned her gaze to Alicia. "I nearly said something to you, I really did, but I kept hearing how busy your brain can be, and I didn't want to overload you any further."

"Did you broach the subject with Flo?" she asked.

"Not directly, no." She held her palms up. "I know it sounds cowardly, but it seemed so outlandish that she would do such a thing! I still wasn't sure it was her, and I was trying to play it smart. If Flo had done it, she must be deranged! And how would she react if I confronted her? We were all stuck up there on that mountain together. A fire raging. No chance of escape."

She shuddered. Sighed. "We danced around the subject a few times, and she knew that I knew. I realise that now. In any case, the message she was giving me was loud and clear. The book club would all be okay. She kept saying that, over and over, and telling me to let it go. I... I had to believe that if she was out for vengeance it had nothing to do with us. None of us knew her brother. I thought that we'd be safe."

"Still, you followed her like a shadow," said Lynette, remembering Ronnie loitering under the fig tree.

She nodded. "I needed to keep an eye on her, just in case. But I honestly thought if she was the culprit, then she was finished. It was over." She turned to Perry. "Then you mentioned that Snowy was still alive and living out on the escarpment..." She thrust a hand to her throat. "I was horrified to hear that! I never would have guessed! That's when I realised that Flo hadn't quite finished yet. I got to Snowy's cabin as soon as I could... but not quite soon enough." She sniffed, tried to smile. "That's why I'm glad I was able to hold his hand through it. It's the least I could do."

"You lied about his deathbed confession?" said Alicia, no judgement in her tone. "To protect Flo."

"To protect *you*, dear! All of you. Snowy told me what had happened, said not to judge Flo too harshly. But I couldn't very well say that! She was sitting right there amongst us! It might enflame her further, and I thought the less you all knew, the safer you would be. I wanted to shut it all down and get you off that blasted mountain, get you away from someone I thought was a friend. I never... never in a million years would I have picked her for a killer. Even when the evidence started to pile up... never."

There was a group sigh as they all shifted in their seats, and then Lynette asked, "Did you know she was dying? Flo?"

Ronnie waggled a hand in the air. "She never said as much, but it was obvious she wasn't well. She had a bath bag full of pills in her bedroom, I knew what was what. She still had so much energy though, which surprised me. I was also surprised to hear she had added that link to my email, lured us all here so sneakily. I didn't even realise she knew how to use a computer! I lied about that too, Alicia. I'm so sorry."

"I know. Flo told us," Alicia replied. "And I'm sorry if you thought I suspected you."

"You *did* suspect me, you wicked thing!" She smiled. "But I don't blame you, dear. I would have made the perfect suspect in a crime novel."

"Speaking of which," said Perry, exhaling again as he reached for a book. "Shall we get on with the next one?"

He tapped his copy of *Still Waters*, the first in the Sandhamn Murders series by a Swedish author called Viveca Sten. It was Perry's job to choose a new author, and he had wanted to try someone more modern than Christie, but with the same clever plotting and endearing ensemble characters. Despite its setting, this was more "Cozy Mystery" than "Nordic Noir", so he knew it wouldn't unsettle jittery Alicia.

Even the title seemed comforting given all they had recently been through.

"Yes, please!" said Missy, wiping her eyes, which had been dripping tears as Ronnie spoke. Just one glance at the book in his hand and her smile was already returning.

"I'm in," said Claire, adding, "at least for now…"

Alicia reached over and gave her shoulder a squeeze. "You can always come back, Claire, be our VIP whenever you get a chance."

"I'd like that. But listen, I might have found my replacement." She took a deep breath, worried how they'd react. "Queenie, Simon's PA. She said she'd love to join this club if you'll have her."

"I bet she would!" said Perry. "The little minx. Are we really going to forgive her for providing Simon with his sneaky alias?"

"It's *because* she came up with that alias that I'm going to forgive her!" said Alicia. "You have to admit, that was pretty smart. And the letter she wrote on Simon's behalf was really lovely. Hate to say it, but I think she'd make a great addition to the club."

"She *is* lovely," Claire agreed. "I've gotten to know her through Simon, and she's very switched on; what she doesn't know about crime fiction isn't worth knowing. I think she might even give you a run for your money, Missy."

Missy's eyes narrowed beneath her spectacles. "There's a challenge I'm willing to accept!"

"Okay then," said Alicia, glancing around the group as they each nodded their approval. "That still leaves us a little short. Do we want to start hunting for more members again?"

Several of them groaned at the very thought, and Lynette said, "Must we? I think I'm done with newbies. No offence, Ronnie."

She smiled sadly. "None taken."

"But that means there's just seven of us," said Alicia.

"And when Claire leaves, there will just be six."

"And then there were—"

"Don't say it!" cried Perry, a hand at Missy's lips. "Do not finish that sentence!"

Then they all broke into laughter—comforting, much-needed, well-earned laughter—as they reached for a fresh new mystery.

~~ the end ~~

ALSO BY C.A. LARMER

After the Ferry: A Psychological Novel

IT'S THE 1990s, pre-mobile phones, and a young traveller must make a terrifying choice: Will she jump ship with a seductive stranger? Or stay cocooned on the Greek ferry with friends and miss what could be the love of her life?

One choice leads to true love.
One choice leads to murder.
But which is which?

"Larmer's plot is a clever one...The characters are finely honed and credible, and Amelia's contrasting lives and personalities are brilliantly rendered and made plausible."
Jack Magnus, Readers Favorite

Killer Twist (Ghostwriter Mystery 1)

KILLER TWIST is the first stand-alone mystery in the popular 'amateur women sleuths' series featuring feisty ghostwriter Roxy Parker.

"A fun read with a well defined protagonist, interesting secondary characters and an easy style. Lots of local flavour which catches the imagination."
Parents' Little Black Book @ Amazon

"Roxy Parker is a compelling character and I couldn't help but adore her. She's 30, hip, very inquisitive, and fiercely independent. A great cozy. I enjoyed it immensely and will be ordering the second in the series."
Rhonda @Amazon

calarmer.com

Printed in Great Britain
by Amazon

STRESS
BEATERS

FOR BECKY

My ocean . . .

STRESS
BEATERS

100 Proven Ways
to Manage Stress

Dr Roger Henderson

metro

First published in hardback in Great Britain in 1999
by Metro Publishing Limited, 19 Gerrard Street, London W1V 7LA

British Library Cataloguing in Publication Data. A CIP record of this
book is available on request from the British Library.

ISBN 1 900512 70 X

10 9 8 7 6 5 4 3 2 1

Typeset by Wakewing, High Wycombe, Buckinghamshire
Printed and bound in Great Britain by
Caledonian International Book Manufacturing Ltd, Glasgow

CONTENTS

Acknowledgements

I have been helped with the writing of this book by a number of people. It would not have even got off the ground without the tremendous support and encouragement I have received from all the staff at Metro, sustaining me through moments when *Stress Beaters* was proving a highly stressful book! A special thank-you to Susanne McDadd, who was foolish enough to take me on in the first instance and who has never been anything less than one hundred per cent supportive when dealing with an enthusiastic and occasionally head-strong author.

My children – Douglas, Sarah and Jack – deserve a special mention for keeping my feet firmly on the ground and reminding me what the truly important things in life are all about. To borrow a phrase from P. G. Wodehouse, without their endless help and enthusiasm this book would have been finished in half the time.

Most of all to my wife, whose quiet encouragement during the writing has been my salvation more times than I can mention. The credit for this book should be hers and hers alone.

R.H.
September 1999

Introduction

Why another book on stress? The answer lies with a remark a patient made to me: 'I never believed anyone could do anything about my stress, but you have, and I still can't believe it. You should write a book on it.' So I have – a book about real people, real situations and real answers. As a family doctor, stress and stress-related problems form a huge part of my workload. Half of each day is spent dealing with patients' stress, and even when they complain of physical symptoms these are often rooted in stress. The thirty-something executive who asks me to cure his palpitations, insomnia and headaches, or the young mother who interprets her profound tiredness as a physical condition alone, won't get better until they deal with the underlying cause of their symptoms. Over the last few years the number of my patients who are suffering from stress has increased, and I am now just as likely to hand out a stress tip as a prescription – a deciding factor in my decision to write this book.

Yet some might say, surely we know everything there is to know about stress – after all, the last thing anyone needs is another self-help book. Before writing *Stress Beaters* I went through some of the existing books on the subject. Certain trends were obvious: Pollyanna books that encourage people to smile at life whatever it does to them; personal audit books in which personality types, questionnaires and the development of a deep and loving understanding of yourself all seem to figure prominently. In theory, there is nothing wrong with these, but in practice most people have already gained some understanding about themselves, their problems and what makes them tick. Also, I do not believe that in order to deal with a problem we need to analyse it endlessly until an answer appears. People want answers not psycho-babble, and this book gives them the answers. What seems to be lacking is a book giving people commonsense advice that they can apply to their situation, rather than spending precious time examining their navels, and hoping some miraculous change will occur in their life. Contentious? Not from behind my desk it isn't.

The word stress is, I think, the most overused one in the language. Its definition is applied in many ways to many people, but usually involves the words or phrases 'pressure', 'tension' or 'physical or mental strain'. The irony is, we all need it. It gets us out of bed in the morning and through the day. A stress-free life would be too dull to contemplate. However, when feelings of strain or tension begin to affect our daily activities for the worse, it is probably time for a quick 'stress MOT' to see if this needs fixing.

Some of the tips in this book are for immediate benefit, while others take a much wider view. I have tried to gear my tips to real life, for example to acknowledge that people often do not have 100 per cent choice in their lives, or the luxury of money and time to put into practice every possible tip that may lower their stress level. So some of my tips are based on making the best of a situation rather than removing it altogether. I hope this book will have something for everyone, in any walk of life.

There are no panaceas. If I had a pound for every time I have been asked for a magic pill to make people's lives better, I would be sitting in a hammock in the Bahamas. Life is a roller-coaster ride for all of us. Sometimes we want to get off, sometimes it goes wrong and leaves us in mid-air, sometimes we can't wait to go round again, and occasionally we are thrown off and badly damaged. The best way of dealing with this roller-coaster is to put away the books and listen to what works in practice for many people. I hope this is what I have done here. Whether you find one tip that transforms your life or benefit from all one hundred, the message is the same – try them and find out what works for you. You have nothing to lose except your stress.

PART ONE

THE BIG
PICTURE

1

Don't put your life in one basket

I was once consulted by a successful entertainer who was well known for his punishing work schedule. During our half-hour he not only took three 'vitally important' phone calls but also jotted down plans for the rest of the week in his personal organizer. He was clearly a very busy man. However, despite his public profile and the pressure of work, he managed to keep both his blood pressure and stress levels low. I asked him how he managed this. He replied that whatever his workload – and the weather – he would spend at least half an hour every day in his garden. This never failed to relax him. The point that struck me was not that we should all take up gardening, but that a personal activity – whether trainspotting, cooking or synchronized swimming – unconnected with work can have huge benefits. Immerse yourself in an activity you enjoy and you will be surprised by how you gain perspective. That crucial meeting with the head of accounts may no longer seem so gruelling, as you realize that there is more to life than work.

In Western society the balance of our lives has changed, with work our main reason for getting up in the morning. We demote friends, family and ourselves and become trapped in a cycle of spiralling work pressure. Yet there is an antidote. Developing other interests – whether a hobby, a sport or a shared family activity – provides a counterbalance to the pressures of work. Balance is the key to keeping stress in its place, while a variety of activities stimulates interest and enthusiasm, two of the best pick-me-ups I know.

So, just as you should spread your financial investments you should do the same with your emotional investments. Then if one fails – work, for example – there are others still there to support you.

Develop a portfolio of interests and activities. Then if you lose one, you will still have a life. Whether these fall into the categories of work, hobbies or family, a *range* of investments is the key.

2

Live once, take risks

I don't hold with Philip Larkin's view that 'Life is first boredom, then fear'. I take the view that in all our lives – even if it is only once or twice – a break comes along which, if we take it, sets us down a different, more exciting path. For many people who sit in front of me in my surgery, the need to make a decision sets off spasms of anxiety and insecurity. They feel they have to seek permission from someone to help them make their choice. This may be a career change, ending a relationship or – on one memorable occasion – deciding whether or not they should pay their gas bill.

When I am dead and buried I will have the inscription 'Life is not a dress rehearsal' inscribed on my headstone. This is one of the phrases I say most to my patients, and all of them have the same thing in common. They have something in their lives that needs to change – an aspect of their behaviour or a problem in a relationship perhaps – but they are afraid to; they would rather stay trapped with their problem and its consequences than take firm action to change their lives. This would involve going down an untried, untested route, and it scares them. Although change is part of human nature, because it is often seen as threatening, people try to rationalize their inability to make a change by saying 'There will always be another day,' meaning they will do something about it next day, week or year. So there are smokers who never give up smoking and people in abusive relationships who never leave. Each broken promise to act encourages feelings of hopelessness for the next time – 'learned despair' – and the pattern continues. We therefore fail not because we have no option, but because we are putting mental stumbling blocks in front of ourselves and then expecting to fail as a result.

I recently spoke to a stockbroker who is widely respected for his daring and highly successful trades in the City. I asked him what advice he had been given when he started his company and he told me it had been simple and to the point – 'Don't take risks.' This was rather like asking a professional poker player not to gamble, he said, but he knew in his heart that if he took that advice he would not succeed. Instead, he viewed it as an opportunity that would happen once only, and accepted there would be low times when he would simply have to tough it out. He suffered from dreadful nerves for the first three months, and wondered on many occasions whether he had made the wrong choice. However, he always listened to the one person he knew he could trust – himself. Many years on he still takes risks, but this time with other people's money! He told me that, had he not taken the chance and broken out from his previous mundane job, he would have spent the rest of his life regretting it.

We don't need to give up our jobs and set up a smallholding in order to change the direction of our lives. Deciding what you want from life and then being ready to accept the opportunities that may – or may not – come your way is good enough. The crime is to notice such opportunities only when they have been and gone.

Grasp the opportunities that come your way. It may take nerve to break out and seize your chance, but you will not regret it.

3

Be positive

There are certain patients I see on a regular basis who always leave me feeling depressed and in a negative frame of mind. This can happen when I have spent only a few minutes with them. These people appear to have one thing in common, an air of negative thinking. Nothing will ever work for them, there is always something worse just around the corner, and when I do achieve the impossible and a symptom disappears, another one rapidly appears to take its place. Patients such as these are labelled 'heartsinks' by doctors, and there is a danger that once such a label is attached to them it sticks, and genuine symptoms can be ignored. Even hypochondriacs have to die of something.

Such people illustrate how their negative thinking rubs off on others and affects their lives. It has the effect of a dripping tap if it is allowed to continue, and drags us down until we lose self-confidence. How many times have you found yourself saying, 'Oh, I couldn't do that,' to someone asking you to do something, simply because you have assumed you could not?

In order to break this pattern you need ordered and regular training – a mental workout, in fact. Books have been written on this subject, but I use three main ways to turn negative thinking around:

 For ten minutes each evening for a week, squeeze a small rubber ball while repeating the phrase 'Do it right, do it now, do it positively.' (You can achieve the same effect by putting a rubber band on your wrist and lightly flicking it.) This links positive thoughts to that action. When you are in situations where negative thinking occurs, squeeze or flick and you will notice a boost of positive thought to help you. After a while you will not need props; simply by squeezing your fist or touching your wrist you will trigger a positive response.

◆ Carry with you, or have near you, reminders of personal achievements or phrases or sayings that make you feel good. These don't have to be well known, in fact, the more personal they are the better. They can be cards carried in your wallet, pocket or handbag on which you have written sayings from the family, your partner or anyone else, as long as they inspire you. Beside my computer I keep my medals for finishing the London Marathon. The fact that I ran a slow time and staggered to the end is irrelevant; they remind me that 'I can do it' despite my reservations. It does not matter what you choose, as long as you have positive images around to challenge negative thinking.

◆ Accept that you will have bad days when you are in a black mood. Instead of viewing these as never-ending, think of the next day as a clean slate on which you can draw what you want to happen. It may not work out quite the way you plan, but half a day of positive thinking is better than none.

Some people use positive thinking almost as a way of distancing themselves from reality. If they think about it hard enough, everything in the world can be all right. This is not only ridiculous but dangerous. Positive thought is not about ignoring how difficult life is at times, but gives you an extra edge at work and at home. Remember, it is your thinking that is negative and not your life.

Think positive. Negative thoughts pollute your life, affecting your behaviour and other people's reaction to you. Positive thoughts breed positive responses.

4

Only two options

A few days before the stroke that killed my father, he quoted the well-known saying 'Grant me the serenity to accept the things I cannot change, the courage to change the things I can and the wisdom to know the difference.' We hugged each other and I drove away. I never spoke with him again.

In this quotation lie the seeds of a major principle – that there are many situations we are simply unable to change. Agonizing about abolishing poverty and famine or wishing everyone could have good health is fruitless. On a much smaller scale we all have daily encounters that seem unfair. We may be stuck in a traffic jam or in the tube, or live in a high-rise tower block in a crime-ridden city. These are situations we *can* change our reaction to. Can we find a way to use our travelling time more fruitfully? Have you tried everything to change your flat or have you become so resigned to the situation you no longer bother?

> **You may not be able to change a situation but you can change your response to it. Unlike politics, there is no third way. If the world will not change, accept it and adjust.**

5

Practise a faith

A Jewish patient once told me a true story about a group of senior rabbis imprisoned in a concentration camp. They were forced to work all day every day except Sunday afternoons when they were allowed a few precious hours off. One such Sunday, a mock trial was organized by the rabbis where God was in the dock for allowing such suffering and misery. It was correctly organized with a prosecution, defence and the rabbis acting as the judges. At the end of the trial the evidence against God was overwhelming and the verdict was guilty on all counts. There was a long silence as all sides considered this verdict and its implications, until an elderly prisoner stood and said, 'Gentlemen, let us not forget – it is now time for our prayers.'

We sat looking at each other for a long time, and I was aware that the patient's religious faith was something he rarely mentioned but which meant a lot to him. I have never forgotten his story. It is probably the best definition of faith I have heard.

It is not my job to moralize or preach to patients; there are other doctors who do that far better. My job is to be the advocate for my patients' health, and there are times, especially when dealing with bereavement or terminal illness, when I am asked the question 'Why?' An answer is almost impossible, but the hesitant and flawed faith that I practise helps me. The effervescent happy–clappy fervour of true evangelism is not for me, because I always feel I have walked into a party three drinks too late. It is quiet reflection and an individual relationship with the person I choose to call God that sustains me through difficult times. If patients ask me, fine. If not, I am not there to impose my beliefs on others.

Religion can help people in many ways. One of these is to provide solutions to their problems that would otherwise be unattainable, and thereby reduce stress. In many cases there is no plan that can solve a problem, but the belief that even if everything collapses around you tomorrow, it will not be the end of the world, can be enough to prevent an increase in stress. If you cannot talk to family or friends about a problem, talking to a higher deity is a safe and healthy way of letting go of suppressed emotion.

There is no right or wrong way to believe. Whether you believe, and what you believe, is an individual choice. The key is that I, and many others, find a quiet affirmation with something or someone is a great way to remove stress. Try it. You may be surprised.

Enormous numbers of people draw immense peace and comfort from religion – conventional or otherwise. If you feel life is empty despite success, find out about faith.

6

'Be', not 'have'

I am very rarely lost for words. In fact, most people say that is the last thing that would happen to me. I also view myself as unshockable – being privileged enough in my job to see people as they really are ensures that – but I remember a particular patient who not only shocked me but reduced me to silence. In doing so he showed me just how destructive 'need to have' thinking is on both our stress levels and our mental health.

James came to see me in a state of considerable mental anguish. I had known him for many years, and had watched from the sidelines as he built up a massive business by the age of 40, along with the trappings of success. These unfortunately included a deeply dissatisfied wife and two children who never saw him from one week to the next. When he asked me what he could do to reduce his stress levels I bluntly suggested he should sell up and get out. I was therefore surprised to hear that he had been thinking of doing just that, but couldn't because his pension fund was not large enough. It was when he told me this fund had 'only' four million pounds in it that silence descended on my side of the desk.

The reality was that James could never have a pension fund big enough to satisfy him, and even if he did there would always be bigger and better ventures after that. He was always thinking about what he didn't have rather than what he had, and so remained deeply dissatisfied.

As expected, my advice fell on deaf ears and James lost his wife and children shortly afterwards, and faced an expensive divorce settlement. He still sees me for advice but freely admits that he is continually moving the goalposts in his life, so that once he has achieved his latest target – bigger bonus, better car, another million – he sets himself a higher one.

Satisfaction can never be achieved if you view life this way. When do we ever have enough? If you list the good points in your life – that you actually have a job in the first place, that your partner does have some redeeming features, that your health is better than some people's – you will actually end up getting more of what you want. If you can focus on enjoying life at home rather than waiting for two weeks in the year when you go on holiday, you will know how to feel good. If for any reason you don't get your holiday you will still have enjoyed yourself.

A lesson we all need to be reminded of is that much of what we have in life is good and satisfying as it is. Look at what you have – house, car, work and relationship – and write down exactly why you feel it needs to be improved. Change is good, as long as you are not simply trying to fulfil an endless wish list.

Many of us imagine happiness involves a bigger house or more money and possessions. But all these do is set more targets and stresses for ourselves. Start investing in the truly important things in life – not just the bank balance.

7

Learn from your mistakes

I don't hold with the philosophy that every single problem is an opportunity just waiting to transform your life radically for the better if only you will let it. This is rubbish. Problems are exactly that – things we would rather not have, since they make a difficult life even more difficult. You need to have a certain masochistic streak to welcome them with open arms. Problems, and mistakes in general, are a fact of life and cannot be ignored, although it is sensible to try to keep them to a minimum. It is essential to remember certain facts about mistakes:

◆　We all make them, so we need to learn to accept them as a fact of life. Making a genuine mistake does not make you any less of a person.

◆　If anyone gives you an unnecessarily stressful time about making a mistake, remember they will have made just as many mistakes as you, if not more. The question 'May I congratulate you on never having made a mistake in your life?' is a useful answer here.

◆　Forgive yourself. It is bad enough having to tell your family you forgot to buy the airline tickets when you are at the airport, so don't hate yourself for being human. Accept the criticism that will come your way and learn from it, although in a case such as this it is unlikely you would ever be allowed not to!

◆　Don't allow mistakes to prevent you from taking future decisions. You forgot the airline tickets this time but this doesn't mean you will never be able to travel abroad in the future. This would imply that all you will ever be able to do is stick to what you know and never try anything new: safe, predictable and dreadfully dull. Life is too short for this.

◆ Don't try to avoid mistakes by not making decisions. In any boardroom there will be people who have perfected this technique so well they spend all their lives sitting on the fence. Their fear of getting something, anything, wrong is so great they are transfixed like rabbits in car headlights to the point of freezing up. They delay endlessly, hoping to guarantee the right decision, and so the cycle continues.

While there is no such thing as a successful person who has not failed or made mistakes, there *are* successful people who made mistakes and changed their life or performance in response to them, and so got it right next time. They viewed mistakes as warnings rather than signs of hopeless inadequacy. Trying never to disappoint people by avoiding mistakes stifles your life in every area.

Never making a mistake means never living life to the full. More useful lessons are learned from mistakes than from success. Children learn to walk because they get up when they fall, not because they stay down. Repeat each morning that to risk failure is to court success.

Project the person you would like to be

Richard Branson is viewed by many people as a decent chap. He does have an interesting tendency to ditch very expensive balloons in large oceans, but he has managed to build his business empire on the back of his image as the type of guy you might bump into in the pub. This has served him well – many people believe he is somehow different from the businessman in a grey suit. Some of his competitors have found this out to their cost, having assumed that anyone who does business in jumpers could not be a serious competitor. They believed that looking like Branson was an impediment to business success. Not true.

Like it or not we are always being judged – appraised by others on our appearance, habits and personality. Yet we forget that what registers most with people are our little kind acts and gestures. We may forget these at the end of the day, but they often stay with other people for a long time. If you have spent all your life being an obnoxious loud-mouthed bore, there is little that can be done for you, but for most of us there are ways to let people see us in a more sympathetic light. They will not turn you into the next Richard Branson, but will almost certainly have beneficial effects in all areas of your life. You can project a positive image in the following ways:

◆ The best Oscar acceptance speech ever made was only two words: 'Thank you.' Showing off is hugely unattractive to most people, especially the British. We like success but prefer it to be quietly understated rather than rammed down our throats.

◆ People will feel better disposed towards you if you always carry manners and politeness with you. It is true that holding

15

a door open for someone may get you trampled on in the rush of another 20 ungrateful people passing through, but it is your action that is important, not theirs, and it will be noticed, whatever you might think.

◆ Those who are at ease with themselves and their values have no need to brag. It is more of an achievement to keep success quietly to yourself unless asked. There is a patient I have known for many years who only told me recently – at my instigation – what he did in the Second World War. I now know I am looking after one of the most heroic and highly decorated soldiers I could meet, but you would never guess it from meeting such a quiet and unassuming man.

Life is a marathon, not a 60-metre dash. The flashy and loud may make an initial impression, but like shooting stars they soon burn out. Small personal victories, shared with close friends or family, are the ones remembered throughout life, and generate the real and deep sense of self-worth that in turn affects how others see you.

Never project your insecurities to the outside world. Carry your sense of worth with you always, but without showing off or bragging. This will transform how others see you.

Remember Shirley Valentine

Before the days of little blue pills for impotence, a bashful young man asked me for help with his sexual problems. He had a forceful and enthusiastic wife, and he felt inadequate. We finally agreed that a course of injections would help. All went well, the desired effect was achieved and I asked him to report back the following week.

When he reappeared he looked sheepish. He had indeed left the surgery in a state of eager anticipation and had rung his wife to tell her the good news, whereupon she told him to pick up a Chinese takeaway on the way home. He arrived home with a cold meal and a deflated sense of self-esteem, which only set his wife off on a tirade. When I asked him – incredulously – why he had not gone straight home and eaten later, he replied, 'I couldn't have done that, I can only do what my wife wants me to.' My suggesting that this pattern of compliance had led to his impotence, lack of self-esteem and a miserable marriage had little effect. To this day this couple remain in separate worlds and bedrooms.

This is only one example of an extremely common problem which causes immense stress – feeling unable to stand up for yourself. For most people a guaranteed way of generating stress is to feel you are living with decisions that have been imposed on you. This can range from being married to the wrong person to hating the colour of your kitchen units – the problem is immaterial, but the effect is always the same. Resentment simmers and eats away at the fabric of a relationship, whether at work or at home. There are a number of ways this can be overcome:

 Be honest with yourself. Write down what is important for you at home, at work and in a relationship. If decisions are being taken out of your hands, who is making them for you?

What right have they to do this? If you're being bullied, learn how to deal with it (see Tip 11).

◆ Be honest with people. Don't keep quiet in discussions when you disagree. That is exactly the time to speak up.

◆ Don't be too dogmatic. We all change our minds and we all make bad decisions. Accept that things won't always go your way, but if they always go against you ask yourself why.

◆ Be prepared not to follow the crowd. Peer pressure is a highly potent force in persuading people to go against their usual principles, and I see dozens of young men in prison who are there simply because of this.

◆ Accept compromise. It oils the wheels of business and relationships more than we think, and should not bother us provided we know why the compromise has to be made.

Remember *Shirley Valentine*? The film gives one of the best examples of suppressed individuality I know, and many people who watch it relate to it. You don't have to talk to the kitchen wall or go to a Greek island – or a psychoanalyst – to free your identity as an individual. You alone know yourself better than anyone, know who you are and what you want. Don't lose sight of that.

Be prepared to stand up for somebody important – you. Don't be forced into other people's orbits. Instead, hold on to your personality and concentrate on your priorities, aims and values.

10

A favour a day

Have you ever done someone a good turn and then waited for them to repay the favour? If you have, you have been doing it for all the wrong reasons. It is a common fault of us all to expect something in return if we have offered to help someone. People sometimes seem to keep a mental score of how many favours they have done, as if the more they do the greater their reward will be. Doing someone a favour does give you a reward, but not in a material way. Expecting some kind of payback is a quick way to disappointment and resentment – a guaranteed way of stopping you doing favours in the future. There are key points about such favours:

◆ Do them for the right reason – because you want to. Any other reason is the wrong one.

◆ Never expect anything in return. Keep the favour anonymous if you want, then you know it is for the right reason.

◆ Remember how good you feel when you do a favour. This is your reward, and it is a deep, long-lasting one.

◆ Favours don't have to be large or dramatic. There is just as much satisfaction to be gained from little acts of kindness as there is from very obvious large gestures.

◆ People often remember kindness and you may get some reward in the future because of this. As you are not expecting this, it is all the more pleasant when it happens – the 'double reward' effect.

At the start of my career as a family doctor, I helped a family cope with their mother who was critically ill. I must have done a number of small favours at the time but within a few weeks had forgotten all about them. Many years later I was looking after someone from the same family, and made the most monumental cock-up with their care. The person concerned was understandably intensely angered by this, and I sat down with him for an open and honest discussion about what had gone wrong. After weighing up what I had said, he agreed it was an honest mistake and no harm had ultimately come of it. The crunch came as he stood up to leave. Looking me straight in the eye, he said, 'I knew you were trying your best because of what you did for Mum.' After he had left I tried to think back to what I had done all those years before, but it was fruitless. He had remembered, I had forgotten, but it had helped me in a way I could never have imagined.

The next time you think 'I want something back' after doing a favour, give yourself a slap on the wrist. It is only when you do favours for others and not for yourself that you will find your stress falling each time.

Do somebody a favour every day, even if it is as small as offering a seat on a bus or doing the sandwich run at lunchtime. Favours cost nothing but you will feel better for doing them.

PART TWO
THE
WORKPLACE

11

Tackle bullies

A highly efficient company secretary came to me with a minor problem. Sensing there was something else on her mind, I asked her what it was. She broke down, and admitted, for the first time, that she was being bullied at work. Having been bullied as a small boy I know how miserable this can make you, and I had every sympathy. Bullying is one of the greatest causes of misery, causing half of all stress-related illnesses at work, and sometimes leading to suicide. Bullies come in all shapes and sizes, and this includes doctors (remember there is no bigger bully than a doctor who refuses to listen). Men tend to be less open than women about being bullied and are often reluctant to admit to themselves that there is a problem. But you *can* do something about it, and it does not take a radical shift in your behaviour to alter another person's attitude to you. Certain principles apply across the board:

◆ The first thing to remember is that bullies are weak or insecure people. Their aggressive front crumbles when they think they are facing someone stronger. Most people work on the assumption that if they do nothing about an unpleasant situation the bully will shut up and life will continue as normal. Nothing could be further from the truth. This simply reinforces the bully's view that throwing your weight about gets results. Believe in yourself, be confident in your own abilities and don't listen to snide or malicious remarks. It may help to memorise a few positive affirmations – 'You cannot touch me' and 'I am winning' are my favourites.

◆ Second, keep calm. The more bullies feel they are losing the argument the louder they will shout. Do not be deflected from what you are saying if they try to shout you down – it shows that you are winning.

Body posture and non-verbal clues are important in helping you stand your ground. *Never* smile at a bully, and do not let them see they are upsetting you. Stand up straight and look the bully directly in the eye. This can be difficult, because if you are angry with someone who you have trouble dealing with, your natural reaction is to lower your gaze in order to hide your true feelings. Take a deep breath and keep your nerve. Bullies will be deeply disconcerted by this, as they feel power is being taken away from them.

If you find it difficult to deal with a bully at work, especially if they are in a position of power, take formal measures. Write down your grievances, make an appointment to see the bully, and then calmly state the reasons why you want their behaviour to stop. If necessary, take a colleague with you as a witness. Follow this up with a letter repeating what you have said and why. Do not forget your legal rights and the relevant complaints procedures. Above all, be as objective as you can.

Memorize and rehearse strategies for dealing with bullies. Soon it will become automatic. Remember to:

- **Make eye contact.**
- **Write down what you want to say beforehand.**
- **Keep calm.**
- **Keep from being deflected.**

Bullies are fundamentally weak, and will move on if you can stay calm, consistent and courageous.

23

12

Build your 'mental wall'

We all find confrontation disagreeable. Bullies capitalize on this, relying on their victim to keep quiet rather than face any more abuse. To counter this we need a strategy to overcome feelings of stress and anxiety generated by such confrontation. I developed the 'mental wall' technique after a particularly bruising psychological battle with an abusive prisoner, and for me this always works to reduce such feelings.

This simple technique works by taking the anxiety out of any situation where you feel you might be threatened verbally. Imagine there is an invisible, clear brick wall between you and the other person. You can see the wall but the other person can't, and they are unable to get past this wall to you. The wall protects you, soaking up any abuse or aggressive language, leaving you able to listen and respond to what is being said in a calm, objective manner. It allows you to keep the other person at a mental arm's length, and puts you in charge of what you filter through. Once you have mastered the technique, try using it in a variety of situations. Imagine you are wrapped in this wall before an important meeting, and 'pin' any important points to it so that your thread of concentration is not lost.

Once the meeting or confrontation is over, mentally roll up the wall and throw it away. As you do so, any feelings of anger and frustration will be thrown away with it. The next time you need it, build a fresh wall in your mind.

This technique is designed to help counter reflex reactions (anger, fear, anxiety) and allow you to think in a cool and objective manner. As you are not being pressurized into making bad decisions, people will soon realize that you cannot be intimidated into doing things you do not want to do.

Of course the mental wall will not protect you from physical abuse. But it will keep you calm during discussions that might otherwise enter the cycle of shouting and name-calling that benefits no one and leaves people feeling stressed and angry.

Use the 'mental wall' technique to keep you focused and calm. Visualize an imaginary wall between yourself and difficult people, and keep the wall at a mental arm's length from you. Try it – it works.

13

Share your problems

No one is an island – we all need friends. We need them as tempo-rary refuges from problems in other relationships. We discuss solu-tions and other ideas with them to get feedback on how realistic they are. Real friends are not 'yes-men', telling you only what you want to hear. They will disagree with you, argue their point and sometimes try to stop you from making a fool of yourself. We can choose to listen to them or not.

It is good to have friends who advise you, but you must fil-ter their advice and use it only as part of your thinking about a prob-lem. Sometimes our intuition about a solution is correct, and some-times we ignore correct advice and fall flat on our face. If we do get it wrong, a good friend will not gloat about being right but will pick us up and get us on our feet again. Love may be blind – friendship simply closes its eyes.

I have been a doctor long enough not to be shocked by human behaviour. Despite this I still raise my eyebrows whenever a patient tells me they have discovered their 'best friend' has been sleeping with their partner. My eyebrows creep up even more when I ask what is going to happen next and they say, 'What can I do? They're my best friend.'

Call me old-fashioned, but that is not my idea of a good friend's behaviour. A real friend is someone you could phone in the dead of night with an urgent problem, who would not think twice about helping you. Real friends are there to help out in a crisis, to give your self-confidence a boost when you are feeling low. Having someone who knows you, who gives you a mental lift or sees you through difficult times, is one of the best ways to reduce your stress.

We choose our friends according to a number of different criteria:

◆ How supportive the person is in times of trouble.

◆ Whether you share common interests.

◆ How much you can confide in them, and whether they can keep a secret.

Physical attractiveness, wealth and humour are other desirable attributes, but good friends always have that key attribute of being a supportive confidant when you need them to be.

Bring perspective to your problems by discussing concerns or fears with people you trust. But don't whinge non-stop, and do remember to filter advice.

14

Anticipate deadlines

My life is one big deadline. If it is not patients wanting the impossible done yesterday, then editors seem intent on filling up my writing diary as quickly as I can empty it. My bank manager is happy, but whether this is good for me is another matter. As a control freak, I must keep on top of any project and have time to spare. This can be a catch-22 situation, since I also need the stimulus of an approaching deadline to focus my attention on finishing a project.

One successful writer I know waits until he has bills that need paying, then sits down at his desk with them in front of him and starts writing – it never fails. If you feel you work best with the adrenalin surge of starting a project a few hours before a deadline, fine. However, this does not allow for unexpected events, which have a nasty habit of occurring when you least expect them. It makes more sense if, mentally, you bring forward a deadline by 48 hours and make sure you complete the work by then, apart from any minor alterations you may need to make. This is especially true if you are giving a presentation, since your anxiety will be less if you have rehearsed what you are going to say beforehand. Public-speaking gurus have this as their main tip, saying the three main ways to speak confidently in public are to prepare, prepare and prepare.

Most deadlines involve a number of people in a team, which means they can be sabotaged by a team member not pulling their weight, or by an unrealistic deadline set by someone not directly involved. This rapidly leads to a loss of motivation and frustration; jobs are either left half-done or not done at all. Although in an ideal world everyone would work efficiently all the time, life is not like that, and a work team is only as good as its weakest cog. Don't let this distract you from completing any work you have to do ahead of time, and to the best of your ability. Even if nothing comes of it in the end, your contribution will add to your self-worth; but do *not* allow other people to hijack your efficiency by getting you to do their work for them. Being efficient is one thing, being used as a workhorse is another. Keep your mental checklist of deadlines ahead of schedule and you will get control back, instead of allowing deadlines to control you.

Plan to meet deadlines early – at least 48 hours before you need to. Some people enjoy the adrenalin kick of working to the last minute, but this leaves no buffer zone for the unexpected.

15

Work smarter, not harder

There is a golden thread that runs through the advice that experts in time management have to give – concentrate not on how busy you are but on *results*. In other words, work smarter, not harder. When I suggest to people they are losing their battle against managing time properly, they refuse to accept this until I ask them the following:

◆ Would you feel lost without your diary?

◆ Do you have more than one diary or calendar?

◆ Are you always looking at your watch when in a queue?

◆ Do you fret about how many jobs you still have to do each day?

◆ Do you always seem to be trying to do two jobs at once?

◆ Do you ever feel too busy to enjoy yourself?

If they answer yes to two or more of these, they have a problem managing their time. Making daily checklists is a good way to overcome the problem, but there are also a number of other key principles which will help:

◆ Remember you will not get any extra reward for perfection. Always do your best, but trying to be perfect at all times is a fast way to major stress.

◆ Spend one day – and one day only – keeping a log of how you spend your time at work. Note how long each job takes, how much time you spend in meetings or getting from A to B. Are you spending periods doing very little? The information will highlight areas that can be improved.

◆ If you have projects to finish and are on a tight deadline, release time by taking shorter breaks during the day or starting earlier. However, this *must* be a short-term strategy only, and should last for no longer than the project.

◆ If you can, delegate work, since many people will often help you if approached correctly.

If you find you are still disorganized, it may be worth seeking professional advice. Some people find this extremely useful, while others do not benefit from it. You may need to invest time and accept disruption in the short term in order to release time in the long term. After I had an electronic appointments system installed in my surgery I spent a week running late, calling the wrong patients in to see me and leaving others sitting in the waiting room while I had my coffee in blissful ignorance. I resisted the temptation to chuck it all in the nearest bin and go back to my old system, and two weeks later my days were running smoothly, with large periods of time released which I could use to deal with administrative matters that would otherwise have kept me late at work.

Seek professional time-management advice if you always seem to be running late or missing deadlines. Simple techniques such as daily lists or phone-free time can add hours to your day.

16

Own your workplace

We work in different places. Many of us do not have the luxury of having our working environment as we would wish – how do you personalize a production line? – but for those who do have some personal space, this is an area that can readily reduce stress.

Most of us spend an enormous portion of our lives at work, yet give little thought to having things around us that would make our working life easier. As a medical student I was told by an eminent professor, 'All you need in your consulting room is a picture of your wife and children. Even if they are not yours.' As a family doctor I know why he said that, but the point is, if you are comfortable in your working environment you stand a greater chance of feeling more relaxed. I have found the following invaluable:

◆ A massive wastepaper bin. Throw junk mail, unwanted papers and clutter into it regularly and ruthlessly. Aim to touch each piece of paper only once before using the '5 Ds' method (see Tip 19) – to decide what to do with it.

◆ Photographs or pictures that mean something to you. Why should you be looking at an office picture inherited from someone else years ago? A small number of personal photographs, mementoes or pictures can lift your spirits during a busy day. Change them frequently so you do not start 'looking but not seeing'.

◆ A comfortable chair. If you have to buy your own, make sure it is fully adjustable in all directions and position it directly in front of a VDU or keyboard if you use one. Don't make the mistake of putting keyboards and monitors to one side of you, and always change your sitting position slightly every 15–30 minutes. Remember to arch your back – so you stretch your spine backwards – at the same time.

◆ A tidy desk. There is nothing more frustrating than having to spend five minutes hunting for files, disks or marker pens in the middle of a busy day.

◆ At the end of each day, tidy up files, paper and work that still has to be done. This will not reduce the workload for the next day, but your heart will not sink, as it will when you look at a desk overflowing with clutter.

There is much at work that is harder to deal with, such as air and noise pollution. Humidifiers and plants can sometimes improve air quality (I never cease to be amazed at just how many office windows cannot open). If noise is a concern, see if separate rooms are available for important matters.

If you have your own work area, make it *your* space. Organize it to suit you, be comfortable in it, fill your waste bin and wage war on clutter.

17

The 3-minute stress fixer

The belief that doctors are models of serenity and calm – an oasis of peace in a hectic, turbulent life – is a fallacy. Most doctors I know spend much of their working day gnashing their teeth and generally under pressure. Their saving grace is that they tend to do this in private, which at least means their patients come back to see them again. I am no different, and after a difficult patient has left, a closed-circuit camera in the consulting room would suggest I was in the grip of madness. Nevertheless, I aim to get rid of my stress before giving my full, calm attention to the next patient. The techniques I use to do this can be applied in any situation, at work or at home.

◆ First, stand as straight as you can and stretch your body. Raise your arms above your head before bending and trying to touch your toes. Repeat ten times.

◆ Second, stand completely still and breathe deeply ten times to a count of five – five on the in breath and five on the out breath. For one minute, think of a favourite mental image – for example, someone you love or admire, a beautiful garden or similar place – and imagine you are actually there.

You should now feel more relaxed, and can say aloud all the things that you wanted to say to whoever has just annoyed you. If necessary, swear. (Privacy is a necessity here!) It is important that while you are getting rid of your stress, you do not stress others.

If you are constantly dealing with difficult people in a busy job, and are unable to de-stress in this way, you can still get the benefit by taking five minutes every few hours and following similar guidelines. Any reduction in your stress will make you more able to cope. The aim is to prevent a build-up of frustration throughout the day, which not only will affect your performance at work but, if left unchecked, may spill over into your home life. Try to dump as much frustration and unhappiness as you can while at work. After that, constructively discuss any remaining problems. This has the added advantage of preventing any feelings of being a 'dumping ground' for another person's problems day after day. This in itself is very stressful.

After a difficult meeting, impossible colleagues or just too much work, blitz your frustrations by taking a few minutes alone to relax. This can be by doing stretching or breathing exercises, swearing to yourself in private or saying aloud what you might have wanted to say at the time but couldn't. Mentally shovel your frustration away, calm down and move on.

18

Develop affirmations

There is a quotation I have been aware of almost every day since I was 15 years old. It has sustained me through all the exhausting times in my life, and is attributed to the 30th American President, Calvin Coolidge. Coolidge stated: 'Nothing in the world can take the place of persistence. Talent will not; nothing is more common than unsuccessful men with talent. Genius will not; unrewarded genius is almost a proverb. Education will not; the world is full of educated derelicts. Persistence and determination alone are omnipotent.'

This has always struck a deep personal chord with me, and I have pinned it to the wall of my consulting room. I sometimes catch patients mouthing it to themselves as they read it, and some have even written it down.

Although this quotation has inspired me through the years, it will do nothing for many other people. This is because remembering such affirmations is a highly individual matter. Being able to speak verses of poetry or lines of prose is a good party trick, but otherwise it does nothing for you. Quotations have to have meaning and relevance for each individual, because they are applicable to *your* life. Otherwise you will forget them.

There are many circumstances where affirmations or phrases can motivate you. Sportsmen often quote such inspirational phrases as 'No one remembers who came second' or, in the case of Linford Christie when he was on his Olympic starting-blocks, 'Go on the B of the Bang!' As much as anything, affirmations focus the mind on the job in hand. The same principle can apply at work when you are under pressure. One senior executive I look after carries a card in his pocket on which is written 'The only difference between a diamond and a lump of coal is that the diamond had a little more pressure put on it.' He looks at this when he feels he is beginning to buckle under his considerable responsibilities, and says it always gives him the motivation to redouble his efforts. Of equal importance, he never lets anyone see the card – if they did, he would feel it had lost its personal meaning for him.

Humorous or ironic phrases are always worth remembering: they can also lighten a stressful day. One that always brings a smile to my lips, and makes me think things are not as bad as I imagine, comes from an American Civil War general. On looking over his barricade to the enemy, he said, 'It's all right boys, they couldn't hit an elephant at this dist . . .'

Learn two or three phrases that are meaningful to you and use them often. They will repay your effort many times over.

Affirmations not only inspire, but also subconsciously influence a person's behaviour. Use those you relate to, and repeat them to yourself every day. Those I use include 'The difference between talent and success is hard work,' and 'Enjoy today – you do not know what tomorrow will bring.'

19

The '5 Ds'

With my patients' consent, I sometimes video my consultations for appraisal by fellow doctors. After showing one such clip, I asked my colleagues, 'What was the first thing you noticed?' To my astonishment, they all agreed on the same thing – how tidy my desk was. Later, I dug out a video from my earliest days as a GP and was interested to see my desk overflowing with papers. What had changed? I puzzled over this, then remembered a seminar on time management I had attended some years previously. There I had heard about the '5 Ds'; a tool for managing stress at work. I must have absorbed the concept.

◆ Do

◆ Defer

◆ Dump

◆ Delegate

◆ Discuss

These '5 Ds' represent the five possible responses to any piece of work, mail or personal or office problem. Do, dump and delegate are decisive, whereas defer and discuss require definite deadlines leading to completing actions. The categories may seem artificial initially, especially if you even hoard junk mail 'just in case'. However, once you get used to selecting your course of action, you will find it is liberating and less stressful to make decisions and stick to them.

'Do' means what it says – sort it out, there and then – no prevarication, no time-wasting; a simple, complete process, whether it is sorting out a piece of paperwork, or launching yourself into a bungee jump. Job done.

'Defer' gives some breathing space while you await further information, or think about your best option. It is *not* an excuse to run away from your problem, or put it off indefinitely. After only a day or two, you must then 'do, dump or delegate' – that is, work out what the paperwork actually means to you, or listen to what your head thinks about jumping off a bridge attached to big rubber bands.

'Dump' simply means bin the paper, the action or whatever. Face the fact that you never want to bungee jump, not ever, and go and find something more interesting to do. This decision is final!

'Delegate' is a subject on which many books have been written. Can someone do the paperwork better than you, or is a teamwork approach possible? Can you ask your best mate to jump off the bridge instead? For this action to be complete, you must ensure that someone actually jumps.

'Discuss' means just that: not moaning because you are uncertain what to do, but seeking advice and sounding out ideas. The object is to clarify in your own mind what is expected of you before committing yourself to acting. If you have jumped off the bridge already it is too late to discuss it.

The '5 Ds' reduce stress because they give you control over what you do, whatever your level in the workplace hierarchy. Used correctly, you should then be able to add a sixth – 'de-stress'.

Do. Defer. Dump. Delegate. Discuss. These can be applied to work, home and anything else you choose. Each in itself is a form of action – even deferring or discussing will lead to doing, delegating or dumping.

20

The 50-minute rule

Concentration is not infinite. We all know the feeling when we are working hard for hours on end – the longer we stick at it, the more difficult it seems to get. At the end of a typical Monday, not only have I forgotten most of the 60 patients I have seen, but find it difficult to put any sensible thoughts together. It is only later, when I am able to relax with a decent glass of wine, that my concentration span rises again. This is because I have spent most of the day breaking my own golden rule – work hard and concentrate as best you can, but remember to rest your brain for five or so minutes every hour. This may involve relaxing, thinking about nothing in particular, doing breathing exercises or spending time on a completely different project. The project should be something of personal interest, such as planning a holiday or thinking about a treat for yourself. It does not matter whether you actually get the treat – it is the thought that counts.

There are of course difficulties with this. Employers – and I am one – do not like their staff to sit with their feet up. However, if you are stuck at a desk for most of the day, simply getting up and doing something different can be effective. As long as your brain is allowed to switch off and float free for a few minutes it will reward you by working better. You may not notice dramatic effects immediately, but jobs that always had loose ends begin to get finished, and the headache at the end of the day will disappear.

This point was highlighted some years ago when I was treating a City trader for stress. His problem was not that he could not do his job. On the contrary, he was very successful in all he did. However, constant pressure – and the thought that he would be criticized if he was away from his desk for any period – meant he became insecure about everything he did. This would have been bad enough if it was just his own money he was dealing with, but when large amounts of other people's money were involved, it was even more important that he felt in control of his actions. After deciding that what would help him most was the chance to have a small number of breaks in his day, he was able to devise a screensaver on his computer that looked like a trading screen, but was actually a dummy image. This would last for five minutes before disappearing, and he would flick this on every hour or two between important actions. It gave him the opportunity to look at the screen and think about nothing, while he cleared his head before starting his next activity.

You do not need to go to such lengths to achieve the same effect. Simply remember that a change is as good as a rest as far as your concentration is concerned.

Give work your best shot for 50 minutes in every hour, then recharge for 5 or 10 minutes. Switch to a different project if you can. Concentrating for long unbroken stretches makes you less efficient, so keep yourself alert and focused.

21

Zap that phone

Edgar Degas is one of my favourite artists. At the turn of the century he dined with a friend who had just had a new invention installed – the telephone. Degas' friend had arranged for someone to phone him during the meal, and when it rang he rushed to answer it. Flushed with pride, he returned to the meal, looking expectantly at Degas. Having thought for a little while, Degas said, 'So that's the telephone. It rings and you run.'

I sometimes think of these words during a busy day when all I seem to do is answer the phone. We have all experienced the situation of the phone ringing when we are rushing out of the house, or a phone call disturbing a special moment. The chances are you probably answered it, making yourself late for your appointment or spoiling a romantic mood. Why should it? It should not be difficult to take charge of your phone and let it work for you, not against you.

It is highly irritating to return someone's call only to find they are unavailable. In many such cases you will get their voicemail or answerphone. When this happens, always leave a message and then get on with your important jobs. Don't go chasing the person again. If it is important they will get back to you. The exception to this is the important call that must be dealt with. In that case it may be you who will need to do the chasing.

Whatever your job, the following principles apply:

◆ If you find you are constantly being interrupted by telephone calls, set aside a time when you will deal with nothing else. Let everyone know what this period is. If this is not practical, use an answering machine to screen your calls and clear your messages at regular intervals.

◆ Buy a caller-display unit and attach it to your phone. These are relatively inexpensive, and allow you to see the number of the person ringing you. You can then decide whether to answer. These units also allow you to see the telephone numbers of people who rang earlier.

◆ Whenever possible, keep calls short and to the point. If key decisions need to be made it is always best to have a meeting face to face. It is much easier for people to mislead or confuse you when they cannot see you.

Do not underestimate how annoying phone interruptions can be to someone who is trying to talk to you. I once had a patient walk out on me after the fourth telephone interruption during their consultation. The fact that the calls all needed my attention was irrelevant, and they were quite right to be upset. The next time they came to see me I made a point of taking the phone off the hook.

Phones are good masters but bad servants. Return a call only once. If it really is important someone will find a way to speak to you. However, remember that you will have to do the chasing if you want to speak to them. If you are under pressure of time, build phone-free time into your day and try to have time-wasting calls screened – this is *your* time that is being eaten into.

22

Become a team player

Many of us have to tread a fine path when dealing with work colleagues. Ideally, we would all work at the same pace and with the same intensity. At the end of each day everyone would go home happy, feeling that there were no weak links in the office and everyone was doing a good job. As we all know, however, things do not work like that. Being part of a team means knowing how your teammates work best. Yet few of us do, and this can cause false and deeply hurtful misunderstandings and assumptions about your performance. Remember:

◆ There will be people in a team who work best alone. It is not a good idea to put such people in a position where they have to manage people. Let the good communicators in the team do that.

◆ Selfishness will get noticed. Taking the credit for something other people have done will only alienate you from them, and make them less likely to help in the future.

◆ Selflessness gets noticed for the right reasons. If you are an expert in a particular field and colleagues are struggling, give them a hand. Do this in an open and friendly manner, but don't expect to get any extra points for it — your help should be a favour. Like many favours, however, you may get a reward in the future when you least expect it.

◆ Be wary of criticizing someone too readily if they appear to be struggling. They may well be doing their best and are embarrassed to say they are out of their depth. This is bad enough in an office situation, but I have seen junior doctors at the start of their career who have never recovered from vicious comments made by consultants simply because, as a result of inexperience, they were not working quickly enough.

Many years ago I went on a 'team-building' course with some of my staff. Our aim was to encourage a closer working relationship and thereby increase efficiency and morale. While this illuminated our good points, it also showed us just how much personalities determine whether a team will work well together or not. Everyone had talents, but these either were not known, or were not being used correctly. People got on well with each other unless someone appeared to be promoting themselves above the rest of the team. The result was general discontent.

Teamwork means there is a common desire to do the best you can, while accepting that everyone in the team has limitations. It was this last point that people on our team found hardest to take on board, and because of this the exercise was ultimately a failure. There was one positive point though – I now know how to build a space rocket out of cardboard boxes and string if I am ever stuck on a desert island with four other people.

At the very least, be seen to be a team player, on the principle that selfishness gets noticed and selflessness can get results. If a project involves a number of people, don't be the weak cog in the wheel.

23

Don't assume you are the cause of other people's bad temper

Recently, I was driving along a quiet country lane on a fine day, and was in a good mood. An old friend drove past me at some speed. I just had time to acknowledge him before he was out of sight, but to my slight irritation he did not respond. Over the next few miles this irritation turned into worry, frustration, and finally mild anger. By the time I got to my destination I needed to take some deep breaths to calm down.

I had fallen into the classic trap of reading a whole book into a situation that was not even worth a line. My thinking ran along these lines:

◆ He saw me but chose not to acknowledge me. I must therefore have upset him and be out of favour.

◆ He knows something I don't. If he knows this (whatever it is) he will have told other people. They now think less of me. It must go against me.

◆ I must have made a medical mistake. I haven't seen him socially for a while, so there has to be a professional reason why he ignored me. What have I done wrong, then? What does he know that I don't? What makes him think he's a better doctor than me?

This type of thinking will continue as long as you let it. In this case it lasted until I came to my senses and realized that probably he had just not seen me. I met him at a meeting some days later and mentioned he had passed me in a hurry. He replied, 'Sorry about that. I was in a desperate hurry to catch a train. I didn't have time to wave and made the train with 30 seconds to spare.' I had turned his mad dash for a train into a professional slight against me.

We are all prone to this type of 'knee-jerk' thinking. The easiest way to stop it is to put yourself in the position of whoever you think you have upset. Have you ever walked through a door held open for you without saying thank you? If you were too busy or distracted to notice that day, why can't someone else be? You will have been late for appointments despite your best efforts – other people are too. Putting this thinking into perspective takes practice, but always pays off. Remember – you do not have a divine right to be the only person having a bad day at the office.

However, this is not an excuse to explain away rude or hostile behaviour. If someone persistently ignores you, they are probably doing exactly that – ignoring you. In such cases you need to find out what is going on. Raising the issue with that person may cause you anxiety, but not as great as the anxiety your knee-jerk thinking will generate if you do not.

If someone is grumpy or rude, don't assume it is your fault. Stop the knee-jerk response of blaming yourself and consider other possible reasons for their behaviour. They may have a hangover, or be late for a meeting.

24

Make 'firebreaks'

I meet many people who are frantically busy. They wear their diaries and Filofaxes as badges of honour, proud to be indispensable and wanted by everyone. Every now and then they will say to me, 'You have no idea how busy I am,' and then look puzzled when I reply, 'Yes I have. I'm busier.'

This is not a macho boast, but fact. The difference shows when I compare diaries with such people. Theirs are crammed with appointments, meetings and social engagements they have often forgotten about until that day. Mine is also booked up well into the future, but there are breaks of 'clear blue water' in each day. They are like firebreaks, and there are usually three for each day, lasting for between 20 and 40 minutes each. *No one* can fill these spaces except me, and if I choose to open them up and use them I can do that only on that day, not before. These 'firebreaks' of time in my diary provide a number of benefits:

◆　They reduce my temptation to commit to more than I can do. I can say 'No' more easily.

◆　If my work is running late I know I have the luxury of being able to use one to catch up and keep to my schedule for the rest of the day. However, you should not get used to doing this; if you find you are always running late, then you need to look at how you are managing your time in general.

◆　If, suddenly, there is something I really want to do, I am not in the position of being so busy I cannot squeeze it into my day.

48

◆ Firebreaks give me the chance to stop and think about my day, my projects and problems, or simply relax and recharge.

◆ I no longer feel everyone is getting something out of me except me and my family. Knowing you have some control over your day makes you more, not less, amenable to requests by friends and family for your time.

I am often taken to task by my patients for the length of time they need to wait before seeing me for a routine appointment. This is often said half-jokingly, as 'You shouldn't be so popular,' but resentment remains. There are two things I have no control over in my work: the number of hours in the day, and the number of patients wanting to see me personally. If I am exhausted and frustrated about trying to squeeze more into the day than I am physically able to, I am of no use to anyone.

As a junior hospital doctor, I once apologized to a patient for keeping her waiting, but a friendly nurse pointed out I was coming to the end of an 80-hour continuous shift, and was slowing down. 'Really? Then take him away and get me a fresh one,' was the patient's reply. I kept my thoughts to myself, but if I had been able to take breaks in that shift, she would have been more charitable.

The firebreaks in your diary may not make your work easier, or your boss more friendly, but they will allow control in a busy day that would otherwise beat you.

Divide your diary into half-hour slots and build in buffer blocks of time for the unexpected – three half-hour buffers each day would be ideal. Avoid taking on more than you are capable of by learning to say 'No'.

49

25

Don't cry wolf

People are interesting. Even those I dislike make me wonder why this is so. I find the way in which people react to situations fascinating, and there is no better example of this than the way in which people react to bad news. Their reactions range from supreme self-restraint to hysterical outbursts, and very often the reaction you expect is the opposite to that which occurs. You have to know someone well in order to predict how they will react to the misfortunes of life, and it is often a mistake to take them at face value. People who constantly tell you how busy they are may be no more – or even less – stressed than you are, but you usually have no way of proving this.

The problem here is the 'crying wolf' syndrome. You can only claim immunity from jobs at work or home because of stress so many times before people stop believing you.

If you tell yourself that you are always too stressed or busy to help other people, is this really the case? Are you deliberately keeping your stress levels high in order to look indispensable, or justify your position? Many people fall into this trap, with some, or all, of the following in mind:

◆ I can avoid more work. I'm obviously so stressed that no one would want to give me any more work, especially menial tasks. Let someone else do those instead.

◆ I like the adrenalin buzz I get from rushing around, no matter how little I seem to get done.

◆ I can avoid personal relationships. I am simply so busy at work that I can't be expected to form any kind of relationship with anyone. Everybody knows that, so no one tries.

◆ I am very important. I must be, because I am busy working on crucial projects that no one else understands. Because I am indispensable, my job is safe.

◆ It lets me behave badly. Everyone will understand if I am in a bad mood, because they know how much stress I am working under.

If any of these apply to you, take a good look at why you need your stress. What gap in your life is your stress filling? Write your goals down, and compare them with what you have in your life. Your stress is not going to protect your job – no matter what you think. Encouraging feelings of helplessness as a way of proving how busy you are is a certain way to work inefficiently, resent everything and everyone around you, and lose any balance in your life. While your work is at a level you can deal with, deal with it. When it goes beyond that, or your workload is inappropriate, then that is the time to make yourself heard. People will then know how serious you are.

Believing you have more work than you do or exaggerating the amount of time you spend on projects is counterproductive. Not only will it encourage helplessness, but after a while people will not believe you. Then, when you do get really busy, you will be on your own.

26

Separate work and home

More people work from home than ever before. This has advantages, but it can also can be a source of stress – 'work pollution' of the home. The ideal set-up is to have a specific room in the house solely for work and nothing else. This is where the phone, fax and computer, desks and other equipment should be. The phone and fax should have a different number from your domestic phone, and the whole should be viewed as an office that is bolted onto the house, rather than a room that is sometimes used for work. If you have to have meetings at home, use this room.

Unfortunately, many people aren't able to put a whole room aside purely for work. Kitchen tables, a bedroom or the lounge can be filled with work papers, which can cause problems leading to stress:

◆ Work is less efficient. You lose papers and documents, since they get moved during normal family activities.

◆ There are more things to distract you – remember there will *always* be just one more job that needs to be done in the house – and if you are bored or finding work difficult, you are more likely to allow yourself to be diverted.

◆ You may find yourself increasingly resenting work because you are always thinking about what you would rather be doing – having coffee with a friend, reading a book or watching television.

◆ When you are not working you may be continuously reminded of it by the work papers around you. You will think of work every time you look at them, however hard you try not to, and therefore you will never feel you can relax.

I used to feel like this until I decided to have a room that I would use only for writing. I put my work hat on when I walk into it and take it off when I walk out. Business calls go through to that room on a business number and I make sure that any papers connected with my media work remain there. The rest of the house is therefore not polluted by work, so I never think of what I should be working on unless I am in the work room.

Where space is a luxury, you can still prevent work stress at home:

◆　Make sure you use a filing system so your work can be stored tidily under a desk or out of sight, even if this is under the kitchen table.

◆　Use one specific part of the house, such as a particular table or chair.

◆　Tidy up at the end of each day.

◆　Work at well-defined times, and make sure you observe them. Do not overrun.

◆　Turn your computer off when you are not using it. When you do this, imagine you are turning your work off at the same time.

A patient who worked at home felt he could never relax there, so he turned his shed into an office. This proved to be very beneficial, since it put some distance – however small – between his work and his home. He now feels completely relaxed about working and says he is 'off to work' when he walks the ten metres to his shed. However you choose to distance your home life from your home work, it will cut down work pollution and stress simply and quickly.

If you work from home, try to dedicate a workspace with its own telephone and fax as a separate part of the house. Never let work pollute your leisure time and space.

27

My boss doesn't like me . . .

For some people, one of the most common causes of stress at work is the belief that their employer dislikes them. Such a belief can be imagined or real, and is made worse by a feeling of impotence at work. On two occasions patients have come to see me the very day they resigned from their job because of a situation such as this. In both cases they withdrew their resignation the following week.

The temptation sometimes arises to walk away from an uncooperative boss. In certain circumstances this is the only answer; however, don't take such drastic action until you have looked at alternative ways of dealing with the stress.

First, ask yourself if there is a real problem. Communication between employees and employer can be notoriously tricky, so if you feel you are disliked, ask if you are. You don't have to be aggressive about it, and it is easier if you have decided what you are going to say beforehand. Arrange a meeting or take five minutes at the end of the day to express your concerns. You will get some idea from this meeting whether your concerns are genuine. If not, regularly appraise what is happening at work and, if it helps, keep a diary of any problems. If the situation becomes worse, you can use this to go back to your employer.

If there is a problem, identifying it is not enough. You will now need to discuss the specific issues that have caused it. Doing nothing will make matters worse. If you have to have another, more detailed meeting, you must be clear about why you are having it. Don't walk in with a list of vague complaints and expect to have all of them dealt with. Think of possible solutions, so you don't sound as if you are simply whingeing, but rather are being constructive. Remember, in such meetings you need to focus on *functions* and not personalities. There are only two possible outcomes. First, your employer will listen to you and discuss your grievances. Ideally this will be followed by a letter outlining a plan of action, and suggesting regular checks to see if the plan is working. Even if the outcome is not ideal, you should still fell less stressed because your employer has listened to you and acted on your concerns.

Second, you may be ignored. Your boss may refuse to see you, reject the possibility that problems exist, or simply tell you that that is how it is. It is often impossible to get past such an attitude, and you then have two options. You can accept that you are working for an unhelpful employer and nothing will ever change. Work is simply the means to pay the bills and your enjoyment either comes from the rapport you have with your colleagues, or is found outside your job. The alternative is to look at the practicalities of resigning. This is a major step, but sometimes there is no alternative. Always remember: if the situation cannot change, change your reaction to it.

If your boss is impossible to work with, you have a choice. Raise the specific issues with your boss and suggest or work out possible solutions; or, if this fails, accept that your work and peace of mind may suffer; or resolve to walk away from the situation. Focus on *functions* not personalities.

28

Be assertive

Anyone can become angry – that is easy. Yet to be angry with the right person, to the right degree, at the right time, for the right reason, and in the right way – that is not. I wish I had said that, but Aristotle said it first. The thought may be thousands of years old, but it is as relevant today as it was when he first wrote it.

Many of us are very good at confusing the practice of arguing our views with being aggressive and forceful. As a result, some of us will let things drop and opt for the quiet life, while others stand up for what they believe in – an example of how different people handle conflict in different ways. An understanding of your particular reaction to conflict is vital if you are to change and be able to state your views coherently but non-aggressively.

Types of arguers include:

- ◆ The 'walkers', those who walk away from conflict, who feel nothing is worth a disruption in their lives. With a serious conflict this attitude can lead to further difficulties. Walking away will not get your opponents running after you. Rather, the opposite will happen, because they will think they have beaten you.

- ◆ The 'duckers and divers', those who avoid immediate confrontation but return to face it after thinking things through. This buys time and gives you an opportunity to prepare, but initially, you must not simply disappear. You need to make it clear to the other party that there is a problem, and that you will be facing this directly. State a time to meet and follow it through. Remember, however, that you may be seen as simply ducking the problem, and as a soft touch in the future. Make a firm plan of action, or the other person may take advantage of you.

◆ The 'dominators', those who try to railroad their plans through whatever the opposition. Occasionally, this is necessary because there is little time, a decision has to be made and no one is prepared to make it. However, people who regularly argue in this way are simply hijacking rules and agendas to gain power. Deal with these as you would bullies (see Tip 11), and don't allow yourself to be rushed into agreeing to something you are unhappy with.

Remember these key points to being assertive without stress:

◆ Be honest and straight with people. They may not always like what you say, but they will know that what you say is what you mean.

◆ Don't fall into the trap of thinking you need to say something at all times. Being silent can be extremely effective. A silence followed by the word 'No' is clear and to the point.

◆ Stay calm. Use the mental wall (see Tip 12) or be angry in private afterwards, but don't let anger pollute your calm assertiveness.

◆ Use body language. A relaxed, open stance suggests confidence and control. Standing with your arms folded, or pointing in someone's face, shows defensiveness.

◆ Listen to the other person, even if you disagree with them. People who know they are in the wrong are more likely to concede defeat if they feel their opponent has listened to them.

State your case consistently. Repeat it if necessary. Don't allow yourself to be distracted by other people's arguments.

Assertion is not aggression. Aggression is believing someone else's needs are less important than yours; assertion is being able to stand up for what you believe in, as an equal with someone else. Calmness and persistence are the watchwords.

Many people think that standing up for themselves means being loud and aggressive. For more effective results, assert your case politely and calmly. Choose language with care. 'I obviously have not explained that clearly enough. Let me go through it again,' gets better results than 'You're just not listening, are you?'

29

Plan your day the night before

This is one of the most obvious tips for relieving stress, yet people either ignore it or do not think about it. The one thing most people are always short of – apart from money – is time. I am no exception. Judging by how my patients start tutting and sighing if I run a few minutes late, it seems most of them hold the same opinion. We seem to have the least time first thing in the morning when we are juggling all sorts of activities: getting up and dressed, organizing partners, spouses, family, the dog, and having, in theory at least, a decent breakfast and trying to get to work. Since many people feel sluggish at this time of day anyway, this is a recipe for running late. It sets up the day in a stressful pattern, which can last all morning. Small wonder that some people do not feel in control of anything until they reach work and stop to draw breath.

Always assume you will not have enough time each morning to get every job done at a steady pace, and plan ahead accordingly. However much time you spend the night before in preparation for the following day, you will save double that in the morning. The main time-savers that work for me are:

◆ Prepare work the night before. Have your bag or briefcase packed and ready, including the children's school things.

◆ Get your clothes ready and lay them out. This saves last-minute ironing or noticing too late your best jacket or skirt needs cleaning.

◆ Get the breakfast table ready before you go to bed. This can be a real chore in the morning and is best done the previous night.

Assume you will need at least 20 minutes longer to get ready than you think you will. This gives you a comfort zone to cope with the unexpected events that mornings throw at all of us.

Once you are in the habit of preparation, you will spend only five or ten minutes to save many more minutes the next day. We all forget things when rushed. Feeling you have enough time to do all that is needed each morning will lessen stress.

While examining a business director very early in the morning, I was surprised to see a full set of pyjamas under his suit. He was so busy thinking about the day ahead and trying to get to my surgery on time he had completely forgotten to remove them before dressing. This was more amusing for me than it was for him, as he had no time to go home and change before catching his train. With a spare tie from me and a shirt bought from the station concourse, he muddled through.

Start the day badly and watch yourself spiral downhill. To avoid this, prepare clothes, breakfast and work things the night before – 10 minutes of preparation will save you 20 minutes of wasted energy the next morning, and you will start the day organized and in control.

30

Use 'trigger pictures'

A middle-aged woman came to see me suffering from symptoms of severe stress. As long as her work was not mentioned she appeared to be in control, but whenever she thought about work she showed all the classic signs of stress. Her problem was a bullying boss who had gradually eroded her self-confidence. She was so upset that she needed to take sick leave. In the end she left the company altogether rather than face returning. She had become conditioned to a certain stress response whenever she thought about work, and for her the only solution was to run away from it.

Fortunately, this response can work in reverse. Just as stressful thoughts can trigger stress responses, pleasurable thoughts can trigger feelings of well-being and relaxation. We can make use of these at difficult times to break a vicious circle of stress, for example before an interview, before speaking in public, or after an unpleasant or stressful encounter. The choice of image is yours, but you should keep it to yourself as a 'mental mantra'. The beauty of this is you can use it anywhere at any time – on the bus, walking down the street or at work. You do not need absolute peace and quiet, but the technique works best if you are not too rushed. Common sources of imagery include:

◆ A romantic encounter that you experienced.

◆ Lying in the sun on your own empty palm-fringed beach.

◆ An achievement you are proud of – however small.

◆ Terms of endearment from family or friends.

◆ Your ultimate fantasy – whatever it is.

Whichever image you choose, it is important to choose the same one every time. Think of it as watching the same video in your head. With each viewing you feel more and more relaxed. This is positive feedback – your body learns to associate your mental picture with feeling better and therefore relaxes.

It is said that the legendary baseball player Babe Ruth thought about the inventor Thomas Edison every time he went to bat. The thought of Edison's success after so many early failures not only inspired him but relaxed his swing. The more he thought of Edison the more he relaxed and the better he played. The results of his 'trigger picture' method speak for themselves.

This tip does not give you permission to use it as an excuse to daydream and avoid those hard decisions that you need to make. It should be used only at times of stress, not as a way of wasting time in the hope that a problem will disappear. You must stick to your goals and aims. Remember that a goal you are not actively working towards is simply a wish, and most wishes never come true.

Build a mental library of images of your favourite places or situations – for example, a family birthday, a success at work, winning a tennis match or walking on a palm-fringed beach. Recall these in times of stress to trigger feelings of well-being and relaxation.

31

Detox

You have an hour to prepare a presentation at work, and your job depends on it. Your spouse has called to say the dog has been sick in your new car and the baby has come out in spots. What do you reach for – a glass of water or an extra strong black coffee? The odds are it will be the coffee. One cup then becomes 15 through the day, although you know it's guaranteed to wind you up.

As a chocolate-loving tea-drinker I have the greatest sympathy for patients when I tell them to reduce their caffeine intake, but the facts cannot be ignored. Caffeine raises the pulse and blood pressure, and studies suggest it may also increase blood cholesterol.

People drink coffee not only for the taste, but also for the kick they get from it. It acts as a stimulant, stressing the body and causing the caffeine 'high'. Unfortunately, as with all stimulants, the high is short-lived, and is followed by a drop in energy, which is not a problem if you have more caffeine. Before you realize it, you are in a caffeine cycle that is driving your stress along.

Cutting down is obviously a good idea, but do you know exactly how much you are drinking? If you make a note of every time you have a cup – or more likely a mug – of coffee or tea, you may end up with a figure of 15 to 20 cups a day. This is a high level of caffeine, which your body has come to expect. Therefore you should not simply stop drinking coffee overnight, as this will cause a major headache. Instead, try the following tips:

◆ Drink a glass of water, fruit juice or herbal tea when you wake up, instead of coffee. If you can't bear it, have just the one cup as a treat.

◆ Substitute one cup of coffee or tea with one glass of water or fruit juice every day. By decreasing your intake in this way, you will reduce it to a manageable level in two to three weeks. Don't substitute ordinary cola drinks, as these either are caffeine-loaded or contain chemicals such as phenylalanine, which may also be habit-forming.

◆ If you crave the 'hit' of a cup of coffee, either drink more of another fluid or eat some fruit. This technique is used very successfully by people who want to give up smoking.

◆ If you miss the taste of coffee, try decaffeinated – although connoisseurs complain it is not as good as the real thing, and the chemical process needed to remove the caffeine deters others. My advice is: enjoy real coffee – not instant – in moderation, drinking fewer than three to four cups a day.

The benefits of reducing your caffeine intake vary, but after a few days you will notice that the symptoms of caffeine withdrawal – such as irritation and edginess – have eased. Within seven to ten days you will have fewer headaches and less indigestion, and will sleep better.

A word of warning. It is probably unwise to give up caffeine and cigarettes simultaneously. Lose the nicotine first. Henderson's law states that stopping smoking is the single most beneficial thing anyone will ever do for their health. Then move on to the caffeine.

Count how many cups of coffee, tea, fizzy drinks or alcohol you drink each day and try driving out bad habits by introducing good ones. Replace half your drinks with water, squash or fruit juice.

32

Use your car. Drive it too

The M6 motorway is not the best place to hold a consultation. If the patient and the doctor are 50 miles apart it becomes even more difficult. I have been rung on more than one occasion by busy executives who were scheduled to see me, but were stuck on the motorway. On such occasions I dispense with general advice, and always tell the patient to use the time they spend stuck in a traffic jam to think about what they are going to say to me when we next meet. Accordingly, when we do meet, they have a concise list of symptoms, or they have thought more about their problem than they would have done otherwise. This is better for them and better for me, as well as a good use of otherwise dead time.

As a doctor, I find that my car is my lifeline. I need it to get me from A to B, but if I add up the time I spend in it I get a frightening result. The same applies to millions of people, most of whom accept delays and wasted time as part of the hassle of commuting. This is a shame; the time can be used to great advantage if you want it to be. There is nothing wrong in letting your mind switch off in stationary traffic and thinking about nothing. Doing breathing exercises at the same time will relax you and quickly clear your mind of stressful thoughts. If you are unable to do this, or prefer to feel you are doing something else, there are a number of possibilities:

◆ Listen to music you enjoy, or do not normally have the time to listen to. I would not inflict loud house music on my family, but find it good fun while doing house calls. Record a tape of your favourite songs and listen to them. Indulge yourself.

◆ Listen to a recording of that book you always wanted to read but never did. Audio books are an excellent way of making boring and frustrating journeys pass quickly. They may include novels, or motivational or self-help tapes. Learn a foreign language using courses on tape. I know one person who learned to speak fluent Italian in a year just listening during his car journeys.

◆ Carry a Dictaphone. Dictate the thoughts you want to remember as they occur. They may range from shopping lists to major plans for life improvement. Listen to them at the end of the day and act on those plans that still sound worthwhile. There may be a lot of dross on the tape but there will be jewels as well.

Remember, you do not need to take a bath in order to sing. The car is a great place to belt out songs, especially if you have a voice like a car exhaust. Look around you the next time you are stuck in traffic – you may well be surprised at how many people are happily singing along to something. They may look daft, but they are probably feeling better for it, and that is what matters.

Traffic jams are a fact of life. Don't waste that time in road rage. Listen to audio books, use a Dictaphone for organizing home or work, or learn a foreign language. Singing, too, is a great stress beater – with the added bonus that no one will hear you.

33

Your best is good enough

Our culture often suggests that there are always greater efficiencies to be made and better results to achieve. This is a commendable thought, but there is a law of diminishing returns – you can only do your very best; more than that does not exist.

I was reminded of this recently from an unexpected source, when I was asked to see a young girl whose parents were concerned about her low mood. Teenagers can be notoriously difficult to assess, and I was having a difficult time establishing any kind of rapport with her until I asked her about her schoolwork. Tears began to well up in her eyes, and the reason for her sadness became apparent as she talked.

She was a bright girl, popular at school, and she worked diligently. She always tried to please her parents, who wanted her to become a doctor or lawyer. However, although she wanted to do as well as she could, she also wanted to spend time seeing the world before deciding on her career. She had recently worked hard for an exam, achieved the excellent mark of 91 per cent, and come top of her class. On telling her parents the good news, she had been crushed by their response – 'What happened to the other 9 per cent?' As a line guaranteed to shatter anyone's self-confidence, this took some beating. Since then she had begun to question why she should bother to achieve at all. It took many sessions to rebuild her confidence, and eventually I had to confront her parents and tell them to let her do *her* best and not theirs, unrealistic as it was.

Being sacked for incompetence is one thing, being fired for not reaching someone else's standards is quite another. The key is whether you have truly tried your best. If you have, and it is still not good enough, you can hold your head up no matter what anyone else may say. It is still a cruel blow to lose your job because a superior cannot see that you have given your all, but you have nothing to apologize for. If, however, you have simply not bothered to try, you probably have no cause for complaint if you are dismissed.

Success is a relative term. Major companies view it strictly in terms of a balance sheet. This is simplistic. People can only do what they can do, and if they do not succeed in someone else's eyes, it does not automatically mean they have failed. I have never failed, but have tried thousands of ways that don't work! View success in this way and it becomes a healthier option.

Success should be judged on how hard you have tried, not on whether you have 'succeeded'. If you have done your best, that is all you can do – give yourself a mental pat on the back.

34

Panic, prepare, present

Anxiety is a major reason why patients come to see me. Driving tests, fear of flying, interviews or exams are the usual things that trigger their stress. Yet there is a simple way to reduce 'nerves' and improve performance – the '3 Ps':

◆ First, panic. Accept that whatever it is that is worrying you will make you nervous. Nervousness will increase the closer it gets to the big day, and you must accept you are going to be nervous and there is nothing you can do about it. It is a normal reaction and everyone suffers from it. A university dean came to me suffering from terrible anxiety because he knew he had to give his annual speech in a few weeks. He had given this for a number of years, and felt more anxious each time. He falsely assumed that because he held an eminent position he should not feel such stress: 'I'm an adult and shouldn't feel like this.' He began to feel better when I told him I would be more concerned if he didn't feel as he did. Anxiety is normal.

◆ Second, prepare. Our fears are usually about what we don't know, and therefore are afraid to face. There is little point in revising what you already know, and thinking you are working well. It is what you know little about that will catch you out; you need to write down what you think are your weaknesses and address them. If you think you are going to fail your driving test on your lack of reversing skills, work harder on those. Think about what questions you are likely to be asked at an interview and rehearse your answers. A piece of music you have to perform in public needs practice in the difficult sections, not the easy ones. Many people think they will succeed by practising what they are good at, and hoping that will be enough – often it is not. The dean was usually too busy to give any real thought to his speech until a day or two beforehand, and then tended to trust to luck and a few notes on the back of an envelope. I suggested he write out his speech in full two weeks before the presentation, and rehearse it every day until it became second nature. This included rehearsing to the empty college hall he would be using.

Third, present. Imagine your driving test is in progress, and the way in which you are going to take each section. Think about things that may not quite go to plan, and accept these may happen. They will not necessarily mean you have failed, and if you have prepared for their occurrence you will be better able to ignore them if they occur. If they do not, so much the better. As the dean stood on stage, although he was nervous, when he looked at his speech it was so familiar to him he felt relaxed about saying it. He remembered standing on exactly the same spot the previous day, and pictured himself talking to an empty hall. Before he knew it he had given what was said to be his best presentation in years. Now he no longer fears speech day, but remembers to use the same routine to prepare every time.

Failure begins well before tests or exams are taken. Identify the sources of your stress, look at your strengths and weaknesses and prepare well in advance. Concentrate on what you want to do, not on anyone else. Remember that anxiety is natural and sharpens your attention.

35

Answer back

The main requirement in my job is the ability to listen. After that comes the ability to talk. These sound simple, but to do both well can be very difficult. We have all experienced the frustration of talking to someone who never gives a direct answer to a question. Whatever you ask is answered either with another question or with a distracting statement that leads away from the point you are discussing. Being direct with such people usually gets results, but decide what type of person you are dealing with beforehand:

◆ The moaner will grumble about anything you say, but never have any solutions of their own. All the time you spend with them will be fruitless, unless you ask what it is they want, and keep asking until they tell you. If they don't, you both know they are simply moaning for no good reason.

◆ The silent person will try to answer every question with a 'Yes' or 'No'. You must ask questions that need deeper answers, and gradually find out what their views are. If there is still little response, let them know your plans or thoughts so they can think them over. Give them the opportunity to return and speak to you later if they wish to do so.

◆ The hesitator will stall at any opportunity. If pressed too far they will not say anything, so gently find out why they are delaying. Say you will help them, and tell them how, but point out that you also need their help to do this.

◆ Nice people can also be difficult to handle. They will agree with everything you say for fear of any argument, since they need to be liked by everybody. They smile even when being criticized. Show them you like them by saying so. Then you can delve deeper to find out what their concerns are.

I took over the care of a woman who, superficially, seemed extremely pleasant. In fact she was an authoritarian bully, used to getting her own way by a mixture of domination and flattery. After several frustrating weeks during which she ignored all my advice, she smilingly said as she was about to leave, 'You must think I'm an awful patient, doctor.' When I replied, 'Yes, sometimes you are,' she was flummoxed. The usual response had always avoided a direct answer, and she took this as implicit that her behaviour was acceptable – and so it continued. No one had actually confronted her about her behaviour for fear of upsetting her. We had a long discussion about why I felt as I did, and understood each other much better as a result.

Humour can be an effective way to defuse conflict, especially if you are uncomfortable about being direct. This does not mean you should tell jokes at random. Where humour is inappropriate, it will make the situation worse. If you hold a position of authority, humour is often seen as patronizing or cruel by your subordinate, so great care is needed. If a joke is reciprocated by another joke, that person may be using your humour to avoid the serious issue at hand. The office clown tries to do this by using up other people's time and energy. Ignore them and be direct if you need to.

People who cause you to feel stressed or who irritate you are likely to continue to do so until you confront them. Don't just suffer in silence. Develop the ability to deflect with humour if you feel uncomfortable about being direct.

36

Reward yourself – you've earned it

We all do things we would rather not do – attend a meeting that we know will be unpleasant, participate in an activity that makes us nervous or sit down to a day's work that stretches far ahead of us. There may be nothing we can do to avoid such tasks, but we can reduce our stress by rewarding ourselves when we achieve them – 'deferred gratification'. The reward can be tiny or substantial, and can be taken immediately after the event or at some time in the future – there are no rules. The point is that you decide your own reward.

I observe the use of deferred gratification almost every time small children are brought unwillingly to see me by fraught mothers. The phrase 'I'll get you some sweets after if you behave' is usually said more in hope than in expectation, but it sometimes works. Little Johnny wrecks my waiting room, is tolerably well-behaved on promises of sweets when seeing me, and resumes his wrecking behaviour the minute he leaves the surgery. It is only when we grow up that an understanding of the 'work today, jam tomorrow' idea becomes apparent.

The editor of a major publication knows each day is going to be chaotic the minute he gets into the office. To counter this, on his way into work he does one of two things. First, he looks at the TV listings for that evening and decides which programme he is going to watch while relaxing with a glass of wine. If there is nothing he particularly wants to see, he then takes out a pocket cookery book and decides on a new recipe he will try instead, often buying the ingredients before he gets to work. These are his two ways of looking past the stress he knows is waiting for him, and helping him get through the day. If you also use the tip of dividing a task into bite-sized chunks, you will at least feel you have some control over your day.

There may be occasions when you cannot claim your reward. You are kept late at the office, so cannot get home to try out that new recipe or watch your favourite programme. Accept that this will happen from time to time, but remember to give yourself a reward later, even if it takes a different form. Should your week be so busy you never pick up any of your rewards, have one large treat at the weekend such as dining out rather than making a meal for yourself. Remember why you have earned your reward, so you have a positive reaction the next time you need to look past a stressful day.

We all have to do things we do not want to from time to time. The trick is to look past them and think of the reward you will give yourself for doing them.

37

Think in concentrated bursts

We constantly think about problems and the decisions we have to make. Most of these are mundane and common. Did I turn off the gas? What do I need to get from the supermarket? Such problems take relatively little thinking time to resolve.

Bigger problems require more thought. We mull these over, amending our views as new information or ideas occur, or as our moods and external events influence us, and then come to a conclusion. Despite the thinking involved, the conclusion itself is often hasty, a half-botched idea that leads to more problems and revisions later as its disadvantages gradually become apparent.

I used to think in this manner until I examined the new managing director of a large company in serious financial difficulties. He had been called in as a troubleshooter to try to keep the company afloat, and was in a constant round of negotiations concerning finance, redundancies and insolvency. Although his reputation was on the line he was remarkably relaxed, and I asked him what his secret was. He told me he knew how to think. When I pressed him for details, he explained that if he had a particularly difficult problem, he set aside 30 minutes of time – away from work, and in the bath if need be – to concentrate fiercely on that problem alone. He used all his powers of logic and thought, making doodles or jottings as he went along if that helped him to think, and then either he had the answer or not. If not, he switched off from the problem and thought about something else until the following day, sometimes waking up with the answer. He viewed any time beyond half an hour spent thinking as counterproductive.

Sir Isaac Newton and Albert Einstein followed a similar procedure when grappling with problems concerning Life and the Universe. If there was no answer they gave up and slept on it, or went off to do something else instead – giving their subconscious minds a chance to deal with it, unconstrained by the more restricted logic of their conscious thought. We may lack the mental agility of great physicists, but the same principle applies to us all. Rather than spending all day half-thinking about a problem, concentrate on nothing else for a set time before making a decision or moving on. This encourages clear thought and makes the lack of an obvious answer easier to accept. Change the way you think about solving your problems and you will spend less time worrying about them.

Incidentally, the troubleshooter saved the company.

Give a problem your best thoughts for a concentrated 30 minutes. If after that you can't come up with the answer, switch off and come back to it another time, or sleep on it and let your subconscious do the work for you. A fresh mind will give fresh perspective.

PART THREE
LIFESTYLE

38

Keep it simple

There is a trend that began in America and is taking hold in this country called 'downshifting', which may be seen simply as making one's life less cluttered. Most of us spend our working hours trying to squeeze more from less, then at home we use up our time doing chores, resenting the feeling that our social lives could be better. There are many books on how to make life simpler, but here are four points that work for me and will reduce anyone's stress levels:

◆ Take one job at a time, however quick or easy it seems. It is tempting to do many jobs at once so they get done in the shortest possible time – cooking while helping children with homework, or writing a report while watching television. Not only does no job get done correctly, but also you will need to do some of them again, so increasing your stress.

◆ Try to do one small job each day. It can be soul-destroying trying to clear a large job over a weekend that has needed doing for months. Instead, do one task as part of what needs to be done – tidying a wardrobe as part of cleaning a bedroom – and when you've done it, stop. Do another small job the next day and gradually the work will get done.

◆ Keep your social circle at the level that is most comfortable for you and you alone. I am always suspicious of people who claim to have hundreds of dear friends who would do anything for them. While it is fun to go to large social events – especially if someone else is paying – the expensive and elaborate social soirées that take all week to prepare are no more satisfying, and certainly more stressful, than a casual meal with a few good friends. These will want to be with you for your company, not to climb a social greasy pole or gain some social cachet. Friendship lasts – meals are usually forgotten.

◆ Don't allow cleaning to dominate your life. I have visited houses where I have deliberately chosen not to sit down, and where my feet kept sticking to the floor. Conversely, I have been in homes where I was obviously the dirtiest object present, and whose owners could not wait for me to leave before re-cleaning an already spotless room. Clean and presentable is one thing, obsessively clean is another. Life is too short to spend attached to a duster.

◆ Try to simplify chores, and ask yourself why you are doing them in the first place. If they are using up time you would rather be spending on yourself or with friends and family, look at ways of achieving the same result in less time. I have yet to meet anyone who said to me on their deathbed, 'You know, doc, I wish I'd spent more time cleaning the house.'

Use the 'Home Four' tips to simplify and de-stress your life:

- **Carry out one job at a time, however small.**
- **Each day, finish one task – this puts you back in control.**
- **Keep social commitments at the level *you* are comfortable with.**
- **Don't become obsessed with cleanliness.**

39

Take a daily stress MOT

When someone is very stressed, I can usually tell within the first 30 seconds after they sit down in front of me. It is never someone bursting into tears that gives the game away, although that happens so often that a box of tissues is one of the most important items on my desk. Rather, it is body language and what is not said that provide the clues. People suffering from stress can be thought of as tightly coiled springs, and the only thing stopping them from going into orbit is usually a constant battle to prevent it. In other words, they know they are very stressed but are so locked into the stress cycle that they cannot get out even if they want to. They sit with hunched shoulders, and knitted eyebrows, and seem to lose inches from their full height when they walk about. When you ask about specific symptoms, the common ones quoted are headaches, muscle aches and neck and back pain – all muscular in origin. A great many will also have a typical sitting or standing pattern at work or home – the sales rep who drives 1,000 miles a week, the VDU operator who has not quite got their computer position comfortable for them, or the mother who has her baby balanced on one hip for most of the day. When we have a pain in one part of our body, we often compensate by trying to get into a pain-free position, which may be more uncomfortable than the first, and so on.

The trick here is to have a few simple exercises you can do in the car, in the office or even when you are standing doing the cooking, which will release these tensions and prevent them from building up. As a result, muscle aches and headaches are lessened and you will generally feel better. The exercises take about five minutes, and you can do them as often as you want during the day, whenever you want. I do them at the end of a busy surgery or during long periods when I am on call. I invariably feel refreshed as a result. Think 'head, neck, shoulders, arms' and you have it.

1   Bend your head forward so that your chin is resting on your chest. Massage your temples slowly with your fingers in a clockwise direction for 10 deep circles. Repeat going anti-clockwise.

2   Bring your head up and press one ear against your shoulder, keeping your shoulder still. Repeat on the other side.

3   Rotate your right shoulder 6 times in a large circle, forwards and backwards. Repeat on the other side. Finish by reaching upwards with each arm as high and as straight as you can. All the time, concentrate on what you are doing. Breathe slowly and deeply with each movement.

When I suggested these exercises to a very successful businessman who was complaining of chronic stress-related headaches he looked at me as if I had just crawled out from under a rock, but I bet him a bottle of claret that if he stuck with them for two weeks he would feel better. A little more than a fortnight later his headaches had disappeared and there was one less bottle of wine in his cellar. We were both pleased with the results.

Recharge every two or three hours by taking five minutes to massage your temples, breathe deeply with your eyes closed and open your jaw as wide as you can five times. Add a positive mental picture for even greater effect.

40

Be generous

Many people feel stressed because they are channelled into a particular way of thinking. They are stuck in a routine at home or at work, and life is different shades of grey instead of new colours. This leads to boredom, frustration in relationships and a lack of self-worth which in turn leads to negative thinking and stress.

Quite by chance, I saw one of the best examples of how routine can damage a relationship when a patient called Alan came to me with a minor problem. Having quickly dealt with the problem we had time to discuss his forthcoming wedding anniversary. He was very much looking forward to taking his wife to the same restaurant they went to every year, and presenting her with a bouquet of flowers at the end of the evening. He told me how much she looked forward to this; it was one of the high points of her year as far as he was concerned. I was genuinely pleased for him and wished him well.

The following day I saw his wife Fran for a routine appointment and asked, almost in passing, whether she was looking forward to her anniversary celebration. Her reply was loud and to the point. Not only was she fed up with going to the same place year after year, but knowing she was going to be given flowers at a certain time in a certain way reduced the gesture to routine. Warming to the subject she told me how she dearly loved her husband, but resented the fact that he never made any impulsive gestures. In all innocence he felt — as many men do — that taking his wife out for a meal once a year was enough to show his affection. For the rest of the year a routine was followed which was driving her to distraction. All she wanted was an occasional, unexpected spontaneous gesture — flowers at other times, a romantic meal at home or even a day together away from home. The more she tried to forget her expectations the greater they became, until they had reached the level where her anniversary was going to be spoiled. Once I had listened to both sides, it was obvious there was a huge gulf between them. It was difficult suggesting to him that he should be more spontaneous, since impulsive acts are just that – impulsive. To plan spontaneity defeats the point. However, I was at least able to point out to Alan that a change is sometimes useful, and he promptly changed the restaurant they were going to. Fran told me later that although the flowers still arrived on cue, she was pleased with them because she knew Alan was trying his best. For his part, Alan now occasionally alters his routine to surprise Fran, and they get on better than ever as a result.

You do not need to spend money to be impulsive. Unexpected compliments can boost someone's confidence for days – but always check you are giving them because you want to, not because you want something back in return.

Give a spontaneous compliment or perform an impulsive act of generosity. These may cost nothing, but can mean everything to others.

41

Learn massage

If I was rich, my daily luxury would be a massage. Massage is the oldest form of therapy for dealing with stress, and its value is as relevant today as it has ever been. Daily tensions and stress make us tense, a state many people come to accept as normal. They have forgotten that time as children when they were attuned to how their bodies felt, and are used to the pain and muscle stiffness that result from a hard day's work.

Hippocrates – the 'father of medicine' – wrote that of all his arts, the doctor must be 'assuredly experienced in rubbing ... for this can loosen a joint that is too rigid'. It is often not until we have a good massage that we realize just how tense we are, how much nervous energy we are burning and how refreshed and different we feel afterwards. Touch is a powerful tool that not only reduces pain but also makes us feel loved and wanted.

The simplest way to relax is to buy some massage oil and spend a quiet evening with your partner learning how to massage each other. You do not need to have a diploma to work out what to do, but if you want to take it seriously there are many books and courses on this subject. Patients often look at me in surprise when I suggest this treatment to them, but when their neck pains or headaches are cured they are delighted not to have tried the usual path of pills and fortitude that many doctors prescribe. If you do not have a partner, you can practise self-massage. Massage those areas where you feel stiff or uncomfortable. The usual places are:

1   Neck and shoulders. Lie on your side and massage the side and back of your neck, using slow, circular movements. Move on to the shoulders and as much of the upper back as you can comfortably reach, then turn over and massage the other side.

2   Back. Sit upright and place the fingers of both hands on either side of your spine. Starting at the bottom, move your fingers up your back, pressing lightly. Do not press on the spine. Work up the back as far as you can reach, then work back down again.

3   Legs and feet. Do this after you have massaged your back. Sit down and stretch your legs out in front of you. Starting on the right, rub upwards from your toes to your hips in small circles. Repeat with the other leg. (If you find it difficult to reach your toes with your legs outstretched, prop your feet up on a stool.)

4   Face. Lie down flat on your back and stroke your forehead with both hands, moving from the middle out to your ears. Move down from there to your chin and rub very gently under your eyes. Finally, give your scalp a brisk rub for five minutes.

A difficulty with self-massage is that you are not able to relax as much as you could if someone else was massaging you, but it is still well worth doing at home, or in a work break. You can even massage your face while sitting in a traffic jam. Listen to what your body tells you and, even if it is only an occasional treat, give it what it needs.

Massage is one of the most effective ways to deal with stress that there is. It works by releasing endorphins – nature's painkillers. Buy a book on massage or enrol on a course, and practise with your partner or a close friend. Remember how you feel afterwards and try to maintain that sense of relaxation.

42

Use daily checklists

Lists can be useful or a waste of time. Some people write lists of things they need to do, and seem to think that by writing the list their jobs will do themselves. Students who write out immaculate revision timetables and lists of topics to be studied are a good example of this. They feel that by writing these they are doing something constructive about passing their exams, when in fact they are wasting what revision time they have. It is completely appropriate to plan ahead for a stressful event, but unless you take action on the basis of those plans you are storing up failure.

The same applies when making a checklist to streamline the day ahead. A checklist is a great way to use time effectively and prevent important jobs from being forgotten, but only if you act on them. Writing a list you never look at is pointless.

At the end of a day take five minutes or less to think about what you must do the following day. You may be tired, but do it then or you will not do it at all. Write down what you feel has to be done, and be ruthless and realistic about it. This does not have to be related to work – it may be getting to a school play or remembering to ring an old friend you have not spoken to for years. Whatever is written on your list, always make sure you finish that day having achieved at least one job on it, however small. Any job that is transferred from list to list every day either will never get done or should have a time limit put on it for the end of that week. If it has not been done by then, take it off the list – it is obviously not that important to you.

Patients often see me with lists of complaints – 'I've been saving them up for you, doctor!' If I do not have the time to deal with every one, or each seems to be a major problem in itself, I will ask the patient to pick the problem they feel is most important. They will always know which this is, and are usually happy if it is dealt with. They can deal with the less important, or more recent, problems next time.

You may know there are certain things that you want to do but which never seem to get done. This may highlight problems in the way you manage your time, or mean you were not keen to do them in the first place. If you never seem to get round to ringing that friend on the list, ask yourself why. Do you really want to talk to them, or are feelings of guilt and duty the reason you write their name down? Be honest, and you will soon learn what is really important to you.

Spend five minutes writing down what you need to do the following day. Then note what you would like to do if you had the time – a wish list. Be ruthless about what is important and try to achieve one thing from the wish list, however small.

43

Keep pen and paper by your bed

Stress affects our sleep, and when this happens many people feel that they must really do something about it. When they see their GP they either are in an exhausted state or have been sent by their partner, whose sleep their insomnia is also disturbing. They are not necessarily looking for a magic pill, but simply want to know how they can prevent their worry from interrupting their sleep.

I learned how to worry less by sleeping more quite by accident. On a home visit to a bank manager, I noticed a large pad of paper next to his bed. The top sheet was covered with a mass of scribbles and deletions, and I asked if he was planning to write a book. He replied that, on the contrary, the scribbles improved his sleep, reduced his stress and worry, and helped his sex life. When I asked what he had to write to achieve this, his reply was 'What you write is up to you. It's when you write it that matters.'

When I saw him next I asked for more details. He told me he had a stressful job, with the very real possibility that he could be made redundant at any time. This had begun a pattern of stress and anxiety, which started to keep him awake every night. He would think through one problem and as soon as this was sorted in his mind another would appear. By the end of the night, not only had he gone without sleep, but he could not remember most of what had kept him awake. He had also begun to realize how little of what he worried about actually seemed to happen.

One night he wrote down some of his worries, initially in order to decide which were the most pressing. In doing this he soon realized that much of what was worrying him was either out of his hands or not worth worrying about. The simple act of writing clarified the real concerns he had, and he then jotted down possible solutions or random thoughts that came to him in the night. At the same time, he determined to look at and act on them the next day. To his surprise he found he was able to get to sleep after only 30 minutes of thinking and scribbling. If he woke in the night worrying about something, he quickly wrote down both the problem and any answer he thought of before putting the problem down with his pen and going back to sleep. The following morning, when he came to look at what he had written, most problems seemed irrelevant or inappropriate, and the rest were either answered or needed more thought. In this way he was able to sort out his real problems, and stop himself from thinking about the same problem night after night. He slept better, and had more control over his work, and so was less distracted when he went to bed, much to the delight of his wife.

Tackle worries that stop you from sleeping by writing them down there and then. Look at your notes the next day. The problem will not seem as bad, or your subconscious may have come up with an answer.

44

Stop, sit, think

Although I do not meditate, some of the most relaxed people I know do. When I have asked them how they think they benefit from it, almost all of them say it is as much the chance to have quiet time as anything. It is often this quiet time that is sacrificed as we attempt to do everything we have to during the day. So we often forget how to stop and simply be quiet. Our bodies become used to adrenalin and activity, never properly relaxing even when we would like to.

In the middle of a summer's day I allowed myself to take a walk in a large park. It was lunchtime, and people had come out of their offices to take advantage of the sunshine. The great majority of these were still animated and busy, moving around or talking to friends, but every now and then I would see someone who was sitting doing absolutely nothing – just sitting quite still and obviously concentrating on relaxing, breathing deeply with their eyes closed and completely oblivious to all around them. After several minutes of this they opened their eyes, focused on the world around them and went back to work. Some may have been meditating, others simply thinking. However, they were all doing the same thing to lower their stress – stopping and relaxing.

Similar opportunities arise when you find yourself walking past an open church. If you can, take five minutes to go in and sit down. Listen to the peace and quiet and compare this with how noisy and rushed you are during the rest of your day. Think about nothing else except how you feel – concentrate on relaxing, and make a mental picture of your stress dissolving. The next time you feel overstretched, remember this quiet time and try to recreate it wherever you are – at your desk, on a train or lying awake in bed.

I look after a sprightly 87-year-old woman who goes to church but is not religious in any way. She makes a point of finding ten minutes at some point in every day to stop, sit and think about relaxing. In her case she feels a church provides the quiet and solitude that helps her, but if she cannot leave her house, she still takes her ten-minute silence. She has been doing this for decades, and swears it is the secret of her healthy life. Although I cannot prove it, I think she is right, as time spent in relaxation is always quality time.

Our lives are so busy that we forget to reflect on the past day, never mind the last week or year. Next time you walk past an open church, go in and sit quietly for five minutes. Store this feeling for times of stress, to help you think more clearly.

45

Eat well, eat right

Stress can be caused by eating habits. This ranges from eating too much junk food, or eating too much or too fast, to eating the wrong amounts at the wrong time of day. The old adage 'Eat breakfast like a king, lunch like a lord and dinner like a pauper' is still a valid one. If you tell someone that if they eat a good breakfast they will end up slimmer, they will not believe you, but this meal reduces our craving for carbohydrates later in the morning. Many people feed cravings with chocolates, crisps or high-fat snacks and therefore put on weight.

Recent research has shown that a low-fat, high-carbohydrate breakfast not only is good for controlling weight, but also may reduce stress. In a study of over 100 people, those who ate cereal every day suffered less stress and depression than those who did not eat any breakfast. Although those who were eating breakfast had a healthier general diet and lifestyle than those who weren't, this alone could not explain their lower stress levels. It is unclear why this occurs, but it may be caused by the calming effect that carbohydrates can have on our moods.

Although no diet can remove all the stress from your life, there are some dietary principles that may help you feel better:

◆ Avoid bingeing and crash dieting at all costs. Overeating, or comfort eating, is a problem in many people who feel stressed.

◆ Eat as much fresh fruit as you can, substituting this for biscuits or chocolate when you are hungry.

◆ Increase the amount of B vitamins in your diet by eating wholegrain bread, lean meat and fish. Stress destroys these valuable nutrients.

Cut out white rice and white flour, and if you are allergic to wheat, buy gluten-free bread.

For many people proteins can be mild stimulants, so small amounts eaten throughout the day can be beneficial. A combination of low-fat, high-protein foods increases alertness and energy levels in a much healthier way than a 'quick fix' of a sugar burst followed by an energy dip.

46

Learn how to breathe

People who are stressed breathe too shallowly and too fast. This can cause palpitations and headaches, although sufferers often don't connect these conditions with their stress.

We all start from a position of strength, in that breathing is an automatic reflex, but nevertheless, we can still alter *how* we breathe. Controlling your breathing controls your heart rate and most symptoms of stress. Getting your breathing right can revolutionize how you feel and perform at any time.

The important point is to breathe from your diaphragm and not from your chest. Chest breathing is shallow, with air moving only through your upper lungs. Oxygen levels fall, and your body becomes stressed and produces an adrenalin surge that triggers palpitations, headaches and muscle spasm. These make breathing even shallower, your body utilizes less oxygen and you may experience a classic panic attack.

It is easy to learn the technique of deep breathing from your diaphragm, and you don't need to be fit in order to practise it. If overweight Italian opera singers can do it, so can you.

1   Lie down in a quiet room. Breathe in through your nose and, as you do, push your stomach and abdomen out. Focus on your breathing and imagine that the air is filling you and rising into your shoulders as you count to 5. Do not force it and keep your shoulders relaxed. If you feel you want to breathe out quickly, don't worry – this urge will lessen as your breathing improves.

2   Hold your breath briefly, then slowly breathe out through your mouth, once again counting to 5. Focus only on what

you are doing and concentrate on your feelings. Repeat this for 2–3 minutes if you can. Breathe normally and feel how relaxed you are before restarting again. Repeat 5 times.

Once you have learned how to relax by breathing deeply, link this to a time of day or an activity, such as sitting down to work at the beginning of the day, or in a daily traffic jam. For a quick fix at times of acute stress, take three or four deep, regular diaphragm breaths, then return to normal breathing for a few moments. Repeat once more. This will be enough to slow your pulse and allow you to concentrate clearly, talk rationally or survive a stressful event such as speaking in public.

Watch famous actors or politicians, and observe how they behave before they speak. They lower their breathing rate in this way and relax their shoulders every time. It does not turn them into Oscar-winners or enliven their speeches, but they feel less stressed as a result. So will you.

Deep breathing, diaphragm breathing and counting techniques are all exercises that can be done anywhere at any time. They are a very useful preparation for stressful occasions.

47

You *can* find the time

When someone says 'I can't find the time for that' they usually mean that a particular activity does not interest them enough to find the time to do it. An example is finding time to visit a distant relative. Although some people explain away the fact that they don't visit by the excuse that they have too little time, most would somehow find it if they were given £100 for each visit. The problem we all have with time is not how little we have, but how we choose to use it.

Of all the solutions that people try in order to reduce the pressure of time, there seem to me to be several worth remembering:

◆ If you have a number of hobbies but never seem to get to grips with any of them, decide which is your favourite and concentrate on that. Having a low golf handicap will be more pleasurable to you than trying half a dozen other activities and hacking around a golf course each weekend. Make priorities for your leisure time. If you are taking up a certain sport, make sure you know how much time it will involve.

◆ Rather than have work spill over into your leisure time, target two days in the week when you will accept a longer working day, but leave work on time the rest of the week. Keep work pollution of your free time to a minimum.

◆ Starting on a Monday morning, make a diary of what you do each day for a week. Plan to spend 30–40 per cent of your time at work, 30–40 per cent at home with family or friends, and put the rest aside for yourself. If work is taking up more than this, there may be little you can do about it – these are the hours you need to work to survive financially.

It is patronizing to tell people in these situations to spend less time at work. If they could, they would. What such people need to do is view each non-working hour as priceless and spend it on something that is important. This may be family, following a football team, or watching television. Whatever it is, once you have decided what is important you should not feel anxious about spending time on it.

◆ Our lives change. Babies, new relationships and everyday stresses and strains mean we must be flexible about time. There are often occasions when individual preferences have to be sacrificed in the short term – for example when a partner is ill, or financial belts need to be tightened during a crisis. View these as temporary measures and remember to look at the big picture – life is a marathon, not a 100-metre sprint.

You would not hand out money you cannot afford, so do not squander your most precious asset – time. It waits for no one. A dying millionaire told me he would burn all his money to be able to regain the time he had wasted. He had acted on the belief that there was always another day, and another after that, so he had never done all the things he wanted to, and now never would. The old cliché of time waiting for no man was his epitaph.

When you say 'I haven't the time', what you are usually saying is 'I haven't the time given all the other ways I choose to use my time.' Take last week's television guide and circle every programme you watched. Do you still think you have no time?

48

Early to bed . . .

Making night visits is a part of my job I never enjoy. It is not the patients' fault, I just like my sleep too much. There is, however, a useful consequence of getting out of bed at 4 a.m. and returning home an hour later wide awake. On such mornings I am reminded of how useful these hours before dawn can be. Knowing that I will never be able to get back to sleep, and that the rest of the house will be up in an hour or two anyway, I use the time to do all the things I should have done but have never got around to doing. This might be filing accounts, catching up on work, reading or writing. On such days I arrive at my surgery knowing I have done half a day's work already, and I can then look forward to a relaxing evening that would otherwise have been polluted by work.

With a young family, quality sleep is at a premium, so I don't make a habit of getting up early every morning – my children do that for me. There are, however, many people who use the early hours to set themselves up for the rest of that day. For example, some people have a body rhythm that makes them function better in the evening than in the morning, and for them getting up an hour early each day simply tires them out. For others, the early hours are when they can do all the things they always meant to do.

Driving along a country lane at 5.30 one morning on my way home from a house call, I came across another patient of mine out for an early-morning jog. This surprised me, as he was not a man who went in for physical fitness. In fact, his motto could have been 'No pain, no pain'. On chatting to him I found out that he got up twice a week at 5 a.m. and went for a short jog to wake himself up. After this he sat at his desk at home and mapped out the day's work and his vital jobs for the rest of that week. Sometimes he just sat and thought about life, and occasionally listened to music he enjoyed.

The important point as far as he was concerned was that this time was his and his alone. He used it as he pleased and got great benefit from it, however he decided to use it on any particular day. He sometimes went to bed slightly earlier on the days he got up early, but found that because he was not getting up early every morning, tiredness did not seem to be a problem for him.

When I got home that morning I spent an hour doing all the things I should have done the week before, and so spent the rest of the day feeling less pressurized. Whether you do so occasionally or every day, by using the early hours for yourself in ways you want to you will be handsomely rewarded.

Getting up one hour earlier than normal can increase your energy – it all depends on what you do with that time. Read, exercise, think – you will feel energized by the sense of achievement this creates. If fatigue is a problem, go to bed slightly earlier.

49

To sleep, perchance to dream

Two things in life I am short of are time and sleep. I sympathize with insomniac patients looking for a cure, but pills are never the answer. When I take a detailed sleep history from such people, the cause of their problem is usually obvious and relatively easy to fix.

Yet why should a lack of sleep matter? We know how awful we feel when we are short of sleep, but forget the longer-term consequences. Poor sleepers have twice the number of road-traffic accidents and spend half as much time at work as those who are good sleepers. Serious accidents at work are more common, with simple tasks becoming more difficult to perform. Decision-making becomes more difficult than ever, causing an increase in stress, which keeps you awake at night.

Alcohol, caffeine and tobacco all affect the quality of sleep. Although people think of alcohol as a relaxant – 'I need a few drinks to get to sleep' – it causes fragmented sleep later in the night, as do nicotine and caffeine. There is a long half-life in caffeine, including that in some fizzy drinks, which can puzzle people who have given up drinking coffee in the evenings but still have a problem sleeping.

I am a great believer in routine and sleep is no exception. Waking at the same time each morning helps the body's natural rhythms, which promotes sleep at night. It is important not to lie in as this throws your body clock out of step. If you spend the night tossing and turning there is no point in trying to will yourself to sleep; this is self-defeating. Get up and do something different instead until you feel tired again. Remember that 'trigger pictures'(see Tip 30), such as an image of an imaginary place, work better than counting sheep or thinking about the day ahead.

Exercise can help sleep but you need to be careful. Exercising late in the evening may exhaust you but will delay sleep.

Get into the habit of exercising each day to improve your sleep pattern gradually.

The bedroom is important. Do not have it too warm as this may wake you in the small hours. Remove the television – the bedroom is for sleeping, not watching television. Sex is an excellent relaxant and nature's best way of promoting deep sleep.

Sleeping pills do not cause natural or restful sleep and there is always the risk of becoming dependent on them. If you do need them, this should be for the short term only, to help break an abnormal sleep pattern. There is no such thing as the right amount of sleep, but most feel satisfied with between six and eight hours a night. You will know what your body needs – ignore it at your peril. Better-quality sleep can be enough to slash your stress level, so take a long hard look at the reasons you cannot sleep and change them.

Combat insomnia by eliminating the most common causes: excess caffeine, excess alcohol, the absence of regular exercise or an overheated bedroom. If the problem persists try 'trigger pictures', relaxation exercises, a hot bath, herb tea or lavender oil.

50

Divide your time into small chunks

I take time to start working efficiently most days, as I am probably at my best in the afternoons. Work and time wait for no one, however, so we all need ways to motivate ourselves to get going, especially on a Monday morning. How many of us wake up thinking about the day ahead, already wondering whether it will ever end? This is bad enough when we are organized, but what about the teenage mother of three in a high-rise block of flats, who views each day as hard graft simply to be endured before the next one starts; or the prisoner, waking each day knowing there are another thousand to go before any chance of release?

There is a simple way of making such long days much more bearable. I realized how it could work when I visited a mother with two small children, who was sleep-deprived at the best of times, even without her new baby. She was managing to cope with all the demands made on her by thinking of each day not as a continuous stretch of time, but as a number of small chunks put together to make up the day. She planned to get through each chunk – two-hour sections – at a time rather than thinking about the end of the day, which depressed her because it seemed a long way off. The breaks in the day were such activities as watching certain children's programmes, walks in the park or set mealtimes. These were, in effect, arbitrary points in her day that she had set up to make each day pass more quickly.

We can all use this principle with variations on the theme to tailor it to our own situation. I put 'firebreaks'(see Tip 24) into my surgery hours so I don't have endless lists of patients waiting to see me at any one time, and I never look at my afternoon workload before I finish my morning. I think of a treat I will give myself at the end of a day and look forward to it during each break. What I always to avoid is thinking further ahead than I actually need to. There is little point in worrying about what you need to do in two months' time when all your attention should be focused on what is happening now. To overcome this tendency use Einstein's thinking technique (see Tip 37) to prepare for events in the future when you have finished your immediate jobs. If a major project is causing you stress, make sure the deadlines are realistic and then cross off one day at a time. Don't waste time worrying about what might happen in the future. Take each task as a small brick in a big wall and mentally tick each brick off as you finish each task.

You can think of time as something you can cut into pieces in lengths that suit you. In this way Monday mornings become much more bearable.

Think of your day in terms of a number of two-hour chunks, each to be crossed off before moving on. Do not look past each chunk before it is finished. For larger timescales, cross off daily blocks.

51

The colour-strip trick

This is a very simple tip, yet it can cause a dramatic reduction in stress levels. I first saw it when visiting a vicar; while talking to him in his study I noticed a small piece of blue paper stuck onto his wall clock. Intrigued, I could not resist asking him what it was doing there, and he replied that it preserved his sanity. Whenever he was writing sermons or doing parish paperwork, often under pressure of time, he would often look at the clock to assess his progress. The blue strip reminded him to relax, calm down and, in his case, draw inspiration from his Creator. It stopped him feeling overwhelmed by pressure and made him realize what he was writing was probably not the most vital thing in the world at that moment. It gave him a sense of perspective.

I was amused by this, but forgot about it over the next few days. Some months later, when I was battling against a number of deadlines as well as juggling all my other commitments, I remembered the trick and tried it. In my case I wrote the word 'relax' on a yellow label and stuck it on my printer. This meant I would see it occasionally, rather than all the time, which would have happened if I had put it on my computer screen. To my amazement, it worked. I would forget it was there, would build up a head of steam and stress while writing, and then would see it. It made me stop, breathe properly for 30 seconds, relax and start again. I hit each deadline feeling as relaxed as I was when I started. The technique can be applied in a number of situations:

◆ At work. If you have your own office, put a colour strip where you will see it occasionally. (This is why a clock is a good example.) If you see it all the time you will become used to it and will end up 'looking but not seeing'. If you have an open-plan office, put it in part of your workspace, for example on the frame of a photograph or on the telephone.

◆ In the car. This will remind you to calm down and accept what is happening on the road – whether it is a traffic jam or road rage. Put a strip on the passenger dashboard. This will not distract you while you are driving but you will see it enough times to remind you to relax.

◆ At home. You can use it here to remind yourself to think about your partner or family. Have you shown them affection today? Are there issues that need to be sorted out before the end of the day? It will lead your thoughts away from the day's stresses and let you think about the important things in your life. Alternatively, if you are feeling exhausted and are hanging on for your holiday, use it to think about that and get through today, to reach your reward later.

The strip can be any colour, and have any word on it as long as it means something to you. Change it regularly so you do not get used to it. You will probably wonder why you have not done it before.

To calm down through the day, stick your favourite colour or word in a prominent position, such as on your computer, phone or clock. Change this often so you keep noticing it. When you do, stop and breathe deeply for 30 seconds before getting back to your tasks.

52

Enjoy a change of pace

Admitting to being bored has almost become a crime. We live in a world in which it seems that if we are not doing something – anything – to move on and achieve more, we are slacking and will never achieve happiness. This is an attitude that is guaranteed to make me seethe, since a constant struggle to fill every minute of every day fills my surgery with stressed patients faster than anything else. It is as if we have become conditioned to always having to 'do', rather than just 'be'.

If this seems a little extreme, ask yourself the following questions:

◆ Do you turn on the TV as soon as you walk into the house, or leave it on when you are not watching it?

◆ Do you have the radio on, even if you are not really listening to it?

◆ Do you clean things that don't need cleaning?

◆ When you are eating, are you thinking about the next course or the next meal?

◆ If you are relaxing, are you thinking about all those jobs you should be doing instead?

The chances are you will have answered yes to at least one of these. Worrying, isn't it? The answer is to learn to be bored, and do something useful with your 'boredom time'. On the next occasion when you say or think, 'I'm bored,' stop yourself and say, 'No I'm not, I'm switching off.' There is no set way of doing this, but always try to spend that time being aware that you are relaxing. Sit still, practise deep breathing and focus on how you are feeling from top to toe. Let your thoughts wander or try to think about nothing at all. After five minutes of this, being 'bored' will have made you feel alert and refreshed.

Initially this can seem unnatural, as we are not used to doing nothing. When I first tried this, I was desperate to go off and do something to fill my time. I felt I was somehow failing by wasting valuable 'doing' time, but within a few days I was feeling relaxed and comfortable when allowing myself to 'be' instead. When other people now say they are bored I reply, 'Good – enjoy the ride.'

Calvin Coolidge, President of the United States, once stood motionless on the deck of the presidential yacht, looking out across the sea for minutes on end. A group of guests watched him, and after a while began to wonder about how he was burdened by all the problems of the nation. As they voiced their concerns, Coolidge walked over to join them and said, 'See that seagull over there? Been watching it for 20 minutes. Hasn't moved. I think he's dead!'

Allow yourself to turn boredom into relaxation and your mind will relax itself, allowing it to be fresher and more alert when you start 'doing' again.

Don't expect to travel in fifth gear all the time. There are always peaks and troughs. Time spent relaxing is never wasted time.

53

It's never too late to change

When someone sits down in front of you and begins quoting from a classic English novel before you have had a chance to say anything, you never forget them. Betty, 76 years old, was a woman I had known as a patient for less than a year. She was a forthright character, and as I opened my mouth to speak she cut me off by loudly saying, 'What man thinks of changing himself so as to suit his wife? And yet men expect that women shall put on altogether new characters when they are married, and girls think that they can do so.' She then sat back in her seat and said, 'There now – what do you think of that?'

I had to confess I was completely nonplussed and must have looked stunned, because she softened and said it was a quote from Trollope she had recently learned. I remained unsure of why she had quoted this passage, and told her so. She related the story of her remarriage after her first husband's death. Unfortunately, there was discord in the second marriage, as her husband wanted to control her life. Having endured this for as long as she could, she wanted my advice. First, she wondered whether a divorce would affect her health for the worse; second, she wanted to know if she was fit enough to take up golf. My answers of 'Possibly' and 'Yes' to these questions were duly considered and accepted, and she went away to think about the situation.

The next time I saw Betty I was walking past a golf driving range. She was swinging her club wildly about, and every now and then would howl with laughter before trying unsuccessfully once more to hit the golf ball. Carefully approaching her from the side to avoid injury, I asked how she was doing. 'Never been happier,' she said. 'Didn't listen to my husband and bought myself this set of golf clubs.'

She told me she had spent her long first marriage doing what her husband wanted. She hoped her second husband would be different but found after they had married that he, too, wanted everything done his way. Rather than end her days frustrated and unhappy she had looked around, remembered that she had always wanted to learn golf and taken it up despite her husband's protestations. For the first time in her life she was doing something for herself, which had brought her happiness.

Today, several years later, Betty is still with her husband, and golfing when the weather allows. Although she is far from happy in her marriage she is pleased she has found an activity that is hers alone. Now over 80, she still occasionally quotes Trollope, and says she is considering writing a book on him when she finds the time. I would not be surprised if she did, just to prove she could.

Getting older does *not* mean you have to stop learning. You can get excitement and satisfaction from projects at any age. You may not be the next Andre Agassi, but you don't have to win a Grand Slam to achieve your personal ambitions.

54

Don't be afraid to swim against the tide

Suzi was a 19-year-old student who came to see me with a problem that was obviously anxiety-related. She was a bundle of nerves, twisting a handkerchief repeatedly as she told me how unhappy she was. She had been brought up in a religious family, and had just left home to begin her university career. After some months she had met a boy she was deeply fond of, but who was pressurizing her to have sex with him.

Suzi found herself with a moral dilemma. She did not want sex before marriage, even if it took many years to find Mr Right. Her boyfriend was nagging her to abandon these views and go to bed with him. She told me she was prepared to give him up, saying that if he respected her he would respect her wishes. I was puzzled about what was troubling her so much, as everything she had told me made perfect sense. It came out that, because she found it difficult to put her feelings into words, her boyfriend and other female students were verbally bullying her to try to make her 'join the crowd', as she put it. She was happy with her life but was being castigated for holding strong views and not being able to express them clearly. This was the cause of her anxiety.

This type of problem causes an enormous amount of stress both at home and at work. Our views often differ from those of our friends and acquaintances, as does our ability to express them. If we differ from our peers – especially as children or teenagers – we can be shunned or kept from participating in friendships and activities, which is deeply upsetting. If you feel you are being pressurized to change your opinions or beliefs, remember the following points:

◆ This is bullying. Treat such people as bullies. (See Tip 11 for how to handle them.)

◆ Take time to think clearly through your thoughts. Write them down and look at why you believe what you do. Keep this list where you can refer to it.

◆ You have to live with yourself. Being coerced into doing something you do not want to do will only ever be a source of regret.

◆ Sticking to your beliefs in the face of adversity is not easy. Expect to be tested – this is normal and most people will accept and respect someone who stands up for their views.

◆ If you change your views, make sure you know why you are changing them. A change is fine, but changing your opinions without knowing why is not.

Suzi went away and wrote out her beliefs, which she found easier than expressing them verbally. This crystallized her thoughts and reaffirmed her views. Her boyfriend left her after he read what she had written, but she realized this showed the shallowness of their relationship and soon recovered. After some months, she has built up a circle of good friends who respect her for who she is, not for what they want her to be. She is now happier and less stressed than she was only a short time ago.

Never allow others to change your opinions. Your opinions are just as valid as those of everyone else, no matter who they are.

PART FOUR
RELATIONSHIPS

55

Talk like a grown-up

I always enjoy seeing the proud parents of a new baby. With a first child in particular, they are immersed in the role of parent, and everything else takes second place. This sometimes causes an unforeseen problem – I call it 'baby babble'.

Several weeks after their baby had been born I saw Simon and Hannah for a routine checkup. I had been treating Simon for many years for an alcohol problem he had managed to overcome, and was delighted to see him looking so happy. The couple were speaking in the usual baby talk most new parents fall into using, and it was difficult to get anything like a normal conversation out of them.

Some months later I saw the family again. It was obvious Simon was drinking heavily, and he and Hannah were no longer talking to each other in an adult way. Whenever I tried to raise the problem of Simon's alcoholism, the talk went straight back to baby matters. The baby was being used as an excuse to avoid serious issues, babble had replaced adult conversation and they were drifting apart. Eventually, I insisted on seeing them without the baby so they could focus on what was being said. Over several sessions they began to talk honestly and openly about what had happened during the previous months, and they shed many tears.

Simon has now stopped drinking, and he and Hannah have a deeper understanding of each other. Each evening they also make a point of saying 'grown-up time', a cue for them to put away the baby talk and speak honestly to each other. They say this has been their lifeline, and I believe them.

However, new parents do not need to have as dramatic a problem as this for communication to dry up. Exhaustion is the norm, sex becomes intermittent or non-existent, and new fathers can resent the attention their partner lavishes on the new arrival. This leads to less, rather than more, discussion about feelings, until there is a major argument about a petty matter, which in turn leads to increased stress.

In this situation it is vital to communicate with your partner. Say how tired you are and ask for help – don't bottle up your feelings. You will come through this trying time intact if you work as a team rather than two irritable, resentful people.

Baby babble arrives with a new baby, at a time when communication between couples is often at its most stretched, so always take the time to discuss adult feelings regularly.

56

Think sex not stress

A patient with sexual difficulties said to me, 'The problem with sex is that men think physical and women think affection.' This may be an overstatement, but I know what she meant. Sex means different things to different people, but it is one of the best ways to reduce stress that there is. A recent study showed that people with fulfilling sex lives – and this does not mean you have to swing from the chandeliers – were more relaxed and in better mental health than those without. Another study of sexual activity and ageing found that couples who made love three times a week looked ten years younger than those who have sex twice a week. Sex keeps you fit, boosts your immune system and releases natural endorphins which relax the body. (It has even been estimated that having sex twice a week for a year will burn up around 10,000 calories!)

Yet where in our busy lives do we find the time to become younger, fitter and free from stress, especially with a young family? As the father of three small energetic children, I know that constantly feeling half-asleep is not a natural aphrodisiac. Tiredness can also start a trend, with the couple's sex life dwindling to virtually zero – and it may be difficult to restore as the children grow up. The old saying of 'Use it or lose it' applies here.

Inevitably, there will be times when sex has to take a back seat. Looking ten years younger is all very well, but if you have a new baby and are only getting three hours' sleep a night, you may happily trade sex for an extra hour in bed. Accept this for the moment, but don't close this part of your relationship for ever. Above all, talk about what is happening. Men find it hard to understand why sex goes off the menu when a new baby arrives, and can easily feel rejected, especially if they also feel threatened by the new arrival. Women may crave affection and understanding rather than sex.

Unless couples discuss their feelings they will reach an impasse. Naturally it is better to continue the sexual relationship, but if you are in a rut, climb out of it now.

Plan a weekend trip away, make love at a different time or in a different place. If children are a problem, find a time when they are not there. Don't forget that 'quickie sex' can be highly erotic and satisfying, and produces the same benefits of reducing stress as prolonged sex. It can also revitalize a stale relationship.

Remember not to expect fireworks every time – think of the sexual rule of three. Out of nine times when you make love, three of these may be just all right, three may be good and three may be spectacular. Whatever your particular ratio is, remember there is no such thing as an 'average sex life'. What matters is that you and your partner are happy.

Having sex is a great way to relieve stress. Make time to enjoy it, and if children dampen your ardour, choose times when they are not around. Quickie sex can be as good at easing stress as prolonged love-making.

57

Resist the argument cycle

Just as you cannot expect to be loved and admired by everyone you meet, you will never be able to win every argument. If you think you always do, think again – this is self-delusion. The problem we have with arguments is that they tend to happen more often with people we are closest to – family and friends. I can argue with a prisoner and forget it happened five minutes later, but an argument with a family member will upset me for some time. Because no two people are exactly alike, compromise is necessary to make relationships work. Sometimes this is smoothly negotiated, sometimes not – hence an argument. As one woman said to me, 'I love my husband deeply, but hate him just as deeply sometimes.' A person may also take flak from an argument through no fault of their own, but because they simply happen to be in the firing line. Examine your reasons for arguing:

◆ The classic reason: you are upset about something that has happened to you and feel wronged or cross.

◆ To get an adrenalin surge, which you need to deal with problems at work or to face up to someone you do not like.

◆ To get attention when you feel you are being taken for granted by someone. The argument may occur away from the person concerned. For example, you may argue at work because it is a 'safe' place to argue compared with home, so there will not be any long-term damage to your relationship as a result.

To let off steam that is a result of frustration. You haven't been able to deal with the frustration properly, and it has built up to breaking point.

All these and more are reasons for arguing with anyone you choose, but before you dive headlong into an argument, take a deep breath and ask yourself why you want to start. If you are rising to a bait dangled by someone else, or automatically challenging a point of view that does not concur with yours, think again. Remember, it may be the other person who wants the argument, not you. If you have thought about it and still choose to argue, go ahead, but remember, if you feel frustrated and upset at the end it was your choice.

A Jehovah's Witness once sat in front of me, challenging me to argue with her stand on blood transfusions. I refused, pointing out that our views would never be the same on this point, and I would not lecture her on the matter. The more she goaded me, the calmer my reply, until she smiled and said, 'Good. I was just testing you to see if you were calm under pressure, because that's what I want from my doctor.' She did not actually want an argument, but was using one as a pretext to check me out. I, however, held very strong views on a point that would have been fruitless to discuss, so kept my counsel. The result for both of us was an improved understanding of each other, and we now have an excellent doctor-patient relationship which would have been in tatters if I had decided to argue.

Do not go hunting the adrenalin arguments create, and stop the cycle of anger and frustration in its tracks. Listen to another point of view rather than automatically getting into fighting mode, and you may well end up winning the argument anyway.

58

The 5 key relationship-busters

Some days I finish my surgery and feel my job description has been changed to marriage-guidance counsellor. Warring couples can see their doctor as an independent referee, arbitrating between them in the (often vain) hope that he or she can put a broken relationship back together. I listen and try to provide common sense and practical advice, but time and again I see the main characteristics that destroy relationships. I call these the 'big 5'. They are:

1   Always be right. Trying to talk to someone who is never wrong is extremely frustrating. Attempting to reason with someone like this over a number of years is a recipe for bitterness and dislike. In my experience, I am afraid that men are probably guiltier of this than women are. Learn to listen to the other side of an argument and remember that no one – and I mean *no one* – is always right. If you think you are, you are lying to yourself.

2   Always be critical. I see this in parents and their children and it saddens me deeply. People who live with constant criticism not only lose their sense of self-worth, but also learn to condemn. A patient for whom I could never do enough was always criticizing my attempts to help him, until one day I asked him if his parents had ever encouraged him in anything. To my surprise he burst into tears and talked at length about how their persistent criticism had undermined him to the point where his defence was to always criticize others. We got on famously after that.

3   Perfect the art of sarcasm. Many couples have learned to use

gentle, or ironic, sarcasm in their relationship and this often disguises a deep affection for each other. This is completely different from the savage and biting sarcasm of condescension, used as a weapon to knock someone's confidence repeatedly and erode their standing within a relationship. This is not only offensive but cruel, and is usually a sign of a weak person trying to bully another. Stand up to it as you would to any other bully and you will see results. When patients ask me to define 'gentle' sarcasm, I remind them of the true story about a petrified young lawyer standing in court for the first time. Facing the judge he could only stammer, 'My lord, my unfortunate client – my lord, my unfortunate client – my lord . . .' Smiling benignly the judge said, 'Go on, sir, the court is entirely with you so far.' That always makes me smile, something raw sarcasm is never intended to do.

4   Become defensive when challenged on any point. It is a rare doctor who does not do this. This is partly a reversion to the days when many doctors thought they were God. Fortunately society and the medical profession now realize that if medicine is to work, it has to be in a real partnership between doctor and patient. This applies to any relationship – if you put up a wall in front of anyone who challenges what you say, however benignly, then the person will probably eventually stop talking to you. Trying to cocoon yourself from any kind of criticism will ultimately leave you isolated. Learn that criticism, when justified, can be useful.

5   Be untruthful. This is the killer. More relationships are wrecked by deceit than by anything else. We all need someone to whom we can talk to as an honest confidant, and we expect such openness in return. This is healthy, desirable and

the basis for a good relationship. Take that away, or introduce the suspicion that one of you is lying, and it is usually only a matter of time before the whole framework crumbles. Lie at your peril, and don't complain if your lies find you out.

There are countless ways to destroy a relationship but the 'big 5' are:

- **Always be right.**
- **Always be critical.**
- **Perfect the art of sarcasm.**
- **Become defensive when challenged.**
- **Lie.**

59

Vary your routine

Routine is important. It gives a sense of order and comfort to our lives, even if we may think we have a set pattern to our day. Unfortunately it is also a source of stress for those who feel they are in a rut and need to break away. A problem arises when they think major changes are needed in order to do this, when in fact only a few minor alterations will make them feel much more liberated and relaxed. Good examples of how you can achieve this include:

◆ Walking to work along a different route, even if this takes five minutes longer.

◆ Wearing brightly coloured socks to work.

◆ Spending your lunch hour in an art gallery, just looking.

◆ Listening to a different radio station in your car.

◆ Ignoring the ironing for once, and spending the time doing anything you want to as long as you enjoy it.

You do not need to think of doing this every day, but if a routine is challenged occasionally, you will have a sense that you are still in control of your day. Remember that these are little victories in your day, and you are doing something for yourself and no one else.

I used to look after Anne, a middle-aged woman who had spent the previous 20 years of her life governed by routine. School runs, family meals, housework and more housework meant she had little time for herself. Yet she had become resigned to this. One day I asked her if she would like to take part in a charity tennis match.

She was delighted, but then frowned and said, 'No, I can't – that will interfere with making tea for the family.' Considering her sons were both in their late teens and her husband was an intelligent man, I pointed out they were hardly likely to starve if she was away from the house for a few hours. After much deliberating, she agreed to attend and thoroughly enjoyed herself – although I did not realize what I had started.

After two decades of being a slave to routine, Anne suddenly found how liberating it was to break free occasionally. She gradually began to play tennis more regularly, to let her sons get their own meals and to do the housework when necessary, rather than at set times as she had always done without thinking. She did not abandon her routine, but simply made it more flexible, with the result that she felt much more relaxed.

Look at your routine and ask yourself why it is like it is. Introduce changes into it as treats for yourself as often as you can. Think of your day as flexible rather than fixed, and use that flexibility to reduce your stress.

Vary your routine. This can be as simple as travelling to work along a different route, or wearing bright red socks. Even the smallest change can pay dividends.

60

Let a conversation flow

We all know how frustrating it is when people we talk to don't let us finish what we are saying. This is a common accusation – often justified – levelled at doctors by patients, who say, 'I came out of his surgery without getting a chance to say what I was worried about.' The doctor is probably unaware of his patient's concerns and carries on in the same manner. The result is a deeply dissatisfied patient and a waste of time on both sides.

How often do we have conversations in the office, at home, or in the pub, when we feel left out in some way, despite saying a lot? Probably frequently, because people often forget that conversation has two parts to it – talking and listening. Being good at only one does not always result in productive discussions.

To overcome this, think of your next conversation as a river. The point is to keep the river flowing as smoothly as you can. It is fine to have white water, calm water and temporary pauses, but it should never stop flowing. Every time you speak or interrupt, you are building a dam in the river. This is removed when you stop talking and the river begins to flow again. However if you, or the person you are talking to, do all the talking, the dam remains and the river stops flowing. This is a sign of a conversation that is too one-sided. In the same way, constant interruptions stop the river flowing smoothly, which is what you are aiming for.

Just as a river gets to its destination more quickly if it is allowed to flow fast and free, you get more out of a conversation if you learn to listen more, interrupt less and let the other person say what they want to say. It sounds so obvious, yet many problems stem from poor communication. People who feel they are able to say what they want to, and get a constructive response in return, not only feel good but also will tell you what is bothering them. Yet if they feel they are always being interrupted, corrected or ignored, the conversation will go nowhere. The next time you are talking to someone, think about how the river is flowing. If it is being held up, is it your fault? If the other person is doing all the talking, listen to what they are saying. Do they have a problem they are desperate to get off their chest, or are they just monopolizing the conversation? If you have to walk away from bores or people who talk non-stop, remember that they stopped the river, not you.

Franklin D. Roosevelt said that as American President he often felt no one listened to what he said at social functions. To demonstrate this he would sometimes greet guests with the words 'I murdered my grandmother this morning.' Invariably the response was one of smiling approval. However, one day he said this to an attentive listener who replied, 'I'm sure she had it coming to her.' After this, the conversation flowed.

Think of a conversation as a river and go with the flow. Don't put up dams to everything that is said to you and learn not to interrupt so much. Then everyone will get more out of the time they spend talking to you, including yourself.

61

Have children, not accessories

Raising children is one of the most satisfying yet stressful things anyone can do. I see many parents who bring their children to me saying they are worried about their development, attitude, schoolwork or a hundred other things. The startling point about almost every one of these consultations is that within five minutes it is obvious that it is not the child who has the problem – it is the parents. Gently suggesting this produces reactions ranging from acceptance to hostility, but it is not my job to pretend something is not happening when it is in front of me. There are certain key points that arise repeatedly:

◆ One or both parents have missed opportunities earlier in their lives. They constantly regret this, and use their children as a way of achieving what they could not.

◆ They view their child's work or sporting abilities purely in black and white – there is no room for the average. There is nothing more soul-destroying for a child of any age who is trying their best than to be told, 'You've got to do better.' Just as your best is good enough for you, so your child's best is good enough for them.

◆ A previously happy relationship between parent and child is soured beyond repair because the parent is constantly putting the child down. There are three other 'Es' apart from education that bring out the best in children – encouragement, encouragement and encouragement.

Understandably, we all want the best for our children but most of us do not put academic achievements ahead of everything else.

A businessman who had put his sons through the most expensive public schooling he could get them once told me how jealous he was of me. I could think of nothing in the world to make him feel like this, but he then said he was jealous of the fact I read stories to my children every night. This was something he had never done, because his children were never at home. He had so much regret about missing out on such a simple act, an act that costs nothing.

On a particular day my waiting room seemed to be full of parents and children. The first family to see me brought their slightly bewildered ten-year-old son because they wanted me to tell him off for not working hard enough at school. He had tears in his eyes as they said this, and I have seldom seen an unhappier young boy. I knew this young boy always did his best, but would never be a rocket scientist. This was not his fault, and I spent the time chastising the parents, not him.

The next family brought in their severely mentally-disabled daughter, who would never achieve any kind of academic qualification in her life. They had accepted her for who she was, and could not have been prouder of her. Despite all the problems they faced, I felt uplifted simply by talking to them. What she could not do did not matter. Being part of a family who were all individuals in their own right did, and the difference in attitudes, happiness and stress levels between those two consultations could not have been more marked.

Don't use your child's achievements as a way of making up for missed opportunities. Be proud of your children for what they are, and live your life while encouraging them to live theirs.

62

Beware the adrenalin buzz

We all work for different reasons. If we are lucky, we get paid for doing what we enjoy. Yet many people tolerate their job simply to pay the bills, and so spend their working life wishing they were doing something else. For others, their job gives them one thing they cannot find anywhere else – adrenalin. You do not need to be a stuntman or firefighter for this. Businessmen looking for the next big deal or people trying to sell their world-beating idea thrive on the buzz of achievement, and seem to appear in front of my desk regularly. There is nothing wrong with hunting success – you do have to look for it, because most of the time it will not just drop into your lap – but it is often at a price.

You can't do two jobs successfully at the same time. If you try to, you will fail. Wanting to be a devoted family man while spending 16 hours a day setting up a company is simply wishful thinking, as is wanting to become rich by spending more time at home or on the beach. Ask yourself these questions:

◆ When you are not at work, are you always thinking there is just one more job that needs doing?

◆ Do people complain about the fact that you seem distracted when you are away from work?

◆ Do you resent time spent away from the buzz of work?

◆ Are you more comfortable at work than at home?

◆ Has success cost you relationships or your health?

If the answer to any of these is yes, write down the reasons why you work. On that list you may well find words such as 'excitement', 'adrenalin' or 'money'. Now look at what you want outside work – family, friends, relationships, good health. Try to work out how the two sides can match up, and you will find you can't. Hunting the buzz can give you material success, but will not add an hour to your life or improve a failing relationship.

The day I wrote the above, I saw a policeman who had to decide whether to take on more commitments at work or accept that he would not be promoted in the future. His marriage was precarious but could be salvaged, provided he spent time and effort on it. He was not especially fond of his job as it was and had often wondered about changing professions, and thought he might like to do so had it not been for one thing – the adrenalin kick he got from being in the front line of the police force. He said nothing came close – not money, sex or relationships. Although I knew he would not take it he asked my advice about what he should do. When I said he could have his job or his wife but not both, he replied, 'I can always get another wife,' and left.

There will never be anything to fill that man's life apart from his job. He knows that, and has accepted the consequences, but I think it will destroy him over the years. If like him you work for the excitement of the job, ask yourself two questions: what do you have when the job stops, and who will remember you?

If you are always hunting the buzz of work and success, ask yourself whether it is preventing you from enjoying life beyond the workplace.

63

Keep your promises

Break a promise at your peril. Its size does not matter – it can involve the washing-up or a major business deal – but its effect is the same. You are seen as less trustworthy than before, and your standing among family friends and work colleagues falls. Keep breaking promises and before long you will be ignored when a decision is necessary. This leads to a loss of confidence and increased anxiety, although you have only yourself to blame.

Most of us make promises to the following people:

◆ To children. One of the ways children learn not to trust is by being lied to, and a broken promise is seen as just that. It can be tempting to promise something to make life easier on a difficult day, but if you know you cannot keep your promise you are simply storing up trouble. Repeated broken promises are not forgotten by children.

◆ To partners or spouses. If you are married or in a long-term relationship, it can sometimes seem the occasional broken promise will do little harm. There may be instances when this is unavoidable, but the reason why should be obvious at the time. Failing to keep your word has a constant negative effect on any relationship and undermines the element on which relationships depend – trust. Lose this and it is hard to salvage a relationship. If you do break a promise, apologize and aim to do better next time, but remember this will not save you if constantly used as a 'Get out of jail free' card.

◆ To work colleagues. If your colleagues think that you will not keep your word they are unlikely to trust you with important tasks. It may also prevent promotion, and make you feel unwanted and at a dead end in your job. Remember, you may be seen as the weak part in a large team simply because you have regularly failed to keep your word.

◆ To yourself. You may not think that breaking promises matters where other people are concerned, but breaking one to yourself does. Diets, exercise, New Year's resolutions or any broken vow – we all fail from time to time, but if we repeatedly excuse ourselves until 'the next time', we are learning how to fail, and this becomes a habit. Be tough on yourself sometimes, and remember how you feel when other people let you down. Learn to keep your promises to yourself and it becomes easier to keep any you make to others.

I once jeopardized the trust of a patient on two separate occasions by forgetting to visit him when I said I would. The first time was not my fault, the second was, and I had a very frosty reception when we did meet. At such times you must be honest, and admit to having broken your word. Covering up a broken promise with deception simply makes things worse, and the other person will guess what is going on anyway. Think of your word as being your most valuable possession. You would not give gold away – why do it with promises?

Never sell your promises cheaply. Just as keeping a promise encourages trustworthiness and reduces cynicism in other people, breaking them repeatedly will shatter their belief in you. Although we all have changing circumstances, don't make a promise you know you cannot keep.

64

Don't exaggerate

Eeyore should be Prime Minister. His ability to understate whatever life throws at him would give him an enormous amount of protection against stress. Saying 'There is an element of damp' while getting half-drowned in the rain is a good example of how to deal with stress — not by thought but by words.

Language is the basis on which we are understood — everything else is secondary. It amazes me how it is tortured, strangled and generally disembowelled when we talk about life's problems. Since I listen every day to people doing that, it quickly becomes obvious how different we all are when trying to describe stress. There are people who need a crisis every day in order to generate excitement in it, while others bear enormous amounts of stress with quiet fortitude.

One of the things that puts doctors on alert is when a patient who does not normally come to see them turns up at the surgery. Because they are not 'regulars' they are listened to with more attention than Mrs Bloggs who turns up three times a day, seven days a week. The Mrs Bloggses of this world are sometimes ill long before doctors believe them, since they have been saying they are unwell for 20 years. In short — they cried wolf once too often.

If everything in your life is a crisis — from burning the toast to finding the right colour shoes to buy — and you tell the world this loud and long every day, who will believe you the day you feel suicidal? The person who says the same thing but restricts dramatizing their words to suitable occasions is believed more readily. Like it or not, this is real life and is how people act.

This point was dramatically brought home to me when I saw a woman who told me — for the first time in 20 years — how she had been brutally raped as a teenager. Her quiet, strong words were more forceful and eloquent than anything she could have said had she screamed at the top of her lungs. When she used the words 'violated' and 'destroyed' they were carefully chosen and therefore carried a huge punch. The next patient was a man who had insisted on seeing me as an emergency and who turned out to be 'gutted beyond all belief' that he had a mild cold. He left the room saying his wife would be equally 'shocked' by the news, and it took me a few seconds to realize he was not joking. It is not difficult to guess who had my sympathy that day.

We live in a media-driven world where bigger and better hype is needed to stimulate jaded palates. Losing a football match is not 'a disaster', but losing a football team in an air crash is. Having a young son ask for an expensive pair of training shoes is not 'a tragedy', but it becomes one when he is blown up by terrorists when shopping for them. The more we moderate what we say, the greater the impact when we use forceful language. Remind yourself of this daily and gain the benefit as a result.

Avoid exaggerated language and choose your words carefully. A flat tyre is not 'a disaster' – your loved one being run over is. Then, if you do choose to use strong or dramatic language, people will sit up and take notice.

65

Have your cake and eat it

I once had the bright idea of trying to count up all the published diets in the world and turn them into *The Henderson Super Diet*, make a fortune and retire. This never got off the ground once I realized there were some 300,000 published diets, and that is an underestimate. Whatever problems I see with patients every day I can guarantee there will always be someone asking for a pill to make them thin. This is sometimes understandable in obese people, but more often than not it is a person who is not overweight. They simply want to be thinner, because that's what they believe society expects.

Our basic body shape is determined at birth, and we are all one of three types: mesomorphs, ectomorphs and endomorphs. Mesomorphs are muscular, ectomorphs are thin and often tall, and endomorphs are rounded with a high fat level. The one thing that diet books will never tell you is – and this is the only thing you will ever need to know about dieting – it is impossible to change your body type no matter what you do. This does not mean you should not try to keep your weight at a reasonable level, since the health risks of obesity are well known. Instead, accept you may never be a size 10 or look like Arnold Schwarzenegger, and try to make the best of what you have. A starved fat person is exactly that, and not a thin person. If you spend your life concentrating on your weight and trying different diets, not only may you be genetically programmed to fail, but you are not concentrating on other, more important things in life. There is an unhealthy obsession with calories, and the only point I ever make to 'calorie-counters' is taste them, don't waste them.

The vast majority of obese people I see compound whatever their basic body shape is by eating too much – it's as simple as that. Added to that we have the following facts:

◆ We can choose to overeat, be badly groomed or untidy, but we have to accept that it will be noticed by others.

◆ Image counts, whether we like it or not. In interviews, a person is judged within the first 30 seconds, and that initial impression usually remains.

◆ You do not need to depend on diet alone to change your image. Clothing, hairstyle and personal grooming are just as important and will be noticed. This need not involve spending huge sums of money and can be as simple as remembering to polish your shoes before an interview.

◆ You do not have to accept being seen as a second-class citizen because of your size, but you may have to work harder to overcome prejudice to get to where you want to be. If you find a change of image too difficult, change your work or home environment to one you are more comfortable with.

◆ Although we all have to live with the shape we are given, it is your choice to choose what image you present. Follow your aims and goals, not other people's.

Like it or not, in this world appearances do count. This may be unfair, but it is the real world and you are living in it. Whatever your size, be comfortable with who you are. Apart from calorie-counting, develop other ways to improve your image, such as clothes, personal grooming, hairstyle and make-up.

66

Commit yourself

At the end of an exhausting day, it is always good to get home and be jumped on by my children. They do not care what sort of day I have had, but simply want me to play with them. The problem is, I would quite like some time to myself first, so what do I do? Simple – I commit. I give them 10–15 minutes of complete attention, knowing that after this I can begin to unwind properly and catch up with what has been happening at home. Once I have done this, I can put the day behind me and turn my attention to my family again in a more leisurely manner. This becomes more significant when you realize that research suggests the total amount of time men spend each day with their children has fallen from an average of 30 minutes a decade ago to as little as 15 minutes today. If you add to this the point that children often prefer quality time with parents rather than quantity alone, it is soon apparent that throwing yourself into what you choose to do is important for both you and your family. Try to remember:

◆ Not to be distracted by outside tasks when playing with your children. You may think they will not notice but they do.

◆ If you must work at home in the evening or at the weekend, have distinct cut-off times for both work and play. If you spend all your time looking over your shoulder at what else you need to do, you will do a bad job of both.

◆ You have your whole life in which to work. You will not have your children for long. Is the occasional 10 minutes of quality time for them too much too ask?

It may seem to overstate the case to suggest that fathers see too little of their children, but it is a common complaint I hear from stressed businessmen who feel trapped in a cycle of work with no way out. What they often do not recognize is that they have the time for their children if they want it, but either choose to spend it in other ways or fritter it away by trying to do half a dozen jobs at the same time and ending up doing them all badly. This leads to frustration and more stress. The same principles apply at work:

◆ You may have three important jobs on the go, but you will only do them all well if you commit to each one exclusively at any one time. Even if you are rapidly switching your attention from one job to another, focus on one and one only.

◆ Try not to take on work unless you are committed to it. This is often not possible – you may have no choice in the work you are given – but even in these cases aim to give the job the best attention you can.

◆ If your workplace has a company ethic of corporate thinking, do your best with this while at work, but always remember to focus on something else at the end of the day.

Throw yourself into what you do. Whether a major project at work, playing with your children, or singing in the choir, never mentally look over your shoulder – focus on the task in hand. Playing horses for your children so they can climb all over you may not be thrilling, but you – and they – will feel better for it.

PART FIVE

CRISIS MANAGEMENT

67

Bereavement need not be fatal

Death, like taxes, comes to us all. It is a part of my job, and I always marvel at the different ways bereaved people react. These vary from a quiet acceptance and a quick resumption of normal life to unspeakable grief, from which there is no recovery and which – I have no doubt – can cause death from a 'broken heart'. We feel grief not only emotionally, but physically, socially and spiritually too. Understanding the natural phases of grief helps people come through one of the greatest crises they can face.

First there is shock and disbelief. I have sat in many homes after a death where all the family are able to say is 'I don't believe it.' They listen but do not hear, and feel detached from the real world. Because shock can cause an outwardly calm appearance, it is often wrongly assumed that the person has accepted their loss, when in fact they cannot even understand what has happened to them. Mary, a 64-year-old woman, was in this position when she lost her husband suddenly because of a heart attack. When I saw her later that day, she was so stunned she hardly recognized me, despite having known me for years.

After this shock – which often lasts until the funeral is over, and occasionally long afterwards – there are intense feelings of separation. The bereaved may see their loved one as a ghost, hear their voice or dream about them constantly when asleep. Mary took to visiting her husband's allotment, still convinced he would be there despite having seen him being buried the week before. This phase can last some weeks, but is usually overtaken by despair and anger.

It is usual for family and friends to rally around a bereaved person at the time of their loss, but this support gradually tails off over the next few weeks and months. This is the wrong way round – the usual time people need most support is several weeks afterwards, when the house is quiet and people have gone away to get on with their own lives. Extreme sadness and depression are common, as is anger, which can be marked. When I was visiting Mary one day she rounded on me and gave me both barrels between the eyes for not preventing her husband's death, even though she knew no one could have done so. She poured out a stream of vitriol and abuse, and I had to sit and wait for the storm to pass before she began to sob, and sobbed for a long time. She later told me how embarrassed she felt about this, but admitted it had made her feel better. She needed to let her feelings out, and I just happened to be in the firing line at the time.

Such despair very gradually gives way to acceptance that the person really is dead, and there is no going back. This can take a very long time (occasionally never) and I always advise people to get past the first anniversary of the death, viewing this as a milestone in their grief. Mary did well, and just after this time had picked up her social life and was coping with being alone.

It is vital not to diminish your loss. Think of life as having stopped, changed irrevocably, and moved on in a completely different way. This may involve having to learn new skills, meet new people or channel your feelings into a new hobby or job. Either way, bereavement means you will be dealing with a new life and if you accept this it is never fatal.

Most people survive the death of a close friend or relative, but it takes time. Accept the loss, express your emotions and – if necessary – distract yourself by putting your emotional drive into a job or activity. Remember to talk to friends and family.

68

Control how you react

We all respond to what other people say to us, no matter how much we try not to. I was made aware of this when I was dealing with Jack, a garrulous man in his 80s, and found I was becoming tense even before he walked into my room. Over the previous months the consultations had followed a typical pattern. Polite enquiries from me were met with dismissive comments, any attempts to find out why he had come were shrugged off, and after ten minutes of going around in circles we were both angry and frustrated. Exit patient, and I ended up seething for the next half-hour, which distracted my attention from others.

What was happening was I had allowed Jack's stress to rub off on me. Instead of sitting back and distancing myself from his emotions to concentrate on mine, I matched his anger with anger and lost the plot. This is the basis of road rage, arguments that spiral out of control and most of the domestic disputes I am called out for. The principle here is simple – you are responsible for dealing with your stress, so let other people deal with theirs. The following techniques may help:

◆ When someone starts to get angry in front of you, take a mental step back from their emotions. However hard it may be, try to listen to what is being said rather than how it is said.

◆ Remember to use the 'mental wall' (see Tip 12) if you need to, and breathe deeply in an effort to keep calm.

◆ When the person leaves, imagine their stress leaving with them. Do not forget to flush tension away afterwards.

Remind yourself that you may be being used as a dumping ground for another person's stress, and that is how they deal with their problems. Don't let them – resist picking up their stress package.

It can often be rewarding if you can stop yourself being polluted by others' stress. The next time Jack came in to see me, I used every trick I could think of so I did not rise to his stress. The calmer I stayed the more he shouted, but a surprising thing then happened. He stopped shouting, went very quiet and burst into tears. He sobbed like a child for many minutes, and when he stopped he began to speak – calmly and politely. Over the next 20 minutes he told his story, and I realized why he had been such an angry old man. For over 50 years he had lived with the memories of what he had done and seen in the Second World War, with nightly dreams of dead colleagues haunting him. We would now call this post-traumatic stress disorder, but after the war no one would listen to him. He had never been able to bring himself to tell anyone, because they always got angry with him beforehand. By staying calm I had given him the chance to open up, and he had. I still see Jack from time to time, and it always reminds me of the benefits of not rising to the challenge of other people's stress. Learn not to, and watch the result.

Don't let someone else's stress infect you. Other people are responsible for handling their stress, you deal with yours.

69

Imagine the worst

In the middle of a busy afternoon surgery I saw Elaine, a mother who had just had a minor car accident while doing the school run. Fortunately she was unhurt, but the car had suffered considerable damage and as her husband had only just bought it, all she could think of was what his reaction would be when she told him the news. She kept saying, 'This is the worst thing that could have happened today,' until I felt I had to intervene. I quietly pointed out that it was certainly highly irritating, but she was alive and well, as were her children. We wrote down a list of what else could have been worse that day, and after ten minutes I called a halt, or we would have writing all afternoon. What I had been able to do was show Elaine how easy it is to think something is worse than it really is, and how stressful such thoughts are. It probably made no difference to her husband's reaction that evening, but at least she had a sense of perspective about what had happened.

The huge majority of our fears and anxieties are in our heads and nowhere else. They have not happened and never will. They are often minor, but by constantly worrying about them we build them up so they become enormous problems. Will I lose my job in the future? Is the car going to break down on holiday? What if it rains on the day of the wedding? These may be worthy worries, but are actually trivial compared with what truly matters in our lives. Whenever I find myself worrying about what-ifs and maybes, I stop such stressful thinking by imagining the worst. What is the most terrible thing that can happen to me? The death of my wife and children – no question. I could probably add terminal illness and hideous wasting illnesses too, but you get my point. When you compare the daily minor anxieties that we all have with such thoughts, they melt away.

Yet what about the rare occasion when your worst fears actually come true? You are made redundant, or your child walks under a bus. How does this help at those times? The simple answer is it doesn't. What it does, though, is prove to you that you are getting through the worst thing that can happen to you. You are surviving. After this, everything else in your life will no doubt fall below this level of stress, and you will see it as such. People who have been through a trial of fire in their life will often say later at times of stress 'Oh, this is nothing compared to when . . .' What they are doing is using their worst fear as a benchmark to judge all the other stresses in their life. Whether these have happened or are in our imagination, the principle is the same. Imagine the worst, look at where your stress is in relation to it, and get your stress in perspective.

It is always worth remembering this joke: 'They said to me "Smile, it could get worse." So I smiled. And, yes, it got worse.' The real punchline should then be 'And I still survived.'

Most of our fears never happen – they are simply in our heads. The American writer Mark Twain said that he had lived through many awful things in his lifetime, but few of them had happened. To break these irrational fears, imagine the worst possible thing that could happen to you, and then think how you would deal with it. You can cope. As Susan Jeffers says, 'Feel the fear. And do it anyway.'

70

Listen, listen, listen

What do most patients want from their doctor? Fantastic medical knowledge, luxurious surroundings, the latest medical technology? No. They want their doctor to do one thing – to listen. Unfortunately, many doctors fail to do this, with the result that many consultations are unsatisfactory on both sides. There is sometimes no fault here – the pressure of time on rushed doctors and patients who want to spend an hour discussing life's problems do not sit easily together – but most of the time listening is a forgotten art. I was once told the best way to learn what is wrong with a patient is, for the first 60 seconds of any consultation, shut your mouth and open your ears. This does not always apply – if someone comes in to me and says, 'Well, what do the tests show?' I am not going to spend the next minute looking at them in silence. It is, however, a very good tip to remember when you want actually to *hear* what someone is saying to you.

When I was growing up my father worked as a Samaritan, taking calls from despairing and suicidal people. I vividly remember as a small boy watching him one evening when he took such a call, and having to find my mother to ask, 'Why isn't Daddy saying anything?' I forget her response, but when I mentioned this to him many years later he smiled and said the hardest thing about that job was learning to bite your tongue and say absolutely nothing, sometimes when the caller was also silent for minutes at a time.

The secret of being a good listener is to put yourself in the place of the other person. People who are forceful or aggressive are usually dreadful listeners – almost to the point of selective deafness. Good listeners encourage people to tell their story in their own words and in their own time, letting them know they have their undivided attention. They do not interrupt or pass judgement, even if what they hear is not to their liking, and they give people the time to think and collect their thoughts if needed.

Before patting yourself on the back at being one of life's natural listeners, ask yourself the following questions:

◆ Have you ever made a judgement about someone simply because of how they look or dress?

◆ Have you ever interrupted someone to tell them you have had a similar experience to theirs, only worse?

◆ Do you finish sentences for people?

◆ Do you look over people's shoulders, or at your watch, when talking to them?

◆ Have you ever heard yourself say you understand their problem while they are still explaining what it is?

Still think you are a good listener? By relaxing and listening better, you will help other people to feel more relaxed with you and to slow down too. People who do not feel they are competing for your attention are more likely to have frank and honest conversations with you. Remember that everyone likes to talk to a good listener.

We are all appalling listeners. Listening is a real skill and to be good at it you need to put yourself in the other person's shoes. Focus on the words they are using as well as non-verbal clues and put your own thoughts to one side.

71

Ask for help

I have lost count of the number of times someone has spent months fighting anxiety and panic attacks before plucking up the courage to tell me about it. This is sometimes because of pride and embarrassment, but also because they see themselves as failures when they have to admit that they have this problem. Nothing could be further from the truth. Time spent trying to snap out of anxiety is wasted time, and any improvement can begin only once it is accepted that there is a problem. This degree of anxiety ruins people's lives, and affects relationships as well as individuals. I always make certain points clear to people suffering from anxiety:

◆ Asking for help is healthy, not asking is not.

◆ You may think you are the only person who feels like you do. You are not; there are hundreds of thousands like you.

◆ Accepting that there is a problem is the first step in doing something about it.

◆ Therapists and doctors have heard your story many times before. They will not judge you. If they do, go somewhere else.

◆ It takes time to feel better. Although just admitting that anxiety is a problem can make someone relax, it is often a long road to being free of worry. There will be ups and downs along the way, but stick with it and the results will come.

◆ If you fail it does not mean you cannot start again.

Getting help for your anxiety should be as simple as walking in to see your doctor. I know this often depends on the sympathy and understanding of a particular GP, and how good the doctor-patient relationship is. (Change your doctor if you are not satisfied.) There are then a number of possible options for getting help:

Your doctor may be able to help you without anyone else being involved. Time spent talking to him may be enough to ease your worries, but will need a number of sessions, which can be difficult in a busy surgery.

You may be able to see a counsellor within the surgery who is trained to help people with problems such as phobias and panic attacks. They are usually able to spend more time with people than the GP, and can achieve excellent results.

Your doctor can refer you to see a psychotherapist, who can counsel you in depth about your problem, your past and possible reasons why you feel the way you do. Knowing these reasons gives you the chance to do something about them. This is rather simplistic, but there is often a great deal of flowery language used to say just that. Counselling has recently become a highly contentious area. In his book *Staying Sane*, TV psychiatrist Dr Raj Persaud is extremely sceptical of much counselling, and the view that every problem has to be referred to a specialist. I basically agree with this, believing the important point is to recognize that you have a problem and then do something about it, even if this is as simple as talking things over with your mates. Doing nothing is not an option.

Don't be afraid to ask for professional help. This is not an admission of failure, but a healthy acceptance of a problem and a declaration you want to do something about it.

72

Don't sabotage your life

There are a group of patients I see who seem to sabotage their lives deliberately. This is either because of a fear of failure or because they think a new relationship could never succeed. Jenny is one – a young single mum who enjoys singing and dancing, and with a consider-able acting talent. It is her dream to audition for the professional stage, but despite my encouragement she always has an excuse why she never has. These have ranged from difficulties with baby-sitters, being overweight and feeling too tired, to not being able to find transport to get to auditions. Some of these may be genuine reasons, but none is insurmountable. The more I see of her the more I know she has a deep-seated belief she is going to be rejected, so she does not try.

This is a common trait. We fear rejection, and if it occurs we take it personally. Failing a driving test means you will never be able to drive, poor marks in an exam mean you may as well give up your course, and a failed relationship suggests you will always be the bridesmaid, never the bride. To understand why you have failed or been rejected you need to do one thing – *analyse*. OK, so you did worse in your exam than you were expecting. If you had not prepared properly, not studied as you should have and not done your best before you went into it then you probably are at fault and need to look at how badly you want to succeed. No one will put success in your lap for you – you need to work for it. If you want success, try again. If you did your best, there are two possibilities. Did you simply have a bad day, as anyone can have, and your mark in no way reflects your ability? Did nerves affect your perform-ance? If so, learn the techniques to reduce these. The other possi-bility is that you *did* do your best, and this is the mark you were given. If so, perhaps this subject is not for you, or are there other ways to get to where you want to be. Look at all the options before giving up on anything.

In the drawer of my writing desk, I keep a copy of a book written by John Creasey, the famous crime novelist. I have never read it, but it is there because it reminds me that he had an unbroken succession of 743 rejections before his book was accepted by a publisher – severe by anyone's standards. At the last count over 60 million of his books had been printed.

If you are constantly being rejected, try not to take it personally. Instead, analyse the cause. Assess if it is unrelated to you, or if you are someone who deliberately sabotages their own life for fear of trying new skills or relationships.

73

Test your friends

At a recent dinner party, I sat next to the hostess, a well-known woman who reminded me of one of Tom Wolfe's 'social X-rays' – anorexically thin and weighed down with jewellery and prejudices. I chatted to her as amiably as I could, while she continually looked over my shoulder, relentlessly scanning the room for bigger social prizes. She enumerated hundreds of dear, wonderful and famous friends she was so lucky to have, and gushed about how they all loved her parties. I felt sorry for her. I knew that nobody in that room was her friend. More to the point, she knew it too.

It may be a cliché, but it is only when your life goes through a difficult phase that you find out who your real friends are. Real friendship means knowing that they will help you at three o'clock in the morning without question if you ask them; it also means being able to resume a deep friendship after a long period without contact. As a doctor, I advise patients who are going through a crisis to lean on their friends as heavily as they need to, but to remember that the best way to gain a good friend is to be one. The people who best survive stress are those who not only have real friends to call on for support, but also are happy with their own company – in a sense they are their own friends.

Friends serve two main purposes. The first is appraisal. They provide objective advice when you are too stressed to think clearly. The quality of this advice may vary, but it can be a useful counter-weight to your own thinking. The second is enjoyment. Few things match the satisfaction and sheer enjoyment that come from a friend-ship based on shared interests and the knowledge that you can count on each other.

I am not a man who joins clubs, and my friendships are forged over long periods. This is partly a result of my quintessential

English reserve – I starch my upper lip every day before facing the world – and because I value the calm and silence that good friends can sometimes share. Friendships between British men are traditionally undemonstrative, but I have witnessed conversations between male friends where more is said by a playful punch on the arm than by any words that pass between them. The superficial appearance of a friendship does not matter as long as a deep and mutual trust exists. To a male eye, female friends seem able to talk about anything, whereas football and cars – safe conversation – are often our talking points, progressing to intimate levels of discussion only when we know no one is going to laugh at what we say – the number-one killer to the male persona.

In *Crocodile Dundee* the hero hears that a New Yorker is seeing his analyst. He responds, 'Doesn't he have any mates?'

As a doctor, I can't beat that.

You only know who your real friends are when you need them in a crisis. Don't spend time with people you don't like purely because of a sense of duty. Have friends you actively like, and who are supportive. Remember – never be afraid to move on from people who are determined to stay in a rut that you want to leave behind.

74

Break your negative thinking

Negative thinkers are some of the most difficult patients I deal with. Consultations take longer and seem to go around in circles, because convincing them that something positive can happen in their life is hard work. There are three main types of negative thinkers I see in my surgery:

♦ The imaginers, who become stressed because they imagine they are always to blame for any negative reaction towards them. A cross word, a look of irritation or a phone call that does not go well is enough to start negative thoughts. What these people need to do is respond only to genuine problems. If someone is really angry with you, they will let you know. Until that time do not waste energy on worrying about what might happen. Most worries are only in our imagination and never happen.

♦ The generalizers, who see everything they do as a constant battle against guaranteed failure in their life. I saw an artist who thought like this after he had failed to sell any of his paintings for months. Before he picked up his brush he believed no one would like them, and this showed in the quality of his work. I suggested he should paint a picture purely for himself, so he knew it could not fail in anyone else's eyes, and I was amazed at the finished result. It could have been painted by a different artist. When I persuaded him to put it in a gallery, he said, 'No one will want to buy my work,' despite the fact that many people had previously. It sold within half an hour.

♦ The black-and-white thinkers, who are the most common

of negative thinkers. You were late for your son's birthday party, so you are the worst dad there has ever been. You had cross words with your husband at breakfast, so the marriage will be over by teatime. What such thinkers forget is that we are all human – Tiger Woods misses short putts and Formula One drivers run into the back of other cars at traffic lights. Everyone makes mistakes. The person who never does is lying to you.

I used to look after a professional snooker player who suffered dreadfully with pre-match nerves. If he got off to a bad start in a match you could see his shoulders sag, and I knew what he was thinking. Instead of forgetting about the frame he had just lost and focusing on the next, he dwelt on the previous half an hour and so began expecting to lose. This meant he did, and his negative thoughts beat him more often than his opponents. I suggested that if he lost a frame he wipe his cue down from top to bottom. This wiped away his defeat, cleared his mind and he could focus on his game. To his surprise he began to win matches again. His ability had not changed but his thinking had. Negative thinking shatters confidence and destroys performance. Whenever you find yourself thinking negative thoughts, mentally wipe them away and start again. Practise this daily and you will soon feel less stressed.

Success breeds success, and defeat generates defeat. Avoid phrases such as 'I knew I'd be no good at this,' and match each negative thought with a positive one.

75

Life is unfair

It is an unfortunate part of my job to see unhappy people sitting in front of me asking, 'Why me?' They may have just received bad news, been told a diagnosis or simply sat down and said how unhappy they are with their lives. Sometimes this question is rhetorical and occasionally it is not – they look for an answer to questions I have no answer to. There is a view as we enter the 21st century that everything has a reason and hence a solution. If such a solution does not exist then someone must be to blame. This is a common situation in bereavement, but I see it at many other times now too. To say 'I don't know' when someone asks an unanswerable question is to invite the response 'Why not?' If someone cannot accept that life is unfair and miserable at times, through no fault of theirs, they are likely to be stressed for far longer at such times than someone who has a more phlegmatic view of life. If you are such a person, say to yourself:

◆ What makes you different from anyone else in the world? You are designed the same, think in the same way and feel the same stresses.

◆ Unfair things are going to happen to you. Family and friends are going to die, accidents will happen and bad people will keep doing bad things.

◆ Accept how life is, and get on with yours in the meantime. If you were to worry about what might happen to you, you would never leave your house.

◆ Many things happen that no one is responsible for, including you.

◆ Time really does help people come through the most awful events. All things pass but you need to remember many do not pass for a long time. Accept that grieving is natural, and there are no rules to it.

◆ Are you reluctant to ask for help? It is at times of greatest stress that true friends show their worth. Lean on them and they will support you. No one is an island and you are no exception.

I have seen terrible things happen to patients in their lives, and initially every one of them felt they could not carry on. They could not understand why they, and not someone else, were suffering, and were convinced they could never recover from such unfairness. Weeks and months later, they all had. Some bounced back quickly, others needed guidance and help, but they had all taken their personal punch, rocked back and recovered. The key with each of them was to accept it was not their fault and things could only get better. This gave them the patience to allow the dust to settle and then pick up the pieces again. You can do the same thing if life turns against you – never forget that.

Everyone has times when life is dreadfully unfair. Just take a deep breath and battle through. With time, even the greatest personal disasters – death, divorce and failed relationships – can be assimilated into your life.

76

Compartmentalize

I look at some people and wonder how they manage not to buckle under the strain of all that is going on in their lives. These can range from the high and mighty – monarchs and presidents – to ordinary individuals struggling to keep body and soul together against huge odds. Although presidents are not patients of mine, I am sure they cope by compartmentalising their thinking. This is a trick many people use to deal with stressful situations and fortunately it is very easy to learn.

Just as we put computer information in files, we can put stressful situations or events into well-defined boxes in our mind. Good examples are bereavements, previous traumatic events or major problems in our lives. If we tried to think about all our worries at once we would either give up and admit defeat or not be able to deal with any of them. Instead we should view each problem as being in its own box, from which we choose to take it out to look at when we want to think about it. When we have had enough or have solved the problem, it is put back in its box and closed up until the next time we need to think about it.

I was recently driving along a country lane when I came across a car accident that had just occurred. The vehicle had skidded on mud and flipped over into a waterlogged field, throwing the driver out. To my surprise I found myself administering first aid to one of my patients, who was remarkably intact apart from a heavy concussion. Some weeks later we met up and I asked how he was getting on. He had been having nightmares and flashbacks about what had happened and had been feeling depressed. I had not seen him at all in this time, so was disturbed to hear this, and asked him what he had done to improve things. Rather sheepishly, he told me he had learned to put the accident and all its effects into a box, and tie the whole thing up with red ribbon. When he felt he was becoming anxious and worried about what had happened, he sat down for five minutes in a quiet place and very deliberately imagined untying the ribbon and opening the box. He then went over the events of the accident before shutting the box up and retying the ribbon. Each time he did this he thought of his family and told himself how lucky he was still to have them. He then felt better and carried on with his life, until he needed to 'open the box' again several weeks later. He had worked out for himself that this was a healthy way of dealing with his near-miss. No one had suggested it to him.

When stressful things happen to us there is no point in trying to pretend they have not. Sweeping things under the carpet only stores up stress for the future. By rationing our stressful thoughts we prevent our lives from being taken over by them, leaving us better able to enjoy the things that matter to us most.

If you have more jobs on the go than you can handle, compartmentalize. Think of each task as sitting in a box, and take it out when you need to work on it. When you have finished, put it back. Deal with upset or trauma in the same way.

77

Is it your problem?

There are two things in my life I have no control over. The first is the number of hours in the day, and the second is the number of problems that come my way during the day. Too many problems in too little time is – another problem. This can lead to a feeling of helplessness. Remind yourself how to say 'No' to unnecessary problems:

◆ Imagine each problem being thrown to you. Is it a hand grenade or a tennis ball? What will happen if you choose not to catch it? Will it explode in your face, or just bounce harmlessly away? Is someone else merely trying to avoid their responsibilities in giving you this problem? Make a mental note about where this problem is on a 'must do/ should do/need not do' list and act accordingly.

◆ If you choose to catch the problem, do something with it. Remember the '5 Ds' principle (see Tip 19) and use it.

◆ Learn to say 'No'. It can be flattering to be asked to help sort out someone's problems, but what is the point of getting involved if you know nothing at all about the question? It is far better to say at the outset 'I'm sorry but I don't know how to help you,' than to get drawn in simply because you are trying to please everybody all the time. Learn what your limits are – a great means of reducing stress.

◆ If personal insults or comments are thrown at you, use this method to ignore them. Don't catch the insult, let it fall to the floor so it has not touched you. If you think criticism is constructive, catch it, think about it and, when you have taken on the helpful criticism, let it go.

◆ If you have taken on more than you are able to cope with, list, in order of priority, what needs to be done, and then work through the list. I worked briefly in a busy casualty department in Canada, and was flooded with urgent jobs. In the middle of this chaos stood the consultant, looking relaxed but working very hard and efficiently. When I rushed to show him an X-ray of a seriously injured motor cyclist he stopped me before I ran off again, and quietly pointed out the other two broken bones I had completely overlooked – I had been too keen to get everything sorted out quickly. All he said was 'Take your time. Get it right and get satisfaction from doing the job right. You are not here to do lots of jobs badly.' It was a salutary lesson, but the more I watched him the more I saw him put these words into action. He focused intently on each job before moving on to the next, and took as much, or as little time as each one needed. He ended up doing less work because so little had to be redone later.

Slow down if need be, focus and finish each job to the standard required. Avoid perfectionist thinking, and mentally tick each job off when it is finished before moving on to the next. Throw each problem ball away when you have sorted it out.

Involving yourself in other people's problems is not compulsory. Learn when you have got your hands full and cannot cope with any more stress. Alternatively, drop one problem to take on another.

78

List and analyse

If I was going to be stranded on a desert island, and could take only one luxury with me to help deal with the stress of finding myself alone in such a place, I would take a pen and paper. Writing things down is one of the best ways of objectively finding out just how bad your problems actually are, rather than how bad you imagine them to be. This can be done with any problem, no matter how large or small, at any time. When I was deciding whether or not to leave a medical partnership, this proved to be the key to making the right decision, and I still do it whenever stubborn problems bother me.

First, write down what the actual problem is as you see it. Below this, write a list of actions you need to take in order to sort it out. Next, list everything you feel you should not do, or which will make the problem worse. On a separate piece of paper, look at what is actually happening in your life as a result of the problem, and compare the two sheets. A number of possibilities will be apparent:

◆　　The first is that you have judged the problem perfectly. Your assessment matches what is happening in your life, and the answers are written in front of you. Therefore you need to do very little to sort the problem out apart from follow your instincts.

◆　　Second, you may have greatly exaggerated the situation. Although you feel there is a major worry in your life, the hard facts show there is not. This should put problems into perspective, and so reduce your stress when thinking about them. You should find this reassuring.

Third, there is a chance you have underplayed the situation. There is a significant problem that has been either ignored – deliberately or otherwise – or underestimated and urgent action is needed to turn it round. Financial stress often shows in this way, and listing money worries and solutions is the first thing bank managers and advisers do when faced with people's financial difficulties. Ignore the problem at your peril. Some people choose to, but at least, having made their list, they are aware of it.

Not all the things you write on the list will carry equal weight. When I was writing mine to decide whether to change jobs, the hard facts were obvious, but my key point on the 'should' list overrode them all. I wrote 'Because I want to.' Over a few days I kept looking at this list, and by the end of a week knew I had made the right decision. I needed to have all the facts of the problem in front of me, in order to know what I had to do and how badly I wanted to do it. At the end of the day it was my gut feeling that proved to be right, but it would have been dangerous to rely on this alone. Learn to look at problems in terms of what is happening and what you want to happen, and you will begin to solve them rather than be beaten by them.

Tackle problems by listing your options. Compare this list with what is happening in practice. Indicate how much (or how little) you need to change to solve the problem.

79

Send it off in a bobsleigh

There are some things in life I think you have to be mad to try. They may be good for keeping mind and body together, but from my experience they can take the body apart first. One of these is going on the Cresta run at St Moritz. Travelling down a sheet of ice at 70 miles per hour holding onto a glorified tin tray is one way of spending your leisure time but is not for me. I am, however, often at the top of an imaginary bobsleigh run as this is a useful trick to stop a problem dominating your thinking.

No matter how hard we try, we can be frustrated by thoughts we can't get out of our heads. This can be an irritating piece of music or a worry we are not able to stop thinking about. It uses up mental energy, which should be put to a more constructive use, and can be exhausting by the end of a day. After you have tried Einstein's thinking technique (see Tip 37), if the problem creeps back then this tip can be ideal.

Whatever your worry – and it does not matter how big or how small it is as long as it is bothering you - imagine you are sitting in a bobsleigh. Your problem is in the seat in front of you, labelled with the name of whatever your stress is. Climb out of the bobsleigh and give it a push. Watch it move away from you, gradually gathering speed until it is out of sight. You will then notice you are not thinking about the problem and can move on to something else feeling better.

The first time I heard about this technique for relieving stress I was deeply sceptical until I had a problem that kept me awake at night. Whatever I tried I could not get it out of my head; I was becoming worn out and obsessed with finding an answer. Somewhat in desperation I used the bobsleigh picture, and found to my amazement that I was no longer turning it over in my mind. The answer appeared the next day, when I was not consciously thinking about it. My subconscious had solved the problem because I had allowed it to work on it. The more I had thought about it consciously, the less chance I had of getting anywhere.

This technique can be applied to any problem, and used at any time, anywhere. Try it and surprise yourself.

Obsessive thinking about work details is mentally draining. Imagine you are climbing out of a bobsleigh and leaving the problem in it. Watch it carry on without you, taking your obsession with it. Weird, I know, but watch the results.

PART SIX

PERSONAL DEVELOPMENT

80

Don't make mountains . . .

Some people seem to spend all their time saying life is terrible, and no one else could possibly have the problems they do. Apart from making others feel less sympathetic, they also run the risk of doing the following:

♦ Getting the balance of their life out of proportion. If you believe something is ruining your life, the belief may become a reality.

♦ Reducing their ability to deal with serious problems when they occur, because they spend so much mental energy trying to deal with imaginary ones.

♦ Forgetting how to enjoy themselves. Some people are so used to thinking life is one long continuous problem, that they feel guilty if they enjoy something.

I knew someone who used to wait for life to slap him in the face, and who almost seemed affronted if it didn't. He never had a cold, it was always the worst case of flu; minor aches and pains were the start of crippling arthritis; and his tension headache was a brain tumour. His hypochondria was something he had learned over years. Yet when his mother became terminally ill he was cured almost overnight. His mother's illness gave him a sense of perspective, and made him think about his minor ailments in a new light. He accepted them for what they were – insignificant compared with the greater problems he encountered.

If you always imagine the worst, practise the following tips:

◆ Accept that you have a problem, even if you cannot stop yourself immediately from worrying.

◆ Start each day with a positive affirmation, but be realistic. For example: 'I may have problems today, but I am bigger than they are and can solve them.'

◆ If a problem seems to be getting out of hand, remember the 'bobsleigh' technique (see Tip 79).

◆ Ask friends and family to tell you when you are worrying inappropriately. Act on what they say.

◆ If a problem still seems insurmountable, write it down and state why you feel you can't cope. This should show you whether it deserves serious attention, or whether it is a minor nuisance that you have allowed to get out of hand.

No one is immune from worry, but if problems seem to dominate your life then it is time to stop and take stock of your attitude. Remember another set of '3 Ps' here – think positive, perspective and proportion.

Don't make mountains out of molehills. Ask yourself if things are really as bad as they seem, and try to get things back into proportion. If you tend to turn everything into a crisis, develop positive mantras or affirmations to use every day.

81

Lighten up

Thomas Sydenham, the famous 17th-century physician, once said, 'The arrival of a good clown exercises a more beneficial influence upon the health of a town than the arrival of 20 asses laden with drugs.' This is a great quotation and one that has as much relevance at the start of a new millennium as it had four hundred years ago.

Humour reduces stress. A good laugh releases natural endorphins, which are nature's feel-good chemicals. I see many people in my surgery who say, 'I just need cheering up, that's all,' and they are right. They do not need drugs or counselling – they need to remember what it is like to have a good belly-laugh. The problem is that they are feeling stressed because of daily circumstances that wipe the smile off their face. To force a grin when life is rotten is absurd, but to look for the humour or absurdity in situations is healthy and can improve our chances of reducing stress. Women suffering from breast cancer who have a positive outlook on their life and who learn to use humour as a weapon against their disease have a statistically greater chance of doing well than those who choose to give in and give up.

◆ Write down, or remember, situations you have found funny in the past. If there is little humour to be found in any one day, think of them for an instant 'lift'.

◆ Keep the company of people you find funny or who seem to cheer you up whenever you are with them. The funniest people in this world are not those we see in the media – they are ordinary people.

◆ Use humour against yourself. People will laugh far more readily at irony than at someone trying to impress in other ways. Remember there is all the difference in the world between irony and sarcasm.

I once attended a charming old lady on a routine visit. After introducing myself I took a careful history and did a fairly detailed examination to reassure myself that she did not have a serious illness. As she was getting dressed again she asked me if I wanted 'to see the meter now'. Puzzled, I asked her what she meant. 'You *are* from the gas board, aren't you?' she said. There was a silence while the penny dropped for both of us, before we erupted in a huge giggling fit.

Abraham Lincoln once said people are as happy as they make up their minds to be. He meant that we can choose to look at life in certain ways, and one of the healthiest is with a smile.

Humour is one of the best stress-relievers. It can be found at the unlikeliest times. Look for the absurdities in day-to-day life, laugh at them and remember that the person it is healthiest to laugh at is yourself.

82

Channel your nervous energy

There is one particular patient whom I see almost on a daily basis, and who wears an expression on her face that marks her out from anyone else I know. It reminds me of a rabbit caught in headlights, with the same look of worry and bemusement, and perfectly reflects her personality. Gemma worries about anything and everything, and on the rare occasions she has nothing to worry about, feels anxious because she is not worrying. This is how she is made, and there is little I can do to change this. However, over the years I have made some progress in getting her to use this nervous energy to her advantage. We have gone through many difficult times in doing this, but at least she can now lead a perfectly normal life, worrying at the same level as the rest of us. She has learned important points to help her:

◆ Worry need not be a bad thing – it sometimes highlights a problem that needs sorting out. Remember to listen to your 'gut instinct' if you are worried about a plan or project you are involved in, but cannot quite put your finger on why you are anxious. If you have an inner anxiety about something, use an analysis list to separate real problems from imagined ones, and act on it.

◆ Channelling energy that would otherwise have been wasted into other activities can be highly effective. Once a day Gemma now goes for a two- to three-mile jog at precisely the same time. This not only burns off much of her nervous energy, but allows her to think problems through while she is running. The fact that she knows she will be doing this also means she copes better with stress earlier in the day, thinking she will have the opportunity to deal with her anxieties during or after her exercise. The added benefit is that she is now far fitter than ever, which also helps her to deal with her stress much more efficiently than she did before.

Gemma now accepts her worry for what it is – part of her. She used to worry she was never able to achieve perfect peace and serenity in her life, but I pointed out that I have yet to meet the person who has. Even the Dalai Lama has his bad days. Worrying is normal, worrying to excess is stressful.

A few days after I wrote this tip, Gemma came to see me, and so I took the opportunity to discuss with her what I had written. She then said, 'You've missed out the real reason not to worry.' When I asked her what this was she smiled and said, 'It's really easy. I know there are only two things to worry about – either you are well or you are sick. If well, there are no worries. If sick, you will either die or get better. If you get better, great. If you die, you only need to worry about whether you go to Heaven or Hell. Going to Heaven means there is nothing to worry about. If you go to Hell, however, you'll be so busy meeting old friends you won't have time to worry!' She has a point . . .

Channel the energy spent worrying into exercise or hobbies. Remember that worrying can be useful if it highlights a problem that needs sorting out.

83

Sculpt your life

I can hardly be called an ageing hippy since I missed the 1960s revolution, and I bypassed the punk era in quiet conformity. I still had the usual amount of embarrassing teenage angst, with hours spent listening to LPs in my bedroom and moaning about how unfair life was. A line from one of these records has, rather annoyingly, stuck in my mind ever since, and influenced my attitude to life. It is from a Pink Floyd record, and its message is that one day, we look back and suddenly realize that the years have run past without us, and feel that somehow we missed the starting gun.

Hardly dramatic stuff, except that it raises the important point that *we* decide what path our life takes. Fate, luck or even predestination is often cited as the reason why our lives follow a certain course, but in real life we all have key decisions to make. No one else makes them for us. At critical times in our lives, should we trust to chance and circumstance or should we try to sculpt what is actually happening to us?

This was the question I was faced with when I realized my medical work had become stale and I needed a new challenge. Fortunately, this coincided with my hearing about the five-ten-fifteen-year plan. This can make life simpler for you.

Take a large piece of paper and draw four vertical lines, one above the other, down the left. Then draw a long horizontal line from the middle of each of these across the width of the page. Imagine the left side to be five years ago. Mark off, at roughly equal intervals along each horizontal line, -5, 0, 5, 10 and 15 years. Label one vertical line 'Family', another 'Work', then 'Finance' and finally 'Personal'. Draw a red line on each, starting at -5 – five years ago – and draw where you think your life was going at that time in each category. Watch the way the line is going – up for good, down for bad. If you then extend this line into the future, you can see your feelings about which direction your life is going in each of these categories. (You can add as many categories as you like, but these are the main ones.) If the trend of all, or any, of them is downwards, it means you should take a long look at this part of your life and decide how to change it for the better.

When I did this exercise, my work red line was falling off the bottom of the page at the 15-year mark. It was at that moment I knew that something had to change, and I could not rely on luck to change it for me. I made the changes – moved jobs, worked part-time and began my writing career – and the plan worked.

These were big changes but they do not have to be. Sometimes you simply need to sit down and look at a map of your life like this to accept that changes need to be made. They can range from a radical overhaul of your whole life to realizing you need to spend more time with friends and family. It does not matter, as long as you take the time to look and are prepared to make that change.

Draw a 5-10-15-year plan up and pin it in a prominent position. Then map out personal detailed goals and targets and notes about how you intend to achieve them. Focus on family and relationships, hobbies, personal and spiritual development, work and finances. Keep checking your progress.

84

If this was your final day . . .

Life can be turned upside down in an instant. We all assume that at the end of each day we will be a day older but little else may have changed. In that same day, however, I may have had to break terrible news to some people and certify others dead – sometimes expected, sometimes not. One of worst memories I have is of having to tell a wife that her husband had been killed in a horrific car accident. This was bad enough, but the double tragedy, and one she has never come to terms with, was that the last words they had said to each other were angry and spiteful. He had left for work rushed and harassed, and a minor point of disagreement had grown into a full-blown argument. Harsh words were said, and both sides went their separate ways in very bad moods. As the day had gone on, she realized how silly the whole thing had been, only happening because everyone was stressed. She had planned an evening reconciliation with a romantic meal and was looking forward to seeing him and making up as they always did. The next time she saw him was in a mortuary.

Several months later, a jack-knifing lorry cut through my car, with me and my children in it, at a combined speed of over 100 miles per hour. I will never know how we survived, but my children did not have a scratch on them and I came home to my wife that night. Who knows why my patient is a widow and my wife is not? Without being morbid, we need to remember that life hangs by a thread for all of us and so make sure there is as little unfinished business or hostility in our lives as possible at the end of each day.

We often spend most of our time being busy for the sake of it. We know there are letters to be written to friends, quality time to be spent with the family, and things we want to say to our parents but never have. Although we realize this, there is always tomorrow and tomorrow can wait. We shrug our shoulders at how busy life has become and drift along without stopping to look at what is important.

◆ If you knew this was your last day on earth, write down all the things left unsaid or ignored that you would want to say or do.

◆ Work out what is stopping you from doing them.

◆ Ask yourself the question 'Why shouldn't accidents happen to me?'

◆ When you know the answer to that question, do something about the list in front of you.

Life hangs by a thread. Ask yourself, if you were to die tonight, what has been left unsaid or unfinished that you would want to change? '*Carpe diem*' – seize the day.

85

Just do it

Much of my time is spent pointing out to patients that it is their choices in life that prevent them from being the person they want to be. The long-haul lorry driver who wanted to study Shakespeare and the managing director who dreamed of resigning and growing roses are good examples. Both had a real passion for what they wanted to do but always gave the usual reasons for not changing their lives: mortgages, relationship commitments, finances and, above all, fear – fear of change and breaking out from a seemingly endless rut. There are reasons for looking before jumping, but I became so frustrated with the lorry driver that I sat him down and asked him to write out what was stopping him from achieving his dream. Once he had his list of negatives, we looked at how big each problem was and what could be done about each one – the list of positives. To his amazement, he found he could afford to take a part-time degree and still work without jeopardizing relationships or family. It took him 12 months to convince himself he could do it, but he is now happily immersed in Shakespeare, quoting huge chunks of the bard as he drives around the country.

If you want to do something you do not have to do it all at once. Remember, you can't be comfortable with yourself without your own approval. Ways of achieving your goals include:

◆ Changing one thing about yourself that you are unhappy with. This can be anything from your hairstyle to your time-keeping. Set a time limit to change and don't use the fact you are trying to change as an excuse for giving up in difficult times – the 'one cake won't hurt my diet' syndrome.

◆ Committing yourself to action. If you want to run a marathon, getting sponsorship to run for a charity is an extra reason for perservering. Telling people you are writing a book is a good way to make sure you don't give up when it gets tricky.

◆ Answering the question 'What do I want to do more than anything else in the world?' It may be impractical: you may not be able to walk in the Himalayas – but you could go mountain climbing in this country.

I asked this question of a deeply depressed teacher, and he immediately said, 'I want to sell flowers.' Although this was an unexpected answer, I asked him to write his positive and negative lists, which he went away and did. Over the next few weeks he visibly recovered from his depression, but was always reluctant to discuss his dream. Some years later I walked into a florist's in another part of the country and was amazed to be presented with a bunch of flowers by the same man. He had looked at his lists every day before going to school and eventually, realizing he had to be true to himself, had resigned his teaching job and taken over a struggling flower shop which he slowly turned around. He earned less, and worked longer hours than he used to, but I have seldom seen anyone as happy in their job. Taking me into the back of his shop he pointed out a framed yellowing piece of paper. He called it his 'qualification' and I recognized the lists he had drawn up four years earlier.

If you ever find yourself thinking 'I could do that,' try it. Surprise yourself and boost your self-esteem at the same time. Overcome obstacles gradually rather than all at once, or you will fail. Remember how to eat an elephant – bit by bit and very slowly.

86

Sweat it out

We are all generally unfit. Obesity is increasing in Western society although slimness and fitness appear increasingly desirable. High-fat convenience food, sedentary travel and a 'couch potato' ethos all contribute to a lack of fitness that usually presents as heart disease – our number-one killer. There is a paradox here; we all know what we should be doing to increase our fitness, but choose not to. Gym culture is more prevalent than it was only two decades ago, and sporting heroes are fêted for sticking to training regimes and self-sacrifice. We appear to have come full circle from the days when corpulence was a sign of wealth: a full, well-fed figure is now available to everyone, while a fit, tanned, slim body is a sign to the outside world of self-restraint and control over one's life. Yet if we had to go back to our days as cavemen, hunting and fighting animals to survive, the smart money would be on the animals.

All studies suggest fit people cope with stress better than those who work out by reaching for another beer. If you improve your fitness you will have:

◆ A lowered pulse rate and blood pressure.

◆ A bigger lung capacity.

◆ More energy throughout the day.

◆ Greater production of calming endorphins in your brain.

◆ Greater blood flow to the brain during exercise.

The list goes on, but there is no arguing – it's good for you. Don't be put off because you think it will mean taking up marathon running or spending all your time at the gym. Having tried the marathon route myself, I know that my knees have yet to recover, and as for spending all my time in a gym, the nearest I get to it now is driving past on another house call. Add in family, friends and home activities and there is not much time left, but even the busiest people can fit in limited amounts of regular exercise and still get fit. Whenever possible, walk or cycle instead of driving. Get off the bus or tube one stop early and walk the final part. Take the stairs rather than the lift at work (common sense applies here – build up to it if you work on the 27th floor!). Work up a mild sweat if you are walking, keep your pulse rate up and remember that brisk walking burns about the same number of calories as gentle jogging. Sustaining such exercise for 15 to 20 minutes is aerobic, and it needn't cost you a penny. Your maximum heart rate should be 220 minus your age, but this is only a goal for the seriously fit.

If you walk the dog, go more quickly – and further – than usual. If you are not used to exercising you may be surprised at how little it takes to raise your pulse rate considerably.

If you decide on a more formal approach, remember non-competitive exercise is often less stressful. You can work at your own pace and enjoy the physical pleasure of using your muscles. When I was running a high mileage every week, actually getting out of the door was the hard part. The really enjoyable bit was the glow of satisfaction afterwards and the feeling of being so fit I could knock down walls. The fittest I have ever felt was ten days after a marathon, having done no exercise in that time – a combination of being fit and having rested.

Although most authorities specify a minimum of 20 minutes of aerobic exercise three times a week, and building up from there, don't worry if you cannot manage it – any exercise is better than none. Try doing it with a partner; you will motivate each other. Classes work in a similar way, as well as giving an opportunity to meet new people. Key aerobic exercises include:

◆ Swimming

◆ Cycling

◆ Jogging or power walking. Both of these are low-impact exercises, where only one foot is off the ground at any one time, so minimizing the risk of joint strain and injury.

It doesn't matter what you do. If you enjoy it, it's good for you – and if you don't you won't keep it up. It is always sensible to get a general medical checkup beforehand, especially if you are aged over 35 and have not exercised for some time.

You don't need to run miles every day to get fit. Start with brisk walking or swimming and build from there if you want to. Twenty minutes of aerobic exercise three times a week will help your heart, lungs and blood pressure as well as making you feel better about yourself.

87

Is my bum too big?

We dress in different ways for different reasons. Some of us, as P. G. Wodehouse remarked, look as if we have been poured into our clothes and have forgotten to say 'When.' Others seem to look elegant in a potato sack, but how we dress usually reflects our personality. This can lead to problems if we are obliged to follow certain dress codes at work with which we feel uncomfortable. Such codes can dampen individuality and cause resentment, but there may be nothing we can do about it. To get over this problem, try some of the following:

◆ If you have to wear a uniform at work, remember it is just that – a company sign. When you put it on, start working for the company. Take it off after work and the job goes with it.

◆ Change as soon as you get home. This puts distance between work and home and reduces any resentment about the clothes you may have to wear for work.

◆ Add individual touches to uniforms, such as fun socks.

◆ Remember, you may do better business in the clothes you would rather not wear. Few people would buy a pension from an adviser dressed in jeans and a T-shirt, even if they were a financial genius. Don't forget possible paybacks from how you dress.

◆ Wear what you feel most comfortable with at other times. This will reinforce your self-image and make you feel you are an individual in your own right rather than a corporate number.

I used to live near a prominent solicitor, who walked past my house to work every morning. He was the archetypal city gent, with pin-striped three-piece suit, umbrella and bowler. He had a hugely successful business, helped to some degree I am sure by his manner and appearance. One evening I went to a barbecue at his house, and was more than surprised to see him in shorts, with much of his skin covered in tattoos and his body pierced in several areas. He told me he detested his work attire, but felt a great sense of rebellion when standing up in court, knowing that no one had a clue about what was under his suit. This constantly reminded him he was an individual, and he quite genuinely believed it made him a better solicitor. You do not have to go to such dramatic lengths to feel the same way, but the principle is the same. Dress for yourself, but pull your work personality on with your work clothes if you have to dress for work in a way you feel uncomfortable with.

There are two ways to dress – for comfort or for public consumption. Sometimes these overlap, but more often different occasions demand a particular style of dress. So, if you have a work dress code that is not natural for you, dress differently away from work to reinforce your personality.

88

Let music work on you

Three centuries ago the English poet John Dryden wrote, 'What passion cannot Music raise and quell?' – an acknowledgement that music has a powerful effect on our emotions. We know now that it can reduce stress by reducing blood pressure and slowing the pulse. Of course the effect music has on us depends on the type of music we are listening to. As a guide, slow, quiet music is more soothing than loud music with a fast beat, and many people find it more helpful to listen to quiet classical music than to pop music or 'easy listening'. However, the choice of music to relax to is individual, and there are exceptions. I know a consultant surgeon who listens to soothing baroque music when coming to the end of each surgical procedure, but also of a bank manager who plays loud Country and Western songs between clients. It does not matter what music you like listening to, but it is important how and when you listen to it. Remember:

◆ You do not need to listen to music for long before you will feel better. Even five minutes in a coffee break will relax you.

◆ To avoid irritating your work colleagues, use a personal stereo.

◆ Have a selection of music you enjoy, rather than listen to the same thing all the time.

◆ When listening to relaxing music, use other techniques at the same time to reduce stress, such as deep breathing and stretching.

◆ Many people find 'New Age' music – combinations of environmental sounds and relaxing music – helps them unwind.

Instrumentals are often easier to listen to than songs with words which you find yourself struggling to remember.

If for any reason you are unable to listen to music, imagine it. When an exhibition of photographs of the great cellist and conductor Pablo Casals was exhibited in America, an elderly gentleman would sit and look at a picture of Casals conducting. After ten minutes he would smile and leave, only to return and repeat the same quiet sitting the next day. After a week, the curator asked him why he liked the photograph so much. Giving him a withering look, the old gentlemen replied, 'Be quiet, young man. Can't you see I'm listening to the music!'

Music can enhance any mood or situation. Tailor your listening to your mood – to soothe or to stimulate you. Even a five-minute break with music can help alleviate tension or lessen your stress levels through the day.

89

List your achievements

Alice was a 38-year-old mother of four who wore the harassed look of a woman constantly in demand by her family. Her husband, although kind and supportive, was always at work and she had the task of bringing up the children. She was a good mother; the children were polite and well turned out whenever I saw them.

I was surprised when Alice came to see me asking for a general fitness checkup. She said she was going to start jogging and hoped to run a marathon one day. She sensed my surprise, stiffened and said, 'I suppose you're someone else who thinks I cannot do anything either.' This was an unusual outburst and she immediately apologized, but there was no disguising how serious she was. After I had checked her over we sat and discussed why she wanted to do something which, on the face of it, was extremely difficult to fit into her busy life. Her reply was dramatic – 'Because I don't do anything for *me* any more.' It was the size of the challenge that had made her mind up, since she felt her identity had been consumed by her husband and her family. Their reaction when she told them what she wanted to do simply spurred her on, and it became her main challenge that year.

Alice knew she would finish well down the field in any race she entered, possibly last. That was not the point. She wanted to do something no one could take away from her. It was something for her, not for her husband or family. This was not selfishness; rather, it was a personal achievement that gave her back some self-esteem and pride that was hers alone. She organized friends to look after her children for an hour each evening while she trained, and I watched her progress. We had an agreement that whenever her resolve flagged she would see me and I would encourage her to keep going, but she never needed to. She ran her marathon just over a year after first walking into my surgery. As expected, she finished way down the field, but she talked about nothing else for days and positively glowed with personal satisfaction.

Alice hung up her running shoes almost immediately and put her finisher's medal away. However, she still looks at it occasionally in times of stress to remind herself of what she is capable of. The medal is hers and hers alone.

You don't have to be like Alice and struggle round 26 miles to feel a sense of personal achievement. Finding the time to read that book you have never read but always wanted to can be equally rewarding. Even in the richest and most intense relationships, we still need to have our own little victories. They make us feel good about ourselves.

Personal achievements, however small, will boost self-confidence. They are yours to keep – no one can take them away from you. Make a list of them and read it regularly.

90

Play to your strengths

If you were asked what your greatest strength was, would you be able to answer? We spend time thinking about which car to buy, what mortgage to purchase or where to go on holiday, but spend a fraction of that time – if any of it – working out our strengths and weaknesses. While this might seem a natural thing to do, few of us bother, which is a big mistake. How can we fight our stress if we don't know the weapons we already have at our disposal? We can probably mention our faults, and certainly those of other people, but not our plus points. There is a simple way to sort this out:

◆ Write down all the strengths you think you have. Do not be too critical or shy. These can be anything from being a wonderful person to always remembering to put the cat out at night.

◆ Ask family and friends the same question, telling them they must be honest. Get them to write down as many points as they can think of.

◆ Compare the two lists and see what they have in common. Make a note of where you and others agree, and whether there are strengths other people see that you have never considered before.

◆ Think about the areas in your life that are a source of stress at the moment. Are you neglecting to use any of your strengths or talents to improve matters? Are there any obvious odd discrepancies? If you are seen as the life and soul of the party, and yet you are walking about with a permanently long face, examine the reasons for this. Being seen as a generous person is great, but if you are always in debt can you alter your spending patterns?

◆ If there are strengths that everyone can see, can you use these to further your career or improve your personal life? You might not think you are any good at doing a certain thing, but if half a dozen different people say you are, they can't all be lying.

At the end of a week's medical course, the organizer asked everyone to name one strength of each person on the course. To my surprise, and without any collusion, a dozen strangers all labelled me as logical. Vulcans with pointy ears are logical, not me, but knowing all 12 could not be wrong I sat down and thought about my stresses in as logical a manner as I could. As a result, my thinking highlighted problems and obvious solutions that I would have either ignored or missed completely. The result? A change of job, less stress at work and more quality time with my family.

It is one of the most common clichés to say a journey of a thousand miles starts with a single step, but I've just said it, and it's true. Learn about your strengths and make them work for you.

We all have strong points, but often do not realize what they are. Ask family and friends to list yours – and tell them to be honest. Nurture and use your talents.

91

Give your mind a workout

We may think about exercising our body, but give little thought to exercising our mind. I was reminded of this when meeting the manager of a highly successful health spa, who had come to see me with stress-related problems. He was a walking advertisement for the physical benefits of his business – fit, trim and physically very healthy – but his mental condition was appalling. He had one particular staffing problem, which he could not see any way to overcome. However, instead of dealing with this in a correct managerial way he had simply tried to ignore it. He thought that by increasing his physical well-being he would somehow solve his business problems. Of course this failed, and he was under severe stress as a result. He had made the big mistake that so many people make, and which is guaranteed to create more problems – he had not taken a long, cool look at what was happening in his life, and what he had to do to put it right. This always raises questions you need to ask yourself:

◆ Have I done everything in my control to try to solve this problem, or am I making a lot of noise about something I have only made a half-hearted attempt to deal with?

◆ If not, why not? Is the problem too big, or do I feel I want nothing to do with it?

◆ If I want to walk away, is it because I am past my level of competence or am I not getting the support I need from the rest of the organization?

◆ Is the failed project a result of events outside my control? Just as you should not judge a book by its cover, there may

193

be occasions when a project should not be judged purely by your contribution to it. This is especially relevant if a team is involved.

In the case of the spa manager, time spent talking to him highlighted all of these points. He had not made a genuine attempt to deal with the problem because he was afraid of confrontation. He felt he could not ask his wife for advice because he thought he would lose her respect, and he believed – falsely – that other senior members of staff would not support him if he asked for help. The underlying problem itself was not that difficult to sort out, and he finally called in a management consultancy to do the necessary hiring and firing he was so anxious about. He does at least recognize he has a managerial weakness here, but instead of pretending it does not exist, he now thinks about this area regularly and asks for advice if he feels unsure of himself. His business has gone from strength to strength, as has his mental health.

Exercise your mind as well as your body. Look at the areas in your life you are unhappy with and plan a step-by-step approach to dealing with them. Think of one area each day – and constantly assess how you are doing.

92

Lose your watch

Retirement may appear to have nothing to do with wearing watches, but this was not the view of an irate foreman who had recently retired. He came to see me complaining bitterly about, among other things, his retirement gift – a watch. For the previous 30 years his job had involved checking times of shifts, lengths of tea breaks and speed of production. He had spent much of his day looking at the clock or thinking about time, and he was given a watch to celebrate his retirement. The irony had been lost on his employers, but not on him, and although he appreciated the thought it was certain he would never take the watch out of its box. All he wanted to do was have days where he simply did what he wanted, when he wanted, without checking the time.

We are not allowed such luxury in our working lives – just about everyone knows their doctor has an average of seven minutes to cure them before the next patient – but we are able to let time stop ruling us sometimes. To achieve this, spend a day not wearing your watch. This will probably highlight the following:

◆ How awkward you feel not knowing what time it is, which may develop into anxiety at times.

◆ How after a while you will feel more relaxed at not having to follow schedules.

◆ How much of your life is spent chasing the clock.

Of course you will not be able to do this on a busy working day. Choose a day at the weekend when you have no appointments or important engagements. If you have to meet friends or take your children somewhere, set an alarm clock. What you are trying to achieve is the relaxation that comes only when you feel there is no need to think about what time it is. I only realized how relaxing this could be when talking to a countryman who had never owned a watch in his life and was now 74 years old. His clock was the country and the changing of the seasons. He got up when it was light and went to bed when it was dark. He was the exact opposite of so many stressed people who know the price of everything and the value of nothing. I once ended a conversation with him by excusing myself to go home for my dinner. He asked if I was hungry and I confessed I was not. 'That's the difference between you and me, lad,' he said, smiling. 'You eat when that watch of yours tells you to, and I eat when I'm hungry.' Although few of us are able to live such a life, the principle is the same. Take a fresh look at how much the clock rules your life, and take every chance to remove this pressure whenever you can.

I often think Groucho Marx should have been a doctor when he said, 'Either he's dead, or my watch has stopped.'

Most of us get used to the clock ruling our lives. Spend a day not wearing a watch – the weekend may be best initially – to show yourself how much you slavishly follow time. Notice how liberated you feel without it once you have got over the initial shock.

93

Blitz your finances

Like it or not, money plays a major part in all our lives. There are more arguments between couples about money than about anything else, and financial problems impose a huge amount of stress on some people, who often come to see me in desperation. They have usually hidden the problem from friends and family for many months, and whatever the sums involved – from a hundred pounds to more than a million – the same mistake is made time and again. They try to ignore the problem and hope it will go away by itself.

I once walked into a patient's living room to find his coffee table overflowing with bills and final demands that he could not face opening. He could have avoided the rising debt he was accumulating if he had taken simple action at the start of his money problems, but instead he had chosen to pretend there was nothing wrong until it was almost too late. This is the main thing to remember when dealing with financial stress – do not ignore it. It will only make matters worse. Other key points include:

◆ Avoid panicking, especially if you have got yourself into serious trouble. Accept that you have a major problem, but recognize that this may be controllable with careful planning.

◆ Realize you will need to get help. Your bank manager or building society can do nothing if they are unaware of what is going on. Get in touch with them, and remember it is in their interests to help you whenever possible. They have heard your story many times before and are used to it.

Talk to people. Let your family and, if you want, your close friends know what is happening. Sit down with pen and paper and look at

197

exactly what you spend your money on each month – you will underestimate your expenses if you do not. Compare this with your income and work out the shortfall.

◆ Look at your major financial commitments. Can you get a cheaper mortgage, house insurance, or car loan? Can flexible budgets such as food and leisure be temporarily reduced?

◆ Do not default on house payments. Most lenders will do all they can to avoid a mortgage default, so work out a temporary deal with them to enable you to stay where you are. Do everything you can to keep a roof over your head. Do not be afraid to include older children in discussions about the problem; you may be surprised at how amenable they are and how ready to accept it and help out.

◆ Be prepared to lower your standard of living if necessary. This is no time to keep up with the Joneses. What matters now are you and your dependants, no one else.

Many people have found that by choosing to reduce their commitment to material things they are not only richer financially, but also have more time to enjoy life as they are not so busy trying to service their debts. Simplify, ration and above all take note of what is happening to your money.

Money causes stress, especially when there is not enough of it. Take a critical look at your finances. List all the ways to improve the situation, such as increasing income and reducing expenditure. Then act on it.

94

Flush tension away

Imagine you are lying on a quiet beach with warm sun on your face, feeling very relaxed. Now imagine your feelings after an argument with an irate driver or dissatisfied customer. You will harbour feelings of anger and resentment after confrontation or a stressful event far longer than feelings of relaxation. Stress plays on our mind and can lead to physical symptoms when the pressure becomes too great. We need to be able to release our tension and stress at the end of a bad day. I was reminded of this when talking to a patient who worked as a prostitute. She had been beaten up by a client and I helped to put her back together again. During the course of treatment I asked how she coped with her job. She said it was simple. At the end of each day (or night) she took half an hour to soak in the biggest, deepest bath she could find and imagined the day washing off her like dirt. When she came out of the bath she felt cleansed and ready to go to work again.

Anyone can have the benefit of such thinking. A similar technique was practised by a consultant psychiatrist I knew who before she went home imagined her day was flushed down a toilet, and with it went all the stress accumulated from seeing her patients. The trick is the same in both cases – picture your stress being taken off you in any way you like. The following are other techniques you might try:

 If you travel to work, pick a landmark about a mile from your home. Imagine your work is in a bag there, and pick this bag up on your way to work. On the way home you drop the bag, with all the day's problems and stresses in it, back at its pick-up point, and travel the rest of the way having left work behind you. How you get to work does not matter; this technique can apply to anyone.

◆ Keep clothes you wear to work and those you wear at home separate. Completely change when you get home, and imagine you are taking off your work problems when you remove your work clothes. Your casual clothes mean exactly that – you are home and cannot be touched.

◆ Choose a personal mantra or saying that you repeat to yourself whenever you leave work. This is known only to you, and in saying it you shut the work door behind you. You can choose to say a different one when you enter work. Think of these as private passwords that allow you into work with all the stresses you will encounter there, but which also shut them behind you again when you leave.

◆ Before you leave work, take a piece of paper, crumple it into a ball and throw it into a waste bin. That ball is the day's stress, and throwing it away closes the day.

It does not matter which of the methods you prefer as long as you use one. Before long it will become second nature and you will have prevented stress from building up as it used to.

If you are a dumping ground for other people's problems, learn to flush away their stress after you have talked to them. This can be done with anything from affirmations (see Tip 18) to a long hot bath. Help other people with their problems by all means, but not at the expense of exploding stress levels.

95

Live in the present

Many people have three lots of stress. They worry about what has happened to them in the past, fret about what is happening to them at the moment and are anxious about what might happen in the future. Deal with this by using 'three-time thinking':

The past: the one thing to use the past for is to learn from. Missed opportunities may only come back if you learn why you missed them and look for them in the future. Avoid saying 'if only'; this means you are looking back – the wrong way to look.

The present: this is happening, this is where your stress is, and this is where you can do something about it. Concentrate on how you feel now, and act accordingly.

The future: the only way we can influence our future stress is by our actions in the present. Make plans by all means, but do not spend your life waiting for a time when your happiness is guaranteed. You may have a long wait. And avoid saying 'what if' – it might never happen.

There is nothing we can do about the past, no matter how much we would like to. And the only way we can influence the future is by our present actions. Avoid phrases such as 'if only' and 'what if'. Don't yearn for what might have been; it didn't happen and never will. And don't live on the promise, or under the shadow, of an imagined future. Be here now.

96

Audit your faults

The term 'audit' is a very popular one in medicine, and one that I usually ignore completely. My dictionary tells me it means 'an official scrutiny of accounts', but it can be used to mean looking at your performance in any activity to see how well you are doing. I feel my rapport with the majority of my patients is such that they quickly tell me if I am getting it wrong, and so they act as my auditors. In the world outside my surgery, however, there is a lot to be said for being able to check your worst faults and do something about them – if you want to. It is important to know what these are, since you may actively have chosen them. Take smoking, for example. There can be few people who are not aware of how bad cigarettes are for their health, and yet smokers continue to smoke. I do everything I can to stop their habit, and explain all the facts in full, but at the end of the day it is their choice whether they smoke or not. As many tell me, 'I enjoy it, doc, so I'll keep smoking.' I have no problem with that *if* they know all the facts – after that it is simple free choice. This raises the essential point – you will not give up a bad habit unless you *really* want to.

Suppose, however, that you have some bad habits that are easier to deal with – for example, always being late for appointments or losing your temper too often. You will need to have a logical approach if you want to improve these. First, write down or remember five of your worst bad habits and deal with them in order; spend a day thinking about each one. Is there an obvious reason for any of them? Are you late simply because you do not prepare in advance? Is there one particular situation which makes you lose your temper? Your answers may be enough to enable you to improve your bad habits, or you may need to go further. If these habits are related to work, is uncertainty the cause? If you are unclear about your position or job description at work, ask. Is your temper a result of frustration at problems at home or in a relationship? Remember that bad habits – smoking or drinking too much, being angry or resentful – are often a symptom of a deeper underlying stress. Only you can work out what these are, no one else can do it for you, and to do this you at least need to look at the problem.

Second, don't try to change everything at once, because you will fail. Work first on those problems you feel you can clear most easily. The sense of achievement you will feel as a result of this will help if you find the bigger problems tougher to deal with. Failing once does not mean you have to give the whole thing up. If that were the case I would never have gone into medicine or started my writing career. Remember your long-term goals, and do not be put off by others who tell you that you cannot do something. That is their problem, not yours.

Keep a mental diary – or a written one – of the things you would like to change in your life. This can range from the amount you smoke to the number of times you lose your temper every day. Review this once a week and bear in mind your long-term goals. Avoid short-term sticking plasters such as treating yourself to an occasional cigarette after giving up 'because you've earned it'.

97

Lose some battles

Why do we argue? It is usually because we hold strong views on something and are unhappy about not getting our point across to others. However, it can also be because:

◆ You feel aggrieved towards someone because of something they have done to you.

◆ You have a sense of being trampled on and need to fight back.

◆ You are having a bad day and want to get it off your chest.

◆ It is a long-running argument in which you feel you have no option but to keep arguing to save your pride, even if you know you are wrong.

◆ You are naturally grumpy.

◆ The buzz you get from arguing is important to you.

There are, of course, many other reasons, and few of us go through life without arguing on a fairly regular basis. This is fine as long as we know which battles to win, since arguing for the sake of it is ultimately fruitless. I see huge numbers of young men in prison who are there simply because they didn't walk away from an argument they should have walked away from. Such arguments are usually over the most inconsequential things, and these men often cannot believe they will be sitting in a prison cell for years to come because of it. Contrary to popular belief, most accept they should have been put in jail, but feel aggrieved that it was for something so stupid.

On another level, I often have to deal with highly argumentative people who are determined to make issues about nothing, and whom I will never be able to please. To deal with such people:

◆ Remember the ways of coping with bullies (see Tip 11), and use the 'mental wall' (Tip 12) to keep their anger away.

◆ If you feel you are right, you will always think that. You don't always need to argue to prove it. Let it go.

◆ Avoid fruitless and frustrating arguments by putting a full stop to them. Say 'We will never see eye to eye on this and must agree to disagree. Now let's move on.' By saying this you are neither giving in nor winning – the two ways most people look at this problem.

◆ If someone persists in arguing after this, they need to know you will not rise to the bait. Remember how to be assertive, not aggressive, and be firm in your manner and speech. If you have done your best in your dealings with such people, more than this means they are taking advantage of you.

◆ It may not be your fault anyway. You may simply be in the wrong place at the wrong time. If an argument upsets you, flush it away at the end of the day.

There are some battles we should not fight, although knowing which these are is never easy. Losing 'no-win' battles is better than trying to save your pride.

98

Don't shoot the messenger

There are many times when a patient sits in front of me and rails against how unfair the world is. Unfortunately this is sometimes true, but often it is not. A good example of the latter is someone who feels everyone is rude to them, and who gets no help from anyone in their life. They are blameless themselves and describe their behaviour in near-perfect terms, but their aggressive and hostile manner suggests they are anything but calm and considerate. This problem of balancing how each of us sees the world against how the world sees us is timeless, and the principles of dealing with it are constant:

◆ If you are consistently told one thing about yourself by a number of people – you are grumpy, they think you are lazy, or you are thought of as always being first out of the taxi and last to the bar – they cannot all be lying. If you think they are, this is not just unhealthy, it is paranoia. Learn to listen to what is being said about you, and don't be in too much of a hurry to dismiss it all as sour grapes. The truth is in there.

◆ You don't have to change your whole personality to get on better with the world. This is impossible anyway – leopards don't change their spots – but you can meet it half-way. If your problem is one of temper, count to ten before rising to bad news. If you are quick to criticize, imagine how you would feel if you were on the receiving end of your sharp tongue. Remember, you are likely to lose rather than win if you feel everyone is against you, because they will turn their back and deal with someone more amenable instead.

If you don't like hearing what someone says about you, it is not going to do you any good if you take it out on them – they are only being honest. I know of a highly respected figure in the industrial world who was invited onto an important advisory panel, chaired by an eminent household name. At the first meeting, and according to his brief, he put forward a series of proposals that were correct but unpopular. At the end of the meeting he heard the chairman say, 'We should all thank Professor Bloggs for his contribution to the meeting, as he will not be attending again.' He recounted this story to me with amusement some months later, adding that most of the committee had subsequently been fired for saying what they thought. In doing this, the chairman rendered the whole project useless, and was soon removed from office himself. Remember – shooting the messenger will ultimately ricochet onto you.

There is always a balance to be struck between what you expect from the world, and how the world views you. Learn to listen to other people's view of you. If they all say the same thing, it is unlikely they are all wrong.

99

What's important?

I was doing home visits one sunny Sunday morning on a large estate in middle England, and was struck by the large numbers of people washing their cars. This in itself was no surprise, but I had driven around the same estate at dawn that day and so remembered some of the cars. A few had been dirty, but just as many had looked pristine and in no need of cleaning. Yet they were being dutifully washed once more. Driving home I reflected on how chores can eat into our leisure time if we let them, with the Sunday car-wash being a prime example. If we are spending all our time on jobs that need not be done we will have precious little left to spend on the important things in life.

You may think routine chores do not affect you, but ask yourself:

◆ Do family, friends and hobbies get put to one side regularly because of routine tasks you choose to do?

◆ Before you start a chore, do you ask yourself if it really needs doing? If not, is it simply being done from habit?

◆ Do you promise to do something with your partner only to have to cancel it because the day's jobs have used up too much time?

Chores are a form of work, and working in your leisure time should be kept to a minimum. You cannot relax properly if you are thinking about the next job that needs doing, or are looking at the clock because meals are always served at a certain time. With a young family, compromises may have to be made, since routine is important and many jobs must be done, but as the family grows up there is more room for flexibility and choosing which jobs can wait.

Look hard at the jobs you do around the house, and ask yourself why you do them. Most will be done out of necessity – clothes do not iron themselves and bathrooms are not self-cleaning – but you will be surprised at how much time you spend on non-essential chores. These can be eliminated and time spent on more productive things that you want to do, even if this means simply sitting and relaxing.

A friend of mine loves relaxing in his garden but hates gardening. He therefore works harder in the week to earn more to pay for a gardener to look after it. He has worked out that the pleasure he gets from the garden outweighs the extra time he spends at work in the week. Whereas he used to resent what he saw as gardening chores – and some people find these relaxing – he now has more time for his relationship and feels better about himself as a result.

Does it matter if the car has not been washed by the end of the weekend or the windows not cleaned? Are you doing chores because they need to be done or out of habit? Is it more important to wash the car or spend that time playing with your children?

100

Life is not a dress rehearsal

My final tip is the shortest and most obvious of them all, yet we seldom seem to think about it, despite the fact that it applies to all of us. There is a golden thread running through this book: it is that the world will not change for you if you sit and wait for it to change. Only you can make things happen to alter your life and so reduce your stress, and there is only one life to do it in – this one.

I am a great believer in trying to beat the odds stacked against you in life, however daunting they may appear. There will be many times you cannot, but by using perspective, the appropriate tips and a balanced view of your stress, you will not be beaten.

I leave the last word to a patient of mine who was diagnosed with a particularly nasty and aggressive form of cancer. She had always led life to the full, and was determined that her illness would not change this. She took this view despite debilitating surgery and chemotherapy. Over many months I watched with growing respect as she took every chance she had to realize her ambitions and learn new skills in order to achieve them. She began to set up the career she had always wanted, and even when she was profoundly tired and weak was always making plans for her future. Her schemes were practical, not just fine theory; she worked hard to set up a five-year plan for the business she hoped to create. When I talked with her about the possibility she might not see the following week let alone the next five years, she said, 'I only have one run at this world and I'm not going to give it up just because I'm ill.' I remembered those words when she died several days later, and they still serve to remind me to do the best I can in my own run at the world. The patient I am telling you about was 18 years old.

No one will achieve your goals for you. Don't wait for the world to change – change yourself and make those goals happen. Life is not a dress rehearsal and we have only one run at it, so don't waste it.

Index